UNBOUND

Published by John Shors, Inc.

ISBN: 978-0-9991744-0-1

Cover design: Caroline Teagle Johnson

Interior formatting: Mark Thomas / Coverness.com

Main Great Wall cover image © Jill Chen/Stocksy

JOHN SHORS

UNBOUND

A NOVEL

PRAISE FOR
UNBOUND

"*Unbound* is utterly captivating—an epic, historical page-turner with a beating heart. I loved it." – Jamie Ford, *New York Times* bestselling author of *Hotel on the Corner of Bitter and Sweet*

"In *Unbound*, John Shors draws us inside the impassioned history of China's Great Wall, through richly intertwined characters determined to live freely, and for love. A haunting tale of the enduring bonds that anchor and save us when all the other chains—poverty, enslavement, cruelty, degradation—have been broken. A gem of storytelling." – Paula McLain, *New York Times* bestselling author of *The Paris Wife*

"An elegant and compelling epic told with Shors' trademark understanding of human nature, and ability to create characters who touch our hearts. The setting—China's Great Wall—is as much a personality in the tale as the husband and wife who live, and love, in its shadow. In *Unbound*, history comes alive and literally takes your breath away." – M.J. Rose, *New York Times* bestselling author of *The Book of Lost Fragrances*

For Allison, Sophie, and Jack

AUTHOR'S PREFACE

The Great Wall of China is one of the most awe-inspiring creations of humanity. But why was the legendary fortification built? And who built it?

Modern scholars tell us that the Great Wall is not actually a single wall, but a collection of ramparts that were raised over a two-thousand-year period. Running from east to west near the northern border of China, the Great Wall was created to protect the Chinese from nomadic tribes, mainly the Mongols and Manchus.

Early sections of the Great Wall were little more than barricades of branches, dirt, and rocks. As the centuries passed, the skills of the builders improved, and by the time of the Ming Dynasty (1368 to 1644), the Great Wall was constructed more as an endless series of small, connected castles than a featureless barrier.

Several million Chinese died building the Great Wall. Some of them were criminals. Others were soldiers. Many were pressured into work through laws designed to reward hard labor with tax exemptions. Everyone toiled under dangerous and often besieged conditions, creating an unrivaled fortification that, if its parts were added together, would stretch for more than five thousand miles.

Once I chose to write a novel about the Great Wall, I was faced with a variety of options in terms of time and setting. I decided to place my story toward the end of the Ming Dynasty. At this time, China had about 150 million people, yet was vulnerable to Mongol attacks. Fierce, mobile, and unrivaled horsemen, the Mongols had struck fear into the hearts of the Chinese for generations. Rather than send armies north to meet and likely be defeated by their foe, the Ming leaders decided to reinforce and expand the Great Wall—a strategy that would become arguably the most ambitious building project in history.

Unbound is loosely fashioned after the famous Chinese legend of a husband and wife who became swept up in the undercurrents of the Great Wall's creation. At the time that Shakespeare's *Romeo and Juliet* was captivating audiences in the West, within China the story of Fan and Meng was being told with equal reverence. The tale of their epic struggle has been since shared from generation to generation, enduring the passage of time with as much resiliency and grace as the stones upon which they are said to have suffered. So it is the setting, not the characters, in this novel that is based on historical fact.

"A journey of a thousand miles begins with a single step."

Lao Tzu

PROLOGUE

Beijing—April 21, 1514

*T*he boy listened to his little sister die. Though a wall separated their rooms, and his mother's weeping obscured many sounds, he could still hear his sister's tortured breathing. Sitting in a corner, with his knees drawn up against his chest and his eyes closed, he trembled at the reverberations of her misery. The way she gasped for air reminded him of how she had screamed months earlier when her feet had first been bound. As was common practice, each of her toes, except for the biggest two, had been broken, one after the other. The broken toes were then forced downward, beneath the sole of each foot, and wrapped tightly with a binding cloth.

Tao would never forget her shrieks and screams. He had been told to ignore them; that miniature feet were for her own good and would help her marry above her station. Someday, it was promised, the pains she endured as a child would bring her comforts as a woman.

Every other morning thereafter the women had bound his

sister's feet tighter, breaking additional bones and dislocating her heels. Her wails had always returned with the women, and Tao had inevitably found himself in the same corner, trying to pretend that the sounds he heard were made by a dragon trapped beneath his house, desperately seeking to find its way into the sky.

At some point amid all the wretchedness, his sister's screams had turned to moans. Something had gone wrong with the binding. His mother wouldn't say what, but Tao had overheard the women talking about an infection, about how the girl's constant writhing and wailing had all but ensured that bad luck befell her.

Now, as Tao tried to ignore his mother's weeping, the trails of tears cooled on his cheeks. He knew that his sister would die soon. She had only been alive for five years, and yet he had many memories of her smiles and laughter. She had warmed his heart, and now that she was leaving him, he felt cold and empty. It was as if a monster had clawed its way into him and then used its talons to carve out his insides. He found it hard to breathe. He ached. He beseeched whoever was listening to his prayers to let his sister's endless suffering end.

As more of his tears fell, as he shuddered from the knowledge of her fate, Tao swore that he would never hear such misery again. In several years a marriage would be arranged for him. Sons would be expected, of course, but he made an oath to himself that if he ever had a daughter her feet wouldn't be bound. He would protect her. Moreover, to make up for the shortcoming of her large feet, he would teach her to be strong. She would learn what he had. She might be poorly suited for wedding proposals, but she would be free. He would call her Meng—after his little sister. In that way, he *would honor them both.*

The nearby wails grew louder. Tao beat his fists against his brow.

He tried to imagine his sister's face, but to his surprise and profound sadness, it was nowhere to be found.

She had departed.

CHAPTER ONE

Farewell

Beijing—September 12, 1548

The room was simple, clean, and warm. Several potted plants, neatly trimmed, occupied one corner. A round, red lacquered table stood on chipped but steady legs. Walls were graced by fading reproductions of classic works of art—renderings of famous calligraphers and landscape painters. The wooden floor bore an oval rug patterned with perpendicular lines, and a low bed covered with bright, cotton blankets and long, tubular pillows.

A man and a woman knelt on the rug, facing each other. Both were young—in their early twenties. The man was named Fan and seemed too tall to be comfortable on his knees. His shoulders were hunched forward. His face was thin, his nose and cheekbones more angular than most of his countrymen. His eyes, not set far apart, dipped slightly toward his nose. A well-kept goatee covered an old scar on his chin. The nails of his oversized hands weren't long and manicured like those of the scholars and state officials whom he saw on the street, men far above him in rank and power.

Fan wore a simple brown robe that was edged in black. The darker fabric matched the color of his hair, which was long and was gathered up at the back of his head in a topknot. When Fan leaned toward his wife, Meng, his robe swayed forward, making him look much heavier than was true. "It's only for three months," he said, his voice soft and refined. "With three months of work, I can spare us from three years of taxation."

Meng looked away, her gaze resting on the words of a long-dead calligrapher. She took two deep breaths, then turned back to Fan. "But winter brings the hardest months on the Great Wall. And you'll be there in winter."

"So you can make me a warm coat."

She made no reply, and he studied her, as he had on countless occasions before. Though she was of average height and build, her face captivated him. Most observers would have thought it to be unremarkable, but he delighted in its design. While his features seemed chiseled out of his flesh, hers were rounded and full. Her eyes were wide and set far apart. Her nose contained not a single straight line but was curved and flowing, reminding him of rocks worn smooth by water. Though she sometimes painted her full lips in red and orange, now they glistened with only moisture. Her long, black hair was pulled back and bound together in buns on either side of her head, just above her ears. She was dressed as he was, though her robe was predominately cream colored, with bands of green, pink, and auburn that were embroidered with small, white flowers.

Perhaps most remarkable about Meng—her feet were unbound. Nearly all women of some rank had bound feet, a symbol of beauty and prestige. Women with large feet were destined to marry poor men and lead difficult lives, working in fields from dawn to dusk. Such women were often teased and insulted by their betters, who knew the agony of broken toes and dislocated heels, yet were proud of their tiny and colorful lotus shoes.

Most even moderately educated men would have been loath to wed a woman with large feet. Yet when Fan's father had arranged the marriage, Fan hadn't been ashamed. His station wasn't so high as to demand a woman with perfect feet. More important, he needed his wife to be free of physical handicaps. Servants were expensive to feed and house, and Fan could afford no such luxuries. He was a craftsman, skilled with stone, but a low rung on the ladder of society's haves and have-nots.

"Not paying three years of taxes will help us," Fan said, taking her hands in his. "We can save that money."

"People say the Great Wall is made from the bones of its workers, that they bury the dead and then cover them with stones."

He squeezed her fingers. "That isn't true."

"How can you be sure?"

"Because I've built such walls. If you filled the gap between the two sides with bodies instead of dirt, the bodies would decay and the walls would collapse."

She glanced away from him. "But where you're headed … it's where the fighting is the worst. What if the Mongols break through? What if you're overrun?"

He saw that her eyes glistened, and he leaned forward to wipe away a tear that had dropped to her cheek. "If the Mongols broke through, they could ride here in a single day. They could knock down the doors to my father's house and harm you. But if I'm on the wall, if I make it strong, they'll never come here. I'll never have to worry about you being hurt."

"But I feel the safest with you. The most at peace with you. The Mongols don't worry me. Losing you worries me."

"You won't lose me, or anything else. I'll make sure of that."

"You're too skilled with stone, Fan. That's why you were noticed. You shouldn't have tried so hard to please them. With masters like them, it's better to remain anonymous."

Fan's mind drifted back to the Forbidden City, where for several years he had been in charge of repairing a section of one of its towering walls. "I'll write to you," he said softly. "I'll send you stories."

"I know you will."

"I'll think of new ones to keep you company. I'll be gone, but my voice will return to you. I won't leave you alone, Meng. And when I'm on the wall, I'll whisper that I love you, even if you aren't listening. Maybe the winds will carry my words."

To his surprise, she tried to smile. "How lucky we are to have been paired together. Most men would make me miserable. You make me happy."

"And most wives would send me in search of a concubine," he replied, trying to lighten her mood. "My friends each have a wife, and if not one concubine, then a slew of courtesans they favor. So, you see, you give me joy, and you save me money. You're my wife and my concubine and my courtesan all bundled together into one person."

"If I save you so much money, why must you go to the Great Wall? Why not just pay your taxes and stay with us?"

"Because one day we'll want our own home, so we must save. And if we ever have a son, we'll need to send him to study. All of that costs money."

"I don't need money to be happy. I need you."

"We've talked about children, Meng. We want them. But we could barely even afford them right now. We'd be too poor to give our sons and daughters the lives they deserve."

She sighed, then shifted on her feet, which she kept hidden from sight. "I want our children to be strong willed. I want to be strong willed. But now … I feel weak. I wish you would stay."

"You're not weak. Far from it."

"But I'll miss you. I'm not the same person without you, especially now, with my father gone."

"Go see your mother. Spend time with her."

"Tell me the story of us. The story you told me on the night of our first anniversary."

He again placed his hand to her face, stroking her cheek with his thumb. "I don't remember my own words."

"Try to."

"Maybe I'll change them a bit. My stories never stay the same."

She shook her head, causing his hand to move against her face. "No. Don't change anything."

His smile dawned slowly, as if cresting over hills and faraway places. "There was once a young, married man who was crippled in an accident," he began. "His wife cared for him thereafter—tending to his wounds, nurturing him with her touch and her voice. She rarely left his side, determined to share her strength and love with him. Yet despite her many efforts, he weakened. One day a physician told him that soon he would die. He then anguished as he thought about how most of his dreams would remain unfulfilled. Distraught, he tried to face his death, and though he'd never favored religion, he looked to it for answers. He read about the different faiths and beliefs, trying to understand the Christian concept of heaven, the Buddhist principle of reincarnation, and the Confucian position that what one did in this life was much more important than worrying about what happens after death."

Meng's eyes locked on his, and she nodded, encouraging him to continue. "But he found no solace in any of those beliefs, did he?"

"No, not much—even as he grew sicker and sicker. His sight failed, he ceased to eat, and his despair grew. Yet even in his worst moments, he sensed her presence. She cleaned his bedsores. She made him his favorite tea, and brought him fresh flowers. No matter how filthy or painful or dreary the task, she undertook it, without complaint, without bitterness. And as he slowly succumbed to the inevitable, diminishing day by day, his love for her swelled. And a day came when he didn't need a religion or a belief. She was his faith, his solace. With her beside him, he was no longer afraid of death. By then she was such a part of him that he believed they could never be separated. Not by distance, or time, or worlds of sun and shadow. His spirit, he whispered to her, had mixed with hers until a unified light had been created. And to him, that light represented the afterlife.

"As he took his final breaths, he was at peace. He smiled at her. He savored the oneness of their unity. His looming death wasn't painful or frightening, but a thing of beauty. Because what he realized in his final moments was that he had been blessed. His journey, while short, had taken him past the most wondrous mountains, the most spectacular sunsets. He'd seen those sights not from a road, but from his bed, even as he lay dying. Because the magnificence that defined her was as glorious as any sight that he'd ever beheld. He knew that whatever afterlife awaited him, hers would be the first voice that he heard. And as he died, he began searching for her voice, her touch, the oneness he knew would comfort him throughout eternity. She felt and treasured that unity as well, and even long after he was gone, she sensed his presence. The light that was their love never wavered—not even in her darkest moments, illuminating the path before her, illuminating her very life."

Fan leaned closer to Meng, wiping a fresh tear from her cheek. "And that's how I see you. That's how I'll always see you. You're my faith, my solace. You'll always be the brightest light in my life." His voice trailed off, and he edged toward her until their knees touched. Gently grasping the jade necklace that fell from her neck, he pulled it out of the folds of her robe and into the light. The coin-size stone was in the shape of a turtle, though only the first half of its body. He wore the second half around his neck. "Soon we'll be reunited," he said. "I promise."

"You can promise ... nothing. But treat yourself, love yourself, as I love you."

"I could never treat myself so well."

Meng nodded, drawing him even closer. "Did he kiss her, even as he lay dying?"

"Yes."

"Show me how."

His fingers intertwined with hers. He leaned forward, and their lips met. Though he tried to hide it, the angst of their looming separation tore at him. He wasn't afraid of dying on the wall, believing that he'd return in only a few months. But being away from her would cast chains around his spirit, and he was afraid of such an imprisonment.

"I have to do this," he whispered, trying to convince himself as much as her. "For you, for our unborn children, I have to go. Otherwise we'll struggle this year, and the next. We'll never have enough money."

"Hurry back," she whispered, kissing him, leaning into him. "And then never leave again."

They toppled backward, still clutching at each other. Their heartbeats quickened and they embraced, passion blooming between them, their fears and troubles momentarily cast aside. They reached into the folds of each other's robe, young and naïve enough to believe that their love had forged a bond that wouldn't be severed.

Their movements quickened.

They caressed and kissed.

Fate had always been kind to them, so they had no reason to flee from it.

CHAPTER TWO

The Pain of Distance

Jinshanling—October 9, 1549

The Great Wall stretched endlessly before Fan. To the east it followed the contours of a ridge, rising and falling over semi-arid, rugged land. He could see about two miles of the structure until it dipped beneath a distant hump of earth, plummeting from sight. Yet he knew it continued beyond the reaches of his vision, knew its every twist and turn.

Most of the men on the Great Wall believed it looked like a dragon sprawled across the mountains. And in many ways it did. The northern top of the wall, the side that faced the Mongols, was crenellated so that projectiles could be fired at the enemy. These notches resembled scales on the dragon's back. Though the body of the beast lay motionless, it twisted slightly to the north and south as it followed the ridge. Every five hundred feet or so, a watchtower rose from around and atop the wall. The stone block and brick watchtowers looked like small castles, complete with battlements and colorful flags. Fan had never been sure what part of the beast they were believed to comprise. The largest could have been its head, the smaller ones its shoulders or hips. In any case, he liked to imagine the Great Wall as his dragon, as the protector of his people and his wife.

Fan had been stationed at the Great Wall for more than a year. His responsibility was to ensure that the fortification remained in good standing from Jinshanling to Simatai—two towns that had sprung up to meet the needs of thousands of soldiers. Fan oversaw about six miles of stonework, a stretch that included twenty-two of the multi-story watchtowers. As this section of the Great Wall was under constant threat, and was often probed or attacked, Fan incessantly looked for damage that needed to be addressed. Both the Mongols and nature took their toll on the mighty wall. The Mongols used explosives and men. Nature fought with water and ice.

The elements had besieged Fan as well. Spending more than a year on the wall had robbed his body of what little fat he'd possessed, darkened his skin, and battered his flesh. His fingers were swollen and scarred. His right knee buckled from time to time, usually when he was carrying something heavy and turned the wrong way. Even his sense of touch was not what it once was—everything felt so very rough and cold beneath his fingertips.

Pushing against the bricks that formed the notched edge of the top of a watchtower, Fan shifted his gaze from the Great

UNBOUND

Wall's outline to the boy beside him. The boy, aged twelve, was a Mongol who had been captured when a group of Chinese soldiers conducted a rare raid on an enemy position. He arrived at the Great Wall at almost the same time as Fan and had been handed over as a slave. Fan was his master.

The boy's name was Bataar, and he was tall and broad shouldered for his age. His round face usually bore no expression, though it could become animated if Fan were telling a story. Bataar's skin was slightly darker than that of most Chinese. He had thin eyebrows and often kept his eyes squinted halfway shut to protect them from the glare of the sun. Bataar had been born with the two middle fingers of his right hand fused together, starting just above the largest knuckles. Like Fan, he dressed in a laborer's tattered outfit. He wore cloth shoes, loose-fitting trousers, and a long-sleeved shirt that parted in the middle like a robe and was tightened with a black sash.

As Fan's gaze was almost perpetually focused on the imperfections of the Great Wall, Bataar usually stared to the north, toward his people. This day was no different. While Fan tugged on bricks and checked for cracks in the mortar between them, Bataar gazed at the barren landscape that dominated so much of his people's territory.

Fan leaned over the watchtower's northern parapet, looking down. Nearly fifty feet below, the reddish earth ran away from the stonework, almost bereft of notable foliage. The top of the wall, where soldiers walked and fought, had been designed to tilt slightly southward, so that water ran to the Chinese side. The land near the southern side of the wall was full of bushes and short evergreen trees, nearly opposite in appearance to what lay immediately to the north. The wall's almost imperceptible tilt discouraged shrubbery, which would allow Mongols to hide, from growing near the north side.

Sometimes sand was also spread out at the base of the enemy's side of the wall, so if a Mongol scout probed the fortification, his footsteps might be detected. Fan placed little faith in this tactic, as the Mongols had learned to smooth out their tracks. Yet he still gazed at the sand beneath him, searching for signs.

"You won't see anything," Bataar said quietly.

"I know. But I must look."

"Before I was captured, I walked under this wall. Twice. And each time I used a bundle of crow's feathers to cover up my tracks."

Fan turned toward the boy. "Was your father with you?"

"He was always with me. Well ... almost always," Bataar added, his voice trailing off.

"If he'd been with you the day you were captured, he might have died. You should be thankful that he wasn't."

Bataar shook his head. "You haven't met my father. Nothing can kill him."

"Because he rides a horse so well?"

"Because he's drunk the blood of a horse. He's fast and agile, and your arrows and cannons will never touch him."

A lizard scurried across the parapet. Fan watched it, making sure it didn't disappear into an unseen crack. The creature stopped an arm's length away, resting on a warm brick.

"You speak our language as if you're one of us," Fan said. "Are you sure you're not Chinese? Perhaps your father stole you from our side of the wall. We merely stole you back."

"I've never been to your side of the wall."

"Tonight I'll tell you a story about our side, about something I saw near the Forbidden City."

Bataar pretended to aim an imaginary arrow, the two fused fingers of his right hand hooking inward, as if gripping a bowstring. "I'll go there with my father, when we break through this wall. We'll dance on your emperor's bed."

Fan smiled. "Why so ill-humored today?"

"I don't know. I didn't sleep well. And I dreamed of horses."

"You'll ride them again soon enough. Just temper that tongue of yours around Yat-sen. He'll hack it out of your mouth if he hears you say such things."

"I'm not afraid of him."

"But I am, Bataar," Fan replied, lowering his voice. "So for my sake, please stay silent. We'll make our escape soon enough."

The wind shifted, causing red banners along the Great Wall to pivot to the north. Though he wasn't nearly as superstitious as many of his countrymen, Fan gazed toward the land of their enemy. He saw nothing but the same rolling, bleak emptiness that usually greeted him. On the broad top of the wall below, four soldiers walked beside one another, heading toward the next watchtower. The armored men laughed as they passed a comrade who was stationed beside a cannon.

Fan wondered why the men were moving. Usually Yat-sen, the commander of this stretch of the wall, kept his men hidden in the watchtowers so that the Mongols never knew which sections of the fortification were most heavily manned.

Fan's lips parted, but his question remained unasked. To the west, four watchtowers away, two dark plumes of smoke rose into the sky. The smoke indicated the presence of Mongol riders. Two plumes meant that a force of fewer than five hundred men approached. A single column of smoke would have announced the sight of fewer than one hundred men. The more columns that were created, the greater was the number of enemy.

"Let's go," Fan said, hurrying from his position. He climbed down a rope ladder, navigated the confusing layout of the level below, and was soon outside, on top of the spine of the Great Wall. The northern and southern parapets rose to the height of his shoulders, protecting his body. He ran, followed by Bataar, toward the smoke. Ahead, alarms sounded as men beat on massive bells. Soldiers hurried from watchtowers, heading toward the smoke, readying their weapons.

Fan wondered if the Mongols would attack the marked position, or if they would simply ride to the east or west as they often did, trying to find a weakness in the endless rise of stone. Yat-sen's men were well disciplined and spread out to their designated areas. Some hurried toward the still-smoking watchtower. Others took up positions along the top of the wall. Fan wanted to be near the action in case the Mongols attacked with force. They might carry explosives and damage what he safeguarded.

Though the day was cool, Fan soon worked up a sweat. He ran on, ascending and descending steps that led to and from the watchtowers. The top of the Great Wall, wide enough to accommodate eight men marching abreast, now bustled with soldiers and horses. A blur of red flashed in the distance. That must be Yat-sen, Fan thought, envisioning the commander in his armor and on his warhorse.

Fan led Bataar to the watchtower adjacent to the one that carried the smoke signals. They climbed to the top level. Five soldiers held notched arrows on bowstrings. Two other men stood near a single cannon. To the north, a cloud of dust came in their direction. Hundreds of Mongol riders approached more swiftly than any storm. The riders moved in unison, shifting directions like a single leaf in the wind. The formation was a thing of beauty and dread. Few of the Chinese soldiers could match the fighting prowess of the Mongols. That was why they had built the Great Wall, and why they now stood behind it, ready to defend their land and their loved ones.

The Mongols approached the nearby tower. Chinese cannons erupted, casting balls of iron forward. As the cannons quivered, the Mongols fanned out sideways into two different directions. Only one horse and rider went down. The rest rode hard, prompting the Chinese to launch their arrows and fire more cannons. The injured Mongol was pulled up by his comrades, who also held down and slew his wounded horse. Not a single Mongol rider fired his bow. Yet the warriors shouted as they continued to ride to the west and east, assessing the responsiveness of the Chinese defenders.

"They always test us," Fan said, glad that no explosions had rocked the Great Wall. Explosions made his life even more taxing, as breeches in the fortification were difficult to fix.

"One day they'll do more than test you," Bataar replied. "Thousands of them will come, and when they do, I hope you're far from here."

Fan took Bataar's arm and led him away from the Chinese soldiers. At the corner of the watchtower, behind the crenellated parapet, Fan turned back to the Mongols. The riders continued to spread out, racing along the Great Wall, just beyond the reach of cannons.

"Is your father out there?" Fan asked.

"He's always out there."

"Looking for you?"

Bataar nodded.

Fan thought of Meng, wishing that such a great distance didn't separate them. He missed her more with each passing day, her absence an ache within him that never left. Yet he could not easily flee to her. Yat-sen had seen to that.

"We're both far from our loved ones," Fan whispered, turning to Bataar. "And we're both slaves."

"You're no slave."

"I want to leave, yet I can't. And I'm working here, against my will. That makes me a slave. Just as Yat-sen captured you, he captured me."

"But you're Chinese. I'm a Mongol."

Fan put his hand on Bataar's shoulder. "Others see those differences, but I only see a man and a boy. I only see two slaves. One must return to his wife, the other to his family."

"So how do we do it? How do we escape?"

"We're patient. We walk instead of run. We whisper instead of shout."

Bataar smiled. "My father said patience is for the indecisive, for the weak."

"I'm not so sure, Bataar. Your people out there—weren't they patient today? Did they charge us or probe us?"

Again came the boy's smile. "That's because my father doesn't lead them. If he did, they'd be attacking you now."

"This wall is strong. It's yet to fall."

Bataar shook his head. "If it's so strong, why must you remain here? Why must you fix it, day after day? My father told me that your wall is like a chain. It's only as stout as its thinnest link, and when my people find that link, they'll attack."

"We'll be gone before then. We'll be safe."

"I don't think so. Not if we're too patient. Winter is coming. Soon my people won't be able to ride as they do now. And in the spring they'll let the horses rest and graze. The time to attack is always in the autumn."

Fan turned to the north. The Mongol riders were barely in sight—tufts of distant dust marking their presence. Though Bataar was only a boy, his words carried weight. Very few men understood the Mongol and the Chinese worlds. Bataar had seen both. He believed that his people were the stronger. Not the wiser or the more artistic or the more humorous, but the fiercer.

A faraway explosion caused the men on the watchtower to hurry to the edge of the crenulated parapet and look to the east. In the far distance, three columns of smoke rose from another tower, meaning that as many as a thousand Mongols had gathered.

"We won't be indecisive," Fan finally replied, still speaking quietly. "But you must trust me, Bataar. You must wait until the time is right."

"I do trust you."

"Good. Then let's hurry toward that smoke. Let's see if your countrymen have damaged my chain."

*

On the south side of Beijing, Meng sat in a garden within her uncle's property. While he wasn't rich, nor was he without some wealth, and his home was large and maintained by several servants. Meng's mother, Hong, had lived there for the past year. She'd arrived at her brother's door several months after the unexpected death of her husband, who had been bitten by a deadly snake while gathering frogs in a marsh.

The home of Meng's uncle was located on one of Beijing's countless *hutongs*. These narrow alleys crisscrossed Beijing like the tendrils of a spider's web. Near the center of the web was the Forbidden City, where the emperor resided. Rich scholars and state officials lived closest to the Forbidden City, and the farther out one went in any direction, the poorer the homes became. The emperor was near fanatical in his desire to separate the classes, and the network of *hutongs* ensured such division.

Meng had been to her uncle's home twice. Women were strongly discouraged from venturing beyond the walls of their father's or husband's property, and only on special occasions had Meng seen the streets of Beijing. Today, because her mother was ill, Meng had been able to visit her, deciding to wear her finest clothes—a robe of homespun cloth that lay beneath a *bijia*, a sleeveless jacket that fell to her shins. Since only the rich were allowed to wear colors of deep blue and red, Meng's garments were an array of green and purple hues. She had selected the smallest of her shoes, though even a child would realize that her feet were unbound.

Meng had ridden through the city in a sedan chair—an extravagance usually reserved for the rich. But traveling as a woman, even with her father-in-law by her side, was a compelling reason to reach her uncle's home as soon as possible.

As she had many times already that afternoon, Meng studied her mother, wondering how she had aged so much in the past year. Her hair was now gray. Her hands trembled. She stooped, was racked by painful coughs, and could barely stand. Her mother was in perfect contrast to the small, walled garden within which they sat. The lush garden consisted of a manicured lawn, neatly trimmed pines, and wisteria vines propped up by bamboo latticework that had been painted orange. A single, male peacock patrolled the grounds, searching for insects between a pair of immense porcelain pots containing koi.

The two women sat on a wooden dais, facing each other. Meng leaned over to pull a silk blanket higher up on her mother's lap. "Where did your strength go?" she asked.

"I seemed strong because you were little. Now that you're older, my true virtues emerge."

Meng shook her head. "No one would believe that. I remember how, when our kitchen once caught fire, you beat at those flames like they were Mongols coming over the Great Wall."

Her mother smoothed out the blanket until its surface was more uniform than the skin of her hands. "That was a long time ago."

"Yes, but that's how I'll always remember you. That's how I want you to be again. You're not old. You're just ill. The rains brought so many maladies to us this year. One happened to find you."

"I think the medicine makes it worse. Why are ginkgo leaves expected to cure everything?"

"Have you stopped making tea with them?"

"It's only because the trees are everywhere. So the medicine is cheap."

Meng nodded, thinking of her father, believing that his demise had weakened her. "Too many people are sick," she said. "It's said that the floods have ruined most of the crops. Famine is coming."

"To many, yes. But you'll be safe in the city. Temples will give out grain, as they always do."

"But, Mother, Fan isn't in the city. He's on the Great Wall, a world away from me. His letters say that he's fine, but I don't believe him."

"Why not?"

"Because he never mentions my words. He doesn't realize you're sick. I know that he's trapped there. He's said as much. But whoever has trapped him must be crueler than he admits. Otherwise my letters would reach him. He'd read them, worry about your illness, and come for us."

The peacock cried out, flapping its wings. In the distance a low reply emerged.

"That bird is restless," Meng's mother said. "Just as you are."

"I want to go to him. Winter will be here soon. A hard winter, I'm told. Fan withers in the cold, and I hate to think of him suffering on that wall. The famine will make everything much worse. Whatever he endured last year will be nothing compared to what he'll go through this winter. What if the cold and the hunger and the misery are too much for him to bear?"

"What will you do? You're a woman of low rank. You can't journey like a man could. Your feet might be unbound, but your free will isn't."

Meng shook her head, reminding herself how her mother might be persuaded. "Women are traveling more these days, despite what the emperor says."

"Rich women who are carried from place to place."

"I made a winter coat, pants, and boots for him. I want to bring them to him."

"Your father—"

"Taught me, Mother. He taught me to read, to think. He longed for a son, yet he still loved me."

Her mother coughed, and Meng thought of her father. As a boy he'd shown so much promise that the leaders of his village had pooled their money to send him to a special school where students studied to take imperial exams. The few who passed the exams became state officials—high-ranking members of society. Those who failed the tests went home in shame. Her father had failed, and though he had been forced to become a farmer, years later he had shared his knowledge with Meng. She had benefitted from his disgrace.

"The journey isn't far, Mother. A week perhaps. At most ten days. I could bring a servant and … and dress like a man."

"A man? But why not just send a man? Send someone to give Fan your clothes."

"Because I need to see him," Meng replied, her voice becoming slightly strained even though she tried to stay strong for her mother's sake. "He's been away for more than a year and I miss him so much. Just like you miss Father. What if you could walk to him? Wouldn't you try? Wouldn't you go to him tomorrow, especially if you knew that you could give him comfort?"

Her mother nodded. "Of course I would."

"Then why shouldn't I?"

"What does his father say?"

"Nothing. He's kind to me, but I can't … I can't tell him this. I'll just go one night. I'll take a servant and go."

The peacock called again, though this time no response was given. Dipping its head into one of the pools of water, the bird drank, then stretched its neck. In the distant sky behind the peacock, several brightly colored kites soared and dove in the wind. Two of the kites were dragons. One was an eagle. Whoever guided the kites couldn't be seen, though surely they were boys. Girls weren't allowed to indulge in such activities.

Meng's mother had always enjoyed watching kites and had once said that she wished she could fly one. The kites seemed free.

"The roads will be dangerous," she finally replied, her eyes glistening. "Fan wouldn't want you to go. Think about his wishes, Meng. Not mine or yours, but his. If something were to happen to you, he would never be the same."

"But I'm not the same," Meng said, then bit her lower lip, trying to restrain her tears. "I'm sad now—sadder than I thought I could ever be. Father taught me to treat others well, to believe in the good in people, just as Confucius said. And I want to act that way. But how can I be noble if I'm miserable? How can I love the world if it gives me so much pain?"

Across the garden, within the house, voices emerged. A man laughed.

"I see your pain," her mother replied. "You hide it well, but hiding suffering from a mother is like trying to hide the sun from the sky."

"I didn't want you to worry."

"Mothers always worry."

"And so do wives. Even young ones."

"Worry is a part of life. It's like the air we breathe, and is always within us. But just because it's present doesn't mean that we should risk everything to make it go away."

"I don't want to be weak, Mother. Father showed me how to be strong. He wasn't afraid of taking risks, or having me take them."

"And now he's gone."

"That doesn't change what he taught me. Or my longing to help my husband."

The older woman coughed, then nodded. "When you were very little, your father wanted sons. He yearned for them, like all men do. But … I could never give him the gift of another child. And so when you were five or six, he began to treat you as a son. He taught you to read and write; to be curious about the world. He wanted to share his knowledge with you."

"And he did."

"And you're correct—he taught you to be strong."

"He was right to do so. Just because we're women doesn't mean that we can't effect change, that we have no influence upon the world."

"Perhaps."

"It's true, Mother. You must believe me."

"The world doesn't care if I believe in you. You could still starve to death on your journey, or be beaten to death, or simply lose your way."

"Please, Mother. Please let me go. I beg you to let me go."

Sighing, the older woman studied the kites, watching them soar and fall. "I've always been superstitious," she finally replied. "And maybe your father failed that awful test for a reason."

"What do you mean?"

"If he'd passed it, we would have been wealthy. He would have rarely been home, and not have had the time to teach you. And even worse, your feet would have been bound, even if he privately abhorred the practice."

"No, he wouldn't have done that to me. One day when I was sick with a fever he told me as much."

"Maybe. Maybe not. He and I would have been under tremendous pressure to do so. Wealthy girls don't have unbound feet. And just as likely as not, today you'd be crippled. You could never walk as you want to walk. So it's good that we were poor, good that you have long, full feet."

"That's right, Mother. I'll look like a man and walk like a man."

"Your father would have gone with you. People would have frowned upon it, of course, but he'd have gone."

"All the more reason for me to go."

Nodding, the older woman slowly wrung the blanket on her lap. Her knuckles whitened. "But you must return, my only daughter. You must come back to me."

Meng reached over to dab at her mother's tears with the corner of the silk blanket. "I'll bring you something back, from the north. Maybe a kite."

"I'd like that. But more important, bring your smile back. You've showed it to me so much in the past. I yearn to see it again."

"I'll smile and laugh again, I promise. I just need to find Fan. Without him I don't feel whole."

"Then find him. Find him and return to me."

Meng squeezed her mother's hand. "Thank you."

"Go now. Go before I change my restless mind. Go before I think about all the calamities that could unfold on your journey."

After standing up, Meng bowed. "You're strong, Mother. If you weren't, you wouldn't let me go."

"Nonsense. The opposite is true."

"Smile when you think of me traveling to him. Soon I'll be happy, and I want to share that feeling with you."

"You will. You have. I adore you."

Meng bowed one more time to her mother, then turned and strode toward her uncle's house. A sudden sense of urgency inspired her pace, and she moved with speed, her feet carrying her ahead in a way that few women could, or would dare, walk.

*

The main room of the watchtower was unusually bright. Oftentimes the thick, wooden shutters on the windows would be closed, whether to keep out rain or Mongol arrows. In those instances, gloom prevailed, the only light coming from the outline of the windows and doors, as well as candles and a small cooking fire in a secondary room.

The interiors of all the watchtowers along Fan's stretch of the Great Wall had been designed to confuse intruders. If an enemy climbed the fortification and broke into a tower, he would find a bewildering array of interior walls, narrow corridors, small and large rooms, and rope ladders leading up to the higher level. While the enemy soldier tried to make sense of his surroundings, strategically placed Chinese archers would fill him with arrows.

The watchtower that Fan stood within was about fifty feet long and forty feet wide, and rose from the ground to surround the spine of the Great Wall, as if a small castle had been placed around the fortification. Two inhabitable levels existed within the tower. The main level was at the same height as the top the Great Wall and featured living and sleeping quarters for up to fifteen soldiers.

The upper level was much more open—only half of it was covered by a stone, two-sided sloping roof that protected a small room. The rest of the level was designed for signaling and battle. Within waterproof, porcelain containers were carefully stacked piles of wolf dung, which, when lit, released dark, dense smoke.

Fan followed his commander, Yat-sen, up the rope ladder to the higher level. The ladder swayed as the men climbed, and Fan was surprised at the strength of his superior. Even wearing armor and a sheathed sword, Yat-sen moved with speed and dexterity. He reached the top of the ladder, told the lone sentry to leave them, and then walked to the northeast corner of the tower. Several spears stood upright in the corner. A single cannon was positioned in the center of the northern, crenulated parapet.

Yat-sen said nothing, so Fan studied him. The commander was dressed, as usual, in magnificent armor—the colors and style of which were usually reserved for a general. An iron helmet covered Yat-sen's head, coming to a rest at his brow. A bright sash of red cloth was affixed to a spike that rose from the helmet, which had been engraved with shiny stars. The commander wore a red robe that flowed to his shins. Over this robe was a thick coat of dark leather that was covered in iron plates the size of a child's foot. Finally, on top of the coat was a red vest embroidered with golden dragons. A curved sword sheathed in stained rosewood hung from Yat-sen's side. The weapon's blade, though unseen, shined like a silver coin. Its hilt gleamed as if gold, though it was brass.

While Yat-sen's armor was elegant, his facial features were not. He wore a thick moustache as well as a tuft of hair on his chin. Deep lines had penetrated his face—etched across his forehead and alongside his eyes and nose. The thick scar of an old burn was visible on the left side of his neck, running down beneath his clothes. Though he was of ordinary height, Yat-sen stood tall, his shoulders held back.

"How much did the barbarians damage our wall?" Yat-sen asked.

Fan gazed toward the next watchtower. The base of the tower was made of massive stone blocks. Eight feet above the blocks, much smaller bricks had been used to erect the tower's four walls. Though the bricks were only two hands long and a hand wide, they were immensely strong, as was the mortar that bound them together. The Mongols often tried to dislodge the bricks but were rarely successful.

Bowing slightly, Fan replied, "The Mongol cannon struck the middle of the tower, but little damage was done. I already have men repairing some cracked mortar and shattered bricks."

Yat-sen coughed, then spat off the side of the tower. "They test us once again, Craftsman. Always probing, always looking for a weakness."

"It will take more than one cannon to topple this wall."

"The barbarians will never bring down the Great Wall. But they seek to scale it. And a damaged wall is easier to climb than the stout one at my feet. That is why they probe. They search for a weakness. We have too few men to stand against a massed attack, so they spread us thin with their antics. Much like a game of *Go*, yes? But then, you wouldn't know, as my pieces always best yours."

Fan nodded but made no reply. Most times, it was better to let Yat-sen hear himself speak. How he loved the sound of his own voice.

"Our twenty-two towers will always be the strongest," Yat-sen said. "As well as the wall between them. My duty is to contain the barbarians within that wasteland. We can never face them on an open field of battle, but we can piss on them from here. We can watch them scurry below us on their flea-ridden mounts like a hawk watches rats."

Fan wondered if the war with the Mongols would ever end. The Mongols craved trade, which the Chinese had no interest in offering. The emperor didn't want the purity of his people to be influenced by the northern nomads, and trade would blend the two distinct cultures together, irrevocably blurring distinctions that were made to stand alone. Though most men in the army agreed with the emperor's belief, Fan had seen the terrible cost of war. He longed for peace.

"The barbarians are hard men," Yat-sen said. "They live in that wasteland, moving from place to place so that their horses can be fed and pitiful crops grown. We have fertile valleys and wide rivers, but these gifts have made us soft. We build and defend an endless wall rather than attack. Our intellect grows, but our ferocity wanes. That is why I am here, Craftsman. Because I'm still fierce. I've been tested by fire and emerged from it only stronger."

"Yes."

"You're soft but wise. You know how to repair these battlements like no other. That's why you remain by my side. My honor rests on the strength of this wall. It won't fall while I still breathe."

Fan searched the distant horizon for enemy riders. "I'm proud to serve you, but … but I've been here for more than one year, far longer than was originally asked of me. Surely there is another who can take my place."

"There is no other," Yat-sen replied. "You will stay. I have the best armor, the best sword, the best men. No one is more important to me than you, as you see the cracks, the erosion, the imperfections of what looks to be perfect."

"But my wife awaits me. We've already been apart for far too long, and I promised her that—"

"Wives do not require promises. And you're in no position to promise any such thing. Until your replacement arrives, you'll stay."

Fan shook his head but said nothing, afraid to anger Yat-sen. Below, along both sides of the Great Wall, red banners rippled in the wind.

Yat-sen coughed once again. "I could chain you, Craftsman. I could keep you in one place against your will. But that would limit your ability to walk the wall." He paused, his hand dropping to the hilt of his sword. He pulled it up, exposing some of the blade. "Should you leave here before I order it, I'll use this steel to take the barbarian boy's feet, and then that misshapen, cursed hand of his. Afterwards I'll cast him into the wasteland so that his people can find him."

"Please don't—"

"But before I do those things, I'll command my men to ride to your home. They will drag your wife into the street. As the wife of a deserter she'll be shown no mercy. She'll—"

"Please stop," Fan interrupted, spreading out his hands, his heart thumping wildly.

Yat-sen stepped toward Fan, his sword sliding farther out of its sheath. "You forget your place, Craftsman," he said. "You'll keep your head because I need you. But you need me as well. Without my good grace the boy and the woman will die. So you'd be wise to please me."

The commander coughed again, placing his free hand against his chest. When his shudders ceased, he straightened. "I know you hate me, as I hate you. We hate each other for different reasons, for we're different men. Yet there can be a peace between us. Keep my wall strong, and the boy and the woman will live. One more winter is all I require. A winter of hardship, yes, but what is one season of suffering compared to a lifetime of joy?"

Fan wavered beneath the intensity of Yat-sen's eyes, shifting his weight, his back suddenly aching. He believed the commander was lying but found himself nodding. Better to make a false peace than to stoke the rage of an enemy. "In the spring I'll leave," he finally replied, his heartbeat slowing. "Until then, your wall will be the strongest. The Mongols will come, but they'll always go."

Yat-sen sheathed his sword. "Keep it strong, Craftsman. All of our fates are tied to it. If it falls, so do we. If it endures, so do we."

"I'll await the spring."

"Do that. Until then, think no more of foolish vows told to women. Instead, go down there and find cracks and chips, weakness and vulnerability. Do what you were born to do and leave everything else to me."

*

Far from the Great Wall, dusk seemed to fall with more swiftness than it did from atop the battlements. Yat-sen rode his stallion to the south, away from his post and toward his home. Beijing was about a full day's hard gallop from the border, and Yat-sen cursed a former emperor's decision to move the capital city so close to the lands of their enemy. In trying to project strength and show a lack of fear, this emperor had doomed his people to generations of warfare. Beijing was so close to the border that surely the barbarians could almost sense its riches.

The countryside through which Yat-sen traveled was hilly and arid. He followed a cobblestone street wide enough to accommodate several ox-drawn carts. Many soldiers, most on foot, were about, as well as merchants who traveled by sedan chair.

These ornate contraptions consisted of an upright, rectangular frame that contained a comfortable chair. Curtains could be drawn across the windows of the frame, which was carried using two stout poles that extended forward and backward. Four or sometimes eight servants carried a sedan chair, gripping the poles and moving their feet in unison to ensure a steady ride.

Yat-sen, like many Chinese, despised merchants, who were of low rank and were tolerated only because of the goods they provided. He spurred his mount past them, coming closer than was necessary to their luxurious accommodations. Though Yat-sen should have heeded men boasting stations above him—men like scholars and state officials—he rode his horse carelessly. He was well known and feared. His unmistakable armor and weapons made him recognizable to most everyone, and without exception people stepped aside to let him pass.

As he rode through the deepening darkness, Yat-sen thought again about the rulers of his land, though now he mused over the present emperor. It was his decrees that had sent Yat-sen's father out into the wasteland, where he led a large contingent of soldiers against the Mongols. His father's force had been surrounded and annihilated, their heads left on stakes for all to see. The defeat had brought great shame upon Yat-sen's family. He'd been only nine, but men had spat on him, and boys had banded together to beat him down. His father had failed the emperor, had failed his people and his nation—an offense that was passed from father to son.

The years of Yat-sen's late childhood had been taxing. A cruel uncle had become his master, ultimately placing him into the army that his father had failed. In the army, Yat-sen's abhorrence for his father and his past had swelled. But his hate served an important purpose—it empowered him. After a decade passed, the men who had belittled him fell under his command. Soon thereafter he reigned over one of the most important sections of the entire Great Wall—a segment of twenty-two towers that the Mongols threatened with frequency.

Yat-sen guided his horse off the main road and onto the path that led to his home. Mirroring his armor, it was grand and spacious, complete with a sweeping roofline, painted walls, and an impeccable garden. A servant boy took the reins to his stallion, as Yat-sen dismounted. The movement provoked a cough from deep within his chest, but he didn't linger near the boy. Instead he walked into his home, ignoring the bows of other servants.

His private quarters featured a red, lacquer bed, desk, and chair, as well as porcelain pots filled with flowers and grasses. Providing additional comforts were silk carpets, paintings, and a small table that held an iron bowl containing warm coals. A red teapot sat on the coals. Yat-sen slid shut the door to his room, then poured himself a cup of the tea, which sometimes settled his cough.

Once his tea was gone, he slowly removed his armor, placing it on a special wooden rack. His dusty and sweat-stained red robe was tossed in a corner of the room for a servant to wash at a later time. Naked, Yat-sen dressed himself in a white undergarment and a red, silk robe. His gaze swept over, but did not settle on, the massive scar that dominated the left side of his body. The scar had come from flames that had nearly consumed him when a cannon misfired atop the Great Wall. The explosion had killed two of his men and knocked him unconscious. When he awoke, he found himself covered in damp strips of cloth and in more pain than he could have imagined. Those had been hellacious days and nights, made worse by the feeling that he had been defeated as his father had, a man he despised above any other.

Clad in a fresh outfit, but still unbathed, Yat-sen closed his eyes, imagining the beauty of Yehonala, a courtesan of the highest rank. He had sought her services for more than a year, and other than defending the Great Wall and restoring his family name, his supreme goal was to buy her freedom so that she could become his concubine and live in his home. But accomplishing this task meant that he would have to pay the man who owned her tea house a vast fortune. Yehonala was one of the most beautiful and admired courtesans in all the land, and her freedom demanded a great price.

Yat-sen walked to his armor. He reached into a secret compartment that had been sewn into the underside of its left flank. A single *tael* of silver had been hidden within the compartment. The piece of silver was an oval shape, slightly larger than his thumbnail, and etched with dragon figures. As the commander of the twenty-two tower stretch of the Great Wall, he was given two-hundred and twenty *taels* of silver each month to pay the salaries of his soldiers as well as to bribe Mongol officers. Yat-sen converted most of the silver *taels* into thin copper coins. These coins, known as *wen*, had a hole in the middle and were the lowest denomination of money. Yat-sen was supposed to pay his men thirty *wen* per day, but he usually paid them twenty-five. He was also expected to bribe the Mongols so as to not attack his section of the Great Wall, but he never did. To bribe the men who

UNBOUND

had killed his father and disgraced his family wasn't something Yat-sen would contemplate. Better to die on their swords.

Since Yat-sen underpaid his men and never bribed the Mongols, he was able to keep a few *taels* of silver each month. Many commanders along the Great Wall acted likewise, though sometimes their men rebelled. Yat-sen paid his soldiers enough so that they would only grumble about lost wages. No one would dare to stand up against him in any case.

Yat-sen carried the silver *tael* to the red, lacquer desk that occupied the far side of his room. He knelt by the desk, listened to ensure that no one was near, and gently lifted up on its right corner. Then he twisted the desk's leg to the left, unscrewing it. With care and silence he worked, pausing only when the leg was completely removed. Still lifting the desk, he stared into the hollow interior of the leg, which contained a small, silk bag filled with silver *taels*. The chamber was lined with thick, cotton padding. Yat-sen now had forty-seven pieces of silver, nearly enough to buy Yehonala from her masters.

After depositing the new silver *tael* in the silk bag and reattaching the desk leg, Yat-sen sat down and opened a small chest. Inside were official documents, as well as more than a dozen letters from Fan's wife. Yat-sen had intercepted the letters before they reached Fan and had read each one several times. At first he only cared about whether Fan was planning some sort of escape, but soon stealing and reading the letters had become an obsession. It was clear that the craftsman's wife loved him deeply. She wrote to him in a way that Yat-sen had never heard anyone speak. It was as if she had left a part of herself on each page, a part

35

to be seen, touched, and adored.

He opened her most recent letter. Within it she spoke about her mother's illness, how the floods had affected life in Beijing, and her desire to see him again. Yat-sen's gaze dropped to the end of the letter. Though most women couldn't read or write, her penmanship was remarkably clear and precise.

I have made a new coat to keep you warm in the coming winter. On the outside, it looks like an average garment, something to be worn by a laborer. But its inside is lined with rabbits' fur. You'll stay warm, my love, warm even though I am not beside you.

I will send the coat to you soon, and when you put it on each day, perhaps you can think of me. Just as I think of you when I look at my necklace and know that you wear its other half.

You have made me a blessed woman, though I miss you more with each passing day. I wish I had tried harder to keep you by my side. I wasn't strong enough to speak my full mind—a failure that haunts me more often than I would like.

Sometimes I try to imagine you working, or perhaps pausing in your labor to glance to the south, toward me. Your letters comfort me and your stories make me smile. But I long for you. Please hurry home. My place is by your side; my heart is yours to keep.

You build wonders within me.

Meng

Yat-sen reread her final words, jealous of them. He would soon go to Yehonala, and she would care for him. She would bathe him, caress his wounds, read him a line of her poetry, and finally make love to him. But she would never say such words to him. To her, he was an escape from a world not of her making. No matter what he did for her, she would never adore him as the craftsman's wife adored her husband.

His fingers nimble, his movements gentle, Yat-sen folded up the letter. He wondered, as he had many times before, how Fan was able to write to her, how his letters avoided detection. Yat-sen would have liked to read them.

But at least he had her words. Though they tormented him, he was glad to see them, night after night. Stealing them from Fan was one of the few joys of his life. Even if the war with the Mongols ended, Yat-sen would never allow Fan to return to Meng. The beauty and joy of their reunion would be too much for him to bear.

Fan would stay on the Great Wall forever. His destiny was to become a part of it, like so many others before him.

CHAPTER THREE

The End of the Beginning

Beijing—October 12, 1549

Unable to lie to him, Meng had decided to ask her father-in-law for his permission to travel. At first he was angry with her request, citing traditions and dangers. But after his initial outburst had subsided, she'd shown him the clothes that she had made for Fan, and passionately explained how without them another cold winter might kill him. Everyone knew that a famine was coming, and life on the Great Wall was harder than it was in most places. Fan's father had already lost two sons to disease, and he feared losing another. Fan was the last of his boys, and only he alone could carry on his family's name.

Because of his love for his son, Meng's father-in-law had ultimately relented. He would have made the journey himself, but he suffered terribly from gout. The pain in his feet made arduous travel all but impossible. So he had done what he could to prepare Meng for the trip, patiently advising her on routes and dangers, as well as giving her a generous amount of money and ordering a strong and trusted servant to accompany her.

Farewells had been exchanged in the dead of night, and now, as Meng walked north along a narrow *hutong*, she tried to keep her breathing calm and deep. She was dressed as a common man, with a blue, loose-fitting robe featuring wide, arm-length sleeves. In the fashion that Confucius had prescribed, the left side of the robe was wrapped over the right and held in place by a black sash. While high-ranking men wore a long robe, Meng's stopped just below her thighs. Beneath the robe, she had tied a silk sash around her chest, greatly diminishing the profile of her breasts. Light-blue leggings covered her knees, shins, and ankles. She wore white socks and black, cloth shoes. A black head scarf covered everything above her eyebrows, including her hair, which had been tied in a topknot. The head scarf was coupled in the back and dropped to the base of her neck. Last, a sheathed, curved sword hung from her side.

Though the sword and the clothes felt awkward, nothing bothered Meng more than her feet. Her whole life she had tried to make them appear as small as possible, wearing tight, stiff shoes that blistered her toes and heels. Now, dressed as a man, she had no choice but to wear oversized, loose-fitting shoes. The change, she thought, was like asking a fish to fly instead of swim. Embarrassed, but unable to show the emotion, she tried to emulate the gait of the servant beside her, who so confidently placed one foot before the other.

Sweat gathering in the small of her back, Meng continued, pushing a small, two-wheeled hand cart that contained the clothes she had made for Fan, as well as food, bedding, cooking instruments, and a waterproof satchel filled with his letters. The alley was packed with people, and she dared not speak to the servant or anyone else she encountered.

To her surprise, the *hutong* opened up, revealing a large, square courtyard that was dominated by a market. Scores of stalls encircled the trading area, the interior of which thrived with merchants who had placed their wares on reed mats. On the stalls and mats, countless goods were for sale—shoes, clothes, knives, jars, vases, tools, weapons, fruits, and vegetables. Several vendors offered warm food to passersby, almost all of it speared with narrow bamboo sticks. Scorpions, grasshoppers, beetles, and caterpillars writhed on row after row of the sticks. If a sale was made, the unfortunate creatures were doused with one of several sauces, set over hot coals, cooked quickly, and handed over. Wherever Meng looked, men dressed in blue or black robes held half-empty sticks. As the men traded, they ate. Only a few women were present, and they tried to make themselves as inconspicuous as possible, staying at the periphery of the market unless they needed to buy something.

Meng followed her father-in-law's servant through the market, heading north. Once again, they walked into a *hutong*, though this one was wider, and the homes on either side were large and ornate. These brick dwellings featured curved rooflines and bright, red trim—a color reserved for the wealthy. Brass dragon-head knockers adorned twin doors at the front of each home. The family name was painted on a rectangular, marble slab above the doors.

Unable to see into the secure dwellings of the rich, Meng wondered what the homes were like, less aware of her feet. She walked on, looking from sight to sight, her fear of being apprehended fading farther away with each new discovery.

Before long, the alley widened into a street that was lined with willow trees, shops, and signs. Meng had never been near Beijing's center, and her gait faltered. The servant asked her to keep walking, gesturing impatiently. Though she increased her pace, she couldn't help but look from pawnshop to noodle vendor to city office. The street teamed with men, most of whom were on foot. Others were carried by horse, donkey, or sedan chair. Hunched figures clad in drab robes swept the cobblestone street.

Following the lead of her companion, Meng continued to walk north, pushing her cart. Up ahead loomed the massive walls of the Forbidden City. Fan had labored on those walls for several years, making a name for himself. Thinking that his feet had touched this same street, she studied the ground, wondering where he had stepped, wishing that she could sense his presence.

As much as Fan often consumed her thoughts, Meng soon found it impossible to consider anything but the magnificence of the Forbidden City. As she drew closer to it, her skin felt as if she had plunged into ice water. The emperor was hard on women, and if anyone discovered her guise, she would likely be put to death. Lowering her head, she looked up at the impressive red walls that surrounded his city. They were thirty paces high and just as thick.

Perched atop them were red-columned buildings with sloping roofs. Tiles painted gold covered the structures. Adding to the glistening display, golden dragons reared up from each side of the roofs. Immense courtyards stretched outward from the walls—a kaleidoscope of bright colors—as elaborately dressed officials hurried about.

Though Fan had never been inside the Forbidden City's walls, he had told Meng that the fortifications protected a hundred palaces and nine thousand, nine hundred, and ninety-nine rooms. Many thousands of concubines, eunuchs, servants, and court officials attended to the emperor's needs.

Meng knew that she was supposed to consider the emperor to be a god, but she only feared him. Rumor said that his predecessor had been buried alongside ten of his favorite concubines, who were still alive when entombed. Despite the splendor of the current emperor's city, Meng increased her pace, grateful for one of the few occasions in her life that her feet were unbound.

It took a long time to proceed past the looming exterior of the emperor's grounds. Finally they were able to turn down a *hutong* and leave the Forbidden City behind them. Meng's breathing slowed. The tremors that had arisen in her hands vanished. Whispering, she thanked the servant. He asked if she would like to stop for lunch, but she shook her head, wanting to move farther away from the Forbidden City, or the center of the universe as the emperor demanded that people think of it.

Though her legs and feet ached, Meng forced herself to continue on. She walked, no longer in awe of her surroundings, but aware of the danger of her situation. The farther she got from Beijing, the better. Equally important, each step she took away from the city brought her closer to Fan.

It was late afternoon by the time Meng and the servant were beyond Beijing's towering walls. They crossed a curved, stone bridge that arched over a river. Men sat in the crooks of pine trees, resting. A lone woman, clad in beautiful robes and sparkling headgear, played a stringed instrument. Meng didn't know what to think of her, having never seen such a sight.

Along the road, merchants led donkeys, which in turn pulled large carts. Soldiers rode armored horses. A substantial crowd had gathered around two men who were dressed as herons and walked on tall stilts.

If she had been a man, Meng would have lingered to watch the performance. But the crowd unsettled her. She had thought that she would feel less vulnerable outside the city walls, but she was still a woman, still in defiance of the laws of her land.

Pushing her cart harder, she hurried forward, wondering if eyes had found and followed her, if someone would betray her and these strangers would come to know who she really was.

*

From the ground on the north side of the Great Wall, the fortification's imperfections were much more visible. Fan and Bataar stood between the fifth and sixth towers under Yat-sen's command. The recent Mongol attack had been to the west, at the twentieth tower. Slight damage had been done to the tower, and Fan's crews were at work repairing cracked mortar and bricks.

Fan had spent some of the previous day at the site, ensuring that his men followed his directions. Once they were almost finished undoing their enemy's work, Fan had decided to travel east, away from the assault. Sometimes Mongols used attacks as diversions, making it easier for them to reconnoiter at other sections of the Great Wall.

Fan and Bataar had been walking outside the northern edge of the Great Wall all day, looking for Mongol treachery. Two Chinese soldiers followed their progress from atop the fortification, ready to drop a rope ladder should Mongol riders appear. Many months ago, when Fan had first arrived at the site, he hated to be on the wrong side of the endless stone dragon. The northern frontier was a wasteland—full of arid soil, unremarkable topography, and countless Mongols. To be caught by the enemy on the north side of the Great Wall was to die.

Yet Fan had grown to appreciate the solitude found outside the stonework. On the ground, Yat-sen could not trouble him. He could think about Meng. The contours of the Great Wall reminded him of the details of her face and body. He often traced his fingers along the massive granite blocks, remembering the many times and ways that he had touched her. In the same manner that he had looked after her when she was ill, he cared for the stonework. If a block was loose or cracked, he would ensure that it was replaced or fixed. His affection was also given to Bataar, who tried to be strong and willful but was still just a boy.

Fan paused, smiling at a sight in the stone. "You see, Bataar, what your countrymen have done?" he asked. "While they attacked us, they were up to their usual mischief."

Leaning closer to the Great Wall, Bataar followed Fan's forefinger as he pointed at iron stakes that had been driven into the mortar between the stone blocks. The stakes weren't much thicker than Fan's finger and had been painted the same color as the stonework. They zigzagged toward the top of the wall, ending several feet short of the summit. Enough of each stake protruded so that a Mongol scout or assassin could use them to scale the fortification.

Fan asked the soldiers above to bring one of his workers to him. The stakes would have to be removed and the holes in the mortar patched. Impressed with the ingenuity of whoever had secured the stakes, Fan took a piece of black charcoal from his satchel of tools. He circled each stake, then patted the stonework, which had warmed in the afternoon sun. Later that day, after the repairs had been made, he would glue a flower to where each stake had protruded. The flowers would anger the Mongol craftsman but also let him know that his skill was appreciated. Fan played many such games with the men who sought to conquer his people. He didn't hate them, probably because of his friendship with Bataar. While the boy often boasted of the ferocity of his countrymen, he also loved and missed his father. And whoever had shaped Bataar couldn't be nearly as terrible as Fan had once imagined.

"I could let you go," Fan said quietly. "But if I did, you might die out there. Bandits or animals might find you before your people did. Or you could perish of thirst."

Bataar nodded. "I won't walk from here. I'll ride from here. To return to my father I must have a horse."

"Why?"

"Because he'll expect me to arrive on a horse. If I didn't, I wouldn't be a Mongol."

Fan wondered if it would be possible to steal a mount. There weren't many on the Great Wall, and each was closely guarded.

"I want to take Yat-sen's stallion," Bataar whispered. "To deliver that gift to my father would make him laugh so very hard."

"Don't," Fan replied.

"Yat-sen smiles when he rides past me on him. He knows that I want him."

"He toys with you is all. Because if you ever put your hand on that horse, he'd cut it from your arm."

Bataar's grin faded. "No, he wouldn't. He likes to mock it too much."

"There's nothing to mock."

"Maybe. Maybe not. But I wish you weren't afraid of him. I wish you'd put your hand on his horse."

"It does us no good to anger him."

"Every night, when you're playing *Go* with him, I expect you to beat him. I know you could, but still you lose, again and again. My father would never lose like that."

"Your father is a horseman. I'm a craftsman."

Bataar shook his head, squinting, as he often did. "But why? Why do you let him beat you? He laughs at you. He thinks he's better than you."

"But do you think he's better than me?"

"No. Of course not."

"I care about your opinion far more than his. So why should it bother me that I let him win at *Go*?"

46

"Because he's your enemy. And you should always crush your enemy."

Fan shrugged. He peered to the north, looking for horsemen. One day they would scale his wall. After all, could a shield of stones forever keep an ocean at bay? For the Mongols were no different than an irresistible force of nature.

"Don't be in a rush, Bataar, to become a man," Fan said, then waved away a wasp.

"Why do you say that?"

"Because you're at the age when you're between boyhood and manhood. A part of you wants to act like a man. But you have your whole life to be serious and strong. It's better for you now to be a boy."

"My father trained me to be strong, to be a man."

"And you'll be one. Soon enough. But don't run toward that moment. You're only young once."

Bataar nodded, but made no reply. Once again Fan studied the horizon, searching for horsemen. Like most everyone on the Great Wall, he was forever on the lookout for threats. "I'm thinking of a new story to send to my wife," he said, still gazing northward.

"About what?"

"A one-winged butterfly that must search for the meaning of life."

"But a butterfly needs its wings. If it couldn't fly, how could it search for anything?"

"Maybe on the ground it could see something that it would miss from the air."

Bataar scratched the paint off one of the stakes. "Could you make it a horse? A three-legged horse? I'd like to know what mysteries such a stallion might discover."

"Aren't your horses always fast? Aren't your lame ones … put to rest?"

"Yes, but this horse could be different. He could find something that the other horses speed past."

Fan put his hand on Bataar's shoulder, wishing that it wasn't so easy to feel the boy's bones. He was far too thin. "I'll tell you the story tonight," Fan said. Then, lowering his voice, he added, "And one day I'll find you a horse. A fast one to carry you to your father."

"Yat-sen's?"

Fan smiled. "I won't beat him in *Go*, so perhaps you'll beat him for me."

"That's right. I'll show you how to do it. Then, when I'm gone, you can beat him, and later find your wife. You can tell her your stories instead of writing them down."

"I'll tell her about you."

"You will?"

Fan squeezed Bataar's shoulder. "You're my friend, Bataar. The Great Wall is as long as China, and no matter where I'm on it, you're my best friend here. Of course I'll tell Meng about you. I'll teach her about horses, as you taught me. And I'll tell her how you rode away, on Yat-sen's stallion, how you brought laughter to your father's voice and tears to your mother's eyes."

Bataar rose taller on his feet, rolling forward on his tiptoes. "If my father comes for me first, I'll let him know not to hurt you. Because he'll hurt everyone else. He says that your men make strong walls, but not strong fighters."

"He's right."

"I don't want you to die, Fan. You're my friend, too."

Fan looked to the west, along the Great Wall. "We should continue to walk. We'll probably find some ladders under that loose soil ahead. Your people never try only one trick."

"Can you tell me the story now, the story of the three-legged stallion?"

"Yes, but it isn't only about the stallion. There was also a boy, Bataar, a boy your age who wasn't in a rush to be a man, who rode the stallion when no one else would."

Bataar smiled, tracing his fingers along the stone blocks while he walked, listening as Fan brought a new world to life.

*

Yat-sen stood between watchtowers number nine and ten. The Great Wall rose steeply from the former to the latter, following the contours of a mountain ridge. Because the rise was so abrupt, it was a difficult position to defend. What few horsemen he had would struggle to gallop to the higher tower. Nor would his foot soldiers be capable of quickly running uphill, especially burdened with their weapons and armor.

Coughing suddenly, Yat-sen cursed his lungs and the smoke of the cooking fires, which seemed to collect within him. Standing beside him was his second-in-command, Li, a large, quiet man dressed in green leather and plate armor. An immense longbow was slung over his shoulder, and a curved sword was sheathed at his hip. Li's face was as expressionless as the stone beneath his feet. Only his eyes hinted that he wasn't a statue, following the movements of Mongol riders to the north. The enemy horsemen rode beyond the reach of arrows or cannon, their formations tight and steady. As usual, the riders moved in unison, shifting to the west, then east. The pounding of two thousand hooves sent plumes of dust far into the air.

Yat-sen considered ordering two piles of wolf dung to be lit on the nearby tower, indicating to his distant countrymen that he could see a large force of the enemy. Reinforcements would arrive from other parts of the wall, grumble at the effort involved with their trek, and most likely watch as the Mongols disappeared to the north.

"If the barbarians come closer, see that two fires are lit," Yat-sen ordered Li. "But if they stay where they are, give them no reason to think that here, on our section of the wall, we panic."

Li nodded, but said nothing.

Yat-sen shifted his gaze toward the lower watchtower to the west. Atop its northern parapet, the small, naked figures of three Mongols had been tied to the stonework. The men had been captured in a recent attack. Yat-sen hadn't bothered to interrogate them yet. That conversation would come later. Nor had he ordered them to be tortured, as he didn't believe in the practice. He would rather shame a man, destroy his pride and his fortitude, than cut him with crude, iron instruments. Though it was rare to capture a Mongol raider, when Yat-sen's men did, he always had the barbarians stripped and bound to the Great Wall. Depending on the season, the elements broke the Mongols in a day or two, at which point they were eager to talk. After they told him what he wanted to know, they were beheaded. His personal seal was stamped on each forehead, and one of his men, usually someone who had vexed him, carried a bag of the heads into the wasteland, where they were left for the Mongols to find. In this way, Yat-sen's name became known to his enemy. The name that they had defiled returned to torment them, again and again.

The Mongols had shamed Yat-sen's family, and so he would shame them—their men, women, and children. He was one of the few commanders along the Great Wall who conducted raids into the land of his enemy. When reports arrived of Mongols massing for an attack on a position distant from his, Yat-sen would accompany his horsemen to the north. They would find Mongol camps, kill the few guards, destroy provisions, and take slaves. Long before the Mongols returned in force, Yat-sen and his men would be back behind the Great Wall, delighting in their victory.

Yat-sen was certain that the Mongols knew of him, and hated him. This knowledge warmed him on cold nights, gave him sustenance when he was hungry. He would never bribe his enemy—a tactic favored by many other commanders. Instead he would show them his strength, forcing them to attack weaker sections of the Great Wall or to come at him with malice in their hearts and arrows in their quivers.

"The barbarians ride out there to frighten us," Yat-sen said to Li. "But they tire their mounts for no good reason. If they truly believed that we feared them, they would attack us right now, with strength. They would amass ten thousand of their horsemen and come at this single point in the wall."

Li's hand strayed to the hilt of his sword, but he said nothing.

"Let them come," Yat-sen added. "Let them break themselves on these stones, on the dragon beneath us."

"Yes. Let them."

"The Great Wall has thousands of watchtowers. We defend twenty-two. A small number to be certain, but we stand in the middle of the dragon, where a crook in its back leaves it close to Beijing. So the Mongols will seek to stand here, to dance in our blood."

"Dead men cannot dance."

Yat-sen nodded, then coughed. "On these stones we would fight them as equals. Out there, in that wasteland, they'll always defeat us."

Li made no reply.

His own words prompted Yat-sen to think of his father, and how he had died beneath the hooves of the barbarians' horses. The commander coughed, then spat toward his enemy. "Soon we'll ride out there again, taking more slaves, burning their crops. But we must wait until their horsemen are far from here."

"Their horsemen are never far. They move like the wind."

"And so will we," Yat-sen replied, flicking a moth from his bright-red armor. "And if I fall, Li, you will hold this wall. You'll protect it as I have always protected it. The barbarians must never enter China through our door."

"Nor any other."

Yat-sen twisted his head from left to right, trying to rid himself of a pain that festered in his left shoulder—one more curse of the exploding cannon. "And watch Fan," Yat-sen added, standing straighter. "I need him, but I don't trust him. He longs to see his woman."

"Then bring her here. Let him see her."

"No," Yat-sen replied, the mere thought of their togetherness causing his pulse to quicken. He could not witness their love when he'd never experience the same. "She would distract him. And I need his eyes and hands on these walls. Without his touch, the barbarians would find a crack to widen. Such a crack could lead to our doom."

Something flashed to the north. The horsemen bunched together, riding into the distance, the dust cloud above them settling, then disappearing altogether.

"Check on the prisoners," Yat-sen ordered. "See if they're ready to talk. If not, we'll wait for tomorrow. Another night in the cold will loosen their tongues."

*

A mile to the northeast of Yat-sen's position, a Mongol scout eyed a familiar section of the Great Wall. It was from this position that, a year earlier, the Chinese had conducted a rare raid on a nearby Mongol camp. The scout, Chuluun, had been away at the time of the attack, which had caught his countrymen by surprise. Most of them were also gone, and their camp had been vulnerable. The Chinese raiders had killed the few Mongol soldiers present, burnt stores of grain, and captured slaves. Six Mongol children, all boys between the ages of eight and twelve, had been taken. One of them, Bataar, was Chuluun's son.

Upon discovering the fate of his son, Chuluun and several other enraged fathers had rushed to the Great Wall, attacking its defenders with reckless fury. Chuluun had been knocked unconscious by explosives dropped from the fortification. When he awoke, he was back at his camp, surrounded by scores of other horsemen. His left leg was broken and had been wrapped in splint. Though he had wanted to rush again to aid his son, he was restrained by his countrymen and, later, by the pain above his ankle.

A full month passed before Chuluun was able to ride again. By this time, a Chinese soldier, whose allegiance had been bought with the copper coins of his enemies, told a Mongol spy that the six children had perished. They had died when a section of the Great Wall they were repairing fell on them, crushing them and several of their masters. Upon hearing this news, Chuluun was beside himself with sorrow and rage. With tears streaming down his face, he'd ridden again toward the Great Wall, looking for the place where Bataar had died, trying to sense the presence of his son. Once more arrows and cannons had sought him out. But he ignored their threat, riding alongside the stone dragon for mile after mile, calling his son's name and struggling to breathe as his chest tightened in angst.

The Chinese traitor had been caught and executed a few days later, but in time Chuluun had learned other details about his son's death. The local Chinese commander, Yat-sen, had ordered the raid and, later, overseen the slaves. Their blood was on his hands, and Chuluun had come to know this man, who always wore brilliant red armor and often rode his white stallion on top of the Great Wall while Chuluun mirrored his movements from a distance below.

Though Chuluun had a wife and three daughters, whom he saw sometimes in a faraway Mongol camp, Bataar had been his greatest source of pride. At age ten, a year before he was captured, Bataar was already a remarkable horseman. Even without a saddle he could ride backwards or could fire his bow while at a full gallop. Such skills were difficult for grown men, and it was almost unheard of for a boy to master them. Yet under his father's constant tutelage, Bataar had learned to think of himself as a part of his horse, as an extension of its body. In this way they were not a mount and a rider, but a single shadow able to race across the plains. As important, Bataar had grown to love his horse in the way that Chuluun loved him—with appreciation for each characteristic, no matter how great or small.

The death of Bataar had killed something in Chuluun. Of course, he still adored his wife and daughters, but his son had been a re-creation of himself. When his son died, his spirit died, or at least the wind that carried it. He no longer sought out the companionship of other fighters, no longer laughed or played games of sport. Instead, he became obsessed with avenging his son. When Chinese faced him and perished, impaled by the shafts of his arrows or trampled beneath the hooves of his mount, Chuluun shouted his son's name, hoping that Bataar's shadow had seen and heard everything.

Now, as he studied the distant wall, Chuluun turned a small, wooden horse over in his hands. He carved a horse every night, as his countrymen ate and drank, plotted and slept. The horses were always different, made of various woods, and shaped in diverse poses. Some galloped; others grazed. Each day he left one of the horses near the wall, in hopes that Bataar's spirit would find one and be entertained and comforted by it. Years earlier, he'd given such horses to Bataar when his son was too little to ride and was teased by his peers for having a misshapen hand.

The horse Chuluun held now was small, dwarfed by his fists. He was a large man, and, though only twenty-nine years old, his face was prematurely wrinkled from countless days of riding under a full sun. His beard was unkempt, especially where it was thicker on his chin and above his upper lip. Ever since Bataar had died, Chuluun had worn black armor dominated by a leather breastplate covered in rectangular pieces of iron riveted to the leather. In the center of the armor was a larger, circular plate of iron. Chuluun chose to wear black armor because he'd been told that the color signified bad luck to the Chinese, who avoided dressing in it.

Chuluun's shoulders were also protected by black leather and steel, as were his thighs and shins. He wore a spiked iron helmet that was lined with rabbit fur. Though he owned a sword, he usually carried only his giant longbow into battle. Fighting against the Chinese rarely came to hand-to-hand combat, and when it did he simply shot an enemy whose sword he admired.

Though his bow was usually slung over his back, and his armor was heavy and unwieldy, Chuluun was faster than almost anyone on horseback. He often thought about his lost son as he rode, usually near the Great Wall, just beyond bowshot of his enemies. They all knew him, he was certain. Spies had spoken of the Black Rider—the man who appeared almost every day, galloping alone, probing the Chinese defenses. Sometimes Chuluun rode straight at his foes, loosened an arrow or two, and then changed his direction. More often than not his arrows shattered into stone, but sometimes he was pleased by the sound of distant screams.

Chuluun had been tasked by his commander to look for weaknesses within the wall, and he took his assignment seriously. His supreme goal was to lead an attack against his enemies, summit their defenses, and kill Yat-sen. Only then would Bataar be avenged. Only then would Chuluun be able to share himself fully with his wife and daughters, loving them as they deserved to be loved.

Spurring his horse to the west, Chuluun followed the contours of the wall, drawing nearer to it. The weapons and armor of his enemies glistened in the distance. They gathered atop the closest watchtower, studying him as he drew nearer. A man dressed in red armor appeared atop the wall from the west—Yat-sen. He was the only Chinese along this section of the fortification to don red armor—the color of his emperor.

Chuluun rode closer to his enemy. A cannon fired, yet he didn't flinch, knowing he was beyond its range. The iron ball, which was slightly smaller than his fist, slammed into the earth twenty paces in front of him. He spat to show his distain, dismounted, and walked to the smoking ball. He placed the small wooden horse on top of it, whispered to his son that he missed him, that he needed to remember to ride with his knees pressing into his mount.

His eyes watered as he thought about Bataar dying alone, under a pile of stones. He climbed back onto his stallion, then, hate filling him as if a storm overwhelming the sky, Chuluun unslung his longbow from his back. He rode closer to the wall. Soldiers upon it lowered themselves behind the parapet. Another cannon fired.

Chuluun notched an arrow and pulled back on his taut bow, grunting with effort. He aimed at Yat-sen, who was about two hundred paces away. The feathers of Chuluun's arrow brushed against his cheek, just beneath his eye. The three largest fingers of his right hand eased open and the arrow launched into the air, which was parted with infinite ease by the darting black bolt. Chuluun shouted his son's name as the arrow arced toward his enemy, ricocheting off the top of the wall, about a spear's length from Yat-sen.

Chinese archers fired in return. Most of their arrows fell short of Chuluun. One neared him, and he had to spur his stallion away from it. He shouted at the men who had killed his son, promising that he would paint the earth with their blood. Raising his bow, he dared them to ride out and face him.

But no Chinese came down from the wall. He called them cowards in their own tongue. Then he started to again draw closer to them but remembered the words of his youngest daughter. She had been sick when he saw her the previous night, besieged by a fever. She'd made him promise to return to her, and so he shouted one more challenge to his foes, turned his mount around, and headed for his loved ones.

His daughter's face would sustain him that night as he held her. He would whisper to her about the wilderness, about its secret and wondrous places. Later, when she was in a deep slumber, he'd kiss her brow, then carve another horse.

After dawn arrived he would leave her, return to the wall, and devise a plan that would leave it in rubble.

*

The embers of the fire crackled, sending sparks into the night sky. Meng and her father-in-law's servant lay on opposites sides of the fire, enjoying its warmth. Though the autumn days were still pleasant near Beijing, the nights were cool and full of hints of the weather that was to come. Gusts from the north caused trees to sway and leaves to fall. Crickets and locusts created a constant buzz, as if each insect were aware of its imminent doom and was protesting its demise.

Though numerous inns dotted the countryside, Meng had opted to sleep, as many travelers did, near the road. She and the servant had made their way into the woods, found a clearing, and prepared their camp. Following the lead of her quiet companion, Meng had cleared a patch of ground free of rubble, spread a woven mat on the dirt, and then placed several cotton blankets on the mat. Because she was cold, she had worn the coat she'd made for Fan. The rest of her possessions remained in her cart, which was near the fire.

Meng would have liked to talk with her father-in-law's servant, but throughout the day her whispered questions to him had been ignored. Back in Beijing, he had seemed to be a capable, willing man who was eager to please her father-in-law. But on the road, alone with Meng, he had turned sullen, perhaps resenting the task of guiding a woman to the Great Wall.

Her feet blistered and aching from walking in oversized shoes,

Meng studied the sky. She had never seen stars such as the ones now above her. Beijing's countless lights obscured the night sky, which she had observed from time to time in her father-in-law's garden.

The stars in the countryside were infinite in number. Meng's father had told her that they were similar in size to the sun, but gazing at their multitudes she found that assertion hard to believe. They must be smaller, perhaps tiny pieces of the sun that had broken off and floated away. One of them occasionally fell toward the Earth, flashing above her before vanishing into the horizon.

Though she remained fearful of being discovered, Meng's emotions had settled since she left Beijing. The farther she'd journeyed away from the emperor, the more at peace she felt. Beyond the walls of the capital, laws seemed less enforced. She had seen middle-ranking men dressed in bright colors, sometimes even red. The boldest wore knee-high boots that were forbidden to commoners in Beijing. And a few women—though always rich—occupied the road, carried in sedan chairs by their servants.

Meng's father had taught her many things, one of which was why the emperor treated women so poorly. The emperor believed in the teachings of the famous Chinese philosopher, Confucius, who advocated that all people should treat one another as they themselves wanted to be treated. Confucius trained his followers to act with compassion, love, and respect toward their fellow man. And while Confucius extended many of his philosophies to women, he was certain that their place was within the home. Though women were to be treated well and respected, their role was to support their husbands.

According to Meng's father, the emperor had forgotten some of Confucius' teachings, but not others. No compassion was shown to the emperor's enemies. Nor were the sick or weak treated with care. Yet women remained banished to their homes, prisoners tormented by thin, wooden walls and dimly lit rooms.

Even the emperor's powers fortunately had limits, and rich women were beginning to test the boundaries of his reach. They could be seen in Beijing's markets, on its streets, and in its parks. They stood on bound feet and watched the world pass by. As a chief form of protest, some high-ranking women wrote poetry, which was published and admired by many. In fact, within certain circles of scholars, some men argued that women's poetry was preferable to their male counterparts.

If Meng had hailed from a rich family, she might have traveled freely to the Great Wall. But poor women did not possess such powers, and so she was forced to dress as a man. She didn't know what would happen if her true identity were discovered, but she could imagine being flogged, or sold to a tea house, or simply killed by one of the emperor's defenders.

Though she didn't know how to use the weapon, Meng pulled her sword closer to her side, keeping her hand on its hilt. Her action caused the servant to grunt, and he rolled away from her. She said good night to him, but he made no reply.

Again, she turned her attention to the stars, wondering if Fan saw the same sight. Whatever they were, the small white dots were remarkably beautiful and settled her emotions. She realized that men had looked at stars for all their lives but that she was witnessing their true beauty for the first time. Her mother had never seen such splendor, nor had her aunts or grandmothers.

If Fan lay next to her, Meng was certain that he would hold her hand and tell her a story about the stars. He would explain their presence. Later, after he was finished, he would ask her what she thought of them. They would talk and perhaps laugh as the moon rose above the distant horizon. Best of all, he would treat her as his lover, as his friend, not as a woman beneath him.

"I'm coming for you," she whispered so quietly that not even the servant would hear her. "You don't know it, but I'm bringing you a coat. I stitched it myself, and it will keep you warm this winter when I cannot."

The wind shifted, causing the fire's embers to redden.

Meng told Fan that she loved him. She reached for her necklace, easing it away from her chest, then stroking it with her thumb. She brought it to her lips and kissed it, remembering how Fan had given it to her. Earlier he'd wound a silk scarf around the necklace, forming an oval with the fabric. He then placed the scarf around her neck, and had slowly unwound the silk, finally drawing the scarf away from her to reveal his gift, which hung from her neck, the half turtle resting between the tops of her breasts. He already wore the other half of the turtle, which he showed her by drawing aside his robe. Turtles, of course, symbolized longevity—both in life and in love.

At that point Fan hadn't spoken of his feelings for her. He hadn't needed to. Instead, he had simply reached behind her, gently pulling her closer to him until they embraced. It was almost as if he were merging them together in the same way that the two halves of the turtle could be held together. And in his embrace, they had become one.

Meng smiled at the memory, kissing her half of the turtle once more. She took a final look at the stars, grateful that she could see them, then closed her eyes and tried to go to sleep.

CHAPTER FOUR

Lost and Found

North of Beijing—October 13, 1549

Meng opened her eyes, blinked at the early morning light, and immediately sensed that something was wrong. She looked around and realized that her cart was gone, as was her father-in-law's servant. Without thinking, she called out to him and then drew back in fear at the sound of her voice. She had only shouted his name once, but women didn't yell, especially a woman pretending to be a man.

Moving slowly, Meng rose to her knees. The fire was out. The ground was damp and she could see fresh ruts from the cart's two wheels, headed back toward Beijing. Traces lingered from the servant's footprints. She had no idea at what point he had abandoned her but thought it must have been in the middle of the night. Weariness had overwhelmed her, and she'd fallen into a deep, dreamless slumber.

Though Meng tried to control her emotions, her eyes filled with tears. The servant was supposed to be her guide, her protector. To make his betrayal worse, he had stolen her cart, which contained half of her money and most of her provisions. All that she had left were a single set of clothes, a woven mat, two blankets, the coat she had made for Fan, his letters, the sword, and the remaining half of her father-in-law's money. She had slept with her satchel of copper coins around her shoulder, beneath her clothes. Surely the servant had been tempted to try to cut it from her, but Meng had rested with her arms around it.

Shuddering silently, Meng rocked back and forth, still kneeling. Her tears dropped to the soil. She felt foolish and naïve for trusting the man, who clearly had never favored her. Now, because of her shortcomings, her journey was in jeopardy. It was dangerous for anyone to travel alone in the countryside, but much more so for a woman. Because of summer flooding, crops had been ruined, and the beginning of a famine gripped the land. Her father-in-law had insisted that she not travel alone because bandits preyed on the solitary, stealing the clothes off their backs and the shoes off their feet.

Meng regretted her stupidity, worrying about Fan. If she turned back, he would have to endure another winter of misery. Her coat would keep him warm, she was sure of that. But how could she possibly get it to him when she couldn't even make it a day without disaster? If she traveled alone, she risked everything. And what good could she do for him if she were dead?

Her fingers digging into and clutching at the soil beneath her, Meng lamented her fate. Fan had been stolen from her, and now, in a way, she had been stolen from him. As a woman, she couldn't be expected, and wouldn't be able, to travel onward alone. She would have to turn back, sneak into Beijing, and endure the gossip of the household. Everyone would know that the servant had tricked her, and that she had failed in her foolhardy task. That failure would affect everyone in her life, but worst of all, Fan, who would continue to suffer on the Great Wall. He would remain ignorant of her search for him, and vulnerable to the winter winds.

Wiping her face free of tears with the backs of her dirtied hands, Meng stood up. The forest loomed around her, far less beautiful than it had been the previous evening. Several other groups of travelers had camped within various clearings and she heard men hacking and coughing, a donkey screeching, and distant laughter. Trembling, she turned toward the source of the happy voices and glimpsed a green kite, far above the trees, seemingly over the road. The frog-shaped kite rose and fell, twisted and sprang. Whoever controlled it was skilled, as the kite resembled a frog hopping along the ground.

The sight made Meng pause. Her mother had always adored kites and said that they made her feel free, even if she was caged in so many ways. Meng had wanted to bring her one; if not to fly, at least to hold and admire. If Meng turned around, if she gave up, Fan would have no coat and her mother would have no kite.

Tapping her right foot, Meng wondered what to do. She had been ready to head south, toward her home. But the sight of the kite had affected her. Certainly she had been meant to see it. Perhaps she could continue on, dressed as a man. She could avoid other people, following a nearby river that led north. If she made herself small, a skill women were more apt at than men, she could disappear from sight, hurrying from place to place, lighter without her cart. She could collect apples, which were plentiful along the river, and buy additional food when needed. The copper coins in her satchel would be more than enough for the occasional meal of wheat noodles.

Her father-in-law had told her the journey from Beijing to Jinshanling might take eight or nine days. How could she turn around when so few steps needed to be taken? How could she fail Fan when the urge to help him nearly overwhelmed her?

Dropping again to her knees, Meng removed Fan's coat, then folded up her mat and blankets. She bundled these items within the coat, then tied it onto her back with an extra cord that she had wrapped around her waist. Of all her possessions, the sword was the heaviest, and she debated trading or selling it. But she decided that the sight of it might deter a bandit, and so she sheathed it, positioning its hilt against her right side.

Meng glanced again at the kite, grateful that someone had arisen early to fly it. A father and son, perhaps—a master and his apprentice.

If I encounter someone, I'll pretend to be mute, she thought to herself, stepping around the fire pit. She knew that the river wasn't far away, and started walking toward it, heading deeper into the forest. The trees drew closer together, soon hiding the kite from her view. The woods darkened, as if morning hadn't yet arrived to the ground beneath her feet. A raven called out, causing her pace to falter. Her hand fell to the hilt of her sword. She didn't think she could use it, but the cool steel was comforting in her grasp.

"I'm coming," she whispered, trying to remember the kite and how it made her feel.

The forest, however, was damp and dim. She sought to walk quietly, but every twig she brushed up against seemed to snap. She longed to be small and unseen, as the emperor expected her to be. Yet she was her father's daughter. Her feet were large and noisy. Her profile was erect and noticeable.

She went deeper into the woods, more like a man than a woman, her mind racing, her hand still on the sword hilt.

Whatever troubles lay ahead, she promised herself, she would try to meet them with confidence and not fear, with purpose and not uncertainty. The world saw her as weak. But her father, her mother, and Fan had seen her as strong. Perhaps her three loved ones were right—maybe the path before her was of her own making.

More ravens called out. Meng walked toward their calls, her breaths quick, but her pace steady.

*

Chuluun lurched out of his dream with a start. The Mongol scout had fallen asleep while riding his horse and had only awoken when it stopped. He'd been dreaming about the day his son, Bataar, had been stolen from him. Chuluun was out raiding that afternoon. Bataar had longed to join him, but Chuluun hadn't wanted to expose him to Chinese cannons. So he had told his son to stay behind, to help an older man mend a crack in his horse's hoof.

Chuluun had missed Bataar's company that day and, after the raid, had galloped back to their camp, eager to find his boy. He'd been surprised to see thick, black smoke smearing the distant sky. While smoke signals were a common sight over the Chinese wall, large fires were rarely seen north of the fortification. His countrymen were careful to preserve their limited amounts of wood, as well as to not give away their positions, and always cooked with the smallest flames possible.

But that afternoon the smoke above their camp was dense. His heart pounding, Chuluun had spurred his mount ahead, seen the bodies of his countrymen, and despaired about the capture of his son.

Since receiving word of Bataar's death, Chuluun often dreamed of that day. Sometimes the Chinese were present at the camp. Sometimes it was a group of red dragons that stole his child. In many of the dreams Bataar called his name, begging for help, but Chuluun could only hear his son's cries. He was never fast enough to save him, never strong enough to do what must be done.

Now, as Chuluun sat on his mount, he gazed at the imposing wall. He saw rippling, red banners atop its watchtowers and the shimmer of distant weapons and armor. A lack of sleep had left his gaze unfocused, and he slapped himself hard on both cheeks. The pain wasn't enough, and he struck himself again, bitter at the freshness of his dream. Though he had spent much of the night comforting his beloved daughter, and to his delight her fever had broken, he hadn't dreamt of her.

Chuluun pulled his horse's reins to the left, guiding it toward the wall. Chinese soldiers shouted at him from the distance. He knew they dreaded him, which pleased him. They had ruined his life. Soon he would ruin theirs.

Because of Bataar's death and Chuluun's subsequent obsession with revenge, the local Mongol commander trusted him. Chuluun had been told parts of a plan that might lead to the breech of the wall. Soon there would be a major attack on a nearby section of the fortification, but this attack was only a ruse. A vast contingent of Mongol horsemen would then assault another area, and Chuluun's task was to determine which section of the defense was vulnerable. He had initially looked at the sections where the watchtowers were farthest apart. These long stretches were the most obvious places to attack, as it would take time for the Chinese to reinforce them with men and cannons. But lately, Chuluun had been thinking about doing the opposite of what was expected.

Two watchtowers intrigued him greatly. They rose, close together, from steep terrain as the wall climbed to the crest of a small mountain. From what Chuluun could tell, and what spies confirmed, Yat-sen used one of these towers as his headquarters. He had stationed many men inside. But if these men were called to fight against Mongol riders who attacked a nearby section of the wall, the towers might be vulnerable. They had never been assaulted before, and so had never been repaired and strengthened. Better yet, if the two towers were captured, they could be held against Chinese reinforcements, allowing hordes of Mongol soldiers safe access to the unprotected stonework between them. If the towers were taken, many thousands of Mongol riders could pour into the Chinese countryside and charge toward Beijing.

UNBOUND

Chuluun smiled at the thought. He continued to ride west, barely beyond the range of the enemy archers. Twisting in his saddle, he reached into his armor and removed a wooden horse that he had carved the previous night, when his daughter was asleep in his arms. The shifting of his weight caused pain to pulsate from above his left ankle. Though the ache of old wounds troubled many of his countrymen, Chuluun didn't mind his sufferings. His son had endured far worse miseries, and Chuluun's leg was one more reminder of his own failures. The pain helped keep him strong and focused.

Turning the small horse over in his hands, Chuluun thought about the wall. Many nights, dressed in his black armor, he had walked along its bottom as his countrymen diverted the attention of its guardians. Chuluun believed that the spring and summer rains, so ferocious this year, had weakened parts of the fortification. In certain areas, the mortar between the stone blocks and bricks seemed to be perpetually damp, suggesting vulnerability.

Chuluun pocketed his carving, then gazed into the distance, studying the two watchtowers that he wanted to capture and hold. They were the key to Yat-sen's undoing. Once the towers were—

An arrow whistled through the air, ricocheting off the top of Chuluun's helmet. The force of the strike threw him backwards in his saddle and left small bits of light dancing in his vision. Instinctively, he spurred his stallion away from the wall, even as he pulled his huge longbow from behind his back.

Another arrow struck one of the iron plates of his armor, slid upward, and nearly penetrated the thick leather that protected

71

his right shoulder. Chuluun cursed, unsure of where his assailant was, but believing him to be close. His aim was far too accurate for him to be stationed on the wall.

Worried for his mount, Chuluun leapt off the stallion, winced at the agony that erupted from his ankle, and notched an arrow on his taut bowstring as he dropped to one knee. He peered toward the wall. Soldiers cheered from its ramparts, but he paid them no heed. Somewhere near was a Chinese killer.

Chuluun closed his left eye, while keeping his right eye open so that he could stare along the bolt of his notched arrow as he gazed into the distance. His forehead, shoulder, and ankle all ached, but he disregarded the pain, whispering his son's name, over and over. Forty paces away, several dense bushes grew from a slight ravine. One of the bushes appeared to shift, though no wind was present.

Without thought, Chuluun fired his weapon and rolled to his right. An arrow flew past his previous position and, before it had struck the ground, Chuluun notched and shot another bolt. A muffled cry broke the silence. Chuluun launched two more arrows into the center of the bush, which then appeared to roll backward.

Notching and drawing back another arrow, Chuluun stood up to his full height and stepped forward, aiming at the bush. He moved carefully, never taking his eyes off this target. The strength required to hold back the arrow was immense, and Chuluun's arms began to tremble. He glimpsed a man's face, shot at the chest beneath it, and then lowered his weapon.

The Chinese soldier was dead. He was dressed in green robes. Scores of twigs and leaves had been painstakingly sewn and tied to his arms, legs, torso, and neck. Three of Chuluun's arrows had embedded themselves within him, and the man must have perished quickly. Though Chuluun's countrymen would have searched the soldier for copper coins or other treasures, Chuluun didn't touch him. He wanted nothing from the Chinese, other than their lives.

Aware that he had become too predictable while surveying the wall, Chuluun promised himself that he would never be ambushed again. He had underestimated the cunning and boldness of his enemy. Once he'd done that before, and Bataar had died as a result. And today, had his enemy's aim been any better, the first arrow would have struck his face instead of his helmet.

Chuluun bent down and placed his wooden horse on the forehead of the man who had nearly killed him. He then stood up, lifted his longbow high above him, and shouted at the Chinese atop the wall, who only moments before had been cheering for his demise. Now they were silent. He saw the glimmer of their steel, yet no one challenged him, not even when he called them cowards and stood over the corpse of their countryman. At some point they would creep out from behind their stone dragon and reclaim the dead man. They would find Chuluun's wooden horse and wonder what it meant. Surely they had already discovered many such tokens—in crevices within their wall, on the bodies of their dead.

Placing his foot on the chest of his enemy, Chuluun shouted his son's name, again thrusting his longbow into the air. One of the Chinese cannons fired, but the defiant shot fell far short of his position. A figure dressed in red appeared on top of the nearest watchtower. Chuluun was certain that Yat-sen was staring at him.

In fact, it was probably Yat-sen who had arranged the attack.

A sudden urge swept over Chuluun—the desire to ride forward and fight his foes. Had he been alone in the world, without his wife and daughters, he would have done just that, waiting until darkness to scale the wall and to kill as many of the Chinese as possible before they took his life. But because of his loved ones, of the way his precious daughter had held his hand, he remained motionless.

"Soon," he whispered. "Soon you'll all burn."

Turning, Chuluun left the dead man. He whistled to his stallion and watched it trot over, wishing that it was his son who admired the grace of the steed and not him. After vaulting onto its back, he rode north, away from the two towers. Though he thought about them, he didn't want to draw attention to them. The aches on his body lessened, as did the beat of his heart. But the need for vengeance felt only stronger. All the Chinese had done was to ignite more fires within him.

*

To the east, near the first tower under Yat-sen's command, Bataar and Fan crept along the top of the Great Wall, studying the bricks and mortar at their feet. The summit of the fortification was about fifteen feet across here, dominated by chest-high parapets on the southern and northern sides. The parapet to the south was uniform and plain. Its counterpart was lined with square openings at the bottom and top through which explosives could be dropped or weapons fired.

The bricks beneath Bataar's feet tilted slightly to the south, encouraging rainwater to flow down shallow grooves to the Chinese side, which was lush because of the heavy summer storms. Fist-size holes led to spouts at the bottom of the southern parapet, allowing the rainwater to drain properly. Bataar thought that his master, Fan, was obsessed with water and how it made its way across stones. If water pooled, bricks were ripped out and later repositioned. If moss grew in a shady spot, the moss was scraped away and later used for the signal fires.

After a cannon was fired, Fan would inspect the stonework beneath it, ensuring that nothing had cracked or separated. The cannons leapt backward when used, a damaging action that tested the strength of bricks, blocks, and mortar. If Fan saw any signs of undue stress, the offending cannon would be moved to a new position of Yat-sen's choosing, and skilled masons would repair the stonework.

As they did once every week, Fan and Bataar would walk from tower to tower, inspecting the area around each cannon. During these trips, Bataar studied his Chinese companion more than he did the bricks, surprised by Fan's patience. Bataar's father had only been patient with horses. With all else in his life, he had plunged forward, often heedless of the potential consequences of his actions. Bataar had always acted like his father, but recently, because of Fan's calming influence, he'd resisted the nearly overwhelming temptation to try to escape. He trusted Fan, who promised that when the time was right they would flee together.

Bataar also expected his father to arrive any day and set him free. Surely his father spent his days and nights planning an attack and an escape. If Fan was too slow, Bataar's father would come, filling the sky with his arrows and the screams of his enemies.

Were Bataar in imminent danger, he would have climbed down the Great Wall one night and set out to the north. And though five of Bataar's friends had died while working on the fortification, he was lucky to have been assigned to Fan. It was Fan who made some of Bataar's loneliness disappear, Fan who made him smile when he missed his loved ones or his horse. While Fan was no fighter, he protected Bataar—not with a sword and strength as his father had, but with his mind and his words.

A servant approached Fan, delivering a bamboo basket that contained their lunch. Fan thanked the stooped man, then walked to some steps leading to the next tower. Sitting down on the second step, he motioned for Bataar to take a seat beside him. As usual, Fan had moved away from the Great Wall's soldiers.

Fan pried the lid from the basket and removed two stacked bowls. Their lunch was a simple meal of fried vegetables, white bean curd, and wheat noodles. The servings should have been bigger, but because of the emerging famine, rations had been cut. Their cook was fortunately a good man and a friend of Fan's. Though he had less produce and meat to work with, his dishes were still delicious and steaming.

"Here," Fan said, passing the heavier bowl to Bataar. "Be careful; it's hot."

Bataar despised many things about his Chinese captors, but their cooking was not one of them. He licked his lips, savoring the scents of garlic and pepper. Using bamboo chopsticks, he stirred his meal, steam rising from the bowl. He accidentally dropped one chopstick, which caused his companion to look up.

"My countrymen believe it's bad luck to do that," Fan said.

"What do you believe?"

"Only that you're hungry and impatient, which is a good recipe for dropping chopsticks."

Bataar began to eat, the noodles nearly burning his tongue. He sucked in air, trying to cool down the inside of his mouth. Despite the heat of the dish, he ate another bite, slurping as he drew the long noodles upward from the bowl.

"Before you choke to death, why don't you tell me something new?" Fan asked.

"Like what?"

"The story of your mother. You talk so much about your father. But what of her? What's she like?"

Bataar wiped his lips with his forefinger. He smiled. "She used to sing to me when I was little. I don't remember the songs, but I can still hear her voice. And we'd walk together. We'd walk until my legs felt like they were going to fall off."

"What else?"

"She thinks my father and I treat life too seriously. She laughs at us for how much we talk about horses and battle. 'Smell a flower,' she says. 'You'll live a longer and a happier life if you do'."

"She's wise."

Nodding, Bataar stirred his food again with his chopsticks. "My sisters are all like her. They laugh a lot. They look for pretty things. Sometimes they tease me and I chase them around."

"But you enjoy chasing them, don't you?"

"I like hearing them laugh."

A man shouted in the distance. Fan stood up, looked over the wall's northern parapet, and resumed his position on the step. "What does your mother think of horses?"

"That they're good at attracting flies," Bataar replied, shaking his head at the thought. "She complains that they stir up the dust, eat too much, and keep the children awake at night."

"She makes a fair argument. Maybe you Mongols should build yourselves a wall and we can all just shoot arrows at one another."

Bataar rolled his eyes. "You build your walls; we'll ride our horses."

"We'll be more comfortable."

"And we'll move like the wind."

Fan chuckled, then ate a bite of his meal.

"Later, when I was older," Bataar added, "she didn't want me to fight, or to go to the wall with my father."

"She was afraid for you?"

"Yes."

"But your father wasn't?"

"My mother once said that my father was afraid of me being different. Because of my hand, I was always different. That's why other boys teased me, why my father taught me to hunt before most of them could even run."

"But difference is good, Bataar. Imagine if every person, if every horse, were the same. There would be no color in the world."

Bataar was about to reply when a clamor emerged to their left. They turned toward the nearest watchtower and saw Yatsen emerge from its main door on horseback. His white stallion could barely fit through the opening, but as soon as his mount was clear of the stonework, Yat-sen spurred it forward. His second-in-command, Li, followed him on a brown mare. Both horses trotted atop the Great Wall, and soldiers hurried out of their way. As always, Yat-sen was clad in his red armor.

Though he knelt and lowered his head as the Chinese officers approached, Bataar watched Yat-sen's stallion, which was magnificent. He longed to ride it and would have happily done so anywhere, but fantasized about stealing it.

The Chinese commander neared. He yanked on his mount's reins, causing it to stop abruptly, its hooves clattering on the stonework. Fan flinched, but Bataar made no move. His gaze swung to the stallion's eyes. He smiled at it, turning his hand over, so that his palm was up.

After giving his reins to Li, Yat-sen vaulted out of his saddle, landing with grace. He took two steps forward. "You feed your slave too much, Craftsman," he said, gesturing to Bataar's bowl. "Slaves are given half-rations and should count themselves lucky to have anything."

Fan straightened himself. "I know. But I need him to be strong. Without strength he's worthless to me and, more important, to you."

"I don't care what you need," Yat-sen replied, then kicked Bataar's bowl into the parapet, shattering it. "If the barbarians can live out there, eating dust, our slaves can survive here on half-rations."

"But we had no meal this morning."

"Neither did I, Craftsman. Because of this famine we will all sacrifice. Day after day, we'll do what is necessary."

"To what end?"

"To protect this wall."

Fan's momentary defiance vanished when Yat-sen's hand dropped to his sword hilt.

The commander turned to Bataar. "And slave, you may look at my horse, but you'll never ride him. You'll never ride again."

Bataar felt his cheeks flush but made no reply. He wished his father was here. His father would kill this devil, steal his horse, and they would gallop away together.

"You want to touch my horse, slave, but you will not," Yat-sen added. "Any part of you that touches this stallion will be cleaved from your body with this sword. Keep that cursed hand of yours away from him. Understand?"

Bataar nodded, saying nothing.

Yat-sen coughed and spat. Grabbing his saddle horn, he swung himself back atop his mount. "When will the rest of the barbarians come?" he asked, glaring once again.

Bataar didn't waiver from Yat-sen's stare. "Soon."

"You think they'll rescue you? That they care about you, even with your half hand?"

"Yes."

Yat-sen laughed. "Your slave has spirit, Craftsman. Much more than you. But remember, boy, if your people come, if they breech this wall, my men will kill you."

Fan leaned forward. "No one will breech this wall. I promise."

"Remember your place, Craftsman. Remember his place. If either of you step from your stations I'll have you bound naked to these stones."

"We understand."

Yat-sen glanced to the north, then spurred his horse forward, up the wide steps. Bataar watched him go, wishing that the stallion would throw him, aware that it hated him just as much as he did. The stallion was simply waiting for the right moment.

Once Yat-sen had disappeared into the watchtower above, Fan turned. "I'm sorry," he said, handing Bataar his bowl.

"I don't want it."

"I know. But you must eat. You're young and you need sustenance."

Bataar shook his head. "I'd rather starve than eat his food."

Fan put his hand on Bataar's shoulder. "Think of your father and mother. Would they want you to eat, to stay strong? How will you ever escape this place if you're too weak to run or ride?"

Massaging his temples, Bataar tried to forget Yat-sen's insults and instead to focus on Fan's words. He was right. Bataar's parents had always fed him as much as he could eat. "Fine," he finally replied. "But only if we share it. I won't eat alone."

The two companions sat on the stonework, using chopsticks to pluck at their food.

"I wish you would stand up to him," Bataar said, then slurped up some noodles.

"I'm not your father, Bataar."

"I know. But you can still be strong. As strong as your wall."

Fan shook his head. "Each man is his own man, has his own way in the world. Your father's strength runs in you, but I'm different. I bow like a reed in the wind because the wind is stronger than me, because that's how I was raised. But just because I bow doesn't mean that I've surrendered."

"Yat-sen thinks you have."

"Fine, let him. I hope he does."

"I'll never let him think that about me."

Fan squeezed Bataar's shoulder. "Resist the temptation to fight him until the time is right. That way you can take him by surprise. That way you can win."

Though he shrugged in ambivalence, Bataar thought about the stallion, and how it waited. Maybe Fan was right; maybe the stallion was right. His father would have never waited, but in this one instance, maybe his father would have been wrong.

"He's cruel to his horse," Bataar said softly.

"How?"

"Watch how he rides him, how he tries to dominate him. He wants to be the master of him. But no one will ever rule that stallion."

*

The trail along the river was barely wide enough to accommodate Meng as she made her way north. Because of the heavy summer rains the water was high, though it had receded from its peak levels, which had flooded the nearby countryside. At one point the trail had been inundated, and it was now covered in dried mud. Nearby grasses, normally chest high this time of year, had been bent backward and lay on the ground, covered in debris. Dark, circular swaths of mud indicated the former presence of pools of water. The carcasses of dead fish lay in the middle of these areas, testaments to the suffering of the trapped creatures.

Meng switched her gaze from the swirling waters to the weeping willow trees that were perched along either bank. Tendrils of thin leaves dragged on the river's surface, creating never-ending ripples that spread out toward either bank. Crows sat in the trees' branches. Red-necked and blue-winged herons occasionally stalked minnows in the shallows. Meng had never seen herons and enjoyed watching them pursue their prey.

She witnessed many new sights while on the trail. Brown lizards sunned themselves on rocks. A broken water wheel nearly the size of a house had been lifted from its perch by the flood and carried far up on the shore. A boy tended to several water buffalo that stood in knee-deep mud, their tails slapping at the flies that besieged them. Meng waved to the boy, saw his smile, and kept walking.

Pleased by her progress, Meng continued to walk briskly. The fears that had gripped her that morning were mostly gone. The sun was out. Birds called to each other. Wild wisteria hung from tree limbs, the vines covered with purple flowers.

Meng had spent quite a bit of time in her family's and her father-in-law's small gardens, which were an attempt to re-create nature on a miniature scale. She had enjoyed each one, but only now did she understand their origins. The beauties of nature enchanted her. Clumps of slender, tall grasses drew her gaze. Moss seemed as soft as silk. Even the wind sounded more melodious than it had in Beijing—rustling scarlet leaves and swaying trees.

Her thoughts drifted to Fan, and she imagined traveling this trail with him. In Beijing they could never walk so openly together.

But here, away from prying eyes, they could enjoy the wonders that abounded in the land of their ancestors. When certain that no one was near, they could laugh and feel the sun's warmth on their backs.

Realizing that such a moment would likely never befall her, Meng thought about the emperor. People said that he was a living god, full of wisdom and strength. But she didn't think he seemed wise or just. If he were, why did he value a state official above a farmer? Why was a man so much more important than a woman? To her eye, a certain tree might have the strongest limbs, but that didn't mean it should receive more light than the trees around it. Nor did the herons seem to group themselves by sex. As far as she could tell, all the birds came and went as they saw fit, each free to fly or fish or simply stare at the water.

Meng was about to step toward the river and watch several birds when she heard a branch crack. She turned and glimpsed three men on the trail, about a hundred paces behind her. She only saw them for a moment, because they ducked into the underbrush, prompting her heart to skip a beat, her pulse to rage. Instinctively she knew that the men were tracking her.

Without a second glance behind, Meng began to run. Unlike boys, who grew up running, she had rarely done so as a girl, and rushing forward was awkward for her, especially in her oversized clothes and shoes. She stumbled, heard the men hurrying after her, and switched directions, plunging into the underbrush as she headed back toward the main road. Branches slapped at her legs, arms, and face. Her lungs heaved, burning with effort. She wasn't sure where the road was, but it couldn't be far.

Shouts were exchanged behind her. The men drew closer. Meng thought about pulling her sword from its sheath but decided that doing so would only slow her. Instead she darted into the thickest parts of the forest, where her smaller size might give her an advantage. She dragged herself between trees, crawled through thorny thickets, and struggled across muddy quagmires. Exhaustion threatened to overwhelm her, but she thought about Fan, terrified that if the bandits caught her, she might never see him again. That knowledge gave her renewed strength, and she threw herself at obstacles, beating them aside. Her hands and face were slashed by thorns and branches, yet she didn't wipe the blood from her wounds. Onward she ran, desperate, but strong; fearful, but empowered.

The men were about twenty paces behind her when she finally broke into the open. The road lay nearby, full of travelers, carts, and men on horseback. Meng rushed toward it, stumbling once again, twisting her right knee, and falling to the ground. Too weak to stand, she sat up and drew her sword. The bandits emerged from the forest, each carrying a knife. They paused, spoke to each other, concealed their weapons, and drew back into the trees.

Meng's eyes filled with tears, but they didn't fall to her cheeks. Trembling, she wiped them away with a dirty hand, blood from a cut on her nose smearing against her fingers. Though still terrified of the men, she also felt something new to her—a profound sense of pride. She had survived their ambush. She had outlasted them. Though she was supposed to be weak and feeble, she had endured. The awareness of her victory over them made her want to shout out, to let them know that they wouldn't rule her, that they should go back to hiding in the woods.

After wiping away more tears, Meng tried to stand up, collapsed, and saw that people on the road were staring at her. Afraid that someone would come forward and talk to her, she rose once again, her legs unsteady, her right knee throbbing. She sheathed her sword, then took several deep breaths, her hands at her sides. Placing one foot in front of the other, she headed toward the road. Now that the chase was over, she felt the sting of her cuts and the ache of her injured knee. Walking gingerly, she merged into the current of other travelers, meeting no one's gaze.

Meng wasn't sure what to do. She had believed herself to be safe on the forest trail and felt naked on the road. Too many people might seek her company. She needed to rest and to plan. Looking around, she studied the sights before her. Several inns loomed in the distance, as did a green and red temple.

Aware that she could walk no farther, Meng limped toward the temple, which was three storied and circular. Around it on all sides was a flagstone courtyard. Immense, long-needled pines rose from square openings in the flagstones. Certain branches of the pines, usually the heaviest and thickest, were propped up by bamboo poles that ran straight into the earth. On the south side of the temple, monks dressed in yellow robes stood behind a long, lacquer table and used ladles to scoop soup into the bowls of strangers. Meng had heard of soup lines before, as they always appeared in times of famine. Though her mouth watered at the smell of the soup, she wasn't strong enough to stand in the line. So she shuffled to the other side of the temple, her emotions settling.

A granite bench had been positioned next to one of the largest pines. The bench was unoccupied, and Meng removed her pack of supplies and sat down. She leaned forward, her elbows on her thighs. The weakness she feared invaded her then, pressing on her, smothering her. She fought back tears, gritting her teeth, unwilling to succumb to sorrows or the notion that she was as feeble as men claimed. Stifling a groan, she straightened up, then pressed her palm against her hidden necklace, drawing strength from it.

Though the other side of the temple bustled with activity, everyone seemed to be near the soup line. The courtyard around her was empty. She decided that if it remained so, she would sleep here tonight. Pretending to be mute, she would stand in the soup line, fill her belly, and then find a quiet place to rest.

How she would go on the following day, she did not know. But she was certain of one thing—she would walk until she was caught or until she saw Fan.

No other fate was possible.

*

On the Chinese side of the Great Wall, away from the dangers of the Mongols, people acted differently than they did on top of the fortification. To serve the soldiers who kept the northern front secure, state officials had created towns that followed the contours of the wall. These bustling communities were filled with street performers, inns, restaurants, shops, armories, and homes.

The sexual needs of countless soldiers were met through an elaborate system of wine and tea houses. The wine houses tended to serve common soldiers, who entered the sites, studied portraits of the courtesans available, and made their selections. Patrons were served food, wine, and opium. Most wine houses had large communal areas, and parties often lasted until dawn.

The tea houses were much more elaborate and refined. Almost all were single story, white structures with blue shutters. Richly appointed rooms surrounded a main gathering area, within which courtesans showed off their skills in fields formerly dominated by men. There were famous courtesan poets, calligraphers, painters, and musicians. Unlike wine houses, where a soldier's needs could be immediately met, the rituals of tea houses required a long and expensive courtship. Men identified courtesans they wanted to pursue, and only after the tea house's madam received a series of expensive gifts could the courtesans be taken to private rooms.

For more than a year Yat-sen had wooed one of the most famous courtesans in the region. Yehonala was seventeen years old—beautiful and a master of poetry. When he had first seen her, Yat-sen's world had changed. All he cared about previously was protecting the Great Wall and restoring his family's name. But once Yehonala had served him tea, recited her poetry, and touched his shoulder, everything was different. Suddenly he became consumed with thoughts of her. He wanted to whisper to her, to touch her, to fall asleep beside her. From that day forward he began to steal some of the funds intended for his men. He hid *taels* of silver so that he could buy jewelry and silk for the madam. Once a week he rode his white stallion to the tea house that she operated, flattered her, presented his gifts, and then sought to capture Yehonala's affections. Her fame was so well-known that initially Yat-sen had many rivals. Most of these men were fellow officers, though some were high-ranking state officials. Yat-sen had come to know his adversaries. One esteemed scholar had been close to paying for Yehonala's intimate services. His jealousy nearly overwhelming, Yat-sen had followed him home from the tea house one night, waited for an open and desolate stretch of road, and trampled him down with his stallion. Over the following months, Yat-sen killed two more of his rivals. Since then men tended to stay away from Yehonala.

Now, as Yat-sen neared the tea house, he hacked, spat, then wiped his lips. He was dressed in his finest robes. In his right hand he carried a silver comb that he would give to the madam. Though he had already paid enough money to secure Yehonala's most intimate services, the next step was to buy her freedom. Once he accomplished this difficult task, she would become his concubine and live in his home. Other than defending the Great Wall, this outcome was Yat-sen's supreme goal. He had to have her at his side. And not at the tea house, where other men could gawk at her, but in his personal chambers.

Yat-sen handed his reins to one of the tea house's servants, then dismounted. He passed through a double-door entrance, removed his boots, and presented himself to the madam, offering his gift after formalities were exchanged. A petite woman dressed in luxurious and colorful silks, she shared additional niceties with him, but he cared not for her words, the perfume she wore, or the smallness of her bound feet. He looked past her, his gaze settling on Yehonala.

He could not imagine anyone more beautiful. Her long, black

hair was pulled back behind her head and shaped into a bun. Ivory picks held it in place, though they were mostly obscured by white orchids that had been sewn into her hair. She wore a silk dress, which looked more like an elegant robe. The garment was cream colored, had several golden buttons, and was patterned with large, white peonies.

The lobes of Yehonala's ears were pierced with golden hoops, the bottoms of which featured dangling ivory feathers. Her lips were painted a faint orange, with a red orb in the middle. Her face was coated with a pale yellow dusting made from flowers and oils. Even her eyebrows were sculpted in the latest style—thin and arching.

Every care had been taken to ensure that Yehonala was presented in the most appealing way. Yet her striking clothing and jewelry were nothing compared to her natural beauty. Her face was perfectly proportioned, with smooth skin, strong cheekbones, full lips, a curved nose, and wide, dark eyes. She was unusually tall and lean. Even more appealing, her feet had been bound so tightly that she was able to wear the smallest lotus shoes.

Staring at her, Yat-sen felt as if he had consumed a cup of wine. His every sense seemed heightened and his aches had disappeared. She was a prize worth fighting for, worth killing for. He had seen every contour of her body, except for her feet, and he imagined the rises of her breasts and hips, his gaze unwavering.

Though most men would have taken tea in the communal room and begun conversation with some of the other courtesans and patrons, Yat-sen bowed slightly to Yehonala and then proceeded toward the private rooms. Hers was the last one on the hallway, and he walked with haste, his feet falling softly on thick rugs. He opened her door, stepped aside to let Yehonala pass by, and followed her in.

Though her room was richly furnished with comforts and works of art, he only looked at her. He took her long-nailed hands in his, delighting in the warmth of her flesh. "I've missed you," he said, the tone of his voice far different than it was on the Great Wall.

"Then why are you so late?" she asked, blinking repeatedly.

"The Mongols delayed me. They grow bold."

She shrugged, having never seen the Great Wall, or the northern frontier. Her parents, poor and starving, had sold her to the man who owned the tea house when she was eight. Since then, she had never left its grounds and yearned to more with each passing day. Her escape, as she saw it, was Yat-sen. He had the power and wealth to take her somewhere else, to save her from the stares of old men and the bitterness of her own thoughts.

Yehonala had never cared much for Yat-sen but pretended to. The madam had taught her well. She showed affection to her chief patron, but not love. If she loved him, he might leave her. It was far less risky, her madam was convinced, to have him wanting more. Better to give herself to him, drop by drop, than to plunge forward and satiate his every emotional desire. She believed that he loved her, and knew that he had killed for her. He had told her how he'd trampled the scholar—knowledge that pleased her far more than she would have expected.

After leading him to a black, lacquer chair, Yehonala knelt before him. She reached for a teapot that sat on the hot coals of an iron brazier, filled a cup, and handed it to him. As he sipped the steaming liquid, she reached for a porcelain dish containing warm, scented water. She began to wash and massage his feet, which seemed impossibly large when compared to the smallness of hers.

"Have you been writing?" he asked.

"I always write."

"Then let me hear you. Tell me your latest poem."

She paused, then pulled up the sleeve of her dress as it was in danger of getting wet. "I'll share a line with you," she said. "When you come again, bearing another gift, I'll tell you the next line."

"When do I hear it all?"

"When I'm your concubine."

"I'm listening."

She took the empty teacup from him. Then she began to slowly undress him. "It begins with darkness," she said. *"In the dusk of winter, the pines do not languish, but smolder, filled with want, with memories."*

He nodded. "What do they desire?"

Yehonala shook her head. She eased his clothes away from the burnt flesh of his left shoulder, massaging the ruined skin. She moved slowly, like the smoke of a dying fire. "Tell me of your enemies."

"Why?"

"Because one day, when you take me from here, they'll be my foes as well."

Yat-sen shifted so that she could remove more of his clothes. "The Mongols will attack soon, before it gets too cold."

"What of the craftsman? I want to hear more about him."

"He does what I tell him."

After pulling his clothes from him, Yehonala began to rub oil onto his legs. Always careful not to soil her dress, she massaged his muscles. She knew he was jealous of the craftsman, jealous of the love between the man and his wife. Envy prompted Yat-sen to steal her letters as they arrived, to read her words and keep them from him.

"What does she say to him?" Yehonala asked.

"Her mother is ill."

"What else?"

"She made a coat to keep him warm this winter."

"Those are just happenings. They're as interesting as dust. What does she feel?"

Yat-sen subdued a cough. "She wishes that she tried harder to convince him to stay in Beijing."

"She blames herself?"

"How could she? It was his choice."

Yehonala shifted her miniature feet, which ached if she knelt improperly. Though she had once wondered about love, she had come to realize that she would never experience it. That private realization was closely followed by bitterness and regret. The bitterness swelled from knowing that men sought her out for her beauty and not her laughter, which had become a thing of the past. The regret stemmed from believing that even if Yat-sen liberated her from the tea house, she would never truly be free. Men had built too many cages around her.

Discarding these thoughts, Yehonala started to massage Yat-sen's thighs, but he leaned forward, reaching for her. He pulled the long pins from her hair, watching its blackness descend on her shoulders and back. Then he unfastened the golden buttons of her dress, exposing her undergarments. She let him do as he pleased, standing up slowly, moving toward him.

Soon she was naked but for her lotus shoes. No wife, concubine, or courtesan would ever show a man her bound feet—not because of their disfigurement, but because the ecstasy of such a sight might be too much for a lover to bear.

"You want the coat she made," Yehonala said as Yat-sen's hands trembled against her body.

He said nothing, looking away.

Yehonala's madam had said that he loved her, but he feared that she would never love him in the way that the craftsman's wife adored her husband. Yehonala smiled inwardly, thankful for the counsel of her madam, believing that she was right.

Yat-sen reached for her breasts, and Yehonala arched backward, as she had been taught. She sensed the eagerness deep within him, yet made no move to touch him. She would only do so toward the end, when his impatience endangered her. Until then she would tease him, increasing his want, his need.

He carried her to a bed covered in furs and silks. Again he touched her, moving with haste and recklessness. His fingers seemed to multiply upon her, squeezing and probing.

Finally, as she grew aroused, she reached for him, thinking of the craftsman and his wife, longing to read all their letters, as jealous of their love as the desperate, wretched man upon her.

CHAPTER FIVE

Tennous Alliances

Simatai—October 14, 1549

At the far eastern section of the Great Wall that Yat-sen oversaw, just beyond the shadow of the first tower in his command, Fan and Bataar knelt next to an iron cauldron filled with water. Both man and boy were positioned at the northern edge of the wall and used ladles to pour water onto the bricks. They watched where the water went, how it drained or pooled. With winter approaching it was imperative that Fan locate and fix cracks in the mortar. If he didn't, freezing rains would fill them and the resulting ice would expand, enlarging whatever weaknesses were present.

Yat-sen was obsessed with having his section of the Great Wall remain in perfect condition. This view was the only one that he and

Fan shared, as the craftsman took pride in his work. He also knew that if the Mongols ever breeched the wall's defenses they could gallop to Beijing in a single day. Most of the city was fortified but if the Great Wall fell, Beijing would certainly follow. Frustrated after being kept out of the Chinese heartland for generations, the Mongols would likely raze the city. Thousands would die.

Fan watched as Bataar slowly overturned his ladle. Water trickled toward the Chinese side of the wall. For several feet, the water moved as it should but then seemed to vanish. Fan set down his own ladle and crept toward the spot. Leaning forward until his eyes were inches from the stonework, he noticed a small crack in the mortar. He removed a piece of black chalk from his pocket, then circled the crack, which his workers would fix later in the day.

"Thank you," Fan said, nodding to Bataar. "I don't know why, but your water always seems to find the right place."

"Because I let it go where it wants to."

"Is that how you ride a horse?"

"No, when I'm on a horse, we go where we want to."

"But what if you want to reach different destinations?"

Bataar set down his ladle. "We never do. What I see, he sees. Where I lean, he leans."

"Oh."

"You'd know that if you'd spent much time on a horse."

"Well, I haven't. Please forgive me."

"You're forgiven. At least this time. Tomorrow you might not be so lucky."

Smiling, Fan filled his ladle with water and flicked it at Bataar, splashing his face. "You're an impertinent child, aren't you?"

Bataar dipped his ladle into the cauldron, flipped it at Fan, and laughed as water struck his chest. "I can't help it if you don't know how to ride a horse. How is that possible anyway?"

"I have two feet. I can walk. I can run. Why do I need to bounce along on the back of some beast?"

Rolling his eyes, Bataar again flicked water at his companion. "Why run when you can fly?"

"Is that what it's like? You feel like a bird?"

"Yes, because the ground is only a blur beneath you. Your body bends and bounces, but your feet hardly stir. So you are flying, in a way."

Fan overturned his ladle on the stonework, watching the water flow. "Maybe someday you can show me."

"But you want to return to your wife, to the south. I have to go north."

"Maybe one day the gates to this wall will be open. Maybe we'll come and go as we please."

Bataar scratched his chin. "No, I don't think so. But you could sneak over to our side. My father won't kill you."

"Why not?"

"Because you're my friend. He'll kill everyone else, of course, so you should stay away from them when his arrows fill the sky."

Fan was about to reply when he saw two distinct columns of smoke rising from a watchtower to the west. He stood up, staring beyond the wall's parapet, out into the wasteland. The ridge of a low mountain obscured his view, and he saw no riders. But he knew they were present, testing the defenders in one way or another.

His countrymen were rushing to their positions or moving to secure endangered spots. Yat-sen was surely charging forward on his stallion, gauging the level of the threat. In all likelihood the presence of the Mongols was only a maddening ruse. Most often they disappeared as they appeared, without announcement or lasting repercussions. But perhaps one visit in ten resulted in an attack. And everyone on top of the Great Wall had to remain vigilant.

"Is your father out there?" Fan asked, deciding to remain where he was.

"He's always out there. And he'll come for me. He won't rest until I'm back by his side."

Fan wondered if he should simply wait for a nighttime attack and send Bataar running to the north. He could be lowered to the ground with a rope and, with luck, would be reunited with his father. Yat-sen certainly would never allow his return to his people. Bataar knew too much about the Great Wall. As soon as his usefulness was over, or when he became too much of a threat to escape, he would be killed.

A cannon fired to the west.

"Why do your countrymen attack Yat-sen's section?" Fan asked. "It's the best defended. And whatever they damage, we repair the next day."

Bataar clucked his tongue, shaking his head. "Because Yat-sen led that raid. He stole six of us boys and so there are six fathers who want revenge. Why would they attack another section when they can see Yat-sen here?"

Fan imagined a child being stolen from him. Though he had

never lifted a weapon, his single purpose in life would be to reclaim his loved one. Surely Bataar was right—his father was out there, looking for him, plotting vengeance and victory.

"When your father comes for you," Fan said, "he should leave with you, and not worry about Yat-sen."

"He'll kill him."

"No, Bataar. That would be a mistake. If your father finds you, you should both flee. Out there, your father is the lord of his land. But on this wall, Yat-sen is the lord. He's walked these stones for five years and knows them like no other. If your father fights him here, he'll die."

"No, he—"

"Yes he will, Bataar. Trust me. So if your father comes, take his hand and lead him away. Ride toward your mother and your sisters. Return to them together, or you won't return at all."

*

Little about the previous night had been restful. Meng had tried to sleep on the bench, lying on one of her blankets and covered by the coat she'd made for Fan. She had propped her sword against her so that its tip bit into the ground and its hilt was in her hand. Though afraid someone might run past and steal the weapon, it looked fearsome in the moonlight, and she hoped the sight would intimidate any bandits.

Without a fire, the night had been cold, and she had spent much of it shivering. To make matters worse, her right knee was swollen and throbbing. When the pain had become too much, she had limped over to an old gingko tree, collected five of its leaves, and eaten them. The leaves were purported to reduce swelling, though they seemed to have no effect on her pain.

The reprieve of sleep had teased Meng until just before dawn when, at last, she had fallen into a deep slumber. She awoke with the smell of smoke in her face. Monks were burning a pile of twigs, needles, and leaves less than twenty paces away from her position.

Sitting up, Meng grimaced at her aches. She reached into her pack, pulled out a scarf, and wrapped it tightly around her knee. After sheathing her sword and eating two shriveled apples that the monks had given her the night before, she slowly stood up. The movement produced a level of pain that wasn't overwhelming, but enough to make her grit her teeth. She tied her pack on her back, waved to the nearby monks, bowed slightly, and began to walk toward the main road, which already bustled with people and animals.

Keeping her right leg straight, Meng hobbled ahead, wincing each time her injured knee had to bear weight. She thought about resting for the day but couldn't imagine sitting still when Fan was so close. A week of walking would bring her to him. If she gave herself a respite from traveling, she might save herself from physical pain, but she would inflict emotional distress upon herself. She couldn't place her own well-being ahead of Fan's, not when he had been laboring for a year and she'd done little more than drink tea and be a dutiful daughter-in-law.

The road, it seemed, bustled with even more travelers than the previous day. Wealthy men and women were carried past on luxurious sedan chairs. Soldiers marched in long columns.

Oxen pulled the carts of merchants, who rode on horseback, or donkeys, or were carried in sedan chairs by servants. Along the roadside, beggars held out wooden bowls. All were dressed in tattered, filthy clothes. Some appeared to be starving. Others were injured or had nearly succumbed to the rigors of typhoid, malaria, smallpox, or dysentery. Most travelers avoided the beggars, as did Meng. At least until she saw a young boy who had only a stub for a leg. She smiled at him, reached into her satchel, and gave him five copper coins. He grinned, then touched her sword hilt, apparently impressed by it. She let him feel the steel until the pain in her knee seemed to increase. At that point she gave him another coin, nodded, and started forward again.

Meng studied the sights along the road in an effort to distract herself from the pain of her knee. Certain areas were inundated with stalls, within which merchants sold food, candy, clothes, shoes, weapons, art, medicine, and walking sticks. Meng wanted to buy one of the polished sticks but feared a conversation.

She continued to limp forward, moving slowly. A large group of Taoist pilgrims leading donkeys burdened with provisions brushed past her, jostling her in their haste. These bumps shifted her balance enough that she was forced to rely more on her injured knee. She had to repress urges to groan and moved to the edge of the road. Yet making progress on the periphery was even worse because merchants sought her gaze, hawking their wares, shoving them toward her.

Her heartbeat starting to race, Meng limped back toward the middle of the road. But men on horseback charged forward, yelling at people to stay clear. Meng moved sideways, then forward, dodged a giant cart, and stepped ahead again. Realizing that she was barely making progress, she grew frustrated. She tried to walk faster but stumbled, nearly falling. Someone cursed at her, saying she should join the beggars. Meng ignored the man's words. Though she felt tears welling in her eyes, she was determined not to cry. She thought of Fan working on the Great Wall—hungry, cold, and covered in grime. This vision prompted her to walk faster, and she shuffled forward, ignoring the growing discomfort in her knee.

Suddenly a group of mounted soldiers charged toward her. People scattered to the left and right, but she was frozen with fear. Men wearing armor and brandishing weapons came right at her, dust rising from the hooves of their horses. Meng bowed, remained motionless, and cowered as the soldiers rushed past. Several of them shouted at her. One soldier came particularly close, purposely whipping her shoulder with his long reins as he rode past. The blow stung and Meng stumbled. She moved to her right, toward the merchants. Though she still fought her tears, they arrived, and she wiped them away in the swirling dust, fearful that someone would see her crying.

The dust settled. Merchants grumbled about the discourtesy of the horsemen and began to wipe off their wares. Meng was glad for the distraction. No one seemed to have noticed her misery. She brushed away her tears, pretending that some grit had gotten into her eyes. Then she limped ahead again.

Meng hadn't gone ten paces when a man approached her, pushing a two-wheeled cart designed to accommodate a passenger. The cart was brightly colored and looked comfortable. The man was slightly smaller than average. He was dressed in a high-ranking state official's crimson-colored robe, featuring a square, ornamental patch on his chest. The patch displayed a white crane with outstretched wings and a red head. Swirling clouds were above the crane, while flowers stretched beneath it. This thigh-length robe was held tight by a black sash. Yellow trousers fell to the man's knees. His black, fur-lined boots looked nearly new. A curved short sword hung from his right side.

"Where are you headed?" he asked Meng, his smile revealing remarkably straight and white teeth.

Meng stopped. She looked around, wondering if he was talking to someone else. When it became clear that he wasn't, she shook her head and ran her hand across her mouth, indicating that she couldn't speak. Her heart pounding so loud that she thought he might hear it, she repeated the gesture.

"I once knew a mute mule," the stranger said, grinning. "Most mules complain from dawn till dusk, but this beast usually kept his mouth shut. I called him Stoneface."

Smiling, Meng bowed slightly, then started forward again.

The official reached for her elbow, stopping her. "In honor of Stoneface, why don't I push you for a bit on my cart? You look hurt. Why limp around when you can travel like the emperor?"

Meng eyed the cart, which featured a thickly padded bench. It looked comfortable. Yet surely the man would expect a large payment. Though tempted, she shook her head.

"Twenty coppers is all," he replied. "Twenty coppers gets you a ride until the sun sets."

She bit her lower lip, surprised at the fairness of the offer. She could afford to pay him twenty coppers, and he might cover a great distance before sunset, much farther than she could make it with her injured knee.

Though Meng wondered why a high-ranking state official would push a cart, she contemplated his offer. Something about the man wasn't right. She studied his face, which was partially obscured by a neatly trimmed beard. His eyes were open and active, darting around like two black and white moths trapped inside his head.

"These are my father's clothes," he whispered. "I borrow them from time to time. That way, no one bothers me."

Meng looked ahead at the road, which remained full of travelers. She tried to bend her knee and winced at the pain.

"Be the emperor for the day," the stranger said. "See what he sees. Feel what he feels. Of course, don't expect me to conjure up too many miracles. I won't have fifty courtesans of the highest rank awaiting you around the next bend."

Though still torn, Meng knew that she couldn't travel far on her bad knee. This man could take her closer to Fan. Better yet, she might be safe on his cart. His clothes protected him from inquiries, and no one would trouble her while she was with him.

Aware that men always haggled, she held out ten fingers and then seven more.

"Seventeen coppers!" he exclaimed. "You don't look like a bandit. But you must have them as brothers. Very well. Eighteen it will be."

Meng nodded, and climbed into the cart, sitting on the bench. The man offered her a red, silk blanket. Grateful, she draped it over herself, pleased that the royal color would elevate her status. The stranger moved behind her, picked up two poles that extended from the cart, and lifted. The cart tilted forward as the man secured a leather strap that ran from the end of one pole, over his shoulders, to the other pole. In this balanced position, the cart bore almost all her weight, and Meng could see that the stranger was able to stand with ease.

"You're heading north?" he asked.

She nodded.

He started to walk, the cart moving smoothly over the road. Meng smiled, feeling at ease for the first time all day. Situated ahead of him, she didn't have to worry about him looking at her face and was relieved. He walked faster than she would have guessed, passing people to his right and left.

"I'm Ping," he added. "I may look to be nineteen, but I'm thirty-one. And you? Oh, that's right, you can't talk, so I'll talk for you. Maybe twenty? You must be a scholar of some sort as your face has rarely seen the sun. How lucky I am to have you as a patron. You must teach me something, Stoneface the Second. What, you ask? Oh, I don't know, but surely someone as wise as you can enlighten a fool like me."

Meng nodded, unwinding the wrap around her knee.

"How did you get hurt? Did a woman knock you out of her bed? That's happened to me twice, though at least I've been able to walk afterwards. I'll tell any man who listens that he hasn't lived if a woman hasn't cast him from her bed."

Two mounted soldiers rode past, sending people scurrying.

"Those fools always act so busy," Ping said. "Like they're single-handedly fighting off the Mongols. They rush around, impressing those less astute than we, but when they reach the Great Wall, all they do is sleep while standing. They've mastered that fine art, believe me."

The stranger's mention of the Great Wall caught Meng's attention. He must have been there. Maybe he'd seen Fan. Resisting the urge to ask him anything, she nodded again, encouraging him to speak.

"You're a merry mute, I'll give you that," Ping replied. "Stoneface the First was much more troubled. He'd try to bite me when I wasn't looking. You won't do that, will you? I can't abide biting passengers, even in times of famine."

She shook her head.

"Good. Besides, you wouldn't find me that tasty. I don't think Stoneface the First even did. At some point I was overcooked."

The cart hit a rock, bouncing up.

"Sorry about that," Ping said. "The emperor would have had me beheaded. Luckily for me, you're much more forgiving."

Meng smiled again. As Ping began to tell her how he and Stoneface the First had parted ways, she watched the countryside pass by. They were moving quickly. This stranger, whom she didn't trust yet liked, was bringing her closer to Fan.

The way to her husband seemed easier. Gradually, as she rumbled ahead on the cart, it seemed that a storm was drifting away from her. This storm had weakened her mind, her body. For more than a year she hadn't been herself. Her appetite for food, conversation, and laughter had ebbed.

In the absence of the storm, her knee ached less; her worries dissipated. She felt free, unburdened by guilt and fear.

On the stranger's cart, moving so swiftly, Meng sensed that she was drawing nearer to Fan. She imagined his face, the feel of his hands against her skin.

Content within this state of sudden and unexpected bliss, she didn't contemplate the dangers and difficulties that surely lay ahead. Whatever problems arose, she would face them. She would do what needed to be done.

*

The Black Rider, as Yat-sen referred to him, was on the move again. He rode his stallion to the southeast, toward Yat-sen's position. The Chinese commander shifted on his own mount, hoping that his foe would come within range of his longbow. Yat-sen hated all Mongols, but he particularly despised the Black Rider. The man was fearless, cunning, brought bad luck to those before him, and had killed more than a dozen Chinese soldiers. All the defenders wanted to see him fall, and all longed to kill him, especially since Yat-sen had proclaimed that any man who struck him down would be rewarded with a *tael* of silver.

For nearly a year, the Black Rider had mocked Yat-sen and his soldiers, riding near the Great Wall, studying its intricacies, and occasionally galloping forward to fire his massive longbow. The Mongol seemed to have an unusual interest in Yat-sen, who was always on guard when he was near. From what Yat-sen had gathered from other commanders, the Black Rider never bothered scouting their positions. For unknown reasons, he was focused on Yat-sen's section, his presence ill omened. Most of Yat-sen's men were superstitious and dreaded the sight of the Mongol, convinced that he brought death to their ranks. Many times he did, as he often led raids. Perhaps worse, the defenders believed that he regularly crept close to their positions at night because every few weeks a solitary arrow hissed through the darkness, shot with such strength and accuracy that it pierced armor and downed men.

Now, as Yat-sen studied the Black Rider, he pulled his own longbow from behind his back, notching an arrow. His second-in-command, Li, mirrored his motions. Nearby, several soldiers readied a cannon. Not trusting the weapon, Yat-sen pulled his horse's reins to the right, turning it away from the cannon. The stallion trotted to an open area of the Great Wall. Li followed.

Yat-sen reflected on his recent attempt to kill the Black Rider. His trap had been well executed and the Mongol was taken by surprise. Yet Yat-sen's man had failed to down their enemy, his arrows missing him entirely or bouncing off his armor. Like hundreds of men on the Great Wall, Yat-sen had watched their battle, cursing when the Mongol had leapt from his mount, discovered the position of his attacker, and killed him.

In a hidden pocket, Yat-sen carried a small, wooden horse that had been found on the forehead of his man. The horse was intricately carved, rearing up on its hind legs. Several similar horses had been discovered after the Black Rider's kills. Yat-sen had cast them all into fires and would do the same with this one. He wanted nothing that the Mongol had touched to remain in existence.

"I long for his head," Yat-sen said quietly, still holding his longbow, watching dust rise from the hooves of his enemy's mount. The Mongol stopped directly across from Yat-sen's position and shouted something. Though he couldn't tell what was said, Yat-sen heard the defiance and anger in the Black Rider's voice.

"If I sent you out there, would you kill him?" Yat-sen asked. "Could you kill him?"

Li shrugged his massive shoulders.

The Mongol suddenly raced forward, yelling again. A nearby cannon fired, the explosion causing Yat-sen to flinch. He drew back on his longbow, aimed and fired an arrow, and then watched the Mongol do the same. Yat-sen's bolt struck the ground beside his foe. Li's attempt was much too high.

The Black Rider's arrow whistled through the air. Yat-sen spurred his mount, ducking. The lone projectile shattered against the stonework near Yat-sen's former position. He swore as the Mongol wheeled around, heading back out into the wasteland.

"Curse that man!" Yat-sen said, still holding his weapon. "Why does he target me?"

Li, who was usually quiet, turned to his commander. "Perhaps you killed someone he loved."

"Why do you say that?"

"Because he seeks vengeance. Slaying you is all that matters to him."

"And the wooden horses? Why does he always leave them?"

Li draped his longbow over his right shoulder, then shrugged.

As he watched the Black Rider depart, Yat-sen pondered Li's words. Perhaps he's right, Yat-sen thought. Perhaps I did kill someone the Mongol loved. But who? When?

Yat-sen thought about the Black Rider's first appearance, nearly a year before. If Li was right, the Mongol must have come to avenge a recent killing. Yet Yat-sen could remember slaying none of his enemies during that time. He had led one successful raid, two months earlier. During that attack, he had downed two soldiers and a sword-wielding woman. He'd also ordered that Mongol boys be taken as slaves. As far as he recalled, all the boys had later died when part of the Great Wall collapsed.

It might have been the woman, Yat-sen thought, trying to remember her. He had been on the ground, and she'd charged him. Sidestepping her attack had been easy, and he'd smashed the hilt of his sword down on her head, crushing the life from her. She must have been the mother of one of the children they'd captured, he thought. That means the Black Rider lost a wife and a son. Or he might be unrelated to her but the father of one of the boys.

Yat-sen tried to remember all of the prisoners. Even though his mind was sharp, it was hard to recollect the slaves. The Great Wall bustled with so many different faces—slaves, servants, soldiers, and craftsmen. The slaves were captured Mongols who were often brought to him. He assigned them to various stations, always under the watchful eye of a man he trusted.

As Yat-sen recalled, the six Mongol boys had been kept together. All were under a weakened rampart when it toppled. All had died almost immediately.

"That woman I slew, the day of the raid, how old was she?" Yat-sen asked.

Li's brow furrowed. "Their women age faster than ours."

"But what do you think?"

"Twenty? Twenty-five?"

The commander coughed, then spat, straightening in his saddle. "I believe she was the wife of the Black Rider. That's why he hunts for me."

Though he nodded, Li made no reply.

"I killed his woman and he seeks to avenge her," Yat-sen added. "The barbarians are a proud race. His honor has been stained."

"So he seeks your head."

"Then we'll have to tempt him with it. Let him come for me and find his death."

Li adjusted his helmet.

Yat-sen stared into the north, once again remembering the raid. "She was brave to pick up that sword," he said. "Foolish, but brave."

"Their women are strong."

"I haven't thought of her since the moment I killed her. But now she returns to me."

Li replied, but Yat-sen wasn't listening. He thought of Yehonala, wondering if she would reach for a sword and fight an armed man. She would, he decided. And if someone killed her, I would avenge her. I would come for him as the Black Rider comes for me.

"He's to be dead before the next full moon," Yat-sen announced. "We'll kill him, tie his corpse to that horse of his, and let it drag him until he's no more."

It had been a long day for Fan and Bataar. They had made it halfway across Yat-sen's section, using their ladles to pour water on the stonework. Fan had found sixteen cracks that concerned him and had circled each with his black chalk.

The craftsman and boy had watched the Black Rider appear. Like most everyone around them, they had witnessed the brief confrontation between him and Yat-sen. Arrows had flown, but no one was injured. The Mongol had shouted in the distance, but his words were indistinguishable.

Now, as sunset approached, Fan and Bataar stood on the upper level of one of the watchtowers. The smell of fried vegetables and rice emanated from below, as dinner was being prepared. Though many men liked to relax within the safety of the lower level, which was almost completely enclosed, Fan and Bataar preferred the open-sided terrace at the top. This platform provided unparalleled views and was free of the gloom and dankness that pervaded the lower level. Besides, when winter arrived, as it soon would, anyone not on guard duty would be forced inside by the inclement weather.

Though most of the top level was open, a small room in the center rose up, protected by a two-sided curved and tiled roof. Four soldiers sat around a table in this room, playing a game of *Go*. The men laughed, grumbled, and wagered bets. Fan liked listening to them play. They were good men. Many were poor, hailing from towns around Beijing. Most had no choice but to fight. They manned cannons during the day or night and otherwise collected

UNBOUND

in the watchtowers to eat, rest, or play games.

Fan knew the men counted on him. If the Mongols breeched a particular section of the Great Wall, many of the soldiers guarding it would die. Though the men weren't cowards, they were often poorly equipped. So many resources went into the construction of the Great Wall that there wasn't much money left for armor, weapons, and horses. Of course, Yat-sen's men were better supplied and trained than most. It was said that for many miles, they were the fastest at lighting signal fires, reloading cannons, and firing their longbows at moving targets.

While Fan thought about Meng every day, he also considered these men and Bataar. He didn't want to betray the men by fleeing. Nor could he leave until Bataar had escaped. If Fan had worried for Meng's safety, he would have helped Bataar run off that very night. But she shared a roof with his father and mother, and they treated her well.

Yet Fan longed for her and was certain that she also missed him. He had always thought himself to be happy, but after they married he realized that his former life had been more incomplete than not. She made him want to be better than he was and awakened him to his true self.

Though Meng was a woman with unbound feet, Fan believed that she possessed the same strength as his stones. She didn't see him as a commoner, but someone she loved. She didn't ask for treasures that he could not afford, but only his affections. She could read and write, laugh and jest. Best of all, she saw the world for what it was but didn't accept its injustices. The world could be better, she believed. And she would do her part to make it so.

113

Leaning against the tower's top parapet, Fan continued to think about Meng while watching Bataar chase a lizard. The boy was quick and agile, rushing from stone to stone, trying to keep the creature from scurrying over the parapet to safety below. Though Fan often advised patience, a virtue that might have led to the lizard's capture, Bataar couldn't help himself. He grabbed and leapt until the lizard was gone.

Smiling, Fan watched Bataar approach. "You almost had him."

"Almost."

Fan turned to watch the setting sun. The days were getting shorter and colder. Autumn had always been his favorite time of the year, though he dreaded spending another winter on the wall. The cold had killed more men the previous year than all of the Mongol attacks.

Bataar nudged his foot. "Tell me a story. I know that you're thinking about one to send to your wife. Can I hear it first?"

"It's not quite right yet. I haven't written it down."

"That doesn't matter. I'm not her. It doesn't have to be just right."

The lizard reappeared, but Bataar didn't stir.

"She's always looking for stars," Fan said, his shoulders hunched forward, as if he were walking into a headwind. "Not that we have many in Beijing, but she often admires the few that we do. So I'd like to write something about two stars."

"Pretend that I'm her."

"You?"

"I'll just act like my mother. Only I won't tell you to listen to your sisters. I wouldn't do that to you."

"You promise not to?"

"Of course."

Fan smiled, then recalled the tale he'd created the previous night, when sleep had been fitful. "Once there were two shooting stars," he said, straightening, trying to remember the words that he'd sought out. "They were very much in love and traveled together, delighting in each other's company. One night, a terrible storm engulfed the heavens, shaking their world, driving them apart. He was cast to the west and she to the east, separated by an unimaginable vastness.

"After the storm settled they began to search for each other. Both were lonely as they sped from place to place, never stopping, always pressing forward, into the unknown. They searched and searched and searched, crossing vast distances, illuminating new skies. For weeks, then months, then years they looked, finding nothing, enduring the blackness alone. Though their despair grew, they never quit searching. And one night, after many years of solitude, they found each other. As this reunion unfolded they were overwhelmed with joy. Suddenly all of the misery was forgotten. All that mattered was their togetherness."

Bataar shook his head. "That's it?"

"No. Because what the shooting stars didn't realize was that they had illuminated the night sky for so many eyes. Their years of travel had given solace to strangers, comfort to creatures both great and small. They had filled night skies with wonder."

"Where are they now?"

"Since their reunion they've always stayed together, throughout the centuries. And whenever you see a shooting star, followed closely by another, you witness their love and happiness."

Bataar nodded. "Is that how you want it to be with your wife? That you'll always be together and happy?"

"Yes. That's exactly what I want."

"But a storm separated the two of you."

"A storm of sorts. But yes, that's right."

Bataar glanced north, standing on his tiptoes as he scanned the horizon. "Is it difficult to be married?"

"Not if you love someone more than yourself. Then it's easy."

"My father loves my mother. He would never write her a story, but I know they love each other."

"I'm sure they do."

"Will I love someone someday?"

Fan started to speak, but then stopped, thinking about how lucky Meng and he had been to be paired together. "The sky is full of stars, Bataar. The trick is finding just the right one. You shouldn't look with your eyes, but with your heart. Ask your father to do that for you. If he does that for you, he'll give you a wonderful blessing."

"I'll ask him. And I'll remember your story. Someday, when I'm married, I'll tell it to my wife."

"I'd like that."

Bataar promised that he would, and then was silent, continuing to stare north.

Fan wondered if the boy was thinking about his family, suspecting that he was. "Let's see what tonight's sky brings us," he said, gesturing toward the horizon, wishing that he could grasp Meng's hand and that they could soar away together.

Meng studied the sunset, still on Ping's cart. The road no longer bustled with people and was almost empty. Though they had passed many inns and homes along the way, this area was dominated by a nearby forest. Meng had been tempted to stop at an inn, but she'd paid Ping to push her until sunset and hadn't wanted to waste the opportunity to make good progress.

Now she regretted her decision to go onward. The forest was dark and quiet, looming around her the way fog engulfs a valley. Every so often a cooking fire pierced the blackness, an orange orb that was both comforting and frightening. After all, people were in the forest, but Meng didn't know if they were harmless or dangerous.

Nor was she sure what to think of Ping. Though he had talked and joked for much of the day, she sensed that he wasn't who he claimed to be. He tended to avoid columns of soldiers, pushed her with more speed than would seem normal, and seemed uncomfortable in his official robes. Yet he had also kept his word, bringing her north, allowing her to rest and the swelling in her knee to subside.

Meng wasn't sure what to communicate to Ping once the sun vanished completely. Their agreement would be fulfilled. He would likely leave her alone, in the darkness, while he continued ahead. She didn't like the idea of asking him to stay with her, but neither did she want to be isolated. Too many bandits roamed the forest. If she made a fire, it would be plain for everyone to see that she was alone.

Sure enough, Ping pushed her across a small bridge, then turned his cart to the right, proceeding to the edge of a creek. He stopped at the base of a large willow tree. Its branches nearly touched the ground and created a protective umbrella of dense foliage.

After setting his poles on the damp soil, he wiped sweat from his brow and turned toward her. "I'd wager that's the best eighteen coppers you ever spent, wasn't it?" he asked. "We traveled far."

Despite her reservations about the man, Meng smiled. Earlier she had reached into her secret satchel and removed the coins she had promised to him. She handed them over, bowed slightly, and took her pack. Though a part of her still didn't want him to leave and was tempted to hire him for the following day, she remained unconvinced that his presence was a good thing.

Stepping away from him, she placed her pack against the willow tree. The sun had set, and darkness had flooded into the forest. In the distance, two fires burned, glowing like the embers of a giant, near-dead inferno. She wanted to say farewell to Ping, and to thank him, but dared not use her voice. Instead she bowed again and smiled.

An owl hooted from somewhere unseen.

Ping started to turn away but then twisted back, straightening out his robes. "We'd be safer together," he said. "Not that the two of us could stop an army. But a pair of swords will make a bandit think twice."

Meng considered her options, none of which excited her. Yet worse than her apprehension over Ping's character was her fear of being alone in the dark—and so she nodded.

"You're a lot smarter than Stoneface the First," Ping replied. "And you never tried to bite me, which I appreciate. I wish your namesake had been as honorable. After all, an obstinate, sullen traveling companion who covets flesh leaves a great deal to be desired."

Believing that a man would collect firewood, Meng began to pick up branches and set them in a small clearing by the tree. Ping tied his cart to a stump, then unpacked a bag that he had hidden beneath the bench. He sang as he worked, his voice off-key, but a welcome presence that blended with the chirps of crickets.

Once Meng had finished her task, she began to arrange her bedding near the fire. She wasn't sure how to light it and hoped that Ping would take the initiative. He did, and before long knee-high flames flickered into the night, illuminating a small sphere of the forest.

"What were you planning to eat tonight?" Ping asked.

Meng shrugged, wishing she could tell him that most of her supplies had been stolen. She didn't want him to think that she was a fool.

"Expect to find a plate of roasted duck awaiting you out here?"

Shaking her head, Meng moved closer to the fire.

"A good thing for you; neither did I." Ping placed a flat stone near the edge of the flames. As the stone warmed, he reached into one of his bags and removed a large, yellow leaf that had been wrapped around something. Now whistling, he unwrapped the leaf, revealing six deep-fried sparrows. If the small birds had been prepared according to common practices in Beijing, they were not only de-feathered but de-boned. They had likely been marinated in rice wine, onion stock, and sugar, then coated in flour and fried in peanut oil.

Still whistling, Ping placed the sparrows on the stone. He sorted through another bag, removed a small, silver container, opened it, and sprinkled salt on the birds.

Meng's eyes widened at the sight of so much salt. The emperor had decreed that only the government could produce and sell salt—a law that created important revenue for the state. Meng had heard of salt smugglers but had wondered if they were real. Anyone caught with unofficial salt could be executed.

"A little salt will have these fellows singing like they were earlier this afternoon," Ping said, closing his silver container. "Made your mouth water, didn't I? Well, lucky for us both, a courtesan in Beijing is fond of me. Hard to blame her, I know. A state official gave her madam mounds of salt, trying to buy her freedom. The official, poor man, died of a fever. But his salt remained at the tea house. So, I told the girl how beautiful she was, as I had many times before. I made love to her like she wanted to be loved, and I left with a pouch of salt."

Meng turned away at the talk of lovemaking. She had never heard a stranger say such a thing.

"True enough, I may be boastful, but you're about to savor the rewards of my affections. And when I go back to Beijing, I'll see her again and tell her how my good friend Stoneface the Second raved about her gift."

Ping pulled a knife from his belt, sharpened a stick, and then used it to pierce one of the sparrows. He handed Meng the stick. "Go ahead. You can thank me later. And if you'd like, you can thank the courtesan. I'll tell you where to find her, and if you treat her well enough she'll give you your own little pile."

Leaning back, away from her companion, Meng began to eat. The sparrow was delicious. Though Meng didn't like how her companion had spoken about the courtesan, she was grateful for the meal and nodded in thanks.

"I bought them earlier when you needed some privacy," Ping replied. "Three birds for you and three for me. Even though you should have paid me twenty coppers, I decided not to hold it against you. Besides, you're so light I hardly knew you were on my cart, a fact that provided me with an epiphany of sorts: Perhaps it's words that give people weight."

The fire cracked, casting sparks into the sky.

Ping bit into a bird, then shrugged. "No, you say? Well, I bet you're not focused on my epiphany and are wondering where I got these clothes. If you must know, I stole them from some fool who had a fondness for rice wine. I stole his cart too. Now don't worry, I won't steal from you. You're too entertaining as a conversationalist. I'd rather push you around, earn your coppers, and listen to your stories—infrequent as they may be. I only steal from the emperor and the dullards who serve him."

Meng stopped eating. The man was a thief. She was alone with him and at his mercy. Perhaps he would do what her father-in-law's servant had done.

"As I said, don't worry," Ping replied. "I never stole from Stoneface the First, and I won't steal from you. To prove it, I'll give you my sword and knife before I sleep. At that point, if anyone should be worried, it should be me. You're the one who knows about my salt. And I have at least eighteen coppers. As far as I know, you have nothing of value other than your wonderful sense of humor."

Meng shifted before the fire, once again leaning away from Ping as he gave her another bird.

"You think I jest, but good conversation is terribly hard to find these days," he said. "It's as if war and famine have made everyone quiet. Almost as bad, I haven't read a memorable book or poem in weeks. So, I have to try to amuse myself. Lucky for you, I'm skilled at it. Did you hear that I once had a mouse for a companion? No? Well, he followed me as I traveled, picking up crumbs that I dropped. You wouldn't think it, but a mouse makes a delightful traveling partner. They don't eat much—far less than you, for instance. And they sense trouble and scurry away long before it comes bounding around the corner."

Ping continued to talk about the mouse, but Meng stopped listening. She finished her meal, bowed to show her appreciation, and went to the stream to wash her face and hands. Needing to relieve herself, she walked deeper into the woods. In her absence, Ping began to sing, his voice drifting to her.

After returning to the fire, she pointed to his sword, asking for it. He handed her the weapon, as well as his knife. She set them on the ground beside her bedding and lay back, trying to get comfortable. Ping spoke about how the famine would soon get worse, how they weren't likely to find fresh sparrows for the price of a few coppers.

Meng paid him no heed. While she remained mistrusting of him, she had little choice but to remain by his side. Of course, she could walk off alone into the night, but with solitude came danger. The worst she thought that Ping would do was to steal from her. But there were men out there, many men, who would find sport in killing her.

Still, she reached for his knife and then, still gripping it, rested her hand on her chest. She wasn't sure if she had the resolve to use the weapon, but it comforted her. At least she looked and acted like a man. No woman she knew had ever handled a weapon or slept outside in the open.

"One of us should stand watch," Ping said, as he returned from the stream. "Since you're exhausted from all your walking, you sleep first. I'll stay awake for now, but when the moon is out, I'll wake you. When I do so, please don't stick me in the eye with my own knife."

Meng nodded, feeling foolish for thinking they could both go to sleep.

"If trouble comes, I'll wake you," Ping added. "At that point you should give me my sword. Don't ask me a lot of questions like you usually do. Just hand me my sword and follow my instructions."

Far away, someone laughed.

Again, Meng nodded to her companion, still wondering if he was a blessing or a curse, but for the moment content that his voice carried into night, warning strangers that she was not alone.

CHAPTER SIX

Games of Chance and Death

Between Jinshanling and Simatai—October 15, 1549

As dawn unfolded, Fan was reminded of how a smile could spread across Meng's face, beginning with a rise of the corners of her lips, then swelling to her cheeks and causing her eyelashes to flutter. Though beautiful sights abounded in Beijing, her smile had captivated him like nothing else, empowering him because often it was his words or actions that prompted this metamorphosis of change, of an empty silk scroll suddenly shimmering in brilliant and wondrous collages of color and art. During these moments, the bond they shared seemed even more pronounced than usual, as if two smiles were the result of two minds merging into one.

Meng's smile brought a light into Fan's life in the way that the sun was now affecting the land. The cold seemed less acute. The distant rises glowed like the golden rooftops of famous temples. Subtle hues spread into a world that only moments before might as well have been no more than a collection of black and white images. The sun empowered the Earth. Meng empowered Fan.

He walked along the Great Wall, thinking of the letter that he'd just sent to her. One of Fan's workers, whom he trusted without reservations, was now walking toward the nearby town of Jinshanling, where he rented a small room. At Jinshanling the worker would mail Fan's letter, ensuring that Yat-sen never intercepted it. Fan was certain that Yat-sen was collecting Meng's messages, a painful act that sometimes left him feeling hollow. All incoming mail and parcels were gathered and sorted in a distant watchtower, where Yat-sen had surely bribed someone to steal Meng's letters. The smuggling of mail out of the Great Wall, fortunately, was much harder for Yat-sen to control.

In Fan's most recent letter he'd written about his daily tasks, his regret and guilt over leaving her, and the story about the two stars. He promised that he would return to her in the spring. While he made no mention of his own discomforts, he warned her about the approaching famine and said that his father should start saving up stores of food. The winter looked to be long and hard. But if they proceeded carefully, their reunion would accompany the emergence of warm weather. In the meantime, the growing cold would only serve to remind him of her warmth.

As Fan continued to walk, he thought about what new story Meng would like to hear. Perhaps a tale about a girl who wished that she was a boy. But then the girl's brothers all died in war.

If she had been a boy, she would have also perished. Instead she was able to give her parents a small measure of happiness, honor her dead siblings, and one day give birth to her own sons and daughters.

Fan was so engrossed in the creation of his story that he didn't notice Yat-sen's approach until the commander was only a few feet away. Though Yat-sen wore his red armor, he wasn't on horseback, which was unusual. Nor did Li accompany him.

"Why do we walk these stones?" Yat-sen asked, his hand on his sword hilt.

Fan shook his head.

"I walk them because I must," Yat-sen answered. "But you, you walk them because out here, away from the smoke of the fires and the stink of the men, you're able to think of her."

"I'm always ... able to think of her."

Yat-sen grunted. "And she thinks of you, always?"

"I wouldn't know. I haven't seen her for a year."

An unseen horse neighed. Both Yat-sen and Fan looked north, scanning the land for Mongol riders.

Seeing none, Yat-sen coughed, trying to rid his lungs of the foulness that gathered within them. "Why do men, who are so much stronger than women, seek their company? Why do we need them?"

Fan started to speak but stopped, surprised at Yat-sen's line of questions. "Because women are everything that we're not," he finally replied.

"Such as?"

"A woman is the light," he answered, thinking of Meng. "A

man is the dark."

"Yin and yang?"

"Perhaps."

Yat-sen pursed his lips. "Women are capable of the same darkness as men. They disguise it as light, but things are never as they appear."

Fan nodded, agreeing with the concept, but not having experienced what Yat-sen was describing.

"You hate me, Craftsman, because I bend your will to mine. But a woman does much the same. She may cloak her intents with silks and smiles, but her goal is no different."

"You bend everyone's will."

"Because I must. Because if I don't this wall will fall; this country will fall. I won't rest until the Mongols bow to us."

Fan thought of Bataar. The boy would never bow to anyone. And if a boy wouldn't bow, his father and mother surely wouldn't.

Yat-sen pulled up on his heavy armor, adjusting it. "We have a sacred duty, you and I. We will defend this wall until dead or ennobled."

"But you seek honor. I don't."

"But you will. Because every man beside me must stand tall or he diminishes the shadow I cast. That's why we fight and die as one, Craftsman. Because I'm the lord of this wall, and if you fail me, you belittle me."

Not far down the wall a cannon fired, followed by another. Yat-sen and Fan turned to watch the gunners practice reloading and then firing again at a distant target, in this case a pile of stones that had been painted white. The balls of iron pummeled the ground near the stones, sending clouds of dust into the air.

"I do my job," Fan finally replied. "I do it well."

"Yes, which is why I'm more forgiving of you than of most of the men beneath me. I allow you to laugh with the boy, to sleep with a half-full belly when I could starve you. But remember that your fate is tied to these stones. If they shatter, so will you."

Fan nodded, though a part of him wanted to further defend himself, to stand straight instead of stoop.

"You see him?" Yat-sen asked, pointing to a faraway and naked Mongol who was tied to the outside of the wall. "I asked him how to kill the Black Rider, but he said nothing. He defied me. I could poke him with hot irons and treat him like the dog he is. But these walls have taught me patience, Craftsman. Why break him with steel when I can with thoughts? Why should you worry about your wife when she is so far away? Perhaps she's already discovered another. Perhaps she's found something in his arms that she couldn't find in yours."

Stiffening, Fan turned toward Yat-sen. "No."

"You don't think it's possible, Craftsman? Women are lonely creatures by nature. That's why they play their games and work their charms. They entice and corrupt. They throw their chains around you while telling you that you're free and loved."

Fan shook his head. "You must ... be with the wrong woman."

Yat-sen stepped closer to him. "Be careful, Craftsman. Unless you want to share that Mongol's fate."

The cannons fired again.

Yat-sen coughed, then spat. "We'll play a game of *Go* tonight," he said. "I'll give you a chance to prove yourself, to show me that you can do more than fix cracked stones. But you'll fail, Craftsman. You'll fail yourself like you failed your woman. She's all alone and you have no one to blame but yourself."

*

Shortly after sunrise, Meng had tried to walk but found that her knee was still stiff and somewhat swollen. With reluctance she'd silently negotiated the cost of another ride on Ping's cart, and they had once again settled on a price of eighteen coppers.

Now, while Ping pushed her ahead, Meng studied the countryside. Mountains loomed to the north—much larger masses of earth and stone than anything she'd ever encountered. The mountains were covered in orange and scarlet foliage, and dotted with mounds of dark rocks. The sky seemed bluer than it was in Beijing, the air free of smoke and stagnancy. In the distance a walled town emerged, though its features appeared to quiver as Ping pulled his cart along the rutted road.

"You don't feel so light today," he said, then wiped his brow. "Did my sparrows fill you up?"

Meng smiled, nodding.

"Maybe I should have eaten them all myself."

She shook her head.

Ping grunted and pushed Meng ahead with what seemed to be renewed strength. On the right side of the road, a bamboo stall materialized. A blue sign hung from its top. Squinting, Meng was able to see that the sign read, "The Society for Liberating Animals." She'd heard about this society before, which was led by educated and wealthy citizens, none of whom ate meat. As often as they could, the society's members purchased animals from vendors and let them go free. It didn't matter if the animal was a duck, pig, snake, frog, or turtle—to the society's members all animals should be destined to run free and not perish on a cutting stump.

Two well-dressed men stood in front of the stall and began to proclaim the merits of setting animals free. While Ping muttered under his breath, Meng listened to their words carefully. She thought about animals in cages, considered how Fan was also trapped, reached into her satchel, and tossed a copper coin to the nearest man. He bowed and thanked her, spreading his arms wide. She smiled.

Ping slowed down. "You haggle with me over the cost of my sweat and blood but are happy to give that fool a coin? He'll use it to liberate a few snails. But what good will your deed do? The snails will simply suffer along until some cart rolls over them. I've stepped on a few myself over the years—never on purpose, mind you, but still, why bother to set them free? If you'd freed those three sparrows you gobbled down last night, you'd be hungry right now."

Though she wanted to tell Ping about Fan's confinement, Meng remained silent.

"I'll save the next snail I see on the road, and you can just pay me a copper," Ping added. "You can call me Ping the Snail Saver. What a magnificent sound that has. Paint me a beautiful blue sign and hang it from my cart. We'll make all sorts of money."

Though Ping continued to talk, Meng stopped listening. The road turned from dirt to cobblestone as they approached a wall that surrounded the town. The main gates were open, but several armored guards were present, and Meng resisted the urge to slump down on her chair. She sat tall, nodding to the somber men, aware that Ping had gone silent.

Once they were inside the wall, the town's features were revealed. Tidy rows of two-story wooden shops and houses ran perpendicular to the road, with the shops adjacent to the thoroughfare and the homes stretching away from it. All of the structures faced southward, which was the direction of good omens and smiling fortune. The north, almost everyone believed, harbored not only deserts and wastelands, but also bad omens.

The usual merchants were about, pedaling their tools, weapons, meats, shoes, clothes, and trinkets. Monks clad in brown robes manned a soup line near a decrepit temple. Several boys ran alongside a wheel, propelling it forward by slapping its top with their open palms. Not a single woman was on the road, though Meng noticed a few in the distance, sweeping doorways and beating dusty rugs. She wondered if their feet were bound or not, if they had ever seen herons on a riverbank.

Ping pulled the cart to a vendor who was selling a variety of freshly cooked meats and fruits. While Ping started to negotiate, Meng got off the cart and handed him five copper coins. He smiled, then turned his attention back to the vendor, ultimately buying sheep tails that had been steamed, then coated with a layer of melted sugar. Ping also purchased two pears, which the vendor proclaimed shouldn't be cut in half, as that act would bring bad luck, resulting in the breakup of a friendship. As Ping collected the food, Meng wondered how many people were standing in the nearby soup line when the vendor before her had a shelf full of offerings. While it seemed that the famine had affected the poor, its ravages hadn't yet touched those with money.

Meng and Ping ate quickly and were soon under way once again. A bend in the road held a variety of beggars, and upon seeing them, Meng felt guilty for her full stomach. She was tempted to give them a few of her coins, but her money was dwindling faster than she would have liked, and there were too many outstretched hands. She dipped her head to the strangers, grateful that no children were present.

The road straightened and Ping increased his pace. Meng turned in her seat, again staring at the beggars, wishing she could help them. But as her gaze drifted from face to face, the beggars began to scream and scatter. Meng didn't understand what was happening at first, but suddenly a thunderous roar pounded against her ears. Shops lurched and toppled. People ran and fell. The world swayed back and forth in front of her eyes. She tried to stand up but tumbled off the cart, landing hard on the cobblestone street. The roar intensified and she momentarily covered her ears, then scrambled after Ping as he pushed his lurching cart ahead. A child was screaming on the ground in front of her. She took his hand and pulled him forward, closer to the town's other wall. But then the earth rose up beneath her, and she, Ping, and the boy were knocked to their hands and knees. Nearby, a three-story home collapsed, silencing screams that had somehow pierced the inferno of noise. Bricks and rubble tumbled into the street, striking down strangers, ricocheting off Ping's cart. Again he pushed it forward, shouting at Meng to follow. Somehow they made it through the town's gate. Dust billowed upward behind them. They struggled to the side of the road and fell down on the pitching, tortured ground. The boy tried to stand up again, but Meng held him immobile, clutching him against her chest.

The earth roiled until Meng thought her ears would burst. Then, almost magically, the shudders ceased. Though people shrieked and yelled, the land had gone quiet. Meng tried to clear her head, now holding it with her hands. She leaned away from the boy and vomited. Without thought she ran her hands through her hair, her tears dimpling the dusty ground.

The boy looked up at her. Their eyes met. He shook his head, easing away from her. She wanted to console him, but suddenly Ping leaned toward her, wrapping her hair up in the fabric that had formerly bound it. He took her hand, pulling her up. She resisted him, but he squeezed her fingers hard.

"They'll blame you," he said, his jaws clenching. "You're a stranger and … and a woman."

Meng shook her head, fearful that the boy's loved ones were dead. She wanted to go to him, to help him.

"Those superstitious fools will kill you!" Ping snapped.

"I'm sorry," she whispered to the boy, who was still staring at her.

Ping yanked on her hand. "Let's go!"

She stood, unsteadily at first, like a fawn that just emerged from the womb. Ping was already running ahead, pushing his cart. She realized then that he wouldn't wait for her. She could run or remain, flee or pray.

She said good-bye to the boy, then turned from him, hurrying forward on her aching knee, tendrils of her hair streaming behind her.

*

The earthquake had been less destructive to the north, shaking buildings and terrifying residents, but inflicting limited damage. Yehonala had been resting when it struck and had rolled under her bed, wincing at the groans of the earth and the shattering of porcelain. Though many other courtesans had screamed from nearby rooms, Yehonala remained silent, grinding her teeth and covering her ears. The floor vibrated beneath her, humming as if it enclosed a million honeybees.

When the land's shudders had finally ceased, Yehonala had lain still until her thoughts and emotions settled. She then stood up, changed into an elegant outfit, and walked into the tea house's communal room. Though other courtesans were also present, she paid these weeping women little heed. They had never cared for her, nor she for them. While her beauty attracted men of all sorts, it spawned envy in the women who competed with her for the attention of wealthy patrons. When Yat-sen had driven all of his rivals away, the other courtesans had eased up on Yehonala, though she would never forget the hostility they'd shown her.

Now, as she sat on a dais and tried to ignore her aching heels, she watched servants tidy the room. Mirrors and paintings had fallen from the walls. Porcelain vases and figurines had shattered. Many of these objects were gifts from patrons, and Yehonala silently cursed her ill luck as surely she would bear some of the cost of replacing these items. The price of her freedom would rise, ensuring that she remained trapped within the tea house for longer than she could stand.

Yehonala thought about Yat-sen, wondering how she could pressure him into stealing more *taels* of silver that could be used to buy gifts for her madam as well as given directly to the owner of her tea house. Yehonala could not remain within these elegantly dressed walls much longer. The conversations she heard, the scenes she witnessed, seemed to drain her of life. A beautiful yet counterfeit world had been created for the sake of men. Yehonala hated men for it; she hated their opium-induced smiles, fumbling hands, stale breath, and simple minds. She tolerated Yat-sen only because he didn't pretend to be someone he wasn't. He was more like her than anyone else she had met. And when she was his concubine, she would rule his house, keeping only quiet, broken servants and enjoying the silence of his absence.

Her hands trembling from the injustice of the day, Yehonala opened a leather-bound notebook, which she placed on her lap. She then pulled a thin, ivory-handled brush from where it was attached to the side of the notebook. The brush was tipped with a narrow grouping of wolf hairs. Twisting to a table beside her, Yehonala carefully dipped the brush into a small, lacquer bowl containing ink.

Her brush descended onto the paper, moving slowly and with grace. She wrote:

The Earth and I are one.
We abound with beauty,
Yet inside we tremble.
We inspire painters and poets,

Yet flee from their colors and rhymes.
Your flowers wilt.
My dreams wither.
People walk on us without thought of what lies beneath.
What does is a tempest—
A shaking of soil and blood.
When we perish will anyone know?

Yehonala set her brush on a brass tray. A servant would clean and return it to her. She looked at her words, wondering if she should change them. But her bitterness was too evident, too revealed. No one could ever see so deeply into her. Feeling as if she betrayed herself, she ripped the offending page from her notebook. She would burn it later, letting the ashes fall instead of her tears.

Closing her eyes, Yehonala tried to remember a time and place when she was happy. She saw herself as a girl, before her feet were bound and misery ensued. Once she had scalded herself with steaming tea. Her mother had cooled her wound with water and the breath of her lungs. Yehonala had felt loved.

But then a series of bad harvests had struck and her world had changed. She was made into something she was not. She was torn from herself.

The little girl with the throbbing wrist was gone.

*

Fan had spent the day walking his section of the Great Wall. Though the earthquake hadn't been as strong as some that he remembered, it had caused the entire structure to vibrate, spawning cracks in the mortar and, in a few places, finger-wide gaps between bricks. Using black charcoal, Fan had circled the damaged areas and determined which locations were in most need of repair. The designers of the fortification fortunately had been aware of the dangers of earthquakes and had built accordingly. Though encased in hard material such as blocks and bricks, the interior of the Great Wall was nothing more than tightly packed soil and clay. This substance, though dense and strong, was inherently flexible. Moreover, the top of the wall was narrower than the base, providing additional stability.

Though Fan didn't often directly supervise repairs, several of the cracks were wide enough that he had ensured that fresh mortar was prepared exactly to his liking—with just the right combination of slaked lime and sticky rice flour. These ingredients would harden to form a nearly impervious bond—bridging separated bricks and older mortar.

The sun had fallen by the time Fan was satisfied that the earthquake hadn't done any damage that required major repairs. At this point he and Bataar returned to the eleventh watchtower in Yat-sen's charge—a small fortress that served at his command post. Several of his senior officers, as well as Fan and Bataar, lived in the watchtower when they were off duty. The largest room in the tower was on its highest level and was protected by a sloping roof covered in clay tiles. Outside this room was a four-sided terrace manned by a guard who stood beside a cannon behind the northern parapet.

Fan, Bataar, Yat-sen, and four other soldiers sat within the room, gathered around a battered table that supported a *Go* game board. The wooden board was two feet long and across— patterned with nineteen parallel horizontal lines and nineteen parallel vertical lines. The lines created three hundred and sixty-one intersections, and it was these intersections that would soon capture the players' attention.

Holding a silk bag that contained one hundred and eighty black, slate game pieces, Fan studied his opponent. Yat-sen rolled one of his white, polished clamshell pieces over and over between his thumb and his forefinger. Neither man spoke, nor did any of the spectators. A fire outside the room's southern wall had been lit and warmed the room through an intricate network of hollow chambers and strategically placed bricks that heated up. All the men had already eaten, and several sipped rice wine.

Yat-sen still wore his armor and his sheathed sword. The weight of these instruments would have caused most men to slump, but he sat tall on a stone block, gazing at the game board. Fan was clad in only his laborer's tattered robes. His shoulders were stooped. Fresh cuts on his fingers, though covered in a healing paste, oozed blood into cotton bandages. He didn't look at Yat-sen, but at Bataar, who stood to his right, shifting his weight from leg to leg. Bataar had been unsettled by the earthquake, fretting over his family and the terrified horses on the Great Wall. As they had worked, Fan had eased his concerns about his loved ones, saying that anyone living in the open would be far safer than the citizens of cities. The horses were another matter, however, as they remained skittish long after the land ceased to tremble.

While Fan studied Bataar, the nearby soldiers wagered on the outcome of the game. No one expected Fan to win, so the men bet by agreeing to give Fan extra points after the game was over. *Go* was won or lost on the premise of accumulating points based on the final position of your stones and the vacant intersections around them. Fan had played *Go* since he was a young boy. The game suited his personality, as it usually rewarded patience over hostility, suppleness over obstinacy.

Yat-sen coughed, and then spat into a silk handkerchief. "Feel blessed tonight, Craftsman?" he asked. "Care to wager?"

Fan shook his head.

"Perhaps if you wagered, you'd play better," Yat-sen added. "Fear is the best motivator."

"I think … we've all had enough fear today."

"The shaking of stones frightened you? Or maybe you worry for your woman? Don't be distracted by her. Couriers have already arrived from Beijing. The capital was mostly undamaged."

"Mostly."

"Maybe if you thought less about her, you could beat me, the man who never loses."

Instead of answering, Fan placed his first piece near the center of the board.

"I hope you'll wager against me someday," Yat-sen said, adding a white piece to the board. He looked at his men. "They think you need an extra twenty points. I'm sure you'll need more."

Fan moved again, envisioning Meng. He had taught her the game, and they had smiled and laughed, moving pieces and trying to best each other. As Yat-sen placed his second piece, Fan thought of how Meng's fingers had looked on the board. They were so thin and delicate—the strokes of a calligrapher's brush. She had always played while kneeling, her posture erect, her movements graceful. If she made a mistake, she would ask him how she could have done better. When she succeeded, she clapped her hands at her ingenuity.

Yat-sen took a far different approach to the game. He moved his pieces with aggressiveness, as if trying to stay ahead of Mongol forces. He surrounded Fan's pieces, denying them access to adjacent intersections, denying him points. Everyone present knew that it had been several years since Yat-sen had lost. News of his prowess had spread along the Great Wall, and sometimes officers and scholars traveled from far distances to play him. He took their coins and their pride. To him, *Go* was war, and few men were as skilled at battle.

"You disappoint me," Yat-sen said, then added another piece to the board. "You play afraid. You run when you should attack, fortify your position when you should besiege mine. Is that because you can only fix things, Craftsman? Because you know nothing about taking land from an enemy and building upon it?"

Fan nodded. His groupings of black stones were surrounded by Yat-sen's white pieces. He studied the board, aware of a potential flaw in Yat-sen's defenses. Though tempted to exploit it, he wasted a piece trying to defend himself against what would soon be an overwhelming onslaught. In the background, Bataar shook his head, unaware of the nuances of the game, but practiced enough to see that Fan was losing.

Yat-sen laughed, prompting Fan to counterattack, to create beads of sweat upon the commander's brow. The pace of the game slowed. Fan thought about Meng, knowing that if she were present, he would have played for her. He would have approached the game in the same way that he did the Great Wall, not only aware of every intricacy, but of how every stone placed pressure against the stones below, above, and beside it.

Though unsure if he could beat Yat-sen, Fan knew that he could make the game closer than he did. He saw Bataar nodding his head, and he understood that the boy was thinking the same thing. But besting Yat-sen would only inflame the commander's anger. As it was, Yat-sen enjoyed winning so much that it was better for everyone if Fan allowed him to continue his dominance.

Fan's father had taken pride in his early mastery of the game. Sometimes, when Fan was battling Yat-sen and wasn't playing to his full potential, he felt guilty, as if he were betraying his father's efforts. He knew that Yat-sen thought he was weak, and that even Bataar was often disappointed in him. At certain moments of a game, Fan would question the path he was walking. It was a path built not to get him to his destination quickly, but safely. Yet so many people in his life would have moved with more speed.

Again, Fan saw an opening in Yat-sen's defenses and considered exploiting it. He didn't have many pieces left to work with, and if he was going to mount a counterattack, now was the time to do it. Yat-sen was confident, perhaps overly so, and that self-assurance had compelled him to neglect a far corner of the board. Through a series of complex moves, Fan could bait Yat-sen into attacking, all the while fortifying a new position. He could score points and better his chances.

"I could never stomach losing like you do," Yat-sen said quietly.

"Maybe that's why I lead and you follow. Maybe that's what separates men like us."

Fan played a strong move, though not one that might have won him the game. "I play for pleasure, not for victory."

"Then you're a fool. A man who doesn't care for victory will only know defeat."

"Contentedness is my victory," Fan replied. "Not the other way around."

Yat-sen's next piece slapped against the board. "You speak like a philosopher but aren't one. You fix cracks. You mend things that other men have built."

Fan bit his inner lip, stifling the desire to trap Yat-sen within a labyrinth of moves and countermoves. Again he played below his ability. "I am content to mend."

"And that is why you will always lose. Why you'll forever stay poor and weak."

"Losing requires as much strength as victory."

"Nonsense."

Someone coughed. Fan let his mind drift away from the board. He thought about Meng, praying that she was safe and happy, that the earthquake hadn't hurt her. He wished that Yat-sen hadn't spoken about how Meng might long for another man. Fan couldn't imagine her betraying him but wished that he would hear from her. He had always believed that Yat-sen intercepted her letters, but it was possible that something else prevented her from writing to him.

Fan let the game disintegrate around him. Yat-sen continued to pile up points. The men who bet on Fan grumbled and began to move away. He bowed to his adversary and forfeited the game, as was his right.

Yat-sen laughed at his timidity and said something, but Fan wasn't listening. He stood up and walked outside the room, toward the southwestern corner of the terrace. The land undulated away from him, a series of rises and falls that were revealed by the light of the moon and stars.

Wishing that Meng was beside him, if only for a moment, Fan stroked the top of the parapet, which was cool to the touch. The air was cold, reaching deep into him, reminding him of what was to come. In the wake of the earthquake and its possible worsening of the famine, Yat-sen had once again cut all of their rations. Fan was hungry and tired. He had spoken of a contentedness, but he did not feel at ease.

A shadow moved next to him. Bataar stepped to the parapet, placing his hands near Fan's. "Why do you let him win?" he whispered.

Fan shrugged. "I don't know … if I could beat him."

"But you could try."

"Yes, though if I won, his power over me, over us, might grow."

"He thinks you're a coward."

"Maybe I am."

"No, you're not. But you look like one. Is that what you want?"

"It doesn't matter what I want."

Bataar shook his head, turning away, hurrying back inside. Fan closed his eyes, his knuckles whitening as he squeezed his fists.

The game replayed itself in his mind. He saw every move, every retreat and surrender. He kicked the stonework, for once glad that his father was so far away, that no one could see the man he'd become.

*

The moon hadn't yet risen when Chuluun handed the reins of his stallion to another rider. The man would await his return, remaining motionless in the slight ravine, among legions of stunted, wind-blown trees. His longbow on his back, and a sheathed dagger tight against each hip, Chuluun crept toward the distant wall, the silhouette of which was illuminated by torches.

Unworried about the feeble light cast by the flames, Chuluun moved like a shadow, blending into the landscape. Spies had said that the Chinese thought the Mongols lived in a wasteland. But what their enemies didn't understand was that to the Mongols, the land north of the wall was precious. Like the rest of his people, Chuluun admired the low, jagged mountains. The streams between them, though shallow and fickle, held fish and clean water. Gazelles, snow leopards, wild horses, bears, goats, wolves, marmots, and eagles were often found near the waterways, hunting or drinking. In the spring, summer, and fall seasons, the Mongols preyed on the animals. In the winter, the wolves sometimes sought revenge, descending in packs on solitary humans.

The combination of limited rainfall and poor soil left the land mostly uncovered by large trees and dense foliage. Yet bushes and waist-high grasses abounded, cloaking countless varieties of lizards, snakes, insects, and birds. Though the land wasn't good for raising crops, it was nearly ideal for grazing horses.

For generations, Mongols had frowned upon farmers and rarely eaten vegetables. Hunting brought food to their tables as well as trained their boys to fight on horseback. Chuluun's father had showed him how to aim his bow while galloping through tall grass, how to not fall from his mount while notching a fresh arrow. He had killed his first wild pig at the age of nine and his first bear two years later.

Chuluun had taught Bataar these same skills at an even younger age, determined to prove to his son that his misshapen hand wouldn't slow him down. They had tracked a snow leopard together into the distant highlands—intent on its rare cloak until they realized that their prey had young cubs. They hunted game both fierce and fleeting, slept alone under the stars, and tried to stay warm in sudden snowstorms. When they were stranded by the elements or by illness, Chuluun had often spoken of how their ancestors' spirits were around them, and how these spirits would ensure their safety. They had often prayed to the spirits, asking for a blizzard to lessen or a fever to break.

Now, as Chuluun crept closer to the wall, he contemplated the spirits, finding no solace in their presence. He didn't pray to them anymore—not after they had abandoned him. Pausing, he collected himself, trying to focus on the watchtower several hundred paces ahead. One of the largest towers in the area, the structure rose from a bend in the wall that followed the twisting contours of a mountain ridge. The tower served as Yat-sen's headquarters, and Chuluun longed to see it vanquished.

Torches burned on each level and corner of the tower but did little to push back the strength of the night. Voices emerged from within the stonework. Chuluun paused, remaining still until he saw the lone sentry. The man faced him from behind a tall parapet at the top of the watchtower but didn't move. Knowing that the Chinese sentries had perfected the art of sleeping while standing, Chuluun snuck closer. If the sentry spotted him, so be it. He wasn't going to wait for certainties.

The wall stretched on either side of Chuluun like a sleeping dragon. He wanted to slay it, to cleave its head from its body. He had heard rumors about dead workers being buried within the wall, and he wondered if Bataar's bones were interred within the stonework. If so, he would learn where they lay. After he'd breached the wall, killed its soldiers, and helped conquer China, he would return to the bricks that encased his son. He would pull them down, one by one, until he was able to collect Bataar's bones and bring him home.

Only twenty paces separated Chuluun from the watchtower, and he moved with speed across this final stretch. Pressing his shoulder against the stonework, he looked up. The watchtower was directly above him, as was the sentry. The man was resting against the parapet, leaning slightly over it. His shoulders, neck, and head were exposed. He was sleeping.

Chuluun weighed his options. He could stay, listen, and retreat. Or he could try to kill the sentry with silence. If the man screamed or raised an alarm, Chuluun would be forced to flee. Arrows and cannons would seek his back. But darkness would protect him, and he would have sent fear into the hearts of his foes.

Taking a step away from the wall, Chuluun lifted his longbow from behind his back. He notched an arrow. The guard was about forty feet above him. Perhaps this man had helped to capture Bataar; perhaps he had been cruel to him while on the wall. Whatever the case, Chuluun felt no constraint or remorse as he closed his left eye and looked down the shaft of his arrow. He aimed for the underside of the man's chin, held his breath to steady himself, and released his arrow.

The guard made no cry as the arrow took his life, knocking him backward. Chuluun waited for a scream, an alarm, or a pounding of feet. But no sound emerged. He replaced his bow on his back, then removed a padded grappling hook attached to a long rope. Stepping farther away from the wall and gripping the rope, Chuluun spun the hook in an upward, circular motion. He spun it hard, finally releasing the instrument as it neared its apex. The hook sailed through the darkness, over the top parapet. After waiting and wondering if an alarm would be raised, Chuluun pulled the rope toward him, feeling the weight of the hook, moving it carefully. He let it rise up the back side of the parapet, hoping that it would catch. Suddenly he encountered resistance. He pulled slightly harder, looking up in case the hook plummeted straight down at him. Yet it didn't, and so he tugged with more strength, finally using all of his weight to test the grip of the iron.

Satisfied that the hook had caught the crest of the parapet, Chuluun began to climb. The voices within the watchtower slowly grew stronger. He didn't speak the language of his enemies but could tell that a group of men was gathered inside one of the tower's many rooms, possibly within the uppermost chamber, which occupied about half of the tower's terrace. Hand over hand, Chuluun went up, his path taking him between the tower's shuttered windows.

Gritting his teeth with effort, Chuluun climbed higher, glad that he had left his armor behind. Finally he reached the summit and peered over the stonework. The bricked, uppermost room contained not a single window. Based on the voices that emerged, he knew that at least four or five men were within the room. No one was on the terrace, except for the body of the dead guard. Chuluun lifted himself over the parapet, then quietly carried the body to the darkest corner of the terrace. Several spears had been affixed to the spot, which Chuluun used to prop up the warrior. To anyone gazing from the distance, it would seem as if the man was simply leaning against the parapet. Anyone close would see the arrow that had killed him, but Chuluun didn't expect visitors. He had watched the towers for countless nights and knew that the sentries almost always stood in solitude.

The roofed room contained a single door that led to the terrace. Again Chuluun unslung his longbow and notched an arrow. He crept toward the door, applying tension to the bowstring. If Yat-sen was inside, Chuluun would slay him, no matter how great the risk. He might be able to take four or five men by surprise, killing them before reinforcements arrived. Then he could wrap his leather-bound arms around the rope and slide down to freedom.

Though such actions would bring terrible risks, Chuluun had never been so close to Bataar's killer, and thoughts of reason fled into the night. His breath starting to catch in his throat, he imagined his wife and daughters, picturing each precious face as he said his good-byes. Though he cherished his family, he would never forgive himself if he allowed Yat-sen to live. And so he leaned toward a crack in the wooden door, trying to see who was inside.

Four men sat in the room around a game board. All were dressed as common soldiers. Yat-sen wasn't present. The men were drinking, talking, and studying the board, moving black and white pieces. Two seemed angry, while two appeared pleased. Chuluun considered killing them. Surely at least one of the Chinese had helped to capture Bataar; surely one had hurt his son.

Anger flooded into Chuluun, threatening to overwhelm him. Yet he kept his footing amid this raging flow of emotion. If he killed the men, there was a strong chance that he would die. And while he would take that chance to slay Yat-sen, he wouldn't risk leaving his daughters fatherless for the heads of four common soldiers.

Chuluun backed away from the door. He could have tried to gain entry into the rooms at the much larger level below but knew from spies that they were connected by a series of confusing passageways. If he entered these passageways, he would most likely be seen and killed.

Having never before been on the wall, Chuluun crept to the southern parapet and studied the land of his enemies. He saw unprotected roads, bridges, and the lights of distant towns. His heartbeat quickened at the prospect of climbing down and walking into the underbelly of his foe. He could kill and terrorize, casting a net of fear wide and far before the sun even rose.

If Chuluun had been alone in the world, he would have tried to seek out Yat-sen. Failing in that task, he'd have hurried south, leaving death in his wake. Yet Chuluun wasn't alone. The faces of his wife and daughters beckoned to him, warming him despite the night's chill.

Gently pushing their faces aside, he studied the main body of the wall as it stretched to the west and east. He looked for weaknesses. Two hundred paces on either side of him a watchtower rose. The towers and the steep and twisting terrain beneath them made this section of the wall appear impenetrable. Yet if two of the towers could be captured and held, thousands of Mongols could pour across the wall between them. Beijing would fall.

Though tempted to try to take the dead guard with him, to remove any sign of his presence, Chuluun left a small, wooden horse in the man's right hand. Yat-sen would find the token and be enraged, prompting Bataar's spirit to smile at the angst of his killer. He would know what his father had done, and perhaps he would think less unkindly of him. His father wouldn't be the man who had abandoned him to a cruel fate, but once again his companion.

One day they would hunt again together, riding across the plains, the thunder of their horses' hooves filling their ears and kinship filling their hearts.

Imagining that glorious moment, Chuluun climbed down the rope, then blended into the night, leaving the sleeping dragon behind him.

✷

The fire danced, gyrating in the slight breeze. Though no aftershocks had followed the earthquake, Ping hadn't wanted to spend the night at an inn, or in the woods. The open countryside seemed safest, and given the abundance of fires, it appeared that many travelers must have felt likewise.

Once the Earth had ceased to shake, Meng had hurried after Ping as he pushed his cart ahead. He hadn't spoken for a long time, nor had she tried to initiate conversation. They had simply walked. Though the ground was stable, each remained off-balance, as if continually reliving the terror of being knocked from their feet.

Movement had eased the stiffness in Meng's knee, and she'd been able to keep up with Ping. Afraid of how he might treat her, now that he knew she was a woman, she'd trailed him by twenty or thirty paces throughout the day. Occasionally he turned around to see that she was following. Her pack was still on his cart, so she'd had no choice but to pursue him.

Finally, late in the afternoon, he had beckoned her forward, to walk beside him. He started to talk as he had the previous day, the sound of his voice nearly incessant. Avoiding the topic of her gender, Ping wondered if she believed the Earth was round or flat. Though astronomers had proved that it was round, Ping disputed their findings. To him, it must be flat. He couldn't imagine walking around on an infinite ball of stone and soil.

The topics of conversation had then turned to politics, literature, and war. Ping spoke on each subject with confidence, finally asking why Meng was traveling north, why she was dressed as a man. She told him about Fan, their long separation, and the coat she'd made for him. Ping grunted at these words but then asked countless questions. Occasionally a fellow traveler would near, and at these moments, Meng went silent, and Ping, while continuing to talk, made no reference to her plight.

Now, as they sat on opposite sides of the fire, having eating nothing for dinner expect for a few worm-riddled apples, Meng wondered again if she should separate from him. He was not her husband, and it was unseemly for them to be traveling together now that he knew she was a woman.

"I should leave you tomorrow," she said, kneeling on one of her blankets. "You've been kind to me, but I should go on alone."

He tossed a stick into the fire, causing coals to cast sparks upward. "Go on alone? You'd be eaten by a pack of wolves or men. Plenty of each inhabit these woods."

"But I'm … a woman."

"So? I've always done foolish things for women. Why should I change now? Besides, to tell you the truth, traveling with you is an undeniable adventure. I enjoyed it when you were a mute man. Now that you're a talkative woman, it's even better."

"But it's not right … for us to be together."

"Why not? Because some old, withered fool in Beijing tells us so? If you travel alone, you'll most likely die. If I travel alone, I'll be bored. Why should you die and I be bored? Both fates seem pointless and unnecessary. I'm headed north, as are you."

"I lied to you. I misled you."

He laughed, his teeth flashing. "I'm a thief, Meng the Misleader. I steal from rich merchants and travel from place to place, keeping ahead of those who would like to kick my corpse down a hill. It doesn't matter that you lied to me. Just be so gracious as to not do it again."

Meng made no reply. She thought about Fan, afraid of what he would think of her, if he knew that she was alone with another man.

"I've met all kinds of women," Ping said as he broke a stick in half and fed it to the fire. "But never someone like you."

"You've met courtesans. That's not every kind of woman."

"Ha! That's what I crave to hear—a challenge thrown in my direction, a threat to my wit. 'You've only met courtesans,' she says. But it's not true. I have a mother, three sisters, and an aunt who fancies herself as a painter."

"That's not what I meant."

"Then what did you mean?"

"You talk like you know everything about women. But how can any man know everything about women when we're usually inside, when you hardly ever even notice us?"

Ping grunted, nodding. "You don't speak for nearly two days and then erupt without end, telling me how the world works. Still, you make a fair argument. But don't forget that courtesans come from every background. They're the daughters of farmers, laborers, merchants, and outcasts. If I've been with dozens of them, haven't I been with every kind of woman?"

"Dozens?"

"Well, perhaps I exaggerate. After all, I'm known for my embellishments. But my point still stands."

"Your point … is pointless. And I still disagree. I don't believe you know nearly as much about women as you think."

Ping threw up his hands, a stick flying from his fingers into the darkness behind him. "I think I liked you better as a mute."

"My father taught me to speak my mind. He encouraged me to speak my mind."

"He taught you well. Too well, perhaps."

Meng smiled. Though she shouldn't be with Ping, the alternative was a night spent alone, and in fear. "Will you promise me something?" she asked, studying his face.

"What? To let you walk all over me, now that you've found your tongue? Or do you want more?"

"You won't … hurt me, will you? Now that you know who I am."

"You're a saver of snails and a slayer of men. Why would I hurt you? If anything, I'm the one who should be afraid. I saw a cloud today that looked like an upside-down dragon. Everyone says that such a cloud is bad luck, but I ignored it, much to my apparent peril."

"You think I'm bad luck?"

"I think people worry too much. Including you. And I promise that you have nothing to fear from me."

Meng nodded, then stood up and began to make a bed for herself, farther away from the fire. A stream ran nearby, and she was tempted to go to it and wash herself but decided to wait until he was asleep. Reaching into her pack, she removed several of Fan's letters and began to read, the fire warm against her fingers and his words. The story she contemplated was one about a monk who scattered flower seeds along roads, trying to ensure that beauty thrived in a land full of misery and ugliness.

"What are you reading?" Ping asked, still sitting by the fire.

"Nothing."

"If you don't want to tell me, that's fine. But don't say that you're reading nothing when I can see paper in your hands and your eyes following rows of words."

She shook her head. "Thank you, Ping. Thank you for helping me today."

"Why, you're welcome, of course. My mother would be angry at me if I didn't help you. And though you don't think I know anything about women, I couldn't disappoint her. She's already much too upset with me."

"Good night, Ping."

"And so she dismisses me. Well, in that case, may your dreams make you smile."

Meng lay down on her blankets, rolling away from him. Though her sword was beside her, she didn't rest with her hand on its hilt. Instead she explored Fan's words and thoughts, then closed her eyes, trusting that there was more goodness than wickedness in the world, that Ping would rather protect her than possess her.

CHAPTER SEVEN

Clashes in the Distance

Between Jinshanling and Simatai—October 16, 1549

In the gentle light of mid-morning, Bataar and Fan walked slowly along the Great Wall, ensuring that the damage from the earthquake had been properly repaired. Fan's charcoal circles were still visible, so it was easy to see where fresh mortar had been applied. As the pair moved from spot to spot, Bataar explained how every horse, like every man or woman, was different.

"They won't let you get to know them at first," he said. "They'll fight you, in their own way. But once they trust you, they'll show you who they really are."

"What about your horse? What was he like?"

"She's young, like me. And playful. Sometimes I run and she chases me. But when it's time to be serious, like when we're hunting, she does exactly what I want her to."

As Fan bent down to inspect a repair, Bataar thought about his filly. He missed her almost as much as he did his parents and sisters. Sometimes, when no one was looking, he pretended to ride her—rushing through an imaginary landscape as they pursued a gazelle and he aimed his bow. In these fleeting moments he was able to forget that he was a prisoner and a slave. All that existed was a feeling forged by countless memories. He felt the cadence of her hooves striking the ground. He heard her sharp intake of breath and smelled the dust kicked up by the frantic gazelle.

Bataar also rode in his dreams, charging across the land, sometimes alone but usually with his father. They hunted, raced, followed the wall over mountains and streams, and rode into camp at midday, surprising his sisters. Awaking from these dreams always left Bataar feeling tired. He tried to go back to sleep, to return to the world he loved, but never succeeded. The voices of his captors, the endless blocks of stone, always kept him trapped in the present.

"What do you dream of?" he asked, as they started to walk again.

Fan's smile was ephemeral. "On a good night, I dream of my wife. I touch her, see her, hear her. We're together like we're meant to be. But when I'm not so lucky, I stay stuck in this place and dream about the wall—fixing it, saving it, watching it topple before my eyes."

"Has it fallen on you … like it did to my friends?"

"I'm so sorry, Bataar. If I had been there, if I had—"

"In your dreams, has it happened to you?"

"Yes. Many times."

Bataar nodded, having experienced the same dream. The blocks fell toward him, slowly at first, but soon picking up speed. They slammed against his shins, thighs, belly, and chest, knocking him to the ground, to a realm of dusty darkness. In this world he heard the screams of his friends as they called for him. But he could do nothing to save them. He called for help that did not arrive, for light that did not dawn. "I hate those dreams," he finally replied.

"As you're falling asleep, think about something that makes you happy. Then you can carry that place into your dreams, into… " Fan went silent, slowing his pace and guiding Bataar to the edge of the southern parapet. Yat-sen and four men, all mounted, had ridden out of a nearby watchtower and were approaching. The men wore armor. Their helmets and the hilts of their swords glistened in the sun. It was unusual to see a group of mounted warriors on the Great Wall as horses were scarce and poorly suited for the bricked surface.

Bataar wondered what the men were doing as he studied their mounts. As usual, his gaze settled on Yat-sen's great, white stallion, which seemed ill at ease under the commander's charge, tossing its head and fighting the reins that guided it.

To Bataar's surprise, Yat-sen halted about ten paces away from Fan and him. Though the other horses stilled quickly, the stallion pranced, half rearing on his hind legs. Yat-sen cursed and yanked on his reins. The stallion quieted.

"Last night we were attacked," Yat-sen said, meeting Fan's stare.
"Where?"

"The Black Rider climbed my watchtower and killed a guard."

"When we were playing *Go*?"

"Maybe. Maybe later. But he has defied me one time too many. Today I'm sending a force out there, to find his camp and destroy his supplies. If he is alone, they'll hunt him down."

Bataar had seen the Black Rider and didn't think that any of the Chinese could ever ride him down. But he said nothing. If the Chinese wanted to venture out from behind their wall and die, he would gladly let them do it.

"I want you to go with my men," Yat-sen said, pointing at Fan.

"Me? But why?"

"Because I may fortify a position out there, build a command post of high, stone walls. Such towers have been raised before, outside the wall. You'd be the man to build one for me. So I want you to look for a suitable site, an arrow's flight from here. If we built on that site, the barbarians would have to circle wide of us, otherwise we could shoot at them from both directions."

"But they'll kill our men in the post."

"No, Craftsman. Not if you build it tall and strong."

"The Mongols will just—"

"Another word from you and I'll carve your tongue from your mouth," Yat-sen interrupted, speaking softly. "I want to stand in their land, in defiance of them. So you'll build my post, and you'll build it well." He paused to cough. "Today Li will lead you. And you'd be wise, Craftsman, to watch him. You lack courage. That's why you fail in *Go* and that's why I'm sending you out into that wasteland. Hurry to the seventh tower and wait for Li and his men. Then, when you're out there, find your manhood, find a place for my post, and return to me."

JOHN SHORS

Yat-sen spurred his stallion forward. Bataar watched him depart, wincing when he kicked the stallion while also pulling back on its reins. "He's going to kill that horse," Bataar said. "Or be killed by him."

Fan nodded but made no immediate reply. Suddenly he turned to Bataar and gripped him by the shoulders. "I'll write a letter, Bataar," he whispered. "A letter to your father. If we find a camp, I'll leave it there. I'll tell him that you're safe, that you have a guardian here, and that you'll come soon, before the snows. Now hurry and go. Get me what I need to write and meet me at the sixth tower. But be careful, and make sure no one sees you."

His pulse suddenly pounding, Bataar turned and ran, rushing ahead, in the opposite direction of where Yat-sen had gone. His heavy shoes were cumbersome and he removed them, feeling much lighter on his feet. It was fortunate that no one was on this part of the wall. He entered the next watchtower, slowed his pace, and ducked into various chambers, looking for paper and ink. For the first time in his life, Bataar wished that he could read and write. He would have liked to tell his father so many things. Instead he would have to whisper to Fan about what to say.

As his mind churned and his breath caught in his throat, Bataar climbed a rope ladder to the level above. The room he entered was vacant. Writing instruments lay on a table that officers used to create dispatches. After glancing around once again, Bataar took everything he needed, stuffing items into a pocket that normally held tools.

The sixth tower wasn't too far away, and Bataar forced himself to slow his pace. He thought what to say, about which words would

160

bring the most joy to his loved ones.

*

The road branched to the east, away from the intended path. Meng studied the distant landscape. She saw large, red structures partly hidden by tall trees. Not far ahead lay the Ming Tombs, the final resting places for China's emperors. Ping had never seen the tombs and wanted to take a slight detour. Though he claimed to have interest in the site, Meng suspected that he hoped to find a rich traveler to pickpocket. After all, the road leading to the tombs was full of well-dressed merchants and pilgrims. Gold and silver jewelry sparkled like stars in a moonless sky.

"People travel for weeks to get here," he said quietly, as they stood off the road, beneath a willow tree. "We're a hundred steps away and you don't want to see what's there?"

Meng shook her head, though she stopped when she remembered how her hair had come loose the day before. She would most likely cut it tonight, she decided. Though she'd wanted to keep it long for Fan, short hair would be safer. "There are bound to be soldiers," she whispered. "Too many soldiers aren't good for either of us."

"You worry about our soldiers? If they're so strong and discerning, why did we build a wall around our country? You see the sword I carry? I stole it from a sleeping soldier. That was three weeks ago, and he probably still doesn't realize it's missing."

"You're going to get yourself killed."

"By that fool? By you maybe, but definitely not him."

"I want to leave."

"Why? Because a woman shouldn't see such sights? Because the ghosts of our fearless emperors will be watching you?"

Meng's gaze drifted down the northern and eastern roads. Her instincts told her to continue to head straight for Fan, but Ping's words reverberated within her. The Ming Tombs were famous throughout the land, and she was a stone's throw from them. Wouldn't it be wonderful to tell her mother about them? Wouldn't she regret passing them by when she was old and reflective?

"Fine," she whispered. "But you're to steal nothing. You hear me? When we're together, you're to steal nothing."

"I'm to be an honest thief with you?"

"That's right. And I'll pay you to be honest, to be my companion and protector."

"Eighteen coppers a day?"

"Ten. Because you're no longer pushing me on your cart."

"Make it fourteen. Otherwise I'll go back to my thieving, diabolical ways."

Believing that she'd be safer with him than she would be alone, Meng agreed, then proceeded ahead, toward the Ming Tombs. The eastern road bustled with activity, but she stayed far from the richly dressed merchants and their servants. Instead she kept to the side of the road, walking briskly. Soon the road widened as she approached a graceful, granite entryway, which was really a series of five connected arches. After passing through the middle and largest arch, she slowed down. Ahead lay a massive, red structure that sheltered several gates, which all were open. The gatehouse looked like a single side of a castle that had been set in the middle of the road. It offered no real protection, as anyone could walk around it, but surely the gatehouse was symbolic of the emperors' power.

After the gatehouse, the road narrowed into a walkway. Meng noticed that it was now comprised of large slabs of gray, granite blocks. The next object to draw her attention was an enormous, three-storied red pavilion. This structure contained a single arched entryway. She and Ping approached the entryway, waiting to pass inside until the crowds of travelers had thinned. What she saw next surprised her, for a stone turtle nearly the size of a house sat in the middle of a vast, vaulted room. Meng wasn't sure what the turtle symbolized, though it had the face of a dragon, and perhaps protected the adjacent grounds.

Beyond the pavilion, everything seemed to change. Gone were the imposing red structures. Instead a row of tall willow trees spanned each side of the long and broad walkway. Interspersed every hundred paces between the trees on both sides of the walkway were pairs of large statues of guardian animals. Meng passed lions, camels, and elephants. Each statue was about twice her height and thicker than the trunks of the nearby trees. Despite Meng's resentment of the emperors, she was awed by the sights. Her pace faltered, and her forehead and back started to perspire. She sensed power here, an ancient strength that was far beyond her comprehension. Suddenly she felt out of place and alone. Yet she remained transfixed and continued onward, ignoring workers who swept the walkway and even armored soldiers who were so still that they might have also been stone.

Once Meng passed the last animal guardian, she approached another series of immense statues, this time paired men, one on either side of the walkway. The men must have been palace dignitaries. They were dressed in thick robes and wore patterned sashes and flat-topped headpieces. The statues of soldiers came next, each clad in ornate, full-length armor and wearing sheathed swords. Some of the soldiers wielded stern expressions. Though the men were stone and had remained still for generations, they sent a chill through Meng. She wasn't supposed to be here. The eyes of the statues seemed to lock upon her, following her as she hurried on.

Fifty paces ahead, a curved, arching stone bridge vaulted over a river. In the hills beyond the bridge were graceful, red buildings that each contained the tomb of one emperor. But Meng, nor any other commoner, would ever get any closer to the tombs. Standing in front of the bridge were at least twenty flesh-and-blood soldiers, several of whom were mounted.

Meng stopped. She stared at the faraway tombs as the wind caused tendrils of nearby willow trees to sway like sea grass. A nearby sign said that the walkway was called "Spirit Way," and Meng sensed the presence of past generations. Yet what she felt didn't put her at ease. Rumors said that some of the emperors had been buried alongside their living concubines and wives. Meng imagined the women suffering and dying in darkness, clad in jewels and gold, but bereft of comfort and choice. Suddenly she no longer wanted to be at the tombs. They seemed haunted, not by the ghosts of the emperors but of their companions.

"I'm leaving," she whispered to Ping. "With or without you."

He looked as if he might argue, but then his gaze settled on hers and he nodded.

They headed back past the stone guardians, moving briskly, Ping's cart rattling over the granite walkway. Only when they had left the grounds did Meng slow her pace. She started ahead on the northern road but soon stepped off the path.

"I don't want to be afraid," she said quietly, half to herself.

"And I don't think you are," he replied. "You're certainly foolish and naïve, but a coward? Most definitely not."

She wiped her forehead, then turned away from the midday sun and looked back toward the hallowed grounds. "I didn't feel welcome there," she replied. "Men built that place. Men treasure and protect it. But still ... it's good that I went."

"Why? You hurried from those tombs like you expected to spend the night in one. What's good about that?"

"I can't explain. But thank you for taking me there. I wouldn't have seen it on my own and am glad that I did. Someday I'll tell other women what I saw."

He rolled his eyes. "You speak in riddles. Is that what you learned in there? Did the ghost of some dead concubine pinch your thigh and tell you that the way to impress men is to confound them?"

Meng tried to smile. "I don't need help confounding you."

"And now she mocks me. She pays me a pittance and she mocks me."

"But you make it so easy, Ping."

He started to laugh and sought to stop himself, but his grin widened.

Not waiting for his inevitable reply, Meng walked back to the trail, thinking about how she would tell her mother what it was like to proceed down Spirit Way, sharing what she was not supposed to have witnessed.

The emperors had been considered to be gods. Monuments had been erected to house them and guardians built to protect them. Meng was just a lone woman. She had been born with a voice but told by society not to use it, born with eyes but told not to see.

Yet her feet and resolve were unbound. And she would travel onward, coming to better know the world that she was a part of, the steps she needed to take to consider herself free.

*

Leaning against the northern parapet, Bataar watched the force leave. He stood about ten paces away from Yat-sen and a group of soldiers. Li led the departing men, who were all on horseback, carried weapons, and were heavily armored. A stout, wooden ramp had been lowered with ropes and pulleys from the top of the wall to the ground. Workers had placed beams vertically under its center to provide extra support. The ramp was only strong enough to handle two horses at a time, one following the other.

Bataar waved to Fan, though his friend did not notice the gesture. The only man in the contingent who wasn't wearing armor, Fan appeared ill at ease on his stallion. Bataar had told him to relax on the horse, to exude confidence and control. Yet Fan seemed incapable of such actions. He sat with a rigid erectness in his saddle as his horse descended the ramp. He should have leaned backward with his feet forward in the stirrups. Instead he sat tall, pulling unnecessarily on his reins, confusing his mount.

When the pair finally reached the bottom, Bataar let out a long exhale. He hadn't even realized that he'd been holding his breath.

The force consisted of thirty soldiers. It had been reported that large groups of Mongols were attacking positions on the Great Wall far to the west. Yat-sen had ordered his men to ride due north, find the nearest Mongol camp, and, if it was unprotected, set it afire. If enemy horsemen were present in large numbers, Yat-sen's men were to turn around and race for the security of the wall.

The flaw in Yat-sen's reasoning, everyone knew, was that the Mongols were far faster riders than the Chinese. If the raiding party was caught out in the open, they would be slaughtered. Their prospects for success lay in the audacity of their attack and the positioning of the Mongol forces. If the reports could be trusted, most of the enemy horsemen were a half-day's hard ride to the west.

Bataar both feared and rejoiced in the prospects of the incursion. Better than anyone, he knew the strengths of his people, and he worried for Fan. His friend was no fighter, and even if he were immensely skilled with a bow and blade, his abilities would be insignificant when compared to the sheer numbers of horsemen he might face. In the event of a confrontation, he would likely be pulled from his mount and captured. Bataar's people rarely tortured their enemies, but Chinese raiding parties were detested, and revenge for previous attacks on loved ones might be in the minds of Mongol horsemen. As likely as not, Fan would be tied to a horse and dragged to his death.

As the troops departed, Bataar continued to watch Fan,

shaking his head at how he rode. Bataar wished that he could switch positions with his friend. In that case, Fan would live, and he might escape. Even if he wasn't able to flee, he could leave Fan's note somewhere. Surely someone among his people could read Chinese. Then his family would know of his situation, his plans to escape, and his love for them.

The soldiers grew distant. Bataar wished that they rode closer together, showing discipline and skill. Yet the force was elongated, ill prepared, and vulnerable. Ten Mongol riders could harass and kill half of its members. Though Bataar rarely prayed to the spirits of his ancestors, he asked them to spare Fan, while he kicked the bottom of the parapet, over and over.

Only when the Chinese had disappeared did Bataar finally turn. To his surprise, Yat-sen stood near him. The commander wore his red armor and his hand was on the hilt of his sword. "You wish, slave, that you were with them?" he asked, his shoulders pulled back, his gaze intense.

Bataar shook his head.

"Why? You think they'll die? That your people are so much stronger?"

His father had once told Bataar that the Chinese had tens of millions of citizens. The Mongols, it was said, had a few hundred thousand horsemen. And yet it was the Chinese who had built a wall around their country. Thinking about these numbers, Bataar shrugged. "My father is stronger."

"Maybe your father is dead. And if I should fear him so much, why hasn't he saved you? Why does he allow his son to be a slave?"

Heedful of Fan's warnings, Bataar held back an angry response.

Yet he straightened. "Your wall stops him. For now."

Yat-sen's smile revealed crooked, stained teeth. "You should be careful, boy. Slaves are hard to come by, and I need them. But not so much that I won't throw you from this spot."

Lowering his gaze, Bataar looked at the tip of the commander's sheathed sword. Though his back dampened with sweat and his heart raced with renewed vigor, he didn't step away from his captor. "Your stallion will throw you," he said softly. "You should find another horse."

"Why? Why do you say that?"

"Because he doesn't like you."

"You don't like me. Does that mean you'll throw me?"

Shrugging once again, Bataar looked up. "I'm not as strong as your horse."

Yat-sen grinned. "You amuse me, slave. Perhaps that's why I allow you to live. Perhaps that's why I talk to a four-fingered boy who is no more significant than the worms beneath this wall. You think your horses are so strong, but where have they gotten you? Your father rides out there, day after day, thinking about you, wanting to rescue you, but what has he done? He's a leaf tumbling from a tree, destined to brown and wither, to be trampled underfoot. Strength is what we stand on; it's what will remain a thousand years after we're all dust."

Bataar didn't reply, thinking again about Fan and the letter he carried.

Yat-sen started to leave but turned back. "You must be conflicted. You hope that your horsemen will appear and slaughter my troops. But if they do, the craftsman will die. If they don't, your people may suffer."

"My people … aren't afraid."

"You're right. But know this, slave—your people honor their horses more than they do themselves. And no race that bows to beasts will ever conquer this wall."

Bataar watched Yat-sen leave. His captor's words echoed in his mind. He wasn't sure what to think. Maybe Yat-sen was right. Maybe his people weren't strong enough to topple the wall. If that was true, they should turn around and ride away, forgetting about the riches and comforts that trade would bring.

Afraid that so much suffering would amount to nothing more than a waste, Bataar kicked the bottom of the parapet. He had taken pride in working with Fan, in etching a horse into a brick and knowing that it would remain visible for generations. Yet the bigger part of him also hated the wall. His people would never rest until it was penetrated, and that achievement might prove to be impossible. What if his countrymen were no more than wasps trying to pierce a sheet of steel?

Bataar didn't want to wait for the wall to fall or for his people to finally flee. He wanted to hunt with his father, to chase his sisters, to see his mother smile at him. Despite his bluster, he was afraid of Yat-sen. His pride, and his belief in his countrymen, made him stand tall. Yet he often longed to simply run away in the night, to return to the embrace of his loved ones.

Only Fan made Bataar's imprisonment tolerable. And now Fan might perish. He was out there somewhere, carrying a letter that might never be read, that might soon be covered in his blood.

Bataar was certain that someone would die today. The Chinese would slaughter or be slaughtered. If he were with them, he would tell Fan to turn around, then he'd ride ahead and warn his people. He would save many.

But he could only stand and hope, wishing for fates that would not befall.

*

The bouncing, gyrating saddle assaulted Fan's thighs, buttocks, and privates. Though Yat-sen had ordered him to look for a suitable building site, all his attention was focused on not getting thrown by his horse. To alleviate his aches, he tried to remain standing in his stirrups, but this position put him higher above the ground and he worried that he'd lose his balance. Whenever Fan had seen men riding at a full gallop they'd looked so serene and free. Yet to him, nothing could have been farther from the truth. The roar of pounding hooves, the dust that assailed his eyes, and the lurching gait of his stallion threatened to overwhelm his senses. It was as if he'd been thrown into the center of a typhoon without time to mentally or physically prepare for its ferocity. All he could do was clutch his reins and hope that his countrymen would stop.

The group went farther than Fan expected, following the contours of a valley that led north. Mountains stretched up on either side of them—rocky rises that bore stunted trees, many of which appeared to glow in autumn colors. Fan managed to turn and was relieved to see the Great Wall. It seemed so much smaller from this vantage point—a long, white line that separated the land.

Someone from their group shouted, and men pulled back on their reins. Fan followed their lead, pleading with his stallion to slow down. As it did he slid forward on his saddle and he had to put his hands against his mount's neck to brace himself. A cloud of dust settled on them. Whispers were exchanged as soldiers pointed at a small column of smoke. Squinting, Fan peered ahead. He couldn't discern much but thought he saw several white, circular structures.

Yat-sen's second-in-command, Li, ordered his men to draw their weapons as he notched an arrow on his longbow and spurred his mount forward. Suddenly Fan was once again struggling to remain on his saddle. He gripped his reins so tightly that his fingernails bit into his palms, causing them to bleed. Around him weapons glistened in the sun and men prepared for battle. Fan had been given a sword but had no idea how to wield it, and the sheathed weapon thumped uselessly against his side.

Fan expected arrows and cries of battle to fill the sky, but neither happened. The war party charged into the Mongol camp, looking for foes. But the camp appeared empty. Six of the strange dwellings encircled a central fire. The light-brown structures were twice a man's height and twenty feet wide. Each was circular at the bottom. The sides rose straight up from the ground until they were head high, at which point they drew toward one another, forming a peak. Stranded near the dwellings was a multitude of wooden, two-wheeled carts that had long poles that could be affixed to horses.

As his countrymen charged into the dwellings with their swords drawn, Fan slid from his horse. His legs trembled. His lungs heaved. Unsteady, he stepped toward the fire. It still burned, roasting a gazelle that had been skewered on a spit. All sides of the meat had been cooked uniformly, and fat oozed into the fire, hissing after it fell.

"They were just here," Fan said without thinking. "They knew we were coming."

Li strode up to him, holding his longbow, an arrow taut against its string. "You're right," he replied, then peered in all directions. "They've gone for help."

"Then we should go too."

Ignoring Fan's words, Li commanded his men to set fire to the circular dwellings. As soldiers began to spread out with burning branches, someone shouted. Li hurried toward the voice, and Fan followed him. To his surprise he saw that a Mongol had been dragged out into the daylight. The man was barely conscious. Bandages, crusted with old blood, were wrapped around his head. A coarse blanket partially covered his legs. He moaned but didn't open his eyes. Li ordered his men to leave him. Fan stayed still, wondering if the man was Bataar's father.

Massive fires began to engulf the nearby structures, sending plumes of dark smoke into the sky.

"I can speak a few of their words," Fan said, kneeling before the Mongol.

"Ask him how many horsemen will come after us."

Fan doubted that he could properly convey the message, but he tried, remembering the words that Bataar had taught him. As he spoke, he glanced at the mountains around them, fearing the arrival of hordes of Mongols. The man moaned again, fresh blood darkening his bandages. He said nothing.

The Chinese soldiers continued to burn anything of value, dragging the wooden carts into the fire.

"We need to leave," Fan said, then remembered Bataar's note.

Li nodded. He drew a dagger from his waist, leaned toward the injured man, and placed the steel against his neck. He slashed the blade to the side, but Fan noticed that he didn't cut the Mongol. He had only pretended to.

"I don't murder wounded men," Li whispered, lowering the Mongol's head. "But don't tell Yat-sen."

Fan didn't reply. He had assumed that Li was a ruthless killer like his commander. Li stood up and hurried away, yelling orders. After glancing around to ensure that no one was looking, Fan pulled out his letter. The Mongol wore a wide leather belt and Fan tucked the letter inside the belt, allowing some of it to show. He then studied the man, who appeared to be near death. One of Fan's greatest fears was that Meng would sicken and die in his absence, and seeing the gravely wounded Mongol rekindled this dread. He thought of her, prayed for her safety, and pulled the blanket higher up on the Mongol. The man's bandages were also slightly askew, and Fan carefully moved them back into position.

Shouts drifted to him. He straightened, realizing that his countrymen were running for their horses. His heart seemed to plummet from its perch in his chest when he saw a cloud of dust just beyond the top of the nearest mountain. The Mongols were coming.

Running to his horse, Fan stumbled, righted himself, and climbed onto his saddle. He didn't need to kick his stallion, which sensed the fear around it and bolted forward. Fan was almost thrown but, crying out, somehow held on. He thought of Meng, longing to see her again, knowing that if he fell he would be slain. He had always expected to die with her beside him, with the sight, smell, sound, and touch of her comforting him. The vision of perishing beneath an onslaught of Mongol blades gave him strength that he hadn't known, and he shouted at his stallion, urging it onward. The beast lunged ahead. Fan's hair unraveled from its topknot and streamed behind him. His eyes watered. He choked on dust but held onto his reins, crouching above his saddle.

Fan turned and saw that the Mongols had crested the mountain. There were hundreds of them. For now the horsemen were too far away to fire their bows, but they would near. Soon their arrows would descend, snatching away dreams and lives.

"Go, go, go!" Fan shouted at his horse, hitting the side of its neck.

The Great Wall seemed so distant—a line of white that could have been a crack in the Earth. Behind the wall, mothers laughed, babies were born, and old men studied calligraphy. Life might have been troubled behind the fortification, it might have been difficult, but it was also beautiful.

Fan longed to look over the Great Wall once again, to be comforted by the stone beneath his feet.

But that sanctuary was too far away. The Mongols were nearing.

*

Enraged that the Chinese would once again come to destroy and kill, Chuluun kicked his stallion savagely. His beloved mount surged forward, drawing in front of his howling countrymen. Slightly crouching above his saddle, he pulled his longbow from behind his back and notched an arrow. Though his saddle lurched back and forth, Chuluun barely stirred. His legs bent with the movements of his horse, absorbing shock and keeping his upper body steady.

The Chinese raiders were barely out of range. Thinking that they had come and stolen Bataar in the same manner, Chuluun imagined the fear that his boy must have felt. Surely some of these same men had captured him, possibly beaten him. They had dragged him away from his loved ones, uncaring that he was still a child and that he'd never raised a weapon against them. Tears streamed from the corners of Chuluun's eyes, driven by wind and anguish. He kicked his mount again, applying slight pressure to his bowstring so that the arrow wouldn't fall off.

One of the Chinese soldiers tumbled from his horse. Chuluun was the first to reach him and could have killed him easily, but his countrymen would finish that task. He raced past the injured man, drawing closer to his enemies, now screaming at them, calling them cowards and the killers of children. The dust in his eyes wasn't felt. The aches from his old wounds didn't exist. Even his thoughts grew dim. All that mattered was the men in front of him. They must die.

The Great Wall loomed larger. He saw that a ramp had been

lowered and awaited the fleeing troops. Soldiers gathered behind the parapets, surely readying cannons. Pulling back on his bowstring as hard as he dared, Chuluun took aim and fired. His bolt sailed through wind and dust, narrowly missing the last rider. Cursing, Chuluun notched another arrow and fired once again. This time the man seemed to spin his saddle, falling hard.

Cannons cracked, sending screaming balls of iron over the Chinese and into the ground near Chuluun. He wondered if this day would mark his death. He wasn't afraid of dying and was comforted that if he were to fall, he would be forever close to Bataar. Yet another part of him wanted to live, to tell his wife and daughters that he'd tend to them during the coming winter.

He shot another arrow, heard a man shriek, and still continued onward. The first members of the Chinese force were riding up the ramp. Chuluun wanted to kill them all, to grind their bones beneath his feet. But he couldn't strike everyone at once, and so he targeted the slowest members of the contingent, another of his arrows knocking a foe from his mount.

A cannon ball seemed to scream as it sped above him, cutting down a Mongol horse and rider.

Let me feel you, my son, Chuluun prayed. If I die, please let me feel you.

More of the Chinese riders were escaping up the ramp. Chuluun was within range of them, and fired his bow again and again. One of the Chinese soldiers, perhaps wanting to make a name for himself, turned his mount around and came charging at Chuluun. The man shot an arrow that thudded into the thick leather of Chuluun's saddle. Chuluun cursed him, drew back his own bolt, and took the man's life.

Though Chuluun had only two arrows left, he again spurred his mount toward the ramp. Cannons seemed to target him, and he glimpsed the red figure of Yat-sen. Enraged by the sight of his enemy, Chuluun shouted at his countrymen to follow him forward. Some did, pressing ahead, their arrows deadly shadows that pierced the blue sky.

Chuluun fired his last arrows, then drew a sword that he'd borrowed when first told of the incursion. He rode toward the last of the Chinese raiders, gaining on them. Three of them saw his threat and turned to face him, two unsheathing their own weapons.

The cannons ceased to fire, the gunners afraid to hit their own men.

Imagining Bataar's face, Chuluun charged the trio of Chinese, his sword held high, his son with him for a glorious, empowering moment.

*

Fan watched in dread as the Black Rider came at him. He'd fallen from his horse while nearing the ramp, and now limped toward the wall. Two Chinese warriors were still mounted behind him, their swords glistening. The Black Rider galloped ahead, not slowing for an instant, even as his horse careened into theirs. One of the men was thrown from his saddle. The other swung his sword, but the Mongol's blade was quicker, blocking the strike, then pivoting and cleaving into the side of the Chinese soldier. He screamed.

Arrows whistled down at the Black Rider, thudding into the soil around him. Fan scrambled toward the ramp, tripping and falling, aware that other Mongols were rushing toward him, their bowstrings twanging. Cannons fired once again, the sound so loud that Fan thought his head might burst. He struggled forward, the Black Rider only twenty paces behind him. The Mongol lurched as an arrow ricocheted off his helmet. Other Chinese turned to face him, their swords sweeping arcs of glistening steel. He met them without pause, maiming and killing.

Fan didn't care if men deemed him to be a coward. He didn't stop and pick up a sword because he didn't want to die. Far above his reputation, his honor, was his longing to see Meng again. He reached the ramp, paused to drag a wounded countryman behind him, and started up. The arrows of his enemies thudded into the wood, one skimming his shoulder. He climbed, seemingly toward the light, toward a world free of blood and madness.

*

Once Bataar saw Fan reach the top of the ramp and topple over the parapet, he turned his attention to Yat-sen, who stood nearby and was screaming at his men to target the Black Rider. More cannons fired, arrows filled the sky, and yet the Black Rider remained unharmed. There was no one on the ground left for him to kill, and the ramp had been pulled up, so he wheeled his mount around and spurred it away. Other Mongols followed his lead, arcing out from the Great Wall.

Bataar looked at the ground and thought about leaping down

and shouting for his people. They might come back to him. Maybe his father was with the men and would hear him. Yet more likely than not, one of the Chinese soldiers would kill him. An arrow would pierce his back, cut him down, and he would never see his family again.

Watching his people ride away, Bataar began to cry. They were so close, yet as always they'd been repulsed by the wall, sent fleeing by the stone dragon. Five Mongols had been downed in the assault, and Bataar looked from body to body, wondering if one of them was his father. He slapped the parapet with his palms, striking it over and over. His father couldn't die out there, so close to him.

If one of the men had moved, Bataar would have jumped down, regardless of the threat from Chinese arrows. But none of the Mongols stirred. Each, it seemed, was dead.

Bataar wiped away his tears, his gaze once again on his people. They were now well beyond the range of cannons and continued to ride away, a cloud of dust following them. He wanted to shout to them that he had been left behind, that they needed to save him next time. But he said nothing, his tears coming once more.

Only when Yat-sen yelled at his men to again lower the ramp so that bodies could be recovered did Bataar remember the letter. He turned, looked for Fan, and ran to him.

His friend was bloodied, but standing. Their hands met, they embraced.

And Fan nodded.

At dusk it had threatened to rain, and Meng had thought about splitting up with Ping to find an inn. Yet the skies, while darkening, hadn't wept. Pleased that she didn't have to hand her precious coppers to an innkeeper, Meng had opted to once again sleep in the open. Ping remained by her side because she had grown to trust him, at least when it came to her safety. After leaving the Ming Tombs, he'd started to position himself between her and approaching soldiers. When alone, they spoke about their loved ones, the role of women in society, and the future. Most men would have never discussed such topics with her, but Ping didn't mind her gender. In fact, he seemed to delight in her perspectives, joking that understanding her point of view would help his chances of finding a good wife.

They had eaten a paltry dinner by their campfire then, as the flames settled, had arranged their bedding beneath a willow tree. She wasn't so close to him as to feel overly improper, but near enough so that they could speak in soft voices.

As Ping talked, somewhat to himself, Meng leafed through Fan's letters. Most of them contained stories. She knew from each weathered envelope what words were inside. Smiling, she imagined his expression when she told him that she'd walked near the emperors' tombs, past all of their guardians. Everyone but a thief had been fooled.

"Why don't you read me one of those?" Ping asked, yawning dramatically. "You're not paying attention to me anyway. I carry your pack, feed you savory sparrows, save your life here and there, and yet you hardly bother with me."

"I've been listening."

"To him, not to me."

Meng considered Fan's stories, wondering if he would mind her sharing a tale. "Sometimes," she said, "he sends me stories he's written for our children."

"But you don't have any. Or are they dressed up as foxes and follow us in the distance?"

"Someday we hope to have them."

Ping nodded, then threw a stick into the fire. "Neither of my parents was a storyteller. Lucky for them, I emerged from the womb and started talking. I joined my first poetry club before I knew what a poem was."

"I'm sure you did."

"So send me to sleep with a comforting tale. Of course, if it's good I may steal his words and tell them to my own children someday."

"Fan wouldn't mind."

"In that case, I'm listening."

Meng thumbed through the stack of letters, settling on one that he'd recently sent to her. "He wants to tell this story to our little ones."

"What's it called?"

"Chen and Chow's Day of Discoveries."

Ping grinned. He sat up, broke a branch in two, and tossed the pieces into the fire. "Tell me what they discover. Dragons, I hope. Eager courtesans would be even better, but that's probably too much to hope for."

"It's a long story."

"So, who else is going to entertain us tonight? Believe it or not, I'm tired of talking."

"I don't believe it."

"That's your right. But saving your skin has worn me out. The least you can do is read me a bedtime story."

Shifting so that the light of the flames colored Fan's words with amber, Meng smiled. "It goes like this … "

"Twice upon a time, two young river otters lived with their parents in a burrow near the edge of a mountain lake. The boy, Chen, and the girl, Chow, were the best of friends. Now I should tell you that this wasn't an ordinary burrow and these weren't ordinary otters. Most of the burrow was as dark as night, and that's how the young otters liked it. You see, Chen and Chow were afraid of the light. Imagine that, if you will—being afraid of the light. It sounds silly, of course, but Chen and Chow were born in the dark and had lived in the dark since they were babies. The light, they were certain, was full of monsters.

One morning, as dark and rainy and wonderful as any other, Chen and Chow's mother sat down near them. They'd just awoken and lay as far away from the burrow's entrance as possible. 'Time to get up, my sleepy sunflowers,' she said, smiling from whisker to whisker. 'Your father and I are about to go find our breakfast. Why don't you come outside with us?'

Chen and Chow looked at their mother as if her tail had suddenly fallen off. Chow leaned closer to her brother. 'Outside? But it's too light up there. Much too light.'

Her mother sighed. 'You can't stay inside forever, Chow,' she said. 'And you too, Chen. There's a big, beautiful world out there. A world full of treasures waiting to be discovered.'

Chow smoothed out a ruffle in her fur. 'We'll go out later, Mother. When we're bigger.'

'We promise,' Chen added.

After their mother and father had left, Chen and Chow played the games they always played. Mind you, these games took place in their small burrow, so they had to be creative. Chow found the marble first in 'Seek and Peek.' Chen won three games of worm racing. And Chow told the funniest story. Now, as I'm certain you know, otters aren't supposed to sit inside and play games all day, and sure enough, Chen and Chow became bored.

Trying to be brave, Chow walked toward the burrow's entrance, peering out. 'It sounds … strange outside,' she said.

Chen started to reply when thunder suddenly boomed. Chow shrieked and ran back to the other side of the burrow. 'That's got to be a monster!' she said, trembling. 'A monster who loves the light!'"

The fire cracked. Meng noticed that Ping had moved closer to her on his bedding. The flames illuminated his face, his faint smile.

"Go on," he said. "You can't stop now, when I'm wondering what will happen to our heroes."

Meng reopened the letter, continuing:

"As time passed, Chen and Chow continued to sit in the corner of their burrow and listen to the thunder. 'Maybe it's a roaring dragon,' she whispered.

'Or a giant snake,' he added.

Chow squeezed his paw. 'Someday we'll go out into the light.'

'But only with Mother and Father,' Chen answered.

Now, please listen carefully, and I'll tell you something. Every spring or two, as older otters know, it rains so hard and long that lakes rise and otter burrows fill with water. And that's exactly what began to happen to Chen and Chow's burrow. You don't need to worry, because the lake only trickled into their home. But still, water rose from their claws to their knees to their shoulders.

Before long, Chen and Chow's parents hurried back to their burrow.

'What's happening, Father?' Chow asked, again holding Chen's paw.

'Oh, the lake's just eating up all of that delicious rain,' he replied, smiling. 'Its belly is getting big.'

Chen stood on his tiptoes. 'Too big!'

'Well, little honeycomb,' their mother said, 'it's time to leave. I don't think we want to swim in our own burrow.'

'But it's light outside,' Chow answered.

'And that's just fine,' her mother said as she took Chen and Chow's paws and gently led them forward. 'Come on now, you magnificent marble hunters. Let's see what discoveries await you outside.'

And so Chen and Chow, their hearts beating as loud as the distant thunder, moved ahead, closer to the light. They were scared and uncertain and unhappy, but they tried to be brave as they stepped outside. And do you know what happened then? No? Well, I'll tell you. A miracle happened, because the storm quieted and a beautiful rainbow stretched across the sky. To Chen and Chow, who had only seen their brown burrow and the brown of their parents' fur and eyes, the rainbow was magical. Its colors filled them with joy and hope and, best of all, light.

'What … what is that?' Chow asked.

'That, my busy bumblebee, is a discovery,' her mother replied, playfully stomping her webbed feet in the lake water. 'Now, do you see any monsters up there?'

'No,' Chow and Chen answered.

'Any fire-breathing dragons?'

'No.'

'Any ghosts or giant bats?'

'No, no.'

Their mother clapped her furry paws. 'Then why don't you go explore? Your father and I need to find us a new burrow. A dry burrow.'

'We'll watch over you while we look,' their father promised. 'So don't worry.'

And with those words, Chow turned to Chen and said, 'We … we could try swimming.'

Chen eyed the lake, which was bigger than anything he'd ever imagined. In the distance, a mountain loomed. For a moment, Chen was afraid of the light, but then he looked up and again saw the rainbow. 'Let's go,' he said, stepping deeper into the water.

Now I should tell you that otters are born to swim. Their slick fur, webbed feet, and sharp minds make it easy for them to explore deep lakes. While girls and boys might naturally be good at running and jumping, otters instinctively know how to swim. And Chen and Chow hurried into that water and swam like a pair of fish. For a while they rode waves, splashing each other, laughing, no longer afraid of the light.

Finally, Chow turned to Chen. 'Mother wants us to make discoveries,' she said.

'So?' Chen asked, happily twisting round and round in the water, making himself dizzy.

'So, let's dive deep and make one.' Before Chen could answer, Chow took a big breath and swam toward the bottom of the lake. To her surprise, she saw schools of fish, a green turtle, and rays of light that must have fallen from the rainbow.

The bottom of the lake was covered with smooth stones. Tucked between two stones, a silver necklace sparkled. Chow carefully pulled the necklace free, showed it to Chen, and then darted to the surface. 'It's wonderful!' she said, not knowing that a girl had lost the necklace in the lake years before, and that the girl had hoped an otter or beaver would find and enjoy it. 'Won't this look beautiful on our wall?' Chow asked.

'Mother will be happy,' Chen said. 'I should find something too.'

Feeling brave, Chen swam toward the other side of the lake. To his delight, he could swim so much faster than he could walk. He swam on his back and let out only a small gasp when the sun suddenly popped into view from behind a cloud. He felt the sun on his face, and it warmed him. Smiling, he returned to Chow and said, 'The light ... it's like one of Father's kisses. It's warm and soft and makes me feel so good.'

Chow nodded, still holding her necklace, agreeing with her brother, which she didn't always do. 'The light isn't scary anymore, is it?' she asked.

'It feels wonderful,' Chen answered.

Now, since you know that otters are curious as cats, you shouldn't be surprised to learn that during the afternoon Chen and Chow explored as much of that lake as possible. They slithered through reeds at the water's edge and discovered a child's toy boat. They took a few steps up the tall mountain and came across a dragon-shaped stone. They picked daisies. They saw a feather fall from a falcon's wing, and they rushed ahead to find it.

Chen and Chow piled all of their discoveries on top of the toy boat and then swam back to their mother and father, who waved from the other shore. And as they swam they saw so many marvelous things—a gazelle drinking from the lake, trees dancing in the wind, their own smiling reflections. And they didn't forget—and I don't want you to forget either—that they wouldn't have seen any of these things if they'd always stayed in the dark.

When Chen and Chow finally arrived at the other shore, their parents waded out to greet them. 'What did you bring home, my darling daredevils?' their mother asked.

'Discoveries,' Chen answered, proudly showing his mother and father their findings.

Chow picked up the necklace. 'We found something to decorate our new burrow with.'

'And something nice to smell,' Chen added, pointing to the flowers.

'And the stone?' their father asked.

'It's a dragon,' Chow replied. 'And it's the best of our discoveries.'
'Why?'

'Because it's our present to you and mother.'

He smiled. 'And you found it in the light?'

Chen nodded. 'We found it under the rainbow.'

Much later, after Chen and Chow had decorated their new burrow with their discoveries, they kissed their mother and father good night and lay down to sleep, near the entrance of their burrow. Now, may I remind you that they'd once slept as far from the entrance as possible? That they'd been afraid of the moonlight? Well, happily, this night was different. They looked out of their burrow and saw the moon and stars. And do you know what they did? They smiled. They saw the light of the night sky, and were filled with joy. They were no longer afraid of the light. The dark and the light weren't so different, they realized. Both held discoveries, and both made their world a more interesting and wonderful place.

The end."

Meng folded up Fan's letter. She looked at Ping.

The thief nodded slowly, as if she'd asked him something. "He loves you," he said. "He loves you very much."

"I know."

"He wrote the story for your unborn children. He wants them … to be free. To not be afraid."

"I think you're right."

"Now I understand why you're going to him. A year apart is too long."

"Will you help me, Ping? Will you please help me?"

He flicked a large red ant from his elbow toward the fire. "We can be Chen and Chow, heading off, finding new discoveries. I suppose the greatest discovery of all will be your husband, though I'm not sure how I'll take him to my burrow and hang him from a wall. I guess I'll leave that to you."

Meng bowed to her companion. "Thank you, Ping."

"Thank me when we find him."

"It's true you're a thief, but in some ways, you're one of the most honest people I know."

"You don't know me well."

She shook her head. "That doesn't matter."

He threw another stick into the fire and lay down on his blankets.

After straightening Fan's letters and placing them back in her satchel, Meng settled on her bedding. She said good night to Ping, smiled at his reply, and drew her necklace away from her chest, kissing it once. Her hands then found her belly, and she wondered if she would become pregnant. She longed for a son and a daughter with whom Fan could share his stories. She would listen as well, perhaps adding a tale or two of her own, memories taken from a journey with a thief, a man whom someday she might consider a friend.

CHAPTER EIGHT

A Longing for Warmth

North of Jinshanling—October 17, 1549

E ven in the light rain, the fires still burned. Chuluun stood
near the center of their destroyed camp, leaning against his
stallion. Very little was left of the *yurts*—the circular structures
that once housed the horsemen. Where each *yurt* had risen,
smoldering, hissing fires remained. The carts that his people
used to transport the *yurts* had also been set aflame. At one point
the fires must have commingled and spread as the grassy area
around the entire camp had been blackened. One of their men,
who was badly wounded and had been abandoned as the Chinese
approached, must have been burned alive. The outer parts of his
body were charred. The Chinese had thrust something beneath his
belt—a warning perhaps. But whatever had been written couldn't

be read. The paper had mostly turned to ash.

While his countrymen shifted through the ruins and searched for anything salvageable, Chuluun closed his eyes. His head ached from when the arrow had struck his helmet. Though the iron had saved his life, a welt had risen above his brow, swelling his flesh. During the fight he'd also somehow injured his lower back, and now movement was painful. He felt so much older than he had the previous afternoon, when the need for revenge had nearly overwhelmed him. At that moment he'd seemed invincible, his aches and fears suddenly gone. But now, in the cold rain, each scar on his body felt as if it radiated pain deep into his joints and bones.

Usually Chuluun didn't mind the fighting, as killing his enemies was a way of honoring Bataar. And yesterday, they'd been close to breaching the wall's defenses. If more horsemen had been present, surely some could have charged up the ramp and into the heart of their foe. But Chuluun had been the first to reach the wall and was practically alone. If he'd gone up the ramp, death would have come swiftly, a demise witnessed by Yat-sen, the murderer of his son.

Chuluun had allowed himself to kill only the Chinese trapped outside the wall. Then he'd retreated. Later, while riders around him had celebrated their victory, Chuluun thought about Bataar, wishing that he'd been present when his boy had died. Bataar wouldn't have been as frightened then. His pain would have been less acute. Even more desirable, Chuluun longed to have switched fates with his son. If anyone should have been captured and killed it should have been Chuluun. His hands and mind had been dampened by blood. Bataar was innocent of everything except for being the son of a killer.

The rain strengthened, lashing at Chuluun's face as wind howled through the valley. The wind had been a constant force in his life, a voice that he found more comforting than not. When he had been young, he'd asked his father why their *yurts* were round, and his father replied that something round couldn't be easily toppled by any wind. His father had also died near the wall, though not by a Chinese arrow or cannon, but by a strange malady that struck nearly as suddenly.

Chuluun considered the plight of his bloodline—that so many of his loved ones had perished within sight of the wall. His father, son, and two of his brothers had all fallen within its shadow. He would also most certainly die there, his blood flowing onto the land that had witnessed their final tears and trembles.

His horse neighed, rearing its head back in the rain. Though his countrymen spoke about staging an unexpected attack, Chuluun was abruptly tired of fighting. He climbed atop his mount, spurred it northward, and ignored the queries of his countrymen. He needed to see his wife and daughters. Without them, the rain would drown him.

The trail was worn and muddy. Chuluun veered off it, afraid his stallion might slip. He let it determine its own path and pace. Lightning flashed in the distance, followed by a low rumble of thunder. The smell of smoke and dust was replaced by scents of damp soil and foliage. Though many people, even some of his countrymen, complained about the endless landscape and patterns of weather, to Chuluun the world was constantly changing. Leaves greened, browned, wilted, and vanished. A thousand different hues colored seasonal skies. Herds of gazelles rushed past the bones of long-dead predators. Streams surged and changed course, weakened and turned to dust. Everything changed, evolved, became something it was intended to become.

Chuluun continued to ride north, deeper into the land of his ancestors. He would have liked to have prayed to them but still felt abandoned by the spirits of those who had gone before him.

The stunted trees around him thinned. No Chinese force, no matter how large, would dare to ride so far away from their wall. Only death would greet them out here. They might thrive in their cities, in palaces of stone and silk, but in this world, Mongol steel would find them.

A hare leapt in front of Chuluun's horse, but his mount didn't alter its pace. The hare bounded ahead, propelled by rain and fear. Chuluun wondered about the location of its burrow, if it would make it there or be eaten by a wolf. As he mused over the hare's fate, he removed his helmet, wincing when he pulled it over his swollen brow. He always tried to minimize his warlike appearance when returning home. His daughters, he felt, shouldn't remember him as a warrior, but as a father.

Chuluun crested a mountain, and a settlement appeared in a valley below. He saw scores of faraway *yurts* and patted his mount, eager to see his loved ones. His horse obliged, moving forward with increased speed, its hooves clattering on rocks. Lightning and thunder came again, illuminating then deafening the valley. Rain ran down Chuluun's back, collecting in his boots.

He whispered good-bye to Bataar, promising that he would

think about him tomorrow, once he'd left his loved ones. But for now he must consider their needs and feelings.

The settlement drew nearer. Chuluun saw horses and people. His *yurt* was on the western side and he headed toward it, his aches lessoning, his spirits rising. He called out, his voice challenging the rain. Flaps that covered the entrance to his home opened. His daughters appeared, laughing as they ran into the rain, their arms outstretched.

Chuluun dismounted. He knelt on one knee in front of his horse, beckoning his loved ones toward him. His daughters shrieked, slipped, and charged into his arms, toppling him. He laughed, clutching them, letting them force him down, into the mud. They held him tightly, and despite their small stature they seemed much stronger than he, so full of life and promise.

After tying his stallion to a post, Chuluun picked up his daughters—one in each arm and one on his back—and carried them toward their home. His wife knelt inside it. Only her face was exposed. Half smiling, she shook her head at him and disappeared, likely to find some fresh clothes for their daughters.

Chuluun breathed deeply, savoring the fragrances of his homeland, of his life. For the moment, the past was forgotten, tucked away into an unseen strongbox where he could contain his miseries, from time to time.

His daughters were speaking, asking him things, inspecting his wound. His gaze settled on each of their faces, and he began to answer them, one at a time. The rain fell harder, but he felt a beautiful warmth that spread through his limbs—the embraces of his girls forging a bond as strong as any of steel or stone.

Fan and Bataar stood near a damaged cannon, staring at the northern mountains. A cold rain fell, slanting toward them, striking their faces and bodies. The tops of the nearby rises were shrouded in dark, low clouds. In places the clouds thinned, leaving a steam-like mist that shifted with the winds. On either side of Fan and Bataar, several hundred paces away, the Great Wall disappeared into the haze. Fan thought that the stone dragon looked as if it had taken flight and was burrowing into magical, empowering clouds.

Turning from the sight, Fan focused his attention on the nearby cannon. During the Mongol attack, the cannon had fired, broken off its carriage, and careened into the top of the crenulated wall. Several bricks had been cracked and partially dislodged. Fan knew that they would need to be replaced, but he wanted to ensure that the overall integrity of the stonework hadn't been weakened. Though the rain made a thorough examination hard, his fingers and gaze swept over bricks and mortar. After locating cracks, he opted to not circle them in charcoal because of the rain but stuck needles into each gap. The work was painstakingly slow, and the rain made him shiver, falling so hard that it often obscured his vision.

Despite the inclement weather, Fan had been ordered by Yat-sen to complete the work. The two of them had spoken after the battle, Yat-sen demanding to know about the Mongol camp and, more important, where the Chinese might create an outpost. Despite his abhorrence to the idea of any of his men working outside the wall, Fan had told Yat-sen where such a tower might be built. He had glimpsed flat, stony ground not too far from where he stood now. A tower could be created at that location. While Fan was dubious of such a fortification's strategic value, he knew that other such towers existed outside the wall. He'd also come to understand Yat-sen's vanity and suspected that the tower would please the commander. It would be an affront to the Mongols, a symbol of Yat-sen's power and indomitable will.

"Do you think someone found our letter?" Bataar asked.

"Yes, I suspect so," Fan answered, pulling himself away from his previous thoughts. "But hopefully they found it before the rain came. I didn't think about that. I'm sorry."

"You were frightened. You knew my people were returning."

Fan envisioned the Mongols charging over the mountain. He could still hear their screams of war. "I'm not ashamed to agree with you. But I was more than frightened. I was terrified."

"Of course you were terrified," Bataar replied, smiling. "And I'm sure you weren't the only one."

"Do you think your father was with them?"

"Yes. And I wanted to call out to him. But I thought I should stay quiet."

"You were patient. Well done."

"I didn't like it."

Fan nodded, wondering if Bataar was right. They had agreed to always assume that their loved ones were alive. They rarely mentioned the danger of disease, war, and accidents. To discuss such threats was to give them life, to acknowledge the possibility of unimaginable loss.

"I thought you were going to fall off that stallion," Bataar added. "I'm glad he was so headstrong. He knew right where to go."

Fan patted his right hip. "My backside still aches. It feels like someone kicked me all the way down the wall."

Lightning flashed above them, prompting Bataar to flinch. "My father can't read. But a few of our people can speak your language. Someone will read him our letter."

"Just stay patient, Bataar. It might take weeks for that to happen."

"Patience, patience, patience. Aren't you tried of being patient?"

"It took patience to build this wall, didn't it? And have you seen anything stronger?"

"That earthquake wasn't patient, and it shook your wall like a toy."

Returning to his work, Fan stuck a needle in a crack. Though the stonework was still stout, he worried about the approaching winter. Water and ice would find each weakness, exploiting it. Spring would bring new Mongol attacks, and if the men here were to survive, the wall had to remain impenetrable.

Fan's hands trembled from the cold. His stomach also rumbled as they hadn't yet eaten. Afraid that Bataar was too thin and therefore vulnerable to illness, Fan had been secretly adding his own noodles and vegetables to the boy's dishes. Bataar's weight seemed to be holding steady. Fan was getting thinner.

"I should show you how to ride a horse," Bataar said, taking a needle from Fan's grasp. "Otherwise you're going to get killed out there."

"Out there is your world, not mine."

"But what if Yat-sen makes you ride again?"

"He—"

"You can't ride like that and expect to live."

Fan glanced to his right and left, seeing no one. Most of the guards were inside the watchtowers as the Mongols rarely attacked in a hard rain, which made footing too treacherous for their mounts. "So show me," Fan replied, then set down the rest of his needles.

Nodding, Bataar leapt up onto the top of the parapet, straddling the stonework. The ground was about twenty feet below him, and Fan reached for his arm, pulling him away from the precipice.

"I'm fine," Bataar said.

"But you could fall."

"And a stone could drop from the sky and split my skull. But neither is going to happen."

Fan started to protest but forced himself to remain silent.

"Imagine the wall is a horse," Bataar said. "See how I have my feet, ankles, shins, and knees right up against it? That's what you need to do. I can stand in my stirrups, but you're not good enough to do that. So you need to ride low and grip your horse with everything you can."

"That wall doesn't move. It's the opposite of a horse."

"You move when you walk. Do you fall down? Don't worry about the horse moving. You just move with him."

"Easy for you to say."

"Get up here and show me."

"Bataar, we can't—"

"Just do it."

Fan bit his lower lip. He thought of Meng, wondering what she would think of their conversation. She would encourage him to do as Bataar had asked and might even climb up on the wall herself.

Moving gingerly because of his sore hips and legs, Fan stepped in front of Bataar and straddled the wall. He placed both his hands on the stonework and, not looking at the ground below, tried to grip the wall with his knees and feet.

"Crouch lower," Bataar said. "Let your horse feel your breath on his neck."

"But yesterday, I was bouncing. I couldn't get close."

"You have to use your knees to absorb the bouncing. That's what you were doing wrong. You were too straight legged and stiff. Pretend that you're a frog or something."

Still shivering, Fan sought to imagine that the wall was a horse. He bent his legs, moving his torso up and down as if a stallion were galloping beneath him.

"That's it!" Bataar encouraged. "You're riding!"

Fan laughed, feeling ridiculous on the wall, but pleased by Bataar's words. "I haven't even fallen. Maybe there's hope for me."

"Maybe so. I'll race you right now, my horse against yours."

"And our bet?"

Bataar didn't immediately reply. Thunder rumbled in the distance, rain gathering in strength. "We'll start like this and you'll count to three," Bataar finally answered. "Whoever is ahead at the count of three wins. If you win, I'll work on being patient. If I win, you'll work on beating Yat-sen in *Go*."

"You have yourself a bargain."

"So count."

Fan pretended to ride, shouting at his imaginary horse to hurry. "One … "

Bataar laughed, jumped off the wall, ran a few steps ahead, and leapt back onto it. "Two, three!" he shouted, thrusting his fist into the air.

"You cheated!"

"I won!"

"But—"

"I finished ahead of you!"

Fan swung his leg over the parapet and dropped to the slippery stonework. "That wasn't a fair bet," he protested, failing to stifle a smile. "You knew you'd win."

"Well, you'd never beat me in a real race. So why pretend that you would here?"

After picking up his needles, Fan turned again to Bataar. The boy was still smiling, and Fan realized that Bataar seemed happier than he'd been in many days. The letter must have given him hope. While Fan understood that without hope, life was lost, he also feared a great rise in Bataar's expectations. If his father didn't come, Bataar would become despondent and rash. He'd try to escape at an inopportune moment, exposing himself to needless danger.

"Your father will find you," Fan said, pointing a needle to the north. "But give him time, Bataar. Racing is good to do on a horse, but on this wall, things move much more slowly. Just be happy that someone will read your words to him and that he'll come for you. Maybe soon, maybe not. In either case, we'll be ready to reach him. When the time is right, we'll run as fast as our legs will carry us. But not a moment before."

Though his smile vanished, Bataar nodded. "I'll try. But I don't like to wait."

"After you escape you can ride as fast as lightning. But move slowly here. Please."

Nodding, Bataar took a needle and bent down, toward the stonework.

Standing straighter, Fan sighed. The rain came at him even harder, dripping from his nose and lips. He wondered if the citizens of Beijing saw the same skies. There the water would run off rooftops, collecting in courtyards and streets, ridding the city of dust. Meng would be happy. She had always liked the rain. Relaxed by its melodies, she might open a book or think about him.

Fan imagined her in their room. He saw her face, smiling at its perfect imperfections, glad that it was dry and warm.

*

Forty miles to the south, Meng hurried through the downpour, trying to keep up with Ping. The ferocity of the rain had caught them by surprise, beating down upon them with no refuge in sight. The road ran alongside a wide, swollen river, which was only a foot or so away from cresting its banks. Only a few other travelers were present, and all of them had umbrellas. Meng's had been stolen by her father-in-law's servant. She had foolishly decided not to buy another, believing that they would always be able to find a warm inn. Yet the farther they had drawn away from Beijing, the wilder the land had become.

Her hands shaking from the cold, Meng stumbled ahead, her shoes heavy with mud. Ping continued to push his cart, cursing its narrow wheels, which left deep ruts. He treated the cart like a living thing, kicking its sides when it got stuck, demanding to know why it didn't try harder to help him. On several occasions, Meng thought that he'd abandon it, yet he never did. Once he drew his sword and slashed at its back side, but shortly thereafter dragged it forward.

Lightening flashed, thunder rumbled, and the rain slanted toward them, driven by northern winds. Meng hadn't eaten all morning and feared that she was losing her strength. Each step seemed to be more torturous than the one before it, each puddle more difficult to wade through. She started to shiver, hoping that Fan was dry and safe, that the Great Wall protected him. Wearing the coat that she'd made for him, she continued to think about him, aware that he disliked the cold more than she did. Though she longed to see him, she was glad that he wasn't with her.

Shouts arose behind them. Meng turned and was surprised to see a mass of red boats drifting down the river. The vessels were all at least thirty feet long and had upturned bows and sterns. Many had green, rounded roofs that were supported by four poles. Several of the largest boats boasted ornate, golden roofs that sheltered enclosed rooms. A single red pole rose near the stern of each vessel. Red and green banners hung limply from the poles.

The boats with the open-sided rooms held about ten men each. They must have been high-ranking court officials because most of them were dressed in fine robes and wore peaked, black caps. Servants used long, bamboo shafts to help guide the boats downstream, thrusting the poles against the river's bottom.

Meng wondered who was in the boats with the golden rooftops. These contained enclosed rooms and surely men of great wealth rested in comfort, likely dozing on silk-covered couches. These passengers were dry and warm, and relied on the sufferings of their servants. For an instant, Meng was jealous of their stature but then shook her head, reminding herself that she could never be satisfied when her contentedness was predicated on the misery of those beneath her. If she was the master of one of the golden-roofed boats, she would be wet with her fellow man or be dry with him. There would be no separation of worlds.

The fleet disappeared. Meng was sad to see them go, as the unfamiliar sight had drawn her attention away from her misery. She continued onward, falling to her knees, rising up, mud slipping off her. Ping turned and saw her distress. He yelled at her to hurry, pointing ahead. She wasn't sure what had drawn his attention, but redoubled her efforts to maintain his pace, shivering despite her exertions.

Ping pushed his cart off the road and toward the nearby river. He hurried to what Meng realized was an overturned boat that lay on the top of the shoreline. The boat wasn't richly colored like the state officials' crafts, nor did it have a roof of any sort. Yet the vessel seemed to be in sound shape, featuring a beaten, yet solid bottom. Ping placed his hand on the upside-down gunwale and lifted up. Though the boat was at least ten feet long, he was able to raise its side from the ground, and he peered underneath. Satisfied, he motioned for Meng to crawl under the craft. She resisted the idea for only a few heartbeats, then dropped to her hands and knees.

The ground beneath the boat was dry. Meng called out to Ping to join her, and he stripped his cart of its goods and pushed them inside. He followed. Once the boat had settled again to the ground, Meng looked around in the dim light. Two benches spanned either side of the craft, and she realized that it must have been used to ferry passengers across the river. The middle section was wide open and tall enough for Meng to sit up. She did so, wiping water from her brow.

"Those fools downstream shouldn't be the only ones to stay dry," Ping said, breathing heavily.

Rain assaulted the wood above them, sounding somewhat akin to a waterfall cascading upon rocks. Thunder boomed, causing Meng to flinch.

"Someone must have upset a dragon," Ping said. "That's what the people say anyway. That's why it rained all summer, why the floods came. After all, it's bad luck to upset a dragon."

"Whose boat is this?"

"It's ours for now, my fellow thief."

"I'm no thief."

"Maybe. But what if I said you stole my heart? You haven't, of course. But if you had, would you be guilty of a theft?"

Meng turned away from him and began to untie the chords that held her pack together. She wasn't comfortable with his question, feeling as if its mere presence was a betrayal of Fan. "How long will the storm last?"

"Ask me after it's stopped. Then I'll have the right answer for you. If I guess now, I'd just be pretending to be wiser than I am."

"But I've come to expect that."

He smiled. "The rain seems to have empowered you. Maybe if all women ran in the rain they'd rule the world."

Shrugging, Meng pulled a blanket from her pack and began to wipe her face. "It seems to me that maybe you men aren't deserving of our rule. We'd surely be kinder to you than you've been to us."

"How so?"

"Oh, I doubt we'd bother binding your big, stinky feet. And we wouldn't stick you inside and never let you see the sun. I'll never understand how you treat women the way you do. It's as if you've all forgotten that you came from us. Without our strength, you wouldn't even exist."

Another crack of thunder came and went.

Ping nodded, then pulled a small, ivory pick from a pocket. He began to clean his teeth. "You're lucky to have good, straight teeth," he said, drawing his lips back. "I'm lucky there too. Have you ever noticed that in all of their portraits, our emperors are unsmiling? Do you think that's because their teeth are crooked? After all, I don't see how a god can have crooked teeth."

"I'm tired. I think I'll rest."

"But haven't you wondered about that?"

"I've wondered what it would be like to rest."

He opened his mouth wider, continuing to pick away. "I don't think a man can be a god and have crooked teeth. On the other hand, if gods were based on perfect smiles you and I would be two of the strongest. Yet here we sit, huddled under an old boat, hiding from the rain."

Meng lay her bedding on the ground, settled upon it, and then covered herself with another blanket. Now that she no longer ran, she was even colder and shivered without end. If Fan were next to her, she would have lain against him, and warmth would have returned to her limbs. In his absence, she could only close her eyes and wrap her arms around herself.

"I'd build you a fire," Ping said, "but the smoke would kill us."

"I'm fine."

"Do you think straight, clean teeth are important in a man?"

"I think honesty is important."

"Show me an honest man and I'll show you a fool."

"Don't you ever get tired of talking? Aren't you cold?"

Ping pulled his pick from his mouth and smiled. "Of course I'm cold. You're cold too. It's a pity that we can't lay beside each other and feel better, but I know that we can't. So we'll both stay freezing. A pair of rabbits would have enough sense to huddle together, but we're much too foolish to do so."

Once again Meng closed her eyes, but she opened them almost immediately. The cold seemed to have penetrated deep into her bones. She wanted to strip her wet clothes away from her body, but with Ping nearby would do nothing of the sort. Her teeth chattering, she continued to hold herself, her knees drawn tight against her chest.

"You're not going to die on me, are you?" Ping asked. "The cold kills plenty of people. But I won't let it kill you. Husband or not, I'll warm you before I'll watch you die."

"I'm not going to die. At least not today."

"Are you sure? You look halfway there."

Despite her misery, Meng smiled weakly. "If I start to die, I'll let you know."

"I'll hope for that moment."

She began to reply but stopped when she heard distant voices. Raising his hand, Ping motioned for her to remain quiet. The voices neared, louder with each passing beat of her heart. It seemed that several men approached them. Ping reached for his sword, his hand settling on its hilt. Meng followed his lead, her discomfort suddenly forgotten.

The men seemed to stop near the boat. They continued to talk, though their voices were muddled. One of them grunted. Something creaked. At first Meng feared that they were lifting up the boat, but she peered under the gunwale and saw boots next to Ping's cart. The cart shifted, then began to roll away. Ping shook his head, slowly drawing his sword from its sheath.

"No," Meng whispered. "Please no."

Ping looked under the gunwale. He cursed beneath his breath. Meng saw that there were five men. Curved swords fell from their waists. Two of them pushed the cart away from the river toward the road. The other three followed silently.

For a terrifying moment Meng feared that Ping was going to go after the men. She felt him tense, felt the boat rise slightly as he lifted. But then thunder cracked and he seemed to go limp.

The men made it to the road and soon vanished.

Because she knew that it would be a gift to him, Meng sat up, reached forward, and squeezed his hand. She kept her fingers wrapped around his for a moment longer than was necessary. "Thank you," she whispered.

His gaze founds hers, and for once he was silent. She nodded and lay back down. When her eyes closed again they did not open for a long time.

∗

The rain couldn't be heard inside the tea house. Replacing its rhythms were bursts of laughter, stringed instruments, and muted conversations. Lying on Yehonala's bed, Yat-sen studied her, wondering how a woman's skin could be so perfect when a man's was often savaged by scars, blemishes, and distortions. She might as well have been covered in gold, he thought, for the sublime rises of her shoulders, breasts, and hips often stole his breath and clouded his judgment. He would kill, steal, and maim for these views. His mere proximity to them left him feeling empowered.

Yat-sen tried to subdue a cough but failed, and once his shudders had ceased, reached toward her. She rested on her side, facing him. The forefinger of his right hand traced the contours of her hip, her belly, her breasts. She had just ridden him until ecstasy had overwhelmed them both, and the memory of their union continued to arouse him. Though she appeared fragile, she was not, and their sexual encounters were often frenzied, loud, and unforgettable.

As he continued to stroke her flawless skin, he wondered what drove her. He knew that anger resided within her, just as it dwelled within him. His rage boiled inside a cauldron of childhood humiliations. But the cause of hers remained unknown. She had never spoken of it.

While their common angst connected them, Yat-sen wasn't

sure if that bond would survive the passage of time. He longed to buy her freedom and for her to be his concubine, to live with him and rule his house. Sharing a home, he could continue to lay waste to his enemies while she kept his demons away. Yet it was possible that her devils might someday join forces with his. If that ever happened, surely she and he would die together in flames.

Yat-sen's thoughts drifted to Fan and his wife. She had written him another letter, which had been intercepted that morning. After finding a private place, Yat-sen read the letter three times, surprised and pained by her words. She wrote that she wanted to travel with him to the sea, sharing its beauty and brilliance. *"If no one is looking,"* she had written, *"we can walk together through the shallows. I'll take your hand and smile at the sound of your voice."*

Yat-sen both admired her courage and derided it. A woman of her station would never travel to the sea. Yet she wanted to go deep into the unknown. Even his best men feared the Mongol wasteland. They dreaded that nameless wilderness. But Meng, the wife of a poor craftsman, wasn't afraid to walk on paths unintended for her. And she wanted to walk them with him.

Breaking his chain of thoughts, Yehonala turned away from him. "If you're going to touch me," she said, "you should think of me."

He drew himself back into the present. "I am—"

"Don't lie."

Outside her room, a man laughed. Footsteps came and went.

Yat-sen reached for a pillow covered in a red, silk slip, then propped up his head. The skin of his burnt side was beneath him, tight yet otherwise without feeling. "She sent him another letter," he said. "It was dated nearly a month ago but arrived today."

"What did she say?"

"She wants him to come home."

"That's nothing new."

"But she longs to … travel with him to the sea."

Yehonala started to reply but let out a deep breath instead. She ran her hand through her long, black hair. "Why does she write about the impossible?"

"I don't know. She's a peculiar woman. Nothing like you."

The scent of opium seeped into Yehonala's chambers. Someone, perhaps in the adjacent room, was smoking.

"Why do you muse over her when you should be contemplating how to buy my freedom?" Yehonala asked.

"I contemplate that every day."

"Several of your gifts to our house were destroyed by the earthquake. You'll have to replace them."

Yat-sen's jaw clenched. "The wall I protect wasn't damaged. Why should I have to pay extra for the thinness of yours?"

She glared at him. "You men made the laws. So abide by them."

His fist tightened. For an instant, he had the urge to strike her. Then his gaze settled onto her feet, which were hidden by miniature, black and yellow lotus shoes. He longed to pull them off her, to see her precious toes and heels.

"I'll get the silver," he finally replied. "I've requested to build a tower beyond the Great Wall, in the land of the barbarians. Because of my reputation they'll give me what I want. And I'll build my tower. But I'll keep a tenth of the wealth they send me."

"When? When will you start?"

"Soon. I've got the craftsman scouting the land."

"Your obsession over him belittles you, distracts you. You should kill him for the same reasons that you slew my former suitors."

Once again his fist tightened. "I need him. If the barbarians best the wall, my downfall will follow. And I'll never come for you."

Yehonala sat up in bed, her shifting breasts drawing his gaze. "So kill her," she said. "Send a man south to end her life. Then you'll be done with her letters, with your fixation on the two of them. They're as great a threat to you as the barbarians."

He coughed, pressing a hand against his sternum. Pretending that an additional cough assailed him, he wondered if she had told her madam about the letters. She probably had, which meant that the old hag was advising her. The madam must want the craftsman and his wife dead, perhaps fearing that they represented a distraction to him, swinging his gaze away from Yehonala. Yat-sen was certain that the old woman had blood on her hands. After all, rumors of her wicked deeds had lingered through the years. Now she wanted to share that blood with Yehonala.

For a moment, it seemed to Yat-sen that Yehonala had aged twenty years. Her body still looked the same, but her mind was much more dangerous and cunning. He asked himself why else she wanted the craftsman's wife dead. Perhaps Yehonala was also jealous of the letter writer's love. Perhaps she feared that Yat-sen would leave her in search of such affection.

Yat-sen had thought about killing Meng. She was a diversion, though also an amusement. Without her letters the winter would be even longer and colder. Not only did he enjoy reading her words, but he also delighted in keeping them from Fan.

Yehonala reached for his hand, lifting it toward her, until it rested on her thigh. "Do you feel me?" she asked.

"Of course."

"If you don't want that feeling to be a memory, you'd better kill her. Because I won't share you with her. If she still lives in a month, I'll find another patron—a task that, as you know, won't be difficult."

Anger stirred within him, his fingers tightening on her thigh. His nails dug into her flesh and she cried out. "Be careful," he said, drawing closer to her. "Don't awake the demons within me."

"But I just want to be with you. I want you think about us, not them."

"You want her life, her blood on my hands. But what are you willing to give me for that blood?"

"I don't—"

"Kill the old hag," he whispered. "She poisons your mind. She pulls you from me. I know that her death won't change your fate. Another madam will merely take her place. But still, I want her gone."

Yehonala slowly shook her head. "I need her."

"Not as much as you need me. So kill her."

"How?"

"When you find yourself alone with her, in a private room, hold your hand over her mouth and nose; and wrap your arms about her. She'll struggle, but she's old and weak. She won't last long. Then straighten her robes, her hair. Set her on a couch and say that she died with great peace and contentment."

Yehonala's eyes glistened, and she bit her bottom lip.

"Kill the old hag and I'll kill Meng," Yat-sen promised, now stroking her thigh. "Do we agree?"

"I—"

"Her past is as tainted as any. And now she taints you. So I say again—do we agree?"

"Yes," Yehonala whispered. "Though not tomorrow, or even the day after. First ... I must talk with her."

"What was your answer?"

"Yes. It was yes."

"Good. Then I'll send a man south tomorrow. And I'll give you a few days to do what must be done."

Yehonala looked away from him.

He sat up and started to dress, thinking about which man would best serve his purposes. Li was strong and deadly, but perhaps too principled. It would be better to send someone else—a desperate man whose allegiance could be bought with silver.

When dressed, Yat-sen turned to Yehonala, who had wrapped a silk sheet around herself. "Remember our bargain," he said.

She nodded.

"Their deaths will draw us closer," he promised, speaking softly. "Unlike other men, I'll never have a wife. I'll never submit to the sad and worthless ritual of marriage. But I'll take you as my concubine. And though you may not think it now, a time will come when you'll thank me for the blood on our hands. Because that blood will bind us, Yehonala. We'll have killed for each other. And when you're far from this place, when you have your own house to rule, and your own children to love, you'll know that what we did was right."

CHAPTER NINE

Strategies for Games and War

North of Jinshanling—October 18, 1549

The Mongols' new camp had been built just below the summit of a midsize mountain. Though the height produced relentless, howling winds that kept all the horsemen awake at night, they had decided that no matter the cost, the Chinese would not surprise them again. Sentries posted on the mountaintop could see for miles, and, better yet, no one believed their enemies capable of riding up the steep incline. For the time being, the riders were safe.

Yet their security did little to appease a strong need to avenge the Chinese attack. Five Mongol riders had been killed during the confrontation near the wall, and each of them had been admired. Their followers demanded a retaliatory strike, which Chuluun had been advocating for months.

Sitting cross-legged in the oversized *yurt* of his commander, Chuluun half listened to the men around him argue about the best strategies to penetrate the wall. He'd heard such conversations hundreds of times and found all of the talk and bluster tedious. Though the officers around him were brave without exception, he knew the wall far more intimately than almost any of them. In time their commander would ask his opinion, but until that moment, he wouldn't argue.

The *yurt* was much more elaborate than the structure farther north that housed Chuluun's wife and children. The commander's dwelling had a diameter of nearly forty feet and could accommodate as many warriors. Though on the outside the circular, canvas wall was uniform and bland, its interior was cluttered with hanging furs, banners, maps, diagrams of the wall, lists of provisions, and reports from scouts. Brightly colored desks and tables, usually red and yellow, formed a circle around the edge of the room. The canvas floor was covered with once-beautiful Chinese carpets that were now stained and frayed. At the exact center of the *yurt*, an iron stove, complete with piping that went straight through the roof, kept the space warm. No fire burnt within it today, as the proximity of so many sitting horsemen produced ample heat.

The majority of the men wore leather armor that featured iron plates or studs. Bows and quivers were fastened to their backs, and sheathed, curved swords rested on their knees. None of the weapons were new or untested. It was an elite group of fighters, and almost every rider in the room had killed. Many had lost comrades and loved ones during the long years of war, and their faces were hardened by loss and disappointments. Their fathers and grandfathers had also struggled against the Chinese. Most likely their sons and grandsons would continue the fight. After all, no peace could ever be achieved until the Chinese opened their empire to trade, allowing the Mongols access to comforts and wealth.

Chuluun had once been proud that Bataar would inherit his weapons and thirst for battle. Now he wished that he'd listened to his wife, who had said that Bataar was too young to see the wall, because anyone who saw it would fight to topple it. Chuluun had thought by training his son as early as possible he'd be better equipped to face his foes, and silence the taunts about his hand. But his wife had been right—Bataar should have remained in the north until he was older and stronger. Either that or Chuluun should have never left his side.

A howling gust of wind caused the walls of the *yurt* to tremble. Though the rain had stopped during the night, the skies were still dark and cold. Chuluun thought about the meal he had shared with his wife and daughters. They'd eaten mutton, potatoes, and cheese. He had also drunk two cups of fermented mare's milk. Though spices were precious, his wife had sprinkled salt on their food for the special occasion.

After dinner, his daughters had taken turns riding on his back, pretending that he was a stallion. Though his joints still ached from battle and the long ride, he'd pushed those pains aside, buoyed by his daughters' laughter and demands. He had bucked each of them once or twice, then pretended to rear up and smash his hooves into their bellies.

Much later, when his daughters were sleeping, he'd let his wife tend to his blisters and welts, and finally lay beside her on a fresh pelt. They had touched and clutched, the rain obscuring the few cries that escaped their lips. Afterwards, whispers drifted back and forth between them. Bataar's name was never mentioned, nor was the distance that since his death had grown between them. Instead they inquired about each other, debated how to best prepare for the coming winter, and watched the sleeping figures of their daughters.

Chuluun was thinking about how often his wife had once smiled when his commander turned to him and asked how he would attack the wall. His mind shifted immediately, his body tensing. He envisioned the watchtowers, the cannons, and the terrain. The endless dragon stretched toward infinity, vanishing over a distant mountain.

"There's no moon in seven nights," he began, staring at his commander. "If we gather our countrymen, we could ride toward a weak part in the wall, where we've attacked before. We could blind those maggots with fear. They'll rush to reinforce this single scale of their dragon, sending men from near and far. And as they do so, a second wave of our men could charge unannounced toward that devil's main tower, from where his wickedness comes to us. His tower and the one to the immediate east of it are the strongest. He won't expect an attack there. But if we capture those two towers, we can seal them up and hold Chinese reinforcements at bay. We can use their own stonework against them. Then thousands of our countrymen could cross between the two towers and pour into their heartland. We could besiege Beijing the following day."

No one spoke as each officer considered Chuluun's plan, which was much more audacious than anything previously advocated. Chuluun had announced it publicly to force his commander to make a decision. While the men in the tent were trusted, such a secret couldn't be kept forever. Seven days might be enough time to gather the necessary men, horses, and supplies for the assault, but perhaps not long enough for Chinese spies to cast their nets.

"Our foes believe us to be beneath them," Chuluun added. "Every day they stand on their dragon and deride us. They mock our fathers, take our children as slaves, and piss on us from above. Are they right? Are we weaker? Do our arrows not fly true and our horses not move like the wind? I see the men around me, and I see strength. I see my brothers. But it's time, brothers, that we prove ourselves; prove that we're worth the blood in our veins. Otherwise we insult the struggle of those who have gone before us."

Voices rumbled. Several men stood, followed by others. Shouts erupted. Chuluun rose to his feet, watching his commander, who caught his gaze and nodded slightly.

The attack would come. Riders would be sent out immediately, instructed to return with more horsemen. An army would be formed.

In seven days Chuluun would ride again to face his foe. He would reach the summit of the wall and hold it through the strength of his sword and of his resolve.

Chuluun wanted to live, to see his daughters grow into women. But he had ensured that they would be looked after in case of his death. And he had no choice but to fight the men who had stolen

Bataar.

Though the horsemen around him wanted to be feared or glorified or loved, Chuluun longed only to be forgiven—both by himself and by the son he had failed.

*

The road was busier than normal, and Meng assumed that they were nearing a village. Though it no longer rained, puddles abounded, and their boots were heavy with mud. Progress was slow, yet they continued north. Meng noticed that the height of the nearby mountains had increased and that many of the trees on them were a dark shade of amber. Autumn was in full bloom—boasting cold winds and flocks of migrating birds.

Since Ping's cart had been stolen, they both walked with a pack of supplies strapped to their backs. As her companion grumbled about the theft, Meng studied the countryside. The road followed the contours of the river, which had been fed by the heavy rain, and ran high and fast. Some of the timber near the water had been felled, and old stumps sprouted ferns and other new life. In the distance, the landscape resembled that which she'd seen in famous paintings—jagged mountains covered partly in pines and mist. Near the summit of the nearest peak, a three-story pagoda reached skyward. The structure featured red sides and a trio of stacked, yellow-tiled roofs.

Meng had expected to see wealth and opulence outside Beijing, but the farther they drew from the capital, the more destitute people seemed to become. As a village loomed ahead, beggars began to congregate at certain sections of the road. All were dressed in filthy, stained clothes. Some were gaunt and starving. Others had boils on their faces. Though almost all the beggars were men, a few women, positioned about twenty paces down the road from their male counterparts, held out bowls. One woman sat with a young boy on her lap. At first, Meng was only aware that he was crying. She neared, realized that his head was swollen to twice a normal size, and stopped in her tracks. The boy was too large to rest comfortably on his mother, and he twisted and turned, tears on his cheeks. He might have been six or seven, and seemed to be in pain. Her eyes tearing, Meng stepped forward, reaching into her secret satchel and removing five copper coins. Though she couldn't afford such generosity, she handed the money to the woman, who thanked her, bowing repeatedly. The woman smiled, stroking her son's hair. For a moment he stopped crying. Meng's eyes found his and she waved. She would have remained standing there, but Ping pulled on her sleeve, leading her forward. After taking a final glance at him, she hurried ahead, hoping that his mother could somehow ease his pains.

The road broadened as they approached the village. It wasn't walled, which meant that it likely contained little of value. Lining the thoroughfare were merchants' stalls, though the offerings were scarce. Dried fish, sickly looking vegetables, and piles of colorless clothes occupied many of the tables. So did fur-lined boots, which Meng realized were much taller than permitted by law. Though the emperor had decreed that any commoner wearing such boots would be beheaded on their doorsteps, many of the merchants wore them. It was simply too cold so far to the north to survive without proper footwear.

As they passed an immense man standing behind bamboo crates of clucking chickens, Ping tugged again on Meng's sleeve. "See how fat those birds are?"

She nodded.

"If you lifted one up it wouldn't be heavy. That giant takes his scrawny chickens and uses a tube to fill them with air. He doubles their size. Of course, everyone here knows the trick. But passing strangers might be foolish enough to buy a bird or two. I've seen chickens like those slaughtered, and when the knife pierces them they practically vanish."

Meng's thoughts drifted back to the mother and boy. She wondered what the woman would do with the five coppers. Would her child's belly be filled? Would she buy him medicine for the pain that seemed to afflict him?

"In times of famine, these rascals use every trick imaginable," Ping added. "They cook with a nearly white dirt instead of flour to thicken pancakes. They sell bags of rice that contain small, white pebbles. You have to be very careful. Otherwise, the delicacies you're eating may end up sickening you. Of course, I shouldn't bother explaining such nuances to you because you rarely pay for anything and eat less than a cricket."

She would have liked to ask him how he knew so much about the merchants' dishonesty, but a few paces ahead, a group of Confucian scholars ambled down the road. The men were dressed in white and brown robes, and wore black, square headdresses. All were long bearded and used walking sticks.

Ping pointed toward circular, head-high structures not far off the road. "Those sad-looking things are storehouses," he said, "and in normal times they'd be filled with dates, ducks, pigs, dried prawns, walnuts, and grains. The merchants here would be selling peaches instead of peddling lies, rolling out watermelons instead of deceptions. But the famine turns everyone into thieves. That's why I feel right at home. Life would be perfect if only I weren't so hungry."

Though Ping continued to talk, Meng noticed a commotion ahead. A large man walked toward her. Bamboo poles jutted out from his back, supporting a variety of colorful objects. One pole propped up a blue and green umbrella that had been affixed with scores of copper bells. When the man moved, the bells trembled, creating a harmonious jingle heard far and wide. Young boys were gathered around the man, reaching toward him, crying out in excitement.

Meng had never seen a similar sight and edged forward. The boys were dressed in worn robes and sandals. The front part of their heads was shaved, but a topknot had been tied above the back of their necks, each bound with a red ribbon. Disregarding the boys, Meng focused on the man, who she now realized was a merchant. The bamboo poles sprouting from his sides carried all sorts of goods—candies, lanterns, flags, caged frogs, and toys of every shape and size. The children buzzed around him, moving from spot to spot, admiring his wares and searching their pockets for coins. Meng saw one child buy a red, corded sling. But the remainder of the boys were left empty-handed. They had no money to offer.

The merchant walked to the south, his bells jingling. Meng

watched him depart, then followed Ping toward the village. It was poor, run-down, and might have been a slum within Beijing. The homes seemed to lean toward each other, as if exhausted from resisting the elements, and seeking companionship.

Off the main road, several larger structures dominated the community. One was an old temple, in front of which a soup line stretched for more than two hundred steps. Another was a one-story, blue and white dwelling. Music emanated from within its walls, as did the occasional bout of laughter.

"Here," Ping said, handing her a piece of hard candy. "You need to eat."

"What?" she whispered, shaking her head. "But where did it come from?"

"Don't worry about where it came from. That's a task for our noble philosophers to ponder. Just eat."

"You stole it, didn't you? From the man selling toys?"

Ping bit on a piece of the candy. "What would you have me do? I only have a few coppers and you're handing yours out as if they're too hot to touch. You haven't eaten anything all day. At this rate you'll waste away before you reach the Great Wall. I'll have to fill you with air just to make you presentable."

"I didn't ask you to steal for me," she replied, her voice louder. "What you've done isn't right. It's shameful."

He turned his hands up in the air. "I'm a thief. What do you expect from me? If you're going to trade coins for smiles, I need to be sure that you have the strength to go on. But I can't do that if we have nothing to eat."

She thrust the candy forward, shoving it into his hand. "That boy was suffering! I'm not. And I won't eat something that's been stolen!"

"Then you're a fool."

"Maybe. But I'm an honest fool."

"An honest fool who will never reach her precious husband, who will weaken and die on the road. You won't reach him because you're unwilling to do what must be done. And that's as shameful as thievery."

His words seemed to strike her, and she stepped back. Suddenly aware that she'd spoken too loudly, that a passerby might have heard her voice, she shook her head. "I think … I think I'll walk alone for a while," she whispered, half to herself.

"Fine," he answered, then pointed to the blue and white building. "You see that? It's a pleasure house—full of thieves and weak-willed women. That's where I'm going. That's where I'll spend the last of my coppers and eat your candy."

"You—"

"The problem with you is that you think we live in a world where fortune favors the good. But that's not what happens. The good suffer and die. It's the strong who survive. And I intend to live."

"Good-bye, Ping."

The tension in his face softened. "I want you to live too, Meng," he replied, again offering her the candy. "Please live. Take it and I'll go with you. But I won't carry you. I won't watch you fade away."

"Enjoy your pleasure house. I hope you find a woman who delights you."

"Wait. Please don't go."

She turned away from him, walking north, over the muddied street. He called out behind her, but her pace didn't falter. While it was true that her stomach was empty and aching, and that her body sometimes trembled from weakness, she wasn't willing to further taint her journey. She'd already pretended to be someone she wasn't. Then she'd held a man's hand and smiled with him as darkness fell.

There was nothing left to do but walk.

*

The skies had darkened with unusual speed, transforming as if a stream's clear water that had been churned by a passing army. The wind had strengthened, blowing from the north, driving rain so powerfully that it slanted nearly parallel to the land. Atop the Great Wall, grooves funneled water toward the fortification's southern side, where spouts directed it forward in streaming arcs, ensuring that it fell as far from the stonework as possible.

The northern frontier was saturated and inaccessible. Even the best of the Mongol riders would struggle to cross the slippery, dangerous landscape. Aware of this weakness, almost all of the Chinese defenders were dry and warm within the watchtowers. Some men slept. Others ate, drank cheap rice wine, or played games of chance.

Deep within Yat-sen's command post, ten soldiers surrounded a *Go* board, studying their leader and Fan. The two men sat on low stools on opposite sides of a table. Yat-sen wore his red armor. Fan was dressed in the robes of a laborer. The room was kept warm by fires that burned outside its walls but heated small, bricked passageways that led to the interior. All of the men had eaten a simple meal of fried wheat noodles and green onions. Though stomachs still rumbled, everyone was pleased to be inside.

Fan barely stirred as he sat before the game board. His neck and shoulders ached from another morning of stooping over small cracks, but he resisted the urge to stand and stretch, or quell his pain with a cup of rice wine. Back in Beijing, Meng used to rub his shoulders when he returned from the Forbidden City, loosening his tight muscles, prompting his aches to flow away. He imagined her hands on his skin, her thumbs pressing on either side of his spine. Though he tried to remember the scent of her hair, it eluded him, darkening his mood. He was tired of living through memories, which had comforted him for so long, yet now seemed so hollow. Once again he wished that he'd listened to her and never left Beijing. He had been rash, failing them both. How angry and disappointed she must be with him.

"Wager with me tonight," Yat-sen said, leaning over the table, his hands outstretched. "Show these men that you're not afraid."

Fan shrugged. "I have nothing to offer you."

"But you do, Craftsman. You see, I want your necklace."

Fan's right hand instinctively rose to his neck, pressing against the second half of the polished, jade turtle. "I won't part with it," he replied, lowering his hand. "Please name something else."

"I named the necklace."

Unseen men encouraged Fan to accept the bet. Bataar pressed against him from behind. Though Fan had planned to try to win tonight in order to please his young friend, he hadn't expected to be asked for such a profound wager.

"The necklace … was a gift," he said softly, the ache between his shoulder blades gone. "My wife wears its other half."

Yat-sen shrugged. "If it matters so much to you, ask me for something of equal value, something I won't want to part with."

Soldiers offered suggestions, but Fan ignored them. He could solicit extra rations, early freedom, or silver. Any of these prizes were valuable, but not worth risking his necklace. He started to shake his head, yet suddenly everything was clear.

"Bataar," he replied, meeting Yat-sen's stare, trying to remain calm. "If I win, the boy goes free."

Silence dominated the room as if the air had been sucked out of everyone's lungs. Men seemed to be frozen for a moment but then recovered, turning to their companions and offering wagers. Fan ignored the growing clamor. His gaze remained fixed on Yat-sen. The commander's face had tightened. He leaned forward on his stool even more intensely.

"The boy isn't yours to wager," Yat-sen said, his right hand dropping to his sword hilt.

"Fine. Then we'll wager nothing. But I'll keep the necklace."

"I could take it from you. I could cut your head from your shoulders."

His heart pounding, Fan bit his lower lip. "But you'd never wear it with honor. Not like you would if you beat me in *Go* and won it fairly."

"Be careful, Craftsman. Dragons should be left sleeping."

Sweat started to bead on Fan's forehead. He wiped it away.

"Why don't we forget the wager? We don't—"

"The necklace against the boy's freedom. If I win, the necklace is mine. If you win, he leaves tonight."

Fan nodded and immediately began to study the board. He focused on it in a way that he hadn't for many years. His gaze swung from side to side, sweeping over each of the three hundred and sixty-one intersections. He knew how Yat-sen would play, with aggression and fury. Fan had always retreated under the commander's advances, trying to protect his black pieces rather than surround and besiege Yat-sen's positions.

After reaching for his first piece, Fan reminded himself of his father's words. He saw himself as a young boy, listening attentively as his father spoke about the strategy of *Go*, and how whoever captured the most territory would win the game. Territory was defined as empty spaces surrounded by stones of the same color. The four edges of the board acted as a natural border, so the best strategies focused on using those borders, as well your pieces, to encircle empty space. If anyone's stone or stones were surrounded by an opponent's pieces, the surrounded stones would be taken from the board. The winner of the game depended on whoever had the most captured territory when neither player could move again.

Fan took a slow and steady breath, placing his first black stone near the center of the board. Yat-sen countered without pause, provoking the soldiers to offer one another additional wagers. Though men spoke loudly and jostled for better position, though Bataar now knelt beside him, Fan was aware of nothing outside the game board. He played quickly, wanting to match Yat-sen's speed, to keep his opponent off balance. Instead of trying to block Yat-sen from clustering his pieces, Fan forced himself to look at the board on a larger scale. He surrounded Yat-sen's positions but did so from a distance, not creating direct threats. Yat-sen focused his pieces as if they were soldiers on a battlefield. And while he scored points, Fan continued to encircle him, remembering his father's lessons. Sweat ran down his back and belly. He glanced at Bataar and recognized the boy's apprehension.

"You build a wall," Yat-sen said, adding another white piece to the board. "I build armies."

Fan nodded.

"But while you build, Craftsman, I score points, I deny you territory."

Continuing to add his black pieces toward the edges of the board, Fan looked for opportunities. His instincts screamed at him to try to defend the center, as he always had against Yat-sen. Yet he didn't do what he'd constantly done. Instead he imagined the northern frontier. He saw fortifications, riders, and cannons. He created lines of black that reached toward those of white, running against them, cutting them off. Points that Yat-sen had scored were taken off the board when Fan surrounded his positions. Now it was the black pieces that began to control the territory. Yat-sen tried to counterattack, but Fan remained one step ahead of him, securing terrain, advancing his forces.

Fan glanced up at his opponent and saw that he had also started to sweat. A vein seemed to bulge across his temple. His fingers often whitened as they gripped a fresh game piece. The board now offered fewer places to play. Yat-sen was forced to move where he didn't want to, wasting pieces and power. Fan's heartbeat further quickened. He saw victory. He imagined Bataar leaving for his family. And he smiled; knowing that the game was his and that Yat-sen would soon surrender.

"I was lucky," he said softly, bowing low to his opponent. "You're the true master."

Yat-sen reached forward, his movements graceful, his fingers pushing apart the carefully arranged pieces. "You should have asked for something else, Craftsman," he replied. "I would have given you wealth or women. But not the boy. He's seen too much of our defenses to ever go free."

"But—"

"Take him!" Yat-sen shouted. "Take him now or I'll have all your heads!"

Fan thought that the soldiers were going to reach for Bataar, but suddenly hands were on him. He resisted them, kicking and struggling, but he was overwhelmed. Bataar screamed. The men lifted him, carrying him forward. Yat-sen shouted again and again at them, but Fan didn't understand his words. Though he'd been betrayed before, this treachery was infinitely more swift and acute. His mind didn't seem to function.

Suddenly they were outside, on top of the wall. The rain smote them all. Again Bataar screamed. The soldiers slowed, seeming to hesitate. Fan didn't understand what was happening. He pleaded with the men whom he'd protected. And for a moment they listened. But then Yat-sen shouted, raising his sword, his voice piercing the storm.

Lightning flashed.

The men grunted, heaving Fan. He reached for their hands, but his fingers missed theirs. He plummeted, twisting toward the abyss below.

The ground seemed to rise up and strike him, instantly suffocating his thoughts and movements and even his terror.

*

Once again, rainfall had transformed the road into a seemingly endless quagmire. Most travelers had long since headed for warm inns or made camps under nearby trees. Meng had considered paying for a room but was worried about not having enough money to make the return trip to Beijing. She'd only eaten some dried peaches for dinner, and in her weakened state, her waterlogged clothes weighed heavily on her shoulders, dragging her toward the mud. She wore the coat that she'd made for Fan. Her intention had been to give it to him in pristine condition, but now the garment was stained, frayed, and well-worn.

Tears descended her cheeks, mixing with rainwater. She carried an umbrella in her right hand and a rolled-up kite in her left. The umbrella had kept her dry for a time but had been overwhelmed by the weather. She'd purchased the kite and umbrella earlier in the day from a boy dressed in tattered clothes. Though the kite was intended as a gift for her mother, it was the sight of the boy that had compelled her to action. At first glance, he'd appeared beaten down. But as she approached, he stood straighter, strength and hope seeming to flow into him. Regardless of how fate might have bullied him, he hadn't surrendered to its will.

After her purchase, Meng had thought of the boy. Then her mind had drifted to Ping, recalling each phrase of their argument. She wished that she could take back some of her words—not because she didn't believe in them but because he had helped her and didn't deserve her scorn. Though she knew such musings were immoral, she wondered what he had done after he'd left her. Surely he'd gone to the pleasure house and found a woman to his liking. The courtesan must have made him smile and laugh, then fulfilled each of his desires, no matter what they were.

Meng wasn't jealous of the woman but also longed to find comfort. With Fan beside her, the cramps in her belly, the trembles of her legs, and the chill deep in her bones would have subsided. She wouldn't have known loneliness so intimately that she could have tasted it, as if it were a steaming, fragrant soup.

Though her body and mind tried to slow her down, to force her to stop and rest, Meng continued forward. She reminded herself of the boy selling kites, and of Fan's enduring fortitude as he labored on the Great Wall. If she stopped, if she yielded, she wasn't deserving of the blessings that had been bestowed upon her. As a woman, she was expected to fall down, to mourn the injustices of the moment. But she would do neither. Her strength was unbound and so was her resolution, despite the laments encouraged by the rain and her longing.

Meng allowed herself to cry; her emotions to escape. To bottle them up would further weaken her when she could least afford it. After all, Fan was less than a week's journey away. She neared him. He had walked this same road, perhaps thinking about her, missing her.

As an attempt to pass the time, she thought about the stories that he'd sent her. In her mind's eye she reread each one, nodding at his attempts to please her, to lessen the distance between them. Though the rain continued to besiege her, she struggled onward, knowing that the decision to go to him had been the right one. Most people believed that a woman couldn't lend strength to a man, that all she could offer him was an heir to his name and a harmonious home. But Meng knew Fan. She understood that he needed her as she needed him. He wrote stories not only to please her, but also to satisfy himself—because an expression of love is a gift savored by both the recipient and the giver.

Meng's right foot slipped on something hard beneath the mud and she fell with a gasp. The hilt of her sword banged against her hip, scoring her skin. She rolled away from the pain, moving to her hands and knees. Lightning flashed, revealing a darkening land, full of towering trees. Night would soon arrive, and Meng realized that she had lost track of time. Orange and red leaves, their colors muted by the weakening light, fell from swaying branches. She looked for a tree that still had some of its canopy, found one, and walked in its direction.

The soil beneath the tree was wet and unwelcoming, but she sat against its trunk, holding the umbrella above her. With her left hand she removed her sword from its sheath and rested the weapon on her knees. It seemed to glisten despite the lack of light. She wondered if its blade had ever tasted blood. She hoped not but saw that its edge was nicked and menacing. If she was fortunate enough to have a son, she would keep him away from weapons. Should she be further blessed, books would elicit his excitement.

With Fan as a mentor, he could become a builder or perhaps a state scholar. His future would be bright.

Now that Meng was still, her hunger grew more pronounced— deep and aching. If Ping was nearby, he would have had a piece of food handy, perhaps stolen, but hopefully not. She would have liked to have shared a fried sparrow with him and remembered their first night together. He'd been kind to her, even after pushing her all day on his cart. Though she would never betray Fan through intimacy with another man, in the deepest and most secretive part of her heart, Meng realized that she'd enjoyed holding Ping's hand under the boat, in a rain like this one. She wasn't sure if that fondness stemmed from forming a bridge to a fellow traveler, or if Ping's character had somehow drawn her toward him. Whatever had happened, she didn't entirely regret the moment and wondered what Ping had thought of it.

The landscape around her seemed stricken, as if ailing from a frightening disease that drained the world of color. Leaves continued to flutter to the ground, passing before shadowy limbs and trunks. The sun must have set because the sky was growing dim. The road was nearby, but she couldn't see it. Nor did fires illuminate any patch of ground. It seemed that other travelers were too wise or experienced to spend the night outside.

Shivering, Meng pulled Fan's coat tighter around herself. Again she thought of food, wondering if she'd resist the stolen candy if Ping offered it to her now. Probably not, she admitted, her mouth watering, her stomach restless and rumbling.

Meng had passed long soup lines that day but had pressed forward without stopping, unwilling to spend time waiting. In

Beijing, the rich would be unaffected by the famine. They would sit in their sprawling homes, sip their tea, and complain about the high cost of servants. Few of them would think about the hungry, the malformed, or the war on the northern frontier. Much to her shame and regret, before her journey, Meng hadn't contemplated the suffering of those less fortunate than she, instead worrying about her unbound feet or the stature of her loved ones.

How many people suffered out here while I slept under warm blankets? she wondered, lowering her umbrella, resting it on top of her head. How many people were hungry when I left uneaten food on my plate?

Fresh tears, driven by guilt, dropped to her cheeks. Only through her own suffering had she glimpsed the angst of others. She felt shallow and weak, insignificant because she had helped no one. The most that she had ever done in her life was to stitch Fan a coat and carry it toward him. She had never cured or comforted, saved or shepherded. Handing out her father-in-law's coins was a sorry effort at being charitable. Yes, those actions had left her an aching stomach, but they had been unplanned and unworthy.

Wondering if Fan had ever glimpsed her failings and thought less of her, Meng rocked back and forth against the tree trunk. Somehow the rain, cold, and hunger had released all her emotions. They came rushing out of her, looking for light, for breath. She wept, her chest shuddering, her sobs obscured by distant thunder.

Many times in her life Meng had felt insecure, but she now felt incomplete, and that sentiment was worse. The gifts fate had sent her had been squandered and unshared.

The rain fell harder. The night grew frigid.

Yet Meng didn't ask for an end to her sufferings. She was glad to shiver and ache. She had begun this journey to find Fan but now felt as if she'd begun to find herself.

As she wiped away her tears, lightning flashed and trees swayed.

Attracted by Meng's cries, two figures crept forward, their boots making no noise on the drenched ground.

★

Fan wasn't sure how long he had remained unconscious. One moment only blackness existed, and the next a wave of light flashed across the sky. Sounds came next, distant groans that resembled a pair of wounded beasts locked in mortal combat. Light pulsated again, its tendrils seeming to reach back into his head, his mind. He blinked. Instinctively he tried to sit up but was instantly devoured by pain. Groaning, he let his muscles relax, finally aware that rain pelted against his face and body. The Great Wall loomed above him. Never had it seemed more imposing.

As his thoughts cleared, Fan realized that he lay on the north side of the wall. He remembered beating Yat-sen in *Go* and the soldiers lifting him up and tossing him over the parapet. Bataar had screamed as Yat-sen shouted. Then everything disappeared.

After taking a series of slow and steady breaths in an effort to collect himself, Fan moved his fingers and toes. He flexed his right arm, then his left, wincing as pain shot through him. Sitting up slowly, he examined his left forearm, which appeared to bulge in the middle. Bending his wrist provoked a new wave of pain, forcing him to bite back a scream. His arm seemed broken. The entire left side of his body throbbed.

Wincing, Fan dragged himself toward the Great Wall, though he knew that it wouldn't provide him with shelter from the elements. Still, he moved through the mud until he was able to push up against it, rising to a sitting position. Though now convinced that his forearm was broken, he understood that the twenty-foot fall could have been much worse. Yat-sen might have easily killed or crippled him. Perhaps the rain had saved him, softening the ground.

Fan thought about the game, realizing that he'd been wrong to openly challenge the commander. Yat-sen's vanity all but ensured a reprisal, and his paranoia toward the Mongol hordes also meant that Bataar would never be allowed to go free. Fan had been foolish to act on impulse, to trust a man he'd believed couldn't be trusted. The only one to blame for his predicament was himself.

With a single, reckless challenge, Fan had put himself in jeopardy. He could have been easily killed, and, equally frightful, Bataar was now surely at risk. Yat-sen would see him as a reminder of his failure at *Go*, of his consequent humiliation, and be eager to vanquish him. It was possible that Bataar had already been punished, though Fan suspected that his own sufferings might be enough to satiate Yat-sen's need for revenge.

Fan's only consolation was that he believed Yat-sen still needed him. No one in the immediate area knew the Great Wall the way he did. As long as the Mongols continued to press and attack, the wall must be repaired. Perhaps, intending to kill him, Yat-sen would finally send for his replacement. But until that man arrived, Fan believed that he would be spared. Bataar, unfortunately, had no such value. He was one slave among many, and Fan would have to devise a way to restore Yat-sen's honor at the boy's expense. Otherwise, Bataar would be killed.

A blast of frigid wind sent rain flying into Fan's face. He used his good arm to protect himself, cradling his broken limb against his lap. He wasn't dressed for the weather and started to shiver. Though tempted to call out, he remained silent, watching lightning illuminate the land of their enemy. Mountains were revealed, then darkened, as if flames that had been extinguished.

Twisting painfully, Fan studied how the lightning brought the Great Wall to life, seeming to fill it with energy and power. Close bursts of thunder echoed off the thick stonework, reverberating around him. He continued staring to the west, aware of the near perfect symmetry of the fortification.

Fan was about to turn in the other direction when something caught his eye—a slight protrusion in the nearby stonework. Though still miserable, his curiosity propelled him to crawl along the base of the wall, holding his left arm against him. Groaning, he drew closer to the sight, soon aware that something had been wedged between two large, stone blocks. Clenching his teeth, he stood up, then pried the object away from the wall.

The small, wooden horse surprised him. Once, many months before, he'd seen a similar horse within a shattered brick. He had tossed it into the underbrush, consumed with making a quick repair. But now, in the driving rain, he turned the horse over and over in his right hand, marveling at its composition. Whoever had crafted the object was an artist, as it was smooth, perfectly proportioned, and elegant. Why the horse had been crudely jammed into the wall was a mystery to Fan. A Mongol must have left it there, perhaps as a warning, perhaps to mark his passage. Whatever the case, Fan wondered about the man. He pocketed the horse, thinking that he'd give it to Meng, once they were reunited. He would never tell her about being thrown from the wall but would describe where he found the carving and what it might mean. Perhaps he'd invent a story about the horse and its creator.

After tucking the horse into his robe, Fan sat against the wall, drawing his knees up against his chest. By now he trembled uncontrollably. His broken arm throbbed as if a blacksmith smote it again and again with a hammer. Though he had usually been able to ignore his aches, this pain was different, pulsating from his wrist to his shoulder. Again he resisted the urge to call out for help. If his spirit, not his arm, had been shattered, he would have, but enough defiance still resided in him that he refused to plead for aid.

Grunting from the pain, he closed his eyes, trying to envision Meng's face. He imagined her lying on their bed, covered in blankets. If he could magically travel to her side, he wouldn't wake her but would simply lie next to her. He'd study her face, his gaze following each contour, each rise and fall. He would lose himself in the beauty, the wilderness that was her. Within this wilderness time would have no meaning, his fears would vanish like mist beneath a bright sun, and he would feel sheltered. When her warmth had spread to him, had bound them together, he would lean toward her, moving slowly so as not to wake her, and gently kiss her fingers, her lips. Only then would he close his eyes. Though she would remain asleep, she'd carry him away.

Fan continued to picture them together as the rain beat upon him. His tears joined the wetness of the night, flowing downward, strengthening in numbers.

Despite Fan's imaginings, Meng had never seemed so far away. He longed to tell her that he loved her, that he was sorry.

But all he could do was weep.

*

Even in the midst of her dream, Meng felt the blade press against her throat. She awoke with a start, but unseen hands held her down, forcing her against the wet soil. A heavily bearded man hissed at her to stay silent, showing her the knife before once again placing it on her neck. Steel met skin, and she kept still, terrified that his hand would move and she'd feel the blade slice deep into her flesh.

The bearded stranger had a much younger companion. His son, perhaps—a child who might have seen ten summers come and go—also carried a knife. Meng glimpsed his thin, nearly gaunt face and saw that he seemed as frightened as she. His eyes were wide open as the older man hissed at him to search her for hidden money. The boy hesitated, and the man used his free hand to cuff him on the side of the head.

Tears welling, Meng tried to stay still as the boy reached inside her coat, pressing against her robe, searching beneath her arms and back. She felt his hands on her bound breasts and closed her eyes at the sensation, suddenly nauseated. Shaking her head, she bit her bottom lip, forcing herself to remain silent, horrified that her identity might be discovered. The boy's hands lingered on her chest but then dropped toward her belly and tugged at her hidden satchel. She had tied it to her waist but the bearded man used his blade to cut it free. Holding it above her, he seemed to gauge its heft, lifting it up and down. He stuffed the satchel into his robes, then reached for her sword, pulling it away from her. Without thinking, she started to rise, but again his knife descended, pressing against her throat. Closing her eyes, she fell back, shaking her head, moaning softly.

The bearded man bound her hands and feet together, connecting them near her belly, so that she was trussed like a pig destined for slaughter. A cloth was stuffed into her mouth. Terror overwhelmed her then, and she screamed, the fabric muffling her cry. The man bent down and struck her hard in the stomach. Suddenly she couldn't breathe. She gasped, writhing on the muddied soil, trying and failing to draw air into her lungs. Though she sought to pull the cloth from her mouth, a rope kept her hands and feet together. She rolled to her right, desperate for air, finally managing to spit out the fabric. Gasping, she turned to her back, letting the rain fall on her face, sobbing now, racked by shudders.

Meng expected to see her assailants, but they had vanished, taking her satchel and her sword. She tried to pull her hands free of the rope but couldn't move them. Her feet were equally immobile. Weeping, she saw that her umbrella and kite still rested near the tree. Wincing from discomfort, she awkwardly rolled toward them, desperate for shelter. Once beside the tree, she struggled against her bonds, thrashing like a fish pulled from water. Yet the man had wrapped the rope around her wrists and ankles so many times that it was impossible to loosen. Meng longed to cry out for help, but doing so might not only invite a savior but also a murderer. Whoever heard her plea would likely realize that she was a woman, a discovery that would place her in imminent danger.

After struggling against the ropes until her wrists were raw, Meng finally stopped trying to escape. She inched under the umbrella, positioning herself so that it covered her face and chest. Someone would find her in the morning. Most likely they would free her, and she could once again pretend to be mute.

As a safeguard against just such a robbery, Meng had slept with half of her coins in her right shoe. She had some money left, at least enough for a few meals. As long as a person of good character rescued her, she wouldn't be forced to beg. She could make it to Fan. She'd be gaunt and haggard, but mostly unbroken. And he would bring her back into the light, mending her as he did his walls.

While the rain continued to fall, Meng's aches started to subside. But then she abruptly vomited, shuddering miserably, moaning into the mud. When at last her body no longer convulsed, she rubbed her lips against fallen leaves, weeping. Not only did she feel as if she had been physically beaten down, but her spirit suffered as well. She was exhausted from trying to be strong, to deny the chains that had been cast around her the moment she had exited the womb. Right now she didn't want to be strong. She longed to be weak, to have someone carry her away to a place of warmth and comfort. Maybe men were right. Maybe she was feeble and of little consequence. She certainly didn't feel like much of anything. She couldn't even last a day on her own without some sort of disaster.

Her tears caused her vision to blur. A sense of loneliness pressed down so hard on her that she found it hard to breathe. She panicked, sobbing, wanting to call out for help but unwilling to do so. The night was too dark for goodness. Whatever walked within it now surely must be evil. Somehow she would have to endure the storm alone.

To keep herself from falling deeper into a pit of hopelessness, Meng thought about her mother, wishing that they could walk along a road together, with no fear of repercussions. She wanted to show her mother so many things—how a road could disappear into the distance, how a stream could feel so good against aching, blistered feet.

Meng's breathing slowed. She stopped shuddering. Rolling onto her back, she looked up into the darkness, raindrops falling against her face. Her chaffed wrists burned, and she started to once again lament her condition, but then forced her mind elsewhere, thinking about the thin-faced boy who had been made to rob her, pitying him, believing that the famine had likely required his family to steal to survive. She'd seen his eyes when he searched her and knew that whatever innocence remained in him had died that night. He had been forced to become someone he was not. Perhaps the older man had as well.

Meng wondered what she would do if her family was starving, if her sons and daughters wept and writhed from empty bellies. She couldn't imagine ever pressing a knife against someone's throat, but innocence would leave her as well, soon a memory that would only give her angst.

Though Meng had always tried to be good, she wondered if circumstances sometimes forced decent people to be bad. Perhaps she was naïve to think that one could always choose between right and wrong. Maybe strenuous moments in life didn't allow for choice. Maybe choice was one more luxury for the rich and fortunate.

Yet her assailants hadn't killed her. So some good must remain in them. And if her coins allowed the boy to eat, to survive the coming winter, Meng would never regret the night's happenings. She was still alive. She would reach Fan.

Shivering, she curled up under the umbrella, her wrists and ankles aching but tolerable. The realization of her assailants' misfortunes, oddly enough, prompted strength to flow back into her—slowly at first, like the light of dawn embracing an open field. For so many years she had doubted herself, afraid that her station as a woman would limit her horizons, her thoughts. But what she hadn't understood was that countless others, including sturdy, resolute men, also had fears and limitations. She was no different than they. She would never sit on a throne or even wear a red robe, but she didn't need to bow to the misfortunes or inequities of life. She could walk forward, most likely never to be seen as an equal to men, but at least on a path of her own making.

The rain fell. From time to time Meng tugged at her bonds, but they remained immobile. Still, she did not panic. The sun would once again be reborn, filling the sky with color and promise. Whatever arrived with it, she would face without regret or reluctance.

Though the rope held her tight, Meng didn't feel like a prisoner. For the first time in her life she understood what it was to be free.

✶

Ping imagined that the room felt like the inside of a cloud might—full of smoke, warmth, and wonders. He lay on an old, four-poster bed, a cotton sheet pulled up to his chest. Beside him slept a low-ranking courtesan he had met on a previous trip. She was twenty-two and liked to laugh, a trait that had immediately drawn him to her. It seemed to him that his country brimmed with infinite numbers of solemn men and women, and discovering her had brought a temporary joy into his life. After they had first met, he'd spent three days and nights in her room, burning through his money as if it were kindling, but uncaring of the cost. She had been worth it.

After his argument with Meng, Ping had headed straight to the pleasure house. A part of him had wondered if he'd purposely disagreed with Meng so as to give him a reason to separate from her. She would never understand his need to rush to the pleasure house, to lose himself in the arms of a woman he hardly knew.

Ping believed that sometimes he had more in common with strangers than he did with his own family. The courtesan understood him. She didn't expect him to be someone he wasn't—unlike his father, who years earlier had all but forsaken him after he failed his imperial exam. He'd studied hard, missing high marks by the narrowest of margins. Still, he had failed, and his father had shunned him. No matter what Ping accomplished in the following months, it was never enough. So one night he'd simply left, stepping outside his ancestors' home and never looking back.

Once Meng had walked away, Ping had hurried in the opposite direction, worried that the courtesan wouldn't be present. But she was, and, better yet, she'd remembered him. After giving her madam the rest of his money and half of his salt, he and his temporary companion had eaten, drunk rice wine, and smoked opium. While she retired to her quarters he bathed in a communal washing room, scrubbing himself until his skin was so wrinkled that his hands looked like those of an old man.

Ping had drifted to her room, the opium seeming to lift him skyward. His aches and worries gone, he celebrated the moment, undressing her with patience and curiosity. He told her that she was a rose wrapped in silk, and she smiled at his attempts to woo her, reminding him that he was a thief and not a poet. She'd been with poets, she said, and they bored her with the weight and self-importance of their thoughts.

After undressing her, Ping had traced his fingers along the contours of her body. For a moment, he imagined that she was Meng, but he forced the image of her away, still buoyed by the drug. Meng had left him. He would never see her again. And so he kissed the woman beside him, his lips alighting on her shoulders, neck, and breasts. She ran her hands over him, teasing him with her nails, prolonging moments of ecstasy. As they began to move together, to rise and fall with unplanned but perfect rhythms, he left the world of stone and water, traveling somewhere distant, shattering into a million gleaming pieces.

Now, as he stared at the ceiling of her room, he felt as if he had fallen down and down, plunging back into a life that he had not intended to live. Though the opium was still partially within him, it had also retreated, leaving him groggy and lethargic. For a while he listened to the courtesan sleep. Her breathing seemed remarkably heavy for someone so lovely.

Ping thought of the night under the boat. He had also listened to Meng breathe, though the sound of air escaping her lips had been almost impossible to detect. Even wet and cold, she hadn't complained of the conditions and had been able to fall asleep. The night had been much longer for him. He'd remembered his failing of the imperial exam, his father's harsh words, and the story of the otters.

Rubbing his brow, Ping wondered about Meng's whereabouts. They had separated fairly late in the day, and she couldn't have gone far, even if her anger at him had propelled her onward. But how high had her ire climbed? All he had done was to try to look out for her. She hadn't been eating enough. The candy would have given her strength. He had been happy to give it her, but she'd turned on him so quickly.

His courtesan would have eaten the candy. She would have laughed at the theft. But Meng was different. She expected more from him. She wanted him to be better. Not for her sake, or even the sake of others, but for his own well-being. The previous day, she had told him that she didn't think any thief could ever truly be content, because true solace couldn't be gained by exploiting a fellow man. At the time, Ping had laughed at her, but now he wondered if she was right. For twelve years he'd lived by using his wit to plunder, and while he'd always seemed happy, perhaps that happiness was an illusion, much like the woman beside him. She had entertained him for a moment, perhaps even made him feel loved. But if he was truly loved, why would he even need to seek out her companionship?

A thump sounded from a nearby room. Ping blinked, his eyelids heavy. He wanted to sleep but continued to think about Meng. Where was she? Had she finally eaten? Did she have enough money to visit an inn and escape the cold? Also, why did she want him to be better? Did she see something in him that everyone else, even his parents, had missed?

Ping turned to his side, away from the woman. With luck, Meng would be resting comfortably, safe within a sound structure of wood and tile. But she was an inexperienced traveler and might have been caught in the rain. In that case, she'd be alone, wet, and vulnerable, both to the elements and to men who would hurt her.

Cursing himself, Ping sat up. His heartbeat quickening, he got out of bed, dressing in silence, afraid of waking his companion. He had planned to steal something from the pleasure house to pay for a meal the following day, but he resisted the urge to glance around her room for valuables. Instead he pulled on his boots and reached for his sword, belting its sheath above his hips.

Glancing at the courtesan, he dipped his head in thanks, then moved to her door. Its hinges were well-oiled and made no noise as he opened it. Stepping into the hallway, he sighed in relief when he saw that no one else was present. Sliding forward on his feet, so as not to produce any sound, he moved toward the pleasure house's entrance. A guard would be stationed outside, though he cared little for any such man. Yet he didn't wish to encounter the madam, as surely she would delay him with questions.

Outside the pleasure house, the night was black. Fine, infrequent raindrops collected on him. A guard stepped forward, inquired as to his intentions, but Ping paid the man no heed. He strode ahead, following a bricked path illuminated by smoke-stained lanterns. The city slumbered, its houses and buildings partially lit shadows. Ping walked, then ran between them, weaving his way toward the main road. Soon he was on it and further increased his pace, using his right hand to try to keep his sword from flapping against him.

A growing sense of loss surged within Ping. He had abandoned Meng as his father had abandoned him. She'd been nothing but honorable and kind. She believed in him. And now, because of his weakness, she might be in danger.

Running at full speed, Ping left the city behind. His boots created deep imprints in the mud, threatening to pull free with each step. Yet he ran as he never had, his left arm pumping, his right continuing to hold his sword hilt. Sporadic lightning flashed to the north, partly illuminating the trail. Ping looked for fires and other signs of life, but the wilderness appeared void of everything but swaying trees and looming mountains. A strange vacancy seemed to have descended into the world, and he began to dread that Meng was dead. The night was simply too empty to have her in it.

Grunting, Ping ran onward, occasionally shouting her name, uncaring of drawing attention to himself, of any danger he might face.

He'd wanted to be a scholar but was a thief. He hoped to have pleased everyone but had failed everyone. Worst of all, he'd failed

Meng, who maintained faith in him when no one else had.

Unlike many of his countrymen, Ping wasn't superstitious. Nor had he ever believed in fate. But as the night seemed to drop down and engulf him, he wondered if he was meant to meet Meng.

Perhaps it was their destiny to save each other.

*

Just before Fan was thrown over the parapet, Bataar had run at Yat-sen, begging that his friend be released. Two soldiers had grabbed his arms, pulling him backward. Bataar had screamed as Fan was tossed into the night. He fought to try to get to the edge of the wall, but the soldiers dragged him away. Though they followed Yat-sen's orders and took him inside, they weren't cruel to him, even as he fought against them. Rage overwhelming him, Bataar kicked the *Go* board aside, casting black and white pieces throughout the room. Spinning around, Yat-sen cuffed him hard on the side of the face, splitting his lip. As he spat blood, the soldiers tied him up, subduing his continued efforts to run toward his friend.

Bataar had been dropped in a corner of the room. Yat-sen had left. For a while Bataar struggled against his bonds but finally gave up. No one told him anything about Fan. The men picked up *Go* pieces and sipped on rice wine. They said nothing, perhaps ashamed of their commander's actions. To Bataar, time passed achingly slowly. He was desperate for news about Fan and pleaded with the men to free him. Unable to imagine his friend hurt or perhaps dead, Bataar worked to untie himself, pulling at his bonds with his teeth. He wept as he struggled, his tears cool against his face.

Finally Li appeared. Yat-sen's second-in-command said nothing but strode toward Bataar, a knife in his hand. For an instant Bataar thought that Li was going to kill him and tried to pull away, but the big man grabbed his wrists and, with several flashes of his blade, cut his bonds. Folded over Li's wide shoulder was a rope ladder. Bataar nodded to him, then rose to his feet and hurried outside.

Rain still fell, though with less ferocity than it had earlier in the night. Bataar rushed to the northern parapet and called out Fan's name. No reply was given, and Bataar pleaded with Li to hurry. The officer started to affix the ladder to the side of the wall, and even before he was done Bataar grabbed the ropes and began to climb down, terrified that his friend was dead. He leapt when still several paces from the ground and tumbled, falling to his side. Immediately he got up. "Fan!" he shouted. "Where are you? Can you hear me? Please answer me!"

Bataar glanced around him and started to run in one direction but paused when he heard his name. He turned and stumbled along the wall, heedless of the muddied, slippery ground. Someone was sitting with his back against the stonework. Bataar rushed to him, dropping to his knees and hugging him, squeezing him tight. "Fan!"

His friend smiled, holding him at bay with his right hand. "You came."

"Of course I came!"

"My arm. You have to be careful of my arm. It's broken."

"Is that all?"

"I think so."

Bataar laughed, hugging him again. "That's nothing! Half our boys break their arms learning to ride. It will heal."

"It doesn't feel like nothing."

Still smiling, Bataar stroked his friend's forehead. "I thought you were dead. I was so afraid, and I couldn't do anything. Yat-sen tied me up. I called and called for you, but I couldn't move."

"I'm fine. Thank you for coming."

"But what have you been doing down here in the rain?"

"Thinking."

"Thinking? About what?"

Fan leaned forward. "About how I've had enough of this wall," he whispered. "About how it's time for us to leave."

Bataar smiled again. "You were right."

"How so?"

"Beating him in *Go* wasn't such a great idea."

"True enough. But we beat him. And we can beat him again."

Glancing up, Bataar saw that Li was slowly making his way down the ladder. Aware that they only had a few moments left to whisper, he again stroked his friend's forehead. "You can't die, Fan," he said, shaking his head. "I don't want you to ever die."

"Someday I will. But not until you're too old to ride a horse."

"Then you'll live forever."

Fan reached forward to grip his hand. "I knew you'd be the first to come for me."

Bataar bit his bottom lip, holding back sudden tears. "When I saw them throw you … I wanted to catch you. But I couldn't. I'm so sorry. It's my fault that you beat him, that he hurt you. Please … please forgive me."

"It's not your fault. Not one bit. Your faults wouldn't even fill a single drop of rain. And look how much it rained tonight."

Shaking his head, Bataar once again hugged his friend, forgetting about his injured arm. He held him tightly, not letting go, even when Li arrived, his sword unsheathed, his eyes scanning the night. The big man nodded, then leaned down to help Fan up.

Bataar rose to his feet. A part of him wanted to focus on Yatsen, to let his hatred give him strength. But he was so grateful for Fan's survival that he couldn't hate. Instead he walked to Fan's left side, pressing his hands against Fan's hip, trying to aid Li's efforts to support him.

The Mongol boy and the Chinese officer walked on either side of Fan, half carrying him to the ladder. He thanked them as he placed his foot on the bottom rung.

Bataar feared that Fan would fall, but Li climbed right behind him, supporting his ascent. They rose as one, nearing the summit, the stonework that both protected and caged them.

Only when Fan struggled over the parapet did Bataar realize that he had grown to love him. Not as he did his father or mother, but as someone who made his world a better place, who would stand by his side when everything else was collapsing.

When war came to the wall, as Bataar believed it would, he'd have to protect his friend from his people. But despite his boasts of strength and courage, he knew his limitations. No one could stop the bloodshed that would arrive, least of all a boy who only felt at home on the back of a horse, riding through tall grass, delighting as he seemed to rise up, over his fellow man, leaving so much ugliness beneath him.

CHAPTER TEN

The Price of Freedom

South of Jinshanling—October 19, 1549

Within her dream, Meng felt hands pull her toward an unseen destination. She resisted the movement, struggling to remain immobile, not wanting to go where strangers asked. It was time for her to walk in a direction of her making. For most of her life she'd done what was expected of her—bowing low to men of stature, keeping within her home's shadows, pretending that she was nothing when she was something.

The hands continued to shake her. Meng felt herself slipping out of her dream. She opened her eyes.

Though darkness still dominated the landscape, brighter colors had started to infiltrate the sky. A man knelt beside her, holding her, whispering something. She started to struggle against him, writing in his grasp. As he spoke, shards of rope fell away from her wrists. Her hands were freed, as were her feet. Still, she raged against him, her fists pounding into his chest. He didn't release her but wrapped his arms around her, repeating a single phrase.

"It's Ping."

"No!"

"I'm here. And I've been looking for you."

"Leave me alone!"

"Meng, it's me—Ping. You're safe."

She stopped fighting, finally focusing on his face. He smiled and a joy brought from recognition flooded through her. Hugging him, she squeezed him with all of her strength, pressing her brow against his chest. Tears dropped to her cheeks, and she felt him stroking her back, whispering that she was fine, that he wouldn't leave her again.

"Please, please forgive me."

Her breath came in gasps. She shuddered against him.

"What happened?" he asked. "Were you … hurt?"

Her mind flashed back to the previous night. She shook her head, which remained against his chest. Though her body ached from being restrained for so long, and she was chilled to her core, her thoughts cleared. "I was robbed."

"They didn't realize you were a woman?"

"The boy, maybe. But not his father."

Ping sighed. "How long were you tied up?"

"I don't know," she answered, still trembling. "But once they left me, I wasn't as afraid. At least I tried not to be afraid. I tried to be strong."

"What a fool I was to leave you. My father called me that a hundred times. I never believed him until I was running through the darkness, looking for you. But he was right—any sense I was given I lost long ago, maybe that day when I fell from a ladder and knocked myself out."

Meng squeezed his hand. "There's still a bit of sense in you."

"If so, it's not much more than a pebble rattling around in a bucket."

"That sounds about right."

"What did they take from you?"

"Half of my money. And my sword."

"The sword we can live without. The money will be a problem, especially if I can't use my few talents to steal."

"We?"

He stood up, extending his hand. "I'm taking you to the Great Wall. I won't leave you again."

Gritting her teeth at the pain brought by movement, Meng rose to her full height. She rubbed her cold hands together, stomped her feet, then stretched her arms and legs, which tingled and ached. "I should go on alone," she said, looking away from him. "It's only a few days' journey. I'll be fine."

He shook his head. "I know you don't need me, Meng. But I need you. If you'll have me, I'm yours. At least until we find your husband. Then I'll go my own way." He smiled, adjusting his sheathed sword. "Now that I know what to look for, maybe I can find a few other women pretending to be men. I can guide them, though of course I won't enjoy their company as much as yours."

"Why not?"

"Because there's only one of you."

She thought of the many women she knew, women who had never traveled beyond Beijing, who obsessed over the smallness of their feet. "You're wrong about that, Ping. But I'll walk with you, if you'd like."

As he gathered up her few remaining belongings, she removed her right boot, dumping her hidden coins into a pocket. He laughed at the sight, took her pack, and bowed low. "We'll see the wall by tomorrow," he said. "It's not far."

"Why, Ping? Why did you come back for me?"

He shrugged. "I was ... disenchanted."

"You were in a pleasure house, and I'm sure that no part of you was disenchanted."

A bird called from a treetop. The sun had risen and was infusing the world with color, chasing away the darkness.

"Did you know, Meng, that you're also a thief?" Ping asked, strapping her pack to his back.

"How so?"

"You force words from me; you steal my thoughts and make them yours. In fact, you're a better thief than me, because what I steal is worth a few coppers. What you steal is priceless."

"Your thoughts are priceless? A moment ago you were calling yourself a fool."

His mouth opened but no words came out. He then smiled. "Maybe I should have left you tied up. I didn't run so far to be humiliated. I could have easily done that somewhere else."

"But you still haven't answered me, Ping. Why did you run? Why did you come for me?"

He started to walk toward the road. "If you must know, Empress of Thieves, I came for you because … because you believe in me."

She paused, waiting until he turned around to face her. "Of course I believe in you. Even more now, after you ran so far to rescue me."

"It was a long way," he answered, smiling. "My feet still hurt."

"I hoped you would come."

"I'm sorry it took me so long. The opium muddled my brain."

"But still, you came, muddled brain and all. Thank you for that."

A bevy of soldiers galloped down the nearing road, their weapons and armor glistening. The men seemed to hurry and headed north, toward Fan. Meng wondered if the Great Wall was under attack. Without thinking, she increased her pace, passing through trees and into the clearing that accompanied the thoroughfare.

"I want to tell you something, Ping," Meng said, rubbing her sore left wrist, still chilled and in discomfort.

"What?"

"I know you think that I give away too much of my money. That I'm careless with it, especially when I have so little left."

"Well, it is your money. I can't say that I agree with the way you spend it, but I'm sure you could also say the same for me. After all, I haven't ever seen you give a courtesan a bag of coins."

"Be serious, Ping. I'm trying to explain something to you."

"In that case, I wish you good luck. It's nearly an impossible undertaking."

She sighed. "Last night, when I was tied up, I thought about what you said. You're right in that I have given a lot of money away. I've tried to help people. But what I don't think you understand, Ping, is that I'm also helping myself."

"How? You're handing out money that could be used for food, for shelter, for entertaining your faithful and gallant traveling companion."

"Because I don't like to think of Fan as being all alone on that wall. I want to think that someone's helping him. You're looking after me. I'm trying to help a few children who I meet along the way. But who's looking after Fan? Who's making him smile and not feel so alone? I'm afraid of him being alone, of no one caring for him."

Ping swatted at a mosquito, then resumed his pace. "I'm certain he's not alone. He's been there a long time. Surely he's made a few friends."

"But maybe if I help people, someone will do the same for him. Maybe there's a balance to life, to fate."

"Maybe, Meng. But don't kill yourself trying to find one. You can't help anyone if you're dead."

"Will we find him?" she asked, stepping toward Ping's side.

A smile graced his face. "I'm glad that you said 'we.'"

She nodded, moving closer to him. "We're friends, Ping. And whenever we walk a road together, it will always be 'we.'"

*

The terrace atop the watchtower was empty of people save Yatsen and Fan. Nearby, banners rippled in a strong wind. A cannon protruded through a notch in the parapet, aiming toward distant emptiness. Near the horizon, a hawk circled, looking for a kill among the bushes and low trees. Autumn was now in full form, and leaves ranged in color from yellow to orange to red. Interspersed throughout the deciduous foliage were low pines, which dotted the landscape with patches of green.

Fan studied the northern frontier, thinking that it looked the most beautiful in the fall. The mountains rose and fell like a series of colorful waves upon an endless, sparkling sea. Soon winter would arrive, and the land would grow bleak. But for now it was a brilliant tapestry, so far removed from the cold, wretched place that he had inhabited the previous night.

Standing with his left arm in a sling, Fan waited as usual, for Yat-sen to speak. The commander was dressed in his red armor and held a spear with both hands, its butt resting on the stonework near his feet. Though some men might have harbored thoughts of revenge toward Yat-sen, had he ordered them thrown from the wall, Fan still blamed himself. If he hadn't won in *Go*, if his pride hadn't needed fulfillment, he wouldn't have been hurt.

According to the surgeon who had set Fan's bone, it was fortunate that the break had been clean and would mend well. The man had wrapped Fan's forearm in bandages soaked in healing oils, then had placed a thin and flat strip of iron on either side of the break. Again, he'd wrapped the arm, though this time with a coarser fabric. Finally, he used a brush to paint the outer fabric with a paste that soon dried and hardened.

Though the surgeon had prescribed several drugs for his pain, including opium, so far Fan had resisted taking any medicine. He was afraid of dulling his mind, as he knew that dealing with Yat-sen would require his full attention.

"Why did you finally decide to try to beat me?" Yat-sen asked, his voice hoarse.

Fan shrugged, flinching at the pain brought by movement.

"Tell me," Yat-sen added.

"Our wager. I wanted to set the boy free."

"He'll never go free. Surely, Craftsman, you must know that. As long as we fight the Mongols he'll remain here."

Fan nodded. "I was naïve."

"Yes you were. And you paid the price for it."

"I didn't ... know that I could win. You're still the better player."

"Maybe. Maybe not. In time we'll play again."

Fan tried to straighten his back, pain emanating from his forearm to his shoulder. His entire left side still ached from his fall. As Yat-sen glanced to the west and east, perhaps instinctively looking for smoke signals, Fan wondered how bodies like his, so weak and feeble, could shape stone into the Great Wall. The fortification was a testament to man's intellect and resolve, he decided, not his physical strength.

"I underestimated you, Craftsman," Yat-sen said. "I won't make that mistake again."

"Of course you won't."

Yat-sen coughed, then spat over the parapet. "I regret the rise of my temper. Not because you broke your arm, but because I can't afford to lose you. I want that observation tower built, and you're the man who will build it for me, broken arm and all."

Fan nodded. "I'll build it. I promise. And the boy will help me.

I need him to accomplish what you want."

"The boy is a game piece that I hold, not you. Fail me again, deceive me again, and he'll cease to exist."

"I won't fail you," Fan replied, turning toward Yat-sen.

"We'll play *Go* again. Soon. But if you play beneath your abilities, I'll see that as one more deception and he'll suffer the consequences."

A cannon fired. Both men turned toward the source of the noise but saw nothing to give them alarm. A sudden gust of wind tore at the nearby banners. As Yat-sen once again studied his surroundings, Fan thought about Bataar, wondering how they would sneak away. Surely Yat-sen had ordered someone to watch them. That person would need to be fooled, to be confused in a moment of chaos or disbelief. Fan was convinced that their best chance of escape lay during a Mongol attack. But he didn't know when or from where such an assault might come.

"Do you understand pride, Craftsman?" Yat-sen asked, turning toward Fan.

"I think so."

"I don't believe that you do, because if you did, you wouldn't have dishonored me in front of my men. The Black Rider dishonors me, and so he'll die. My men hunt for him, lay traps for him, as we speak. Soon I'll catch him and I'll hurt him—not by cutting his flesh or bleeding him to death, but by breaking his mind. I'll learn what he holds dear and destroy it. What do you hold most dear, Craftsman? The boy? Your wife?"

For the first time during their conversation, Fan felt fear sweep into him. The ache in his arm seemed to double. His legs weakened.

"Please don't … hurt them," he said, his voice unsteady. "I'll do as you ask."

Yat-sen smiled, removing something from within his armor. The morning sun illuminated an envelope. "A letter from your wife," Yat-sen said, stroking the paper with his thumb. "It arrived last week. I've read it more times than I can count. I feel as if I know her as well as you do; her every hope, her every thought. She's a bright girl, fearless in her own way. What she treasures in you, I'll never know."

Fan extended his right hand, which trembled. "Please. May I please have it?"

"Why does she love you so much? What have you done to make her feel that way?"

"I don't know. But … but I've always loved her."

"Yes, she says as much, time and time again. That you loved her from your wedding night forward, that you held her unbound feet and spoke of your contentedness."

"Please give me her letter. I haven't heard from her in so very long."

"I know where she lives, Craftsman. She's another game piece in my grasp, not yours. I could use her in so many ways. But for now, I will keep her in reserve. Please me, and perhaps she'll not be exploited."

Nodding, Fan bowed low, continuing to hold out his hand.

Yat-sen coughed, then extended his arm, as if he was going to pass over the envelope. But he withdrew the gift, taking it in his hands and tearing it apart. He ripped and ripped, tiny pieces of paper catching in the wind, fluttering like leaves. After tearing at the envelope until only shards remained, Yat-sen walked to the edge of the parapet and tossed the remnants of Meng's words over the wall.

"I can treat flesh as I do paper," Yat-sen said, turning away. "Remember that, Craftsman."

Fan didn't watch Yat-sen walk away. Instead he dropped to his knees, using his good arm to reach for the few scraps of paper that remained on the stonework. He hadn't heard from Meng in so very long, and to be so close to her words, to her, overwhelmed him. Tears dropped to his cheeks as he lifted up the bits of paper, searching for her voice. He found a few words, a few strokes left by her hand, but these traces of her presence only served to deepen the sudden despair within him. He clutched these discoveries in his fist, next to his heart, and ran to the wall, looking over it. The wind tugged at the few visible pieces of paper, sending them tumbling into distant stones and bushes. Fan cried out, looking for some sort of ladder, a means to bring himself to her. But no such bridge existed—at least not here.

His tears still falling, Fan spun around and ran toward the interior of the tower. He stumbled, banged his injured arm against a wall, but hurried ahead, awkwardly descending a rope ladder. After rushing through the lower level of the tower, he emerged onto the main part of the wall, running toward a cache of supplies that contained another ladder. He opened the box, which was empty. The ladder had been removed.

Finding it hard to breathe, desperate to hear from her, Fan ran to the edge of the wall that was nearest to the watchtower. He scanned the ground for Meng's words but saw nothing.

The wind had carried her away.

*

Glancing at the faraway wall, Chuluun clicked his tongue, guiding his horse forward. Its neck, shoulders, and hips were covered in small handprints, left by his daughters. The previous morning they had pressed their palms against wet clay and then his stallion. The gray clay contrasted with the black stallion, creating a highly visible collage of prints.

Chuluun and his wife had watched their daughters decorate his horse. As the girls laughed and experimented, Chuluun sharpened his wife's cooking and cleaning knives. Once the horse was completely covered in handprints, the girls turned their attention to their father, ignoring his concerns as they applied more clay prints to his armor and helmet. Chuluun laughed at their determination, glad that they were strong willed. When finished with his armor, they hurried to him and his wife, damp hands seeking cheeks and foreheads.

As Chuluun rode his horse toward the wall, he thought of his daughters, grateful that their brother's death hadn't ruined them. Each bore scars brought by his departure, but each had also learned to once again laugh and play. They had one another, a simple fact that gave Chuluun enormous solace. His daughters would survive, someday becoming wives and mothers, living as their ancestors had. Their lives would be hard, but not bereft of joy.

Chuluun worried far more about his wife. The loss of her

firstborn had aged her, slowing her movements, stooping her shoulders. A woman who used to enjoy walking, during recent months she often sat, weaving more than was necessary, staring toward the south. While Chuluun's sadness had transformed into rage, her loss had doused the fires that once burned within her. She was vacant. And though she had only said as much on one occasion, he knew that she blamed him for taking Bataar to the wall, for his fate.

The distance that Chuluun felt from his wife was present in part because he believed that she would never forgive him for the loss of their son. In her mind, his determination that Bataar be the best horseman and fighter had led to his death.

Though Chuluun wanted to restore her to her former self, as well as to be forgiven in her eyes, he usually lacked the vigor to heal the wounds that he'd inflicted upon her. Upon returning home from the southern front, he gave most of his remaining energy to their daughters. Whatever passions he had, they consumed. To his dismay, little of his strength remained for his wife. He had failed her, he knew, and some failures couldn't be redeemed.

Covered in handprints, Chuluun had left his family, his jaw clenched. His daughters had chased him down the trail, asking him to bring them something from the south, as if he might magically vault over the wall and return home with an armload of treasures.

As his daughters had chased him, Chuluun wondered why the Chinese bound the feet of their women. He couldn't imagine his girls confined to small spaces, unable to run or leap. While it was true that the Chinese were far more advanced than his people in terms of medicine, agriculture, weaponry, architecture, and science, he couldn't understand why bound, crippled feet would be desirable to any man. His daughters were strong. Certainly they would have a place within the homes of their husbands and much would be expected of them, but they would never be treated as if made of porcelain.

A sudden gust of wind buffeted against Chuluun's face. He glanced at the distant wall, then his stallion, smiling at the handprints. Studying them carefully, he tried to determine which was left from each of his daughters. The cleanest, most precise prints were likely from his eldest. The messy prints must have been from his youngest. Imagining their faces, he patted his horse's neck, his hand falling on a small print.

The wall stretched to the east and west like a white line that had been cut into the colorful horizon. In only a few days, his people would throw themselves at it, at first to the east, drawing defenders away from the true prize—Yat-sen's command post. Then several thousand of the Mongols' best riders would attack the two towers, killing every defender, securing the towers against Chinese reinforcements while many more thousands of Mongols poured over the wall between them. Chuluun would be at the head of the main charge, his goal, his supreme need, to face and kill Yat-sen. Once the Chinese commander was dead, Chuluun would interrogate one of his officers, learning where Bataar had died. He would find his son's bones and return them to his homeland, leaving him to rest on a summit that overlooked grazing horses.

Thinking of carrying Bataar to the site caused Chuluun's eyes to tear. He shook his head, trying to focus on the distant wall, imagining how the battles would unfold. His commander had asked him to once again scout out the area, looking for the best approaches, the easiest terrain through which to move two armies. He had also been ordered to hide caches of arrows at several positions near the wall. His horse carried large, leather satchels full of arrows that Chuluun would empty once darkness fell. He was to stash them at landmarks near the wall, so that any Mongol knocked from his horse would know where to arm himself.

The wall loomed, growing larger with each step his stallion took. Because he knew the Chinese feared him, Chuluun slipped his longbow off his back and notched an arrow. He was now close enough to the fortification to barely make out individual defenders. Red banners rippled in the wind. As it always did, the sight of his son's killers ignited a sudden hatred within him. He wanted them all to burn.

A cannon fired, followed by another. Chuluun was well out of range, and the smoking balls of steel crashed into the soil fifty paces ahead of him. He held up his longbow and shouted, calling the gunners cowards in their own tongue. No reply was given, nor did the cannons fire again. Time passed slowly. Chuluun tugged his reins to the right, forcing his stallion to turn west. Opposite his position, a red figure appeared at the top of the nearest tower. Chuluun shouted again, defiantly raising his longbow. He tried to count how many defenders were on the wall, though he knew that most of the Chinese were in the towers. Hidden within the stone, their numbers were impossible to guess.

Wishing that Bataar rode beside him, that they were hunting an antelope, Chuluun closed his eyes. He tried to remember his son's voice, his scent, his touch. But no such pleasures entered his consciousness. Instead he smelled gunpowder and felt only the rhythmic trotting of his stallion.

"In three days I'll find you," Chuluun whispered. "I'll bring you home."

His fists clenched as he turned the stallion toward the wall. Again a cannon fired. This time the soil erupted closer to him. He pulled back on his reins, provoking jeers from his enemies. If the attack hadn't been planned, Chuluun would have charged his foes, drawing back on his bowstring and sending death into the air. Instead he dropped from his saddle, tied his mount's reins to a stunted pine, and walked toward a boulder. He placed one of his carved horses onto the boulder, positioning it carefully.

Chuluun sat down, his gaze on his carving. He would await here until darkness. Then he'd ride toward Yat-sen's tower and complete his duties.

His mind wandered, traveling to his wife and daughters. He saw their faces, their smiles.

What he didn't see, what he was too far away to see, was that the wall's defenders were throwing loops of rope to the ground.

They were laying a trap for him.

*

The soldiers were on foot and had formed a barrier across the road. Each wore armor. Some carried sheathed swords while others leaned on spears. There were at least twenty of the men, most of whom had beards or long mustaches. Approaching travelers had formed a line in front of the soldiers and stood quietly, patting their donkeys or shifting on their feet.

"Our noble heroes are taking bribes," Ping said, grabbing Meng's shoulder, forcing her to stop. "Anyone who fails to pay them will be turned around."

"Bribes for what?" Meng whispered.

"For keeping the road safe. But that's just what our heroes say. Any copper handed to them will be spent on wine and women."

"We don't have anything to spare. Can we go around?"

Ping smiled. "How you make me happy. My humble humanitarian wants to break the law."

"Only because they're breaking it."

"Come. Follow me."

Meng turned and walked behind Ping as he headed off the road and into the forest. She remembered running through it, getting chased by thieves. Then a second memory unfurled—a vision of being tied up as a knife was held against her throat. Her pace increased. She looked from tree to tree, her gaze settling on potential ambush sites. The forest here was thick and damp. Colorful leaves covered the ground. Birds squawked. Freshly disturbed dirt lay outside burrows. The river was nowhere to be seen.

Her mind settled on Fan. She was only a few days away from him. What would he look like, she wondered, after so long? How would he react to her arrival? Surely he'd be stunned, but he would also realize that she came in secret and that her true identity must not be revealed. She hoped that he'd be able to leave the Great Wall for several days. Perhaps they could travel to a nearby city and rent a room. Were that to happen, she wouldn't leave that space, no matter how small, until she must. She'd hold him, whisper to him, and the discomforts of her journey would be rendered meaningless. If fortune smiled upon them, she would become pregnant, as the timing would be right. Some people believed that a coupling made on a mountain or by a stream provided a better chance at conception than one occurring within a city's polluted environs.

"Do you want to be a father?" Meng asked, moving to Ping's side.

"I'm afraid I wouldn't be much good at it. My father wasn't. So how would I know what to do?"

"You'd know."

"I know that I'm frightfully hungry, that my feet ache. Right now those thoughts test the limits of my mind. It doesn't have room for imagining what it might be like to be a father." He stopped and reached into his coat, producing a porcelain flask. It was capped with a cork, which he pulled out and held between his fingers. "Care for a dash of rice wine?" he asked. "It helps in vexing times like these."

"How did you get that?"

"I didn't steal it, if that's what you're asking. It was a gift."

Meng considered his offer. She had never drunk wine with any man other than Fan, nor was she supposed to. "I'll take one sip," she answered. "Just because my feet hurt too."

"Then sip and dance through the forest. Dancers make the best lovers, by the way. They move like swans."

"Don't seek to be a poet, Ping. It doesn't suit you."

He smiled as she sipped. "Be careful you don't taint yourself too much."

"It's good."

"Of course it's good," he replied, reaching for the flask. "I wouldn't give it to you if it wasn't." He took a long drink, then placed the flask back in his coat. "You walk like a man, drink like a man, and even think like a man. Are you sure you're not one of us? Maybe you've been mistaken all these years."

"Let's go."

"And you order me around like a man. You must be one. Either that or I've turned into a woman."

Meng laughed, increasing her pace. A faint trail led to the northeast. She followed it, aware of the wine in her system. The landscape seemed slightly more picturesque, its colors richer. She wasn't hungry for the first time all day. Nor did she notice the blisters on the tops of her toes.

The companions continued onward, the forest seeming to rise and dip with the contours of the land. To Meng's surprise a home appeared, perched beside a small lake. The home was decrepit, really nothing more than four half-broken wooden walls that leaned against each other. Unlike most homes in Beijing, this dwelling had neither a sloping roofline nor a single drop of paint. It had been hewn straight from the forest and looked as old as the land.

A man sat on a stump in a small clearing. His clothes were tattered and his hair and beard were white. Someone had beaten him, as the skin beneath his eyes was black and swollen. Dried blood also stained his clothes. Beside him were several bamboo cages that appeared to have been broken. Brown feathers were strewn about the area.

The old man made no movement as Ping and Meng approached. He didn't seem to see them. A small sword lay at his feet.

"Are you alright?" Ping asked.

The stranger shrugged slowly, his gaze unfocused.

Ping cleared his throat. "What happened to you?"

"My ducks. They took my ducks."

Meng turned from side to side, studying the area.

"Who took your ducks?" Ping continued. "Soldiers? Thieves?"

"Men."

Ping reached for the hilt of his sword. "When were they here?"

"Yesterday. They left my rice. Take it if you want. I won't need it."

"Why not?"

"My ankle … it's twisted. I can't move. If I can't move, I can't collect my ducks. I won't last the winter."

"I thought they took your ducks."

"Some. But some escaped. Ducks are good at that."

"Why does every old man I meet talk in riddles?" Ping asked, throwing up his hands in frustration. "Does someone teach you this new language? How can I learn it?"

"Just leave me. Take my rice and go."

"We're not going to take your rice. Stop saying that."

"Take it."

"Stop!"

Meng tugged on Ping's sleeve, pulling him toward her. Rising on her tiptoes, she whispered into his ear, "Can we collect his ducks?"

"I don't know. Can we?"

"Can you what?" the old man wondered.

"Can we find your ducks?"

"It's not so hard."

Ping cursed, then removed his pack. "How does one find a duck? Do you call to them?"

"You walk toward them with your hands outstretched, carrying food, singing softly."

"Are they ducks or lovers?"

"Just ducks. But treat them like lovers."

"My lovers don't have feathers and beaks."

The old man smiled, grunted as he stood up, and limped into his home. He reemerged a moment later, grimacing, though he held a small burlap bag. "Open your hands," he said. "Cup them together."

Meng did as he asked, watching him pour grain onto her palms. She kept her hands pressed tightly together. He gave Ping some grain as well, then explained how to walk to the far side of the lake and lure the ducks by singing and holding out the grain. After they appeared and fed, they could be picked up and returned to their pens.

As Ping grumbled about their task, Meng followed him to the far end of the lake. Though she was only a few days' journey from Fan, she didn't mind the delay and was pleased that the detour had brought them to the old man.

"We didn't even look at his ankle," Ping complained. "Maybe it's not even twisted."

"And I suppose his face wasn't beaten either."

"How does one sing to a duck anyway? Do they enjoy ballads? Or dancing?"

"Something soft, I'd think."

"We should at least take one for our troubles. I haven't had roasted duck in many moons. My stomach aches at the memory."

"We're not taking anything."

The end of the pond was thick with reeds. Much of the foliage had browned and fallen over, but plenty of cover remained. Meng and Ping walked to the edge of the water, avoiding numerous black droppings.

"Go ahead," Meng said. "Sing."

"You sing."

She laughed, spilling some of her grain. Thinking back to her childhood, she drew a deep breath and then gave life to a lullaby that her mother had sung to her when she was ill. Aware that the old man might hear her, she sang quietly, though her words carried across the water. She had always believed that she was unskilled at more things than not but had also been aware that she'd been blessed by a beautiful voice. Light and constant, her melody seemed to rise upward, taking flight on invisible wings.

The ducks came. There were seven of them, two males and five females. They emerged from the reeds and headed straight toward Meng. Surprised, yet pleased, she crouched down, extending her hands. The ducks entered shallow water, waddled forward, and dipped their heads toward her cupped hands. Resisting the urge to step back, she laughed as their long bills pinched her palms. They fought for position, several heading to Ping once he settled down.

Soon the grain was gone.

"How do you carry a duck?" Ping asked. "Won't they bite?"

"He didn't seem to think it was hard."

"That's because he's crazy. He wouldn't think flying was hard either."

Meng reached for one of the larger ducks, then lifted it out of the water. It didn't struggle against her, even as she cradled it against her chest. After repeating the process with a smaller duck, she headed back toward the old man.

He smiled when he saw her approach, struggled to his feet, and lifted the top off an unbroken pen. Meng set the two ducks within the pen, then headed back toward the lake. She passed Ping, grinning as three ducks thrashed against him. He cursed her.

After lifting up the final two ducks, Meng returned to the old man's home, setting her load within the now-full pen. Hobbling on his bad foot, the stranger secured its lid and thanked them. Meng bowed to him, preparing to leave, but he reached out and squeezed her forearm.

"You'll want my eggs, dear," he said, his smile revealing only three crooked teeth.

"Dear?"

"You're a woman pretending to be a man. I may be old, but I'm not a fool."

"But—"

"Don't worry. I won't tell anyone." He shuffled slowly into his home, disappearing from sight. A thumping emerged, a bang of wood against wood. Finally he reappeared, carrying a small box that was filled with moss and four eggs. "The thieves missed my eggs," he replied. "They always do."

"Maybe you should hide your ducks too," Ping said.

"They're usually in the pond," the old man replied. "But I can fatten them up better in their cages. Once a week they sleep with me."

Meng crossed her hands, refusing the box. "You should eat your eggs."

"I've eaten a thousand eggs. A million. Now that you've returned my ducks, why would I want these four?"

"Are you sure?" Meng asked.

"People think that the old can't hear," he answered. "That we're all as deaf as stones. But not me. The rest of me might have fallen apart, but my ears are still young. And I heard your song, your voice. What a beauty you are."

"I'm no beauty."

"If you're not, then neither are those mountains around us." He handed her the box. "I had a daughter once. You remind me of her. So be careful out there. She wasn't. Neither was I. So you be very careful." He handed her the small sword, which she tried to give back to him, but he forced it beneath the sash around her waist.

Meng shifted her weight, her gaze meeting his. "How else can we help you?"

"You've caught my ducks. You've given me another winter. And you've reminded me of my girl. What more could I need?"

Ping, who had been repairing one of the broken pens, rose to his feet. "We'd better go," he said. "We still have a long way to walk."

Meng shook her head. "But what about him?"

"As soon as you leave I'll butcher these ducks and dry the meat. I'll hide it well. Without the ducks, no thief will waste his time with me."

"And in the spring? What will you do then?"

"The ducks will come again. They always do. I'll sing to them and feed them grain."

Meng glanced toward the trail, then back at the old man. "Are you sure we shouldn't spend the night?"

"It will rain tonight," he said. "No one will smell my fire, my birds. So go find yourself a warm, dry place. Eat my eggs and think of me no more."

Nodding, Meng said good-bye, then followed Ping as he walked away from the lake, back toward the road. She carried the box of eggs carefully, singing softly, hoping that her voice would remind the old man of happier days.

*

Yehonala's room was a cocoon of sorts, largely unaffected by what was happening in the outside world. Though nightfall had arrived, darkness wasn't seen. Though rain had started to soak the land, wetness wasn't felt. Sometimes laughter, music, or the smoke of opium pipes seeped through her walls, but for the most part, her room was its own sanctuary.

A new, four-poster, canopy bed occupied the center of the space. Made from a dark hardwood, the base of the elaborate bed was two feet off the ground. Three of its sides were dominated by a web of geometrically patterned wooden rails. Four graceful posts supported a semi-open roof that was draped with wide bolts of red silk.

The bed had been a temporary gift from Yehonala's madam. An older courtesan's freedom had been purchased by a wealthy scholar, and once the girl was gone, Yehonala received her bed, which the madam believed brought luck to whoever slumbered upon it. Yehonala had been pleased with the addition, which gave her even more stature. She'd lain on it for two days and nights, awaiting Yat-sen's return.

He now rested in the middle of her bedding, on his stomach. A short time earlier, a noted physician had visited Yehonala's quarters, deftly inserting dozens of acupuncture needles into Yat-sen's legs, buttocks, back, arms, shoulders, neck, and scalp. He'd been complaining of his aches, and Yehonala's madam had immediately sent for the physician, who was used to such summonses.

Once the physician had inserted his needles, Yehonala had asked him to leave. She was capable of removing the thin instruments and wanted to be alone with the patient. Besides, the physician was beneath them both in stature and had no place in her room.

Now, as she sat beside Yat-sen, she admired her nakedness in the mirror across the room. Though fearful that one day her breasts and stomach would sag, she knew that she was in her prime. As any poet would profess, however, time was fleeting. Soon she must secure her future with Yat-sen. He was better positioned to free her than anyone else. He probably even loved her.

"Do you feel better?" she whispered, running her fingers alongside his thigh.

"Much."

"I'll pull them out soon. But in this one thing, we must be patient."

"And where should we be impatient?"

She leaned closer to him, letting her long hair drop to his buttocks. "I want out of this prison. You must buy my freedom or I'll go mad like every caged creature does."

"I will," he replied, then stifled a cough. "My request to build a tower in the wasteland has been approved. Soon I'll have more silver than I'll know what to do with."

"You'll know exactly what to do with it."

"I—"

"Better yet, why not get a loan against it? Free me with the loan."

"No, it's better to wait. Otherwise tongues could waggle."

Yehonala sat up, her hair lifting above his skin. She moved toward the end of the bed, careful that her lotus shoes didn't scuff against the silk sheets. Several needles had been placed in the soles of each of his feet. She grasped one, twisting it slowly, pulling it out, and setting it on a black, lacquer plate.

"Wait too long, and I'll bring another suitor to this bed," she whispered, reaching for a second needle.

"Be careful, Yehonala. Be very careful."

"With the needles?" she replied, shrugging. "But of course."

"Anyone else who came here would die. And you'd share his fate."

She grasped a third needle, applying slight pressure against it, pushing it downward before freeing it from his flesh. "So sorry. That one was stuck," she said, moving to his other foot.

"People who play games with me do so at their own risk," Yat-sen replied, perfectly still.

"Who plays games with you?"

"The craftsman. He pretended to be feeble at *Go* when he was extraordinarily skilled. After he beat me, I had him thrown from the wall."

"Did he die?"

"Fortunately, no. I still need him."

She pulled out another needle, watching as a small drop of blood formed on his heel. Using her thumb, she rubbed the blood against his skin, thinking it matched the color of her bedding. "What of his wife?" she asked. "Has she been killed?"

"No, not yet. My man went to look for her, but she's gone. No one seems to know where. And since we speak of killing, I see that your madam still stands and plots."

"For how long has his wife been missing?"

"Six days. A servant said she left in the night. But he doesn't know where."

Yehonala plucked another needle out of his foot, considering possibilities. Perhaps the woman had gone to visit her ill mother. But if that were the case, why would she leave in secret? Why would she travel at night? No, she thought, there has to be another reason. Might she have a lover? Doubtful, as her letters to the craftsman were adoring. Of course, she might deceive him.

Yat-sen cleared his throat. "Maybe she's lost in an opium den."

"For six days?"

"It's happened."

"No, I've read her letters. Her mind is too keen for that world. She's strong, not weak."

"A man. Could it be another man?"

"She loves him too much to go astray. And no woman could leave her father-in-law's house for so long and expect to ever return. He must agree with whatever she is doing."

Yat-sen grunted, still unmoving.

Twisting a needle in the back of his thigh, putting slight pressure upon it, Yehonala weighed other possibilities. Could the woman be ill and seeking treatment? Might there be a problem with an impending child?

As she considered various scenarios, Yehonala moved about Yat-sen's body, removing more needles. The sight of his nakedness and several more drops of blood aroused her. She found herself pressing against the needles, hurting him ever so slightly. As she worked, she let her hair glide over him. Once his buttocks were free of needles, she leaned ever lower, brushing her hard nipples against his skin.

She reached toward his low back, then paused, straightening. "What if … "

"What?"

"Perhaps she travels to him. That would explain the secrecy, why her father-in-law would let her go."

"Impossible. No woman of her stature could make that journey alone."

"And why not?"

"Because she'd be arrested."

"Not if she looked like a man."

Yat-sen finally shifted, rising to one elbow. "But why? Why take such a risk?"

"Because she loves him. You've kept him prisoner for a year and she wishes to see him. What's so impossible about that? You can't go a week without seeing me, and you expect her to go years without him? Even when they're more in love than we could ever hope to be."

"How can you speak about their love? About what they have and what we lack?"

"We've read her letters. She doesn't speak to him with her mind, but with her heart. Don't you understand the difference? They give each other their love freely. You and I pay for it, each in our own way."

"Still, for her to travel to him seems … outlandish."

"So does your precious wall. And yet it's there."

He dropped back to the bed, and she began to quickly pluck the needles from him, tossing them on the plate. If she was right, if the woman was headed north, she could be intercepted.

"If she comes for him, they'll have to die lovers' deaths—another pair of sufferers for poets to immortalize," Yehonala said, pulling out the final needle. "You'll have to kill them."

"Why?"

"Because if you don't they'll run away together like true lovers do. And you'll be humiliated. Whatever honor you've restored will be dragged through the mud."

"Perhaps."

Yehonala nodded, helping to turn him over, hoping that the woman would come. She and her husband had grown to be a major distraction for Yat-sen. Yehonala wanted his sole focus to be on her.

"Lay a trap for her," Yehonala whispered, and kissed his lips. She slowly swept her nails against his skin, encircling his nipples then his navel. He grew aroused but didn't move. Again she leaned toward him, this time lifting his right hand to her mouth and gently biting his fingers, one by one, teasing them with her tongue. His breath quickened. His chest rose and fell.

"I'll never be truly yours until you free me," she said, her nails again gliding down, toward his privates. "I'll never love anyone until I'm free. Do you understand that?"

"Yes."

"I can't live in this cage. Everything about it is a lie. It makes me a lie."

"I understand. Please, let's talk of this later."

"I want to talk of it now."

"Why?"

"Because this place is slowly killing me. You must get me out of here. Soon."

"Why—"

"Buy my freedom or I'll die in flames. Buy it soon and I'll be yours. Fail me and my hate will be without end."

*

As it had so often that spring, summer, and fall, the rain strengthened as darkness spread across the land. No thunder or lightning accompanied it that night, but the incessant splatter of infinite raindrops drowned out every other sound. Along the Great Wall, the rumble was even more pronounced, as bricks, blocks, and mortar resisted the elements.

At the base of the wall, Chuluun crept, his black armor rendering him all but invisible in the moonless and starless night. He had finished hiding several stashes of arrows and now moved toward Yat-sen's watchtower, imagining how the coming assault would unfold. Ladders would be set against the fortification, which the Chinese would try to push backward. It would be up to Mongol archers to keep the defenders away from the ladders. Yet to accomplish this task, the Mongols would be forced to stand near the wall, well within range of Chinese cannons. The only hope of the Mongols would be to attack with near complete surprise. If fortune smiled upon them, their diversionary attack to the east would work, and many Chinese would rush to that part of the wall. Otherwise, the attack on Yat-sen's tower would be disastrous.

Drenched and chilled to the bone, Chuluun studied the landscape as well as the wall. The Chinese had removed trees, shrubs, and even boulders from the immediate area, stealing any sort of ground cover from an assaulting force. Attackers would be terribly exposed to enemy archers and gunners. Chuluun could see no recourse for his countrymen but to fight in the open, or to bring in portable barriers from which to stand behind and fire arrows. He wondered what could be built, transported on horseback, and quickly erected at the site of the battle. Though unskilled as a carpenter, several ideas emerged as he stood unmoving in the rain. As soon as he returned to his camp, he'd share the concepts with his commander.

The night was as black as any that Chuluun had seen. A few covered torches illuminated the wall above him, but their faint orbs were overwhelmed by the elements. As he once again crept forward, he thought he heard whispers and stopped, leaning against the wall. The downpour seemed to intensify as he listened to his surroundings, hammering at his helmet and armor like ten thousand miniature fists. His heartbeat started to quicken. Someone might have been moving above him, behind the wall's parapet. He heard a scrape of steel against stone, or at least he thought he heard it, but couldn't be sure, as his imagination might have been overly active. Still, he decided that he would back away from the wall, that he'd touched it one time too many.

Eying the dimly lit parapet, Chuluun took a deep breath, steadying himself. Moving as slowly as possible, he pulled his longbow from his back and then notched an arrow. He started to creep away from the wall, wishing he hadn't placed so much faith in the cover provided by the storm. Usually almost all the Chinese stayed in their towers during inclement weather, but someone was sitting or standing almost directly above his position, though he wasn't certain if that person was aware of his presence.

His bowstring taunt, Chuluun kept the tip of his arrow pointed just above the parapet. He continued to backtrack, unaware of the rain that assaulted him. Suddenly lightning flashed, revealing a dozen Chinese faces. They shouted, and Chuluun released his arrow. He didn't know whether or not it struck home, because something seemed to grab at his ankle, yanking him from his feet. He was spun to the ground, falling awkwardly in the mud. He stood up and tried to run away, but again, something knocked him down.

Chuluun realized that a rope was tight around his right foot. Cursing, he withdrew his dagger and cut himself free. Yet at that moment a single, unseen arrow slammed into his right thigh, spinning him around. He cried out in pain, struggled to his feet, and started to limp away. Drawing his sword, he shuffled through the darkness, aware that the Chinese were likely clamoring over the wall to capture him. He tried to run, but his wounded leg was unresponsive, and so he half dragged it behind him. The words of his enemies reached his ears. He debated turning to face them but decided that if he were to wait, he would be overwhelmed.

The voices came closer. Chuluun thought about his wife and daughters, imagining them asleep, warm, and dry. He then spun back toward the wall, his sword arm extended, his blade nearly invisible. It bit into something and a man screamed. Chuluun reversed his strike, swinging in the opposite direction. A deeper voice cried out. But then shadows seemed to leap forward, smashing into him. He dropped his weapon, was knocked to the ground, and struggled against the blurry figures. They tore off his helmet, gouged at his eyes, pummeled his face and stomach.

Terror swept through him—not a fear for himself, but for failing to avenge his son. With the terror came rage, and he managed to half stand, throwing men from him, fighting like a trapped beast, using his teeth and fingernails. Something smashed into his side, knocking the breath from him. He was forced back into the mud. The Chinese shouted as they fought, their own wrath empowering each strike.

He tasted blood, perhaps his own, perhaps that of his foes. Then the flat of a sword cracked him on the side of the head. He crumpled, falling face first into the mud. His attackers shrieked in triumph, stripping his armor, leggings, and boots from him. Soon he was naked and barely conscious. Men stomped on him, forcing him down. He thought that he would black out, but somehow his mind remained partially lucid. To his profound sadness, he wondered if Bataar had been captured this same way. Surely his son would have been screaming for him, begging for help that never arrived.

The Chinese dragged him toward their wall. He wished that death would come for him, but it didn't. Instead a rope was tied around his chest, beneath his arms. Unseen men hoisted him into the air. He was pulled over the parapet and dumped onto the stonework. There he lay still.

Chuluun's mind remained focused on his son. At least, once the Chinese killed him, the two of them would lie near each other. Perhaps their spirits would sense their closeness and reunite.

Though Chuluun hated the wall, if he was going to die, it was better that he die on it, as Bataar had.

A large shadow, or perhaps it was a man, came into view. A powerful voice emerged. Chuluun didn't resist the hands that bound him. He was tired of fighting.

His death would bring peace.

CHAPTER ELEVEN

Farewell

Between Jinshanling and Simatai—October 20, 1549

Chuluun awoke slowly, his subconscious reluctant to part with dreams of warmth and laughter. He tried to go back to the world that had enveloped him, keeping his eyes closed, willing himself to ignore the aches that assailed him. His wife smiled, his daughters skipped, his son stood on a white stallion. He stayed with his loved ones for as long as possible.

Finally Chuluun opened his eyes. He expected to find himself in a prison but instead was greeted with a view of his homeland. His captors had strapped him to a latticework of posts that rose from behind the parapet of the wall. He hung vertically as a vine might, ropes binding his wrists, elbows, chest, waist, thighs, and ankles to the posts. To his surprise, he saw that the arrow had been removed from his leg and the wound bandaged. A thick, oily paste had also been applied to abrasions on his face, knuckles, and knees.

Someone had taken care of him. Yet he'd also been strapped, naked, to the posts. He was perched directly above the wall's edge. The rain had fortunately ceased, and the morning was clear and fair. Chuluun had rarely seen his land from such a height and marveled at its beauty. The valleys and mountains were vibrant with the colors of autumn, far lovelier than any painting, carpet, or carving. He realized then that everything would go on without him. His wife and daughters would survive, finding pockets of joy in the landscape of life.

Though his captors surely sought to torment him, Chuluun realized that they'd unintentionally given him the most glorious of gifts. His land and his loved ones were worth dying for. He had always known that, of course, but now he saw so much. The wilderness of his father's father stretched into and beyond infinity.

Chuluun hadn't reached out to the spirits since Bataar had died, but now he whispered to his ancestors, asking if Bataar had also seen this view before he'd perished. As if to reply, the wind stirred, prompting Chuluun's eyes to water. If his son had looked to the north, had glimpsed the wonders of his land, perhaps loneliness and despair wouldn't have overwhelmed him. His land might have given him strength and solace.

Again Chuluun whispered to the spirits, his lips swollen and covered in paste. He prayed that Bataar had been reborn, that he was eying the same land. Perhaps, once Chuluun was dead, their paths might cross. They might ride together, not as father and son, but as friends.

Tears fell to his cheeks. Now that he was close to death, he wanted to follow in his son's footsteps. There was no point in lingering, in appeasing the Chinese. He would tell them nothing, resisting them until their blades drained him of life.

"Why do you weep?"

The question surprised Chuluun. He looked down to his left and saw a small man who stood next to Yat-sen. The Chinese commander was dressed in his red armor and held a long spear. The smaller man spoke again, repeating the question.

"I'm tired," Chuluun answered in his native tongue.

The interpreter translated his reply, turning to Yat-sen. The smaller man nodded as Yat-sen spoke, then bowed slightly.

"Your wounds have been treated," the interpreter said. "If you tell him what he wants to know, you'll be executed with mercy."

Chuluun looked north. He said nothing.

"Commander Yat-sen doesn't deal in torture," the small man continued, after conferring with his superior. "He believes that it's a stain on everyone's honor. And nothing is more important to him than honor. He will let the wind, the rain, and the cold break you."

"I was born in the cold."

Again, the Chinese men spoke.

The interpreter straightened. "He wants to know why you hate him, why you have tried to kill him so many times."

"What does it matter?"

"It doesn't. But still, he'd like to know."

"Tell him that he stole my son. He murdered my son when he

brought him here."

As the interpreter relayed the message, Yat-sen coughed and spat, placing his free left hand against his chest.

"He says that sons die in war," the small man said. "But that if your son died here, building our wall, then he died creating something infinitely more wondrous than himself. You should feel blessed."

Chuluun turned, straining against his bonds. "My son blessed me, and my people. Your wall is nothing more than a pile of stones. I've pissed on it a hundred times."

As the Chinese spoke, a gust of wind battered a nearby banner.

"My commander says that if that's true, then you've also pissed on your son. His bones are a part of this wall."

"Then I'll tear it down and bring him home."

The small man laughed, then spoke with Yat-sen.

"Do you know, barbarian," the interpreter asked, "why your people will never enter China?"

"Because we'd rule you."

"Because your blood is impure. You're nothing more than a breed of masterless thieves. Our emperor is wise to keep you in your wasteland. After all, if you can't kill a rabid dog, you keep at it bay until it dies of its disease."

"Your words or his?"

"His. Always his."

"Tell him that if he were the man he pretends to be, he'd cut me down and face me."

The interpreted shrugged and then turned to Yat-sen. They spoke at length.

"My commander says that it's easy for you to talk now, when you feel strong. But after a few days tied to our wall, you won't be so boastful. No one will come to change your bandage. No one will save you. And after you die, your body will be carried deep into China, far away from your son. You'll never rest near him but will be dumped into a pit of refuse, a site where you belong— where all Mongols belong."

Chuluun shook his head. "Tell him that my son was a better man than he'll ever be."

"Your son was a coward. He died weeping like one."

A gust of wind burst through the parapet's openings. Chuluun turned away from his captors, looking across his land. No more would he speak about Bataar with them. To mention his son to his killers was to dishonor him.

"Remember," the interpreter added, "tell him what he wants and you'll be executed with mercy. Resist him and you'll rot on this wall. You'll die the slowest, most desperate death imaginable."

Chuluun disregarded the words. Again, he whispered to the spirits, asking them to shelter his wife and daughters, to give them reasons to hope and smile.

Then he asked for the strength to not shame his people.

*

The road had begun to undulate, following the land's increasingly pronounced features. Fewer travelers and pilgrims were about, but greater numbers of soldiers and merchants were present. After all, the soldiers were needed to defend the Great Wall, and the merchants provided extra food, clothes, and comforts to the fighters.

Dawn had been a dull, listless affair, but the skies had slowly thinned and lightened. Rain no longer fell. Recent storms had stripped colorful leaves from many of the nearby trees. The leaves blew in the wind, skipping along the ground. The naked trees swayed like tall blades of grass, seemingly ill prepared for the coming winter. A few of them had already fallen over, their roots' grip on the soil weakened by floodwaters. Only the trunks of these trees remained—their limbs had long ago been chopped up and carried off to serve as firewood.

The mountains seemed to loom larger with each passing step. Ping expected to see the faint outline of the Great Wall at any moment and from time to time looked up, gazing ahead. He had to often slow his pace because Meng was limping. She'd said that her feet were blistered. Though he had wanted to stop and tend to them, she'd refused his advances, claiming that her wounds wouldn't worsen. Now that they were so close to the Great Wall, she didn't want to waste any time.

Ping's stomach rumbled. They had shared only a handful of roasted walnuts for breakfast. Between them, they had twenty coppers left—enough, perhaps, to make it to the Great Wall. But what Ping might do after their journey ended remained a mystery to him. He really had only two choices: to return to his thieving ways or enlist as a soldier. Though fighting the Mongols didn't interest him, a half-full belly did. Perhaps he'd spend a year standing on the wall, searching for men who would come to kill him. His vision was excellent and he was capable with a sword.

In any case, stealing from the weak and foolish no longer appealed to Ping. He wasn't sure why he'd undergone this change in perspective but knew that Meng had something to do with it. Unlike his father, she believed that he could be more than who he was. Greatness was probably beyond his reach, but decency wasn't, and he wanted to summit that plateau.

A group of people had formed ahead, on the right side of the road. Suspicious of any gathering, Ping took Meng's elbow and directed her toward the opposite side of the thoroughfare. He noticed that ten paces ahead an older man had taken the same action with a young man who was dressed in fine clothes—except the elder had rubbed his companion's hip before leading him aside.

"Boy love," Ping whispered to Meng.

"What?"

"The old man pays the young man. In that way the young man eats and the old man … well, he gets what he wants."

Meng nodded but made no other reply. The sight wasn't uncommon, and Ping wondered why he'd mentioned it. Meng had been unusually quiet that morning, and he realized that he missed her voice. Suddenly he wanted to hurry ahead of the gathering, so that he might once again talk with her in privacy.

The crowd neared. Ping moved to the other side of Meng, his hand falling to the hilt of his sword. His pace faltered slightly when he realized that people were staring at a line of at least ten hanged men. The men hung within bamboo cages, their feet far off the ground, their hands tied behind their backs, and their necks encircled by a piece of wood that was supported on all sides by the bamboo bars. Ping had seen criminals executed in this manner before and knew that the men had been lifted into the cages. After the wood had been placed around their necks whoever had carried them had stepped back. Usually the condemned would thrash and scream. The grip of the wood around their necks wasn't tight enough to kill them. Instead, death arrived slowly, excruciatingly.

A sign on each cage proclaimed that the men had been thieves. Ping shook his head at the sight, then noticed that Meng was slumping beside him. Her head rolled back, her weight shifted sideways. He caught her as she fainted, lifting her up and into his arms. She weighed much less than he might have guessed, and he wondered if it was hunger or the sight of the dead men that had caused her to fade.

"Maybe those men," he whispered, "hurt the old man. Maybe they stole his ducks."

She didn't respond.

He continued ahead, walking as quickly as he dared, wanting to put distance between them and the gathering. As he moved, he studied Meng's face, wishing that he could touch her cheeks, her lips. She looked so pale, and he longed to comfort her. Instead he gritted his teeth, briefly closing his eyes to steel himself.

"You're too heavy," he said. "Have you been readying yourself for winter? Stuffing your belly with all sorts of treats?"

She made no reply, though her eyes opened. She blinked, then appeared to recognize him.

"It's me, your humble servant." He stumbled over something unseen but continued to carry her. "If you're tired of walking, you don't have to pretend to faint, you know. Just order me to carry you. Use your sternest voice. Threaten me with all sorts of evils."

"I fainted?"

"You've been drinking more of my wine, haven't you?"

"But those men ... what happened to them?"

"They died quickly," he lied.

"Really?"

Ping nodded, then stopped. He would have liked to carry her for the entire day. But in his weakened condition, he was worried that he'd drop her. "I have to put you down. Otherwise, we may end up in a heap."

She allowed him to set her on her feet. He didn't let go of her though, continuing to grip her shoulder until she told him that she could walk.

"Why don't we rest?" he asked.

"Later."

Holding her forearm, he followed her as she moved ahead. She breathed deeply, as if trying to clear her body of the filth behind them.

"Thank you, Ping," she said, finding his gaze.

"I'd be lying if I said it was nothing. You nearly toppled me over."

She didn't smile. "Sometimes ... I'm ashamed of my country, of my people. We could be so much better."

He shrugged, once again noticing her limp. "You should rest before your feet fall off."

"I miss him, Ping. I want to be strong, but right now I really miss him."

Ping wasn't sure what to say. Her words stung. He had carried her, sheltered her, but now she thought only of her husband. "You'll be with him soon," he finally replied. "A few more days is all."

"Good. Because I'm tired. I'm tired of all the suffering. I need to see something that will make me happy."

An idea occurred to Ping and he squeezed her arm. "I'll show you that something. It's not far ahead."

"What is it?"

"I've walked this road before. I know its blessings and evils."

A galloping horse approached, ridden by a heavily armored soldier. Ping and Meng stepped aside to let them pass. The remainder of the road was empty, both to the north and the south. For the moment, Ping and Meng were alone.

"Come," he said. "It's not far."

"I thought you wanted me to rest."

"That was before you got all melancholy, a trait I deplore in a traveling companion. If I wanted to weep as I walked, I'd whittle onions."

"No you wouldn't. We'd make a fire and roast them."

He started ahead, walking toward a bend in the road, hoping that the medical dispensary still existed. He'd used it once before, when dysentery had struck him down. For generations Buddhist monks had run the operation, ensuring that the dispensary was filled with the proper medicines and staffed by a constant supply of doctors who donated their services. The dispensary gave free care to the needy, and Ping could only imagine how besieged it might be that day.

The landscape trickled past. Meng walked with a renewed sense of purpose. Ping spied a thin trail of smoke rising beyond the bend. His spirits lifted.

The dispensary, built just off the road, was as he remembered it—a series of small, one-story rooms near an old temple. In front of each room stretched a line of people. Monks clad in yellow robes held notepads and went from patient to patient, ensuring that people's names, addresses, and symptoms were properly documented. Once they reached the front of the lines, patients slid open a door to the rooms and entered, always bowing. They soon emerged holding a paper prescription, which they filled at a stand-alone structure that was farthest from the road.

The lines were populated by people of all shapes and sizes. Old and young were present. Women held babies or moved on handmade crutches. Men hacked and beat fists against aching chests. Many injured patients were present as well—farmers who'd been gouged by plows or kicked by donkeys.

Ping guessed that there might have been more than two hundred patients. "They all receive free treatment," he whispered. "The rich give the monks silver, which they use to buy the medicine. The doctors are all volunteers."

"Those children," Meng said, pointing to a screaming infant, "they'll get treated too?"

"Of course. Actually, that's what I like best about this place. The children are saved."

Meng bit her bottom lip, her eyes tearing.

"Wait here," Ping said. "I'll be right back."

She nodded but said nothing.

He walked toward the structure that held the medicine. Only a few people were in line. He stood behind them, waiting his turn.

When it soon came, a white-haired monk gestured that he come forward. The old man's face was deeply pockmarked, perhaps from some childhood disease.

"Where's your prescription?" the monk asked, his hand outstretched.

"All I need is some ointment for blistered toes," Ping answered. "My companion is in terrible pain, but we don't have time to wait in line. Our master is an impatient man. He'll have us beaten if we linger."

The monk stiffened, then nodded and shuffled inside the room. He soon emerged carrying a smooth stone and some small strips of cloth. On top of the stone was a dollop of glistening ointment. "Use this," the monk said. "But wash his toes first. Add the ointment, and then bandage them."

Ping bowed deep and low. "Thank you, sir," he replied. "Thank you for doing exactly what you do."

"I merely share what has already been given to me."

After reaching for the supplies, Ping returned to Meng. He asked her to follow him, and they walked away from the dispensary, the tumult of a hundred conversations fading into the distance. A trail appeared, branching off from the main road. Ping followed it, heading into a forest of nearly leafless trees. He walked until coming to a stream.

"Would you please wash your feet?" he asked.

At first it seemed that Meng might resist the idea, but, after an initial pause, she moved toward the water. Ping didn't watch her as she washed but sat down and tried to pretend that his stomach wasn't rumbling. It was a distant earthquake, he told himself. The land was famished, not him.

"I'm finished," Meng said.

"Take this," Ping said, handing her the stone. "Dab the ointment on your blisters, then wrap and tie these bandages around your toes."

"Thank you."

Ping would have liked to apply the ointment himself, to stroke it against her blistered flesh. But he knew that a woman's feet were sacred. He couldn't touch them without dishonoring her. Still, he was unable to resist glancing down, his breath catching when he saw large and open blisters on the top of each toe. Every step she'd taken that day must have sent pain rushing up her legs. Yet she had never complained.

Meng worked slowly, and from time to time, Ping looked down, following her progress. He saw her ankles, as well as the grace and beauty of her feet. He had never seen a woman's feet and his heartbeat quickened. Though he longed to kneel down and help her, he forced his gaze away, toward the treetops.

When she finally rose, he wasn't aware that she had even moved. But she stood nearly shoulder to shoulder with him. "My toes … feel better," she said quietly.

"Good."

"But that's not why I'm happy."

"Are you going to make me guess?"

"I'm happy because you reminded me about the good of my people. The sight of those monks gladdened me. It gave me strength when I didn't have any left."

"You have as much strength as any man. Perhaps more, much

to my dismay."

She reached for his hand, squeezing it. "I love my husband, Ping. You know that. But also know that you've crept into my heart as well. I wouldn't have made it this far without you. And I'll be forever grateful."

For once words fled from Ping. He was speechless.

She turned away from him, heading back down the trail. He stood still, closing his eyes, remembering the sensation of her skin against his.

*

His broken arm aching, Fan walked beside Bataar. They were ostensibly looking for cracks in the top of the southern parapet, but in truth, they sought safe places to talk. It seemed that the entire length of the Great Wall was abuzz with news about the capture of the Black Rider. Though neither Fan nor Bataar had any desire to see him in chains, they had heard that he was bound near the side of the wall. Soldiers of all ranks hurried toward Yat-sen's tower, eager to witness the humiliation and suffering of the man who had tormented them for so long. Saddened by the capture of his countryman, Bataar wanted to stay as far away from the spectacle as possible. Fan could hardly blame him, having no desire to watch Yat-sen gloat over the fate of a helpless man.

Pausing near a cracked section of mortar, Fan removed a piece of chalk from his pocket and circled the damaged area. He started to ask Bataar a question but stopped when four soldiers hurried toward them, presumably eager to see the Black Rider. The men rushed past, their sheathed swords banging against their sides.

Fan shook his head. "I'll miss him," he said quietly, rolling the chalk between his thumb and forefinger.

"The Black Rider?"

"I liked to watch him ride. He's the only person I've ever known to be completely unafraid of Yat-sen."

"How long will he last?"

"Not long. The nights are getting too cold. If it rains again he'll freeze to death."

Bataar flicked a pebble toward China. "A lot of my people aren't afraid of Yat-sen. And you stood up to him when you beat him in *Go.* You weren't afraid."

"You can stand up to someone, Bataar, and still be afraid of him."

"Do you think the Black Rider is afraid now?"

"Yes."

Bataar looked away.

Fan saw his friend slump and realized that he should encourage him. "I want to tell you something. Something important."

"What?"

"My year on the wall has been the hardest of my life. More than my arm has been broken here."

"You're not broken."

"I know. But that's because of you." Fan turned to Bataar, placing his good hand on the boy's shoulder. "I've wanted a son for many years, but I've failed myself and my wife. Yet you've changed things. You've given me a wondrous gift, because you're more than a companion to me, more than a friend. And though

I'm not your father, I'd be proud to call you my son."

A smile dawned on Bataar's face. He straightened, running his right hand along the top of the parapet. "And I'd be proud to call you my father," he replied. "Even though you don't know how to ride a horse."

Fan laughed. "You could teach me."

"And you'd try to learn?"

"For you? Of course."

Bataar's fingers raced along the stone, prancing like a stallion. "Maybe someday this war will end. My father and I could visit you then. We could teach you. We could teach your son."

"I'd like that."

"Or you could visit us."

Several more soldiers stepped out of the nearest watchtower and headed in their direction. Fan turned his attention back to the stonework, circling the section that already bore marks from his chalk. When the soldiers had faded into the distance, Fan turned again to Bataar. "We're going to escape soon," he whispered.

"How?"

"I'm not quite sure. But I'm close to knowing. And I'll tell you two things."

"What?"

"I'm going to steal a horse for you. Then, after you're free, I'll head south, and I'll steal Yat-sen's treasure."

Bataar's eyes widened. He glanced to his right and left. "How do you know he has treasure?" he asked, his words barely audible.

"Because one of China's great weaknesses is that many of its officials are corrupt. Yat-sen is given silver each month to pay for his men, for food, for material. But I've heard the men grumble about missing wages. And I've also learned the location of Yat-sen's house. Surely hidden within it is a horde of coins."

"You'll be rich."

Fan shook his head. "I'll just keep a little. He owes me that much. But the rest will go to the poor."

A crow landed on the opposite parapet beside a red banner that fluttered in the breeze. The bird squawked, shifted on its thin legs, then used its beak to pick at something deep in its feathers.

After glancing around to ensure that no one was near, Fan leaned close to Bataar. "Do you know why I'm telling you this?" he whispered.

"Because you know it will make me happy?"

"Because I want you to know that we're going to win, going to beat him in the grandest game of *Go*."

"If he catches us, he'll kill us."

Fan nodded, his mouth dry. He had two enormous fears in his life. One was that he would never see Meng again. The other was that his actions would lead to Bataar's death. Either outcome would slay him as easily as any blade.

"Are you as good a rider as you say?" Fan asked. "Truly?"

"Yes."

"I hope so. Because for what I have in mind, you'll have to be as swift as the wind."

Yehonala stood before a full-length mirror, studying herself. For not the first time in her life, she wished that her reflection was plain rather than beautiful. Had she been born with such a face she might not have been sold to the tea house. Instead, she might have been able to help her parents, allowing them to resist the poverty that later forced their hand. With luck, she would have married and borne fine sons.

Instead, because of her splendor, she was seen as a prize at even a young age. Her father must have always known that she could be sold. She could save his family if his crops failed. So she'd never been sent out into the fields to labor. In the fields the sun would darken her skin. Worse, she might become disfigured through an accident. Though her mother didn't have bound feet, she'd consulted with women who did. Yehonala's toes had been broken, her heels dislocated, at a very young age. She could still remember her screams, and being held still by her weeping mother. The bandages that bound her feet were replaced day after day, each wrapping tighter than the one proceeding it. Every session brought more shrieks, tears, and anger. At one point her right foot had become infected, nearly killing her.

In time her feet were as small as any.

Still standing before the mirror, Yehonala studied her lotus shoes. They were bright red with yellow, exaggerated stitching. The shoes might have been pure gold for how strongly they attracted men's stares. Yet none of her admirers knew what she did—that her feet were deformed, reeking incarnations of what had once been beautiful.

A woman's muffled laugh seeped through the walls of Yehonala's room. She could have gone to the communal area but hated its environs. Within its colorful confines men would seek to flatter her while women would pretend she didn't exist. It was far better, she believed, to wait in her room for Yat-sen. He was the man who could save her.

Yehonala walked to a rosewood desk near her new bed. She opened a letter that the craftsman's wife had written to him, her gaze passing over familiar and loving words. Shaking her head, she wondered how two people could find so much joy in each other. The knowledge that she couldn't relate to such love saddened her. She felt hollow and incomplete, as if her creator had forgotten to give her the very best of human emotions. She was a home with no roof, a field bereft of flowers. She was nothing.

Her tears dropped to the letter, staining it. A candle burned near the edge of her desk, and, without thought, Yehonala held the paper over the flame. It blackened, caught fire, and rolled up as if to protect itself. She held a corner of the letter until the last possible moment, dropping the charred paper to her desk. As smoke wafted upward, the flames dwindled, leaving ashes behind. She waited for the remains to further cool, then picked them up and patted her hands together. Though her exquisite turquoise robe was soiled, she paid it no heed. Instead she opened her fist above a small lacquer bowl that contained ink. Miniscule bits of ash fell into the ink. Yehonala rubbed her hands together, then wiped them on a nearby cloth. She used her ivory-handled writing brush to mix the ash with the ink. When satisfied that the two components were now one, she reached for her leather-bound notebook, leafing through its filled pages, ignoring poems that she'd written months before, when she still thought herself capable of love.

Finally she came to a vacant page. She leaned closer to her desk, dipped her brush in the gritty ink, and began to write. Her poem took shape swiftly, seeming to create itself.

Mirrors
Are liars,
Purveyors of untruths.
True wilderness will never come to these woods again.
They have been stricken of light, of soul.
A courtesan's beauty is said to be ephemeral—
A cherry blossom in the spring.
Yet beauty is a feeling,
Not a scene on silk.
Lacking love,
There can be no beauty.
Lacking beauty,
There can be no me.

Yehonala reread her poem. She set her brush down, carefully. Then she stood up and walked to her bed. She lay down and began to cry.

*

Chuluun didn't realize that he was such a prideful man until he had spent a day bound naked to the Great Wall. As soldier after soldier came to mock him, he closed his eyes, trying to ignore their taunts. Though no one hurt him, they laughed at him, spat at him, and insulted him in every conceivable way. It wasn't that their affronts overwhelmed him, but he felt that his entire race was being belittled. The men who had fought before him, the women who'd lived such hard lives, all seemed to somehow be represented by him, and his humiliation was a shared experience.

Seeing the men who had murdered his son rekindled the flame of hatred within him. Immediately after his capture, he'd felt vanquished and listless, but now, even in his weakened state, he longed to free himself, grab one of his Chinese tormentors, and leap from the wall, killing his foe and himself. Such a death would restore honor to his name and his people. It would show the Chinese that the horsemen would never surrender.

The previous night had been dreadful. Though it had never rained, the wind had been strong, chilling Chuluun so profoundly that even his bones seemed to beg for warmth. He'd been cold many times in his life, but even in those moments, as the rain or snow besieged him, he had been astride a warm horse. Heat had been shared.

The wind had cut through him during the night. He had been bound with his arms and legs spread wide apart, so he couldn't curl up to warm himself. In the blackness he hadn't even been able to take solace in the sight of his land. Few stars had been out. At some point, when no guard was near, he'd whispered to his loved ones, telling them to seek out happiness, to please forgive him for his failings. Later he had reminded himself of the many good moments they had shared, of how his daughters had once sheltered a young falcon, of his wife's long-lost laughter, of how he had tied two of his fingers together and kept them bound for a full month, proving to Bataar that any task could still be done.

After a seemingly endless absence, the sun had finally risen. He'd trembled at the sight of it, his teeth still chattering. Though warmth did not arrive for some time, he felt somewhat rejuvenated. It was easier for him to imagine his loved ones in the light. He could envision what they were doing.

Now, as Chuluun studied the afternoon light, flies buzzed against his bloodied bandage. His leg throbbed from the arrow's bite. He no longer shivered, which he thought to be a good sign. Perhaps the wound wasn't infected. But he was unsure if he could endure another night on the wall. If it rained, he'd most likely die.

Chuluun wanted to live just two more days. He longed to see his countrymen attack, summit the wall beneath him, and bring death to their foes. Though certain that the Chinese would kill him at the first sign of the assault, he craved the possibility of seeing fear in their eyes. He would smile as their swords fell upon him, calling out Bataar's name so that his son would look for him, for surely, however Bataar had been reborn, he would hear the screams of his countrymen and come to celebrate their victory.

The sky was dark and ominous. As Chuluun wondered if it would rain, he saw Yat-sen approach on a magnificent stallion. The horse resisted the man upon him, snorting in frustration, rearing its head back. The small interpreter lurched away from the agitated mount, clearly ill at ease. For a moment, Chuluun imagined riding the stallion along the top of the wall, replete in his armor, his sword bloody and wicked.

"The commander wants to know how your night was," the small man said, moving to the edge of the parapet and grabbing one of the bamboo poles that kept the prisoner immobile. "Were you afraid of never seeing the sun rise again?"

Chuluun shrugged.

"Silence won't save you. Answer him."

"My people aren't afraid. You're the ones who hide behind stone."

"He says that's not true. When your countrymen are captured and suffer on the wall, they always end up being very afraid. Once they're broken, they tell him what he wants and then they die."

"I'll just die."

The interpreter conferred again with Yat-sen. He then cleared his throat. "Answer his questions and you'll be granted mercy. Your execution will be swift. Resist him and you'll suffer."

"The spirits grant me what they wish. His mercy? I spit on it."

"He asks me to say that once you're dead he'll find your woman. He'll make her his."

"As a pebble might try to tame a mountain."

"Perhaps a daughter then? You Mongols breed like rats so you must have daughters."

Chuluun shook his head, reminding himself not to talk about his loved ones with Yat-sen. They were so far above him that to think of them in his presence was to defile them. Besides, Yat-sen would never find them. The Chinese weren't strong or bold enough to travel far into the wilderness. They would never survive outside their walls.

The interpreter said something else, and the red shape of Yat-sen drew closer. But Chuluun ignored them. He watched a hawk soar above the wall, heading east. The bird rose up over a distant watchtower, disappearing from sight.

Chuluun kept his head turned to the right, away from his captors. He studied the wall as it stretched from him. Red banners rippled on its parapets and soldiers manned its cannons. Only two people moved—a tall man and a boy. They were an arrow's flight away and seemed to examine a series of wide steps. Perhaps some bricks had come loose. The man's arm was in a sling, so the boy seemed to do most of the work, tugging at something unseen. Chuluun wondered if he was a slave or an apprentice of some kind.

The pair of workers straightened and came closer. Because Chuluun didn't want to turn in Yat-sen's direction, he continued to study them, even as his captor spurred his great stallion away. They moved slowly, their faces downcast, their robes billowing in a gust of wind. The boy looked up. The sun caught his face, illuminating what had been dark, stealing the breath from Chuluun's lungs.

He gasped, then bit his bottom lip so hard that it bled. Everything but the boy disappeared.

Bataar was alive.

Chuluun closed his eyes, shook his head, and once again stared at his son, wondering if the spirits were toying with him, if he was envisioning a dream he'd had countless times over. Bataar's image seemed to swell and ripple, to explode into a thousand pieces of light and joy and love.

Yet the sight before him was no dream. Bataar stood, now facing north, staring at his homeland. Chuluun wept. His chest heaved. He found it hard to breathe. He wanted to shout out to his son, but even in the midst of his overwhelming euphoria he realized that to call Bataar's name would be to kill him.

Chuluun turned in the other direction. Such a profound relief flooded through him that his vision blurred and his strength failed. The world seemed to spin around him. He sagged against the ropes that bound him, bowing his head, mumbling his thanks to the spirits, over and over.

Though he was still imprisoned, though death would likely still claim him, Chuluun had been set free.

CHAPTER TWELVE

Wings of Dawn

Jinshanling—October 21, 1549

The second-to-last watchtower at the western end of Yat-sen's territory had been under repair for several months. Fan had earlier determined that the engineers who originally designed the tower had failed to adequately address how the spring runoff from a nearby mountain might create a seasonal stream that could ultimately reach the southern side of the wall. That year's flooding had created such a waterway, which while temporary, had affected the land beneath the wall, causing it to erode slightly. While the watchtower had been mostly unaffected, several troublesome cracks had appeared in the mortar.

Weeks earlier Fan had devised a plan to redirect any future spring runoff and had examined the tower from top to bottom. From time to time he visited the site to ensure that the improvements and repairs were proceeding to his liking. He now sat in one of the tower's interior rooms, hunched over a game of *Go*. Yat-sen had just beaten him in what was their closest game to date. The contest could have gone in either direction.

For the first time since they had started playing, the two men had battled against each other with no one else present. Yat-sen had asked for such a match, and Fan was happy to please him. He had tried to win until the very end, at which point, he made a series of almost imperceptibly passive moves. Yat-sen had then struck at the perfect moment, gaining territory and points. Fan had tried to counterattack, but the battle was lost.

Fan had wanted Yat-sen to win in the exact manner that he had. Wiping his brow of perspiration, he bowed slightly. "I'm lucky we wagered nothing," he said, gathering his game pieces.

"Pride is always wagered," Yat-sen replied. "Though you didn't lose much of it today. You played well."

"Thank you."

Through several open windows, the morning's light slanted into the room. Like so many of its predecessors, the day was gloomy. It had rained for some of the previous night, and the air felt damp and cool.

"How is your arm?" Yat-sen asked, nodding towards Fan's sling.

"Healing, I think. The surgeon doesn't expect any lasting damage."

"If your woman were here, Craftsman, how would she treat it?"

Fan started to speak, then stopped, aware that Yat-sen's eyes had narrowed. "She'd heal my mind first."

"It's broken?"

"It's lonely. And loneliness is a disease like any other."

Yat-sen coughed, stood up, and spat outside the window. "Everyone on this wall is lonely, Craftsman. What makes your needs any different?"

"I didn't say they were."

A gust of wind swept through the room, causing particles of dust to fill the air.

Fan looked back toward the *Go* pieces, trying to gather his thoughts. He'd silently rehearsed what he would say to Yat-sen, practiced which words might best open the doorway to freedom.

"The men are gloomy," he said quietly, touching his pieces, replaying the last part of the game. His heartbeat quickened. A drop of perspiration rolled down his chest. "But if you'd like to hear it, I have an idea as to how to please them."

"Speak."

"I've found the perfect site to build the tower you want, outside the wall."

"Where?"

"Not far across from our seventh tower is a mountain with a flat top. I'd build the tower there, as it would give us an unparalled view into the Mongols' land."

Yat-sen's brow furrowed. "I know this mountain. It might work. But what does that have to do with pleasing the men?"

Shifting on his short chair, Fan leaned backward, the wood creaking beneath him. He was afraid of saying the wrong thing, of Yat-sen's keen mind. But he had to do something. Otherwise he and Bataar would spend the winter on the wall.

"We know the men like to gamble," he finally replied, meeting Yat-sen's stare. "But let's give them something bigger than a game of *Go*. Let's give them a horse race—a race from the base of this wall to the top of that mountain. We give them that race, let them celebrate the victor, and then break ground on our new tower."

Yat-sen subdued a cough. "You'd have us celebrate on the barbarians' land?"

"Why not? As you've told me before, why are we the ones who always have to hide?"

"How long will it take to build that tower?"

"With enough men, two months. Keep the Mongols off my back for that long and the tower will stand."

"Tell me my duty again, Craftsman," Yat-sen replied, his hand dropping to his sword hilt, "and your head will grace this floor."

Fan bowed. "Forgive me."

"But your idea pleases me. We could have a race. We could piss in the faces of our foes."

"Yes. And if you'd like to wager against me, I have one more idea."

"The last time we wagered you nearly died."

Nodding, Fan lowered his gaze. "True. But this time I offer an honest bet. Let Bataar ride in the race. I think he'll win."

"The slave boy?"

"Put your best rider on your stallion, against him."

"He'd simply ride away."

"No he wouldn't," Fan replied, shaking his head. "If he rode away you'd kill me. And he won't be the cause of my death."

Yat-sen walked once again to the window. "If the slave wins, what do you receive?"

"Your vow that he'll never be harmed while he remains in your care."

"And if he loses?"

"If he loses, I'll give you my necklace. And I'll build you the best watchtower in the entire empire."

"You'll build that for me anyway."

Fan stood up. He moved toward Yat-sen, moved so close that it would be difficult for him to unsheathe and wield his sword. "I know, Commander, that your father died on that mountain," he said quietly, trying to subdue his rapid breathing. "That's why you command this section of the Great Wall and that's why I want to build the watchtower there. You're right—I'll build you the best watchtower in all of China regardless of whether the boy wins or loses. But I'd like him to win. I think he can win."

Yat-sen turned from the window to face Fan. "You play dangerous games, Craftsman," he said, shaking his head. "You make too many assumptions for your own good."

"I—"

"Because I want the tower, I'll let you live. And you'll have your bet. But the price of failure just increased."

Fan said nothing, his gaze low.

"If the boy loses," Yat-sen continued, "you'll give me the necklace, and you'll give me the tower. But build it strong, Craftsman, because you'll spend the spring and summer imprisoned within it. If it falls, so will you."

Fan felt weak. His arm ached. "And in the autumn?" he asked quietly.

"In the autumn, if you still live, you'll go free. That's our bet, Craftsman. The race will be as you say, a week from today. I'll see that the slave gets a good horse to ride."

"And … and to train? A ride on your horse, here on the wall, to train?"

Yat-sen chopped down with his right hand, striking Fan's injured forearm. The pain was instant and overwhelming, blinding Fan with its intensity. He crumpled to the ground, bending over, rocking back and forth in agony. "You ask for too much, Craftsman," Yat-sen said, shaking his head. "That disfigured half-breed will never touch my stallion, will never taint him. But I'll send a good horse his way. He'll get one afternoon to train."

Fan tried to speak, but only a moan escaped his lips. He nodded repeatedly, still rocking on his knees.

Yat-sen coughed, collected himself, and left the room.

His forearm still afire, Fan gritted his teeth, barely able to think.

"I'm finished with this place," he whispered. "No more."

In two nights there would be no moon. That's when Fan and Bataar would break out, when they would rush headlong toward a fate that would be either cruel or kind.

★

The Great Wall was a white line in the distance, following the summits of a ridge of mountains. The fortification looked unimpressive from so far away, little more than a crack in the landscape. But it loomed slightly larger than it had at first light.

Meng and Ping had been awakened near the road by four soldiers. The men demanded to know their intentions and, later, a bribe to ensure their safe passage. When Ping protested that they were down to their last few coppers, the men smiled and struck him, and Meng emptied her pockets. She'd given them everything.

With no money remaining, it made little sense to stay on the road. Though they might stumble upon a soup line, all the other food was overpriced and in high demand. The famine had ensured that the cost of everything had more than doubled in the past few weeks. While merchants ignored pleas from hungry travelers, beggars held out their upturned palms. Unable to help anyone and pained by the sight of so much misery, Meng had wanted to leave the road, despite the dangers of the forest. For once Ping hadn't argued with her.

The companions had walked for most of the morning on a seldom-used trail that led toward the Great Wall. The previous night's rains had left the ground damp. Fallen leaves had lost their color. Tree branches, now mostly naked, still reached and fought for sunlight. Few animals were about, as most species had been hunted to near nonexistence. At one point, Ping had contemplated cooking some snails that they'd found in a stream. But the discoveries seemed too small to bother with and had been tossed back into the water.

They had fortunately come upon a wild chestnut tree. Neither would have recognized it, but an old woman had been scavenging through the leaves, searching for fallen nuts. Once she'd explained to Meng and Ping what to look for, they had found several dozen of the spiky, husked prizes. Grateful for the information that had been shared with them, they had given her ten of their nuts, then proceeded to smash open the rest of their finds and eat the damp, nourishing interiors.

The chestnuts hadn't done much to quell their hunger pains but had given them some much-needed energy. They had continued heading deeper into the woods, talking in quiet voices, their hands always on their sword hilts.

Now, as they reached the summit of a low mountain, they paused to study the Great Wall. It appeared slightly more formidable than it had during their last break, stretching across the entire northern horizon. As she had many times already that day, Meng wondered where Fan was and what task he might be undertaking. She smiled without thinking, eager to reach him.

"You've been doing that all morning," Ping said, scratching his chin.

"Doing what?"

"Grinning like you passed your exams."

She wiped sweat from her brow. "I'm excited to see him."

"I know you're excited to see him. My old mule, Stoneface the First, would have sensed as much."

She turned to him, her smile still present. "Are you jealous, Ping the Petulant?"

"Of him? He's spent a year on that row of rocks and will probably spend another year on it. Why would I be jealous?"

Shrugging, she started to walk again, following the trail as it dropped toward thicker woods far below. "I'll find you a woman," she said, nodding to herself. "A good, strong woman who will stand her ground."

"I'd rather you find me a weak-willed courtesan who bends with the winds."

"No you wouldn't."

He slipped, then righted himself. "How do you know what I want? Is clairvoyance another one of your gifts?"

"Maybe."

"Then why does my stomach growl like a rabid dog? Why didn't you know those soldiers were coming before they kicked me in the ribs?"

"Maybe I did know they were coming. Maybe I wanted to go this way."

He muttered something beneath his breath, then added, "You're as clairvoyant as I am honest."

"Then I can see everything. You're a changed man, remember?"

He slipped once again. "Damn these boots. How are your feet anyway? Still blistered and bleeding?"

"I don't think so. You healed me."

"How do you even know where he is? The wall is endless. What makes you think you'll find him between Jinshanling and Simatai?"

"Because his letters tell me as much. That's where he's stationed."

"And you expect to just walk up, find him, and give him his coat?"

"I think—"

"But why so much trouble for a coat? You could have died. I could have died."

"We didn't. We won't. And I don't want him to be cold this winter. He could freeze to death up there. Thousands do each year."

"I think I liked you better as a man. You weren't so domineering."

"I was a lie."

He clucked his tongue. "I don't believe you're going all this way to simply give him a coat. There must be another reason."

She started to respond but slipped on a wet, exposed root and fell to her backside. Ping helped her up from behind, grasping her beneath the shoulders. She offered her thanks, then said, "I love him, Ping. That's my other reason. I want to see him."

"If you love him so much you should run away with him. Don't just give him the coat."

Stopping, she almost slipped again. "What do you mean?"

"Maybe give him the coat, but leave a letter in it. Say that you'll wait for him at a certain inn."

"I don't—"

"For once in your life, act like me, act like a thief. Only you'll steal him."

Meng stood still. She had imagined running away with Fan but had never considered actually doing so. The thought was both thrilling and terrifying. If they were caught, they'd be killed.

"Your coat might save him from the cold," Ping added. "But not from an empty belly or a Mongol's arrow. You should run away with him and never look back."

"They'd find us."

He shook his head. "Then don't think like them. Think like a woman and take him to a place that they'd never go."

An unseen bird squawked. Meng considered her options. A part of her was tempted to give Fan the coat and then quietly return to Beijing. But another part of her, the stronger part, pondered Ping's words. "Maybe you're right," she whispered, as if afraid of the statement.

Ping slipped, then straightened. "I know how much you love him. I can see it in your eyes."

"I think that—"

"Why not put those big feet of yours to good use? Take his hand and just start running. Run and run and run and don't ever let him leave you again."

*

A gust of wind tugged at Chuluun's long, unkempt hair. Still bound and naked, he turned away from the sun, looking east. That simple movement sent a wave of pain rolling from his head to his feet. He groaned. The ropes around his wrists, arms, legs, ankles, and torso weren't tight but, because of the pull of his weight, pressed hard against him. At first his extremities had tingled, but now they ached. His upper back throbbed, and he longed to lie down.

He hadn't been given anything to eat or drink in a full day. Yet it wasn't hunger or thirst that had nearly killed him the previous night. It had been the rain, which started after the moon reached its zenith and had lasted until almost dawn. The wetness brought such cold to him that time seemed to stop. He shivered, convulsed, and finally felt the life flowing out of him. If he had still believed that Bataar was dead he'd have let himself fall into an endless sleep. But the knowledge of his son's well-being kept him fighting, kept his heart beating. The only way he could stay alive was to move, and so he fought against his bonds, writhing like a fish in a net, never stopping. Though the ropes cut into his skin, the pain was a gift, as it kept him awake. At one point he started to sing, trying to remember his mother's words, aware that he must also continue to think, to force his mind into action.

Chuluun had been in dozens of battles, but the one he'd fought against the rain had been the most difficult and painful. The elements were a nearly irresistible force that beat him down with as much power as any weapon. He imagined that he was fighting, and had been knocked from his horse, time and time again. After each fall, he dragged himself up out of the mud and climbed back onto his saddle. When his enemies attacked him, he flexed his sword arm, envisioning Chinese warriors dying beneath his blows. Yet they always came back at him, their blades not steel, but ice. When it seemed that they would finally defeat him, he whispered his son's name and tugged at his bonds, his strength dissipating but still present. He would never surrender while Bataar lived, and so he continued to generate warmth by twisting and pulling and sometimes even shouting.

At last, when it seemed that he could endure no more, the rain had ceased. The skies had slowly cleared, revealing stars. Chuluun wept at the sight, still shivering and miserable, but believing that he'd live to see another sunrise. Dawn had been glorious, each shade of orange and amber impossibly vivid and profound. Chuluun had never seen such beauty, not even in the faces of his loved ones. The splendor made him feel as if he had died in the night and been reborn into a new and better world. The wall was still there. The ropes still held him. But something deep within him had changed. Suddenly he no longer cared about taking the lives of his enemies. Instead he wanted to find Bataar, flee to the rest of his family, and ride far away. His father had once told him that to die in war was his destiny, but now he wasn't sure. His sword had been bloodied on enough occasions, his ancestors made proud more often than not. Now it was time for different deeds, triumphs seemingly small in stature, but with his loved ones at his side. The evil that men made was often permanent, his father had said. But couldn't good deeds and joys also be eternal?

If he could endure one more night on the wall, he'd witness his countrymen's arrival the following eve. They would attack at a distant site, but once the Chinese had been diverted, the horsemen would throw themselves against Yat-sen's great watchtower. If Chuluun loosened his bonds and escaped right before their attack, he could find Bataar. In the ensuing battle they could flee north. The problem was that Chuluun wasn't sure if he could survive another night on the wall. Not if it rained. He was already too weak and battered.

Studying the sky, Chuluun looked for clues as to what the day would bring. A gathering of low clouds moved swiftly, which concerned him. Sunlight was intermittent. Though the air had warmed, he wished that it were dry. As it was, his nostrils filled with moisture. Rain would most likely fall, he decided, either later in the day or once again at night.

Though he was almost overcome with weariness and he wanted to sleep, Chuluun forced himself to stay awake. As he thought about his situation, he realized that two choices faced him. He could give Yat-sen a single piece of information in exchange for food or a blanket. Or he could escape that day and return when his countrymen attacked.

Aware that he would never betray his people, Chuluun decided to escape. He glanced to his right and left, saw that no soldiers were near, and began to work at his bonds. Soon he could tell that he'd loosened them in the night. Though he couldn't see behind him, the area was silent, and he believed that he was alone. He started to twist his right wrist. The rain had left the ropes damp and pliable. He strained against his bonds, clenching his teeth as he moved his right hand up and down, trying to stretch the rope. Barely healed wounds reopened, yet he paid them no heed. Instead he thought about Bataar, imagining how they would ride together, hunting deer instead of men, laughing instead of plotting. No moment would be wasted, no question unheard. Whatever Chuluun had left to give, he would give it to his son, daughters, and wife. The spirits had listened to him. They had sustained him through the night and shown him a perfect sunrise when he most needed to see it, when it could sustain him.

Chuluun wouldn't waste the spirits' gifts. He would love as he had fought, with boldness and passion. He would take joy in life, not death; rising upward, forever grateful for the return of his son. A new, better man, he would be, more tender and content. If the sun could emerge after such a long and wretched night, then so could he.

Feeling intact for the first time in more than a year, Chuluun continued to pull and twist with his right hand. A loop of rope loosened, slipping down his palm, over his fingers. He smiled.

ROCm

But then, from behind him, a harsh voice called out. A shadow loomed. He tried to protect himself as gloved fist swung toward his face. The blow snapped his head backward, smashing it into a bamboo post.

Darkness flooded into Chuluun, sweeping away pain, weariness, and even thoughts of his loved ones.

*

Only a few watchtowers away from his father, Bataar sat on a gray and black stallion. He still couldn't believe that Yat-sen had agreed to Fan's suggestion for a race. The previous night, standing on an open stretch of the wall, Fan had whispered the details of his plan to Bataar. There would never be a race, he said. Instead, they would soon escape under the cover a moonless sky. Fan had concocted the idea for a race so that Bataar would have access to a horse. If he was allowed to train on one, if the Chinese saw him riding, they would be less likely to question him during his escape.

Upon first hearing Fan's plan, Bataar had resisted, saying that he wanted to pit himself against the best Chinese riders, believing that he could beat them. His pride had overwhelmed his reasoning, and he'd pleaded with Fan to delay their escape. If he could beat the Chinese, he would have a story to tell his father, his people. That story would make his endless days on the wall worthwhile.

Fan's rebuke had startled Bataar. He'd never seen his friend angry, but Fan's face had colored with frustration. Once the race was over, Fan argued, Bataar might not ever again have access to a horse. He would remain trapped, forever at risk. The time to escape was now, and the race was of no consequence. What was victory, Fan reasoned, compared against a reunion with his family?

In the end, Bataar had agreed. Fan hadn't shared every detail of his plan but had said that they would both escape during the moonless night. Bataar was to be ready.

Now, as Bataar sat on his restless mount, he patted its broad neck, whispering its name. Nearly a dozen men were gathered around him. Fan was present, as was Li, Yat-sen's next in command. Li had been ordered to kill Fan if Bataar tried to escape and had his hand on the hilt of his sword. The other Chinese were in the process of lowering a ramp from the northern parapet to the ground below. A single Chinese horseman would accompany Bataar as they galloped in front of the wall. The ground was still damp, but Bataar wasn't worried about his stallion slipping. He'd promised himself not to ride too fast.

"Don't make me pull out this blade," Li warned, shaking his head. "I like our craftsman."

Bataar nodded. "So do I."

Soldiers began to grunt as they lowered the ramp using pulleys, winches, and ropes. Other men held bows and arrows at ready positions, just in case a Mongol war party was nearby and tried to ride up the incline. Two cannons were also primed and prepared to fire.

Out of habit, Bataar glanced to the west, then east, searching for smoke signals rising from the wall that would announce the presence of his people. The air was clear of such signs, however, still but for red banners that fluttered in the wind.

The ramp reached the ground. Soldiers then positioned a smaller, sloping platform on the inside of the parapet, allowing horses to reach the top. The Chinese rider carefully spurred his horse ahead, keeping a firm control on its reins. The ramp was about four paces across, plenty wide to accommodate a confident horse. But any mishap would send a mount and its rider plunging toward a likely death.

Bataar watched the other rider, ignoring the ache of his stomach. Neither he nor Fan had eaten anything since the previous day. The entire garrison of defenders was on half rations as the result of the worsening famine. The upcoming race, Li had told Fan earlier, was a good distraction.

"Show them how to ride," Fan said, smiling.

Bataar's pulse quickened. He nodded, holding his reins tight, his knees pressing against the stallion's sides. He tried to slow his breathing down until it matched that of his mount, then twisted slightly in his saddle toward the men behind him. "I'll show the spirits," he finally replied. "And they'll tell my father."

Fan stepped away from the ramp. "Good luck."

Focusing ahead, Bataar gently spurred his stallion forward, clucking his tongue. The animal stepped onto the smaller ramp, its hooves thumping on the thick wood. Bataar reached the summit, paused for a moment, and tapped his heels against the horse's ribs. The stallion snorted, resisting him. He repeated his command but this time was slightly firmer with his feet. The horse shifted its weight and took a step down the ramp, which featured raised cross planks so that hooves couldn't slip far.

The Chinese rider was waiting for him below. Leaning back on his saddle, so that most of his torso was nearly over the stallion's rear legs, Bataar again clucked his tongue in encouragement. His mount neared the bottom, increased its speed, and trotted onto familiar soil. Bataar couldn't help but smile at the other rider. It felt so good to be on a horse that he forgot all about Fan's plans of escape, his own hunger, or the moans of an ill soldier who had died in the night. In all the world, only this particular moment mattered. He closed his eyes, more aware than ever of the horse beneath him. It wasn't afraid. If anything, it was restless and ready to run.

"I'll race against you," the other rider said. "But not today. Today let's just ride."

Bataar nodded, using his thighs to grip his mount, raising his bottom over his saddle. He leaned forward. "Let's ride."

The Chinese soldier shouted, spurring his stallion ahead.

Laughing at the sight of the accelerating horse, Bataar nodded to himself, leaning forward and backward above his saddle. Suddenly he used the end of his reins to swat his stallion's neck. It lunged forward as if its legs were catapults that had been released. The horse's power surprised Bataar, pulling him back. He righted himself, kicking his mount as it sped into a gallop, the wall rushing past on his right side. Bataar could hear men shouting from above. He wanted to see them, and so he angled the stallion away from the stonework. Red banners and gleaming cannons flashed by. He called for more speed, free for the first time in many months, feeling as if he'd been reborn—lifted up from the muck and misery of life into an infinitely more wondrous realm.

The landscape flashed by. Forgetting his promise to himself to be careful, he kicked the stallion again, his body moving in perfect cadence to its movements, his cries in synchronicity with its snorts. He caught up to the Chinese rider, ignored his orders to slow down, and charged ahead, rising and falling over the undulating land, the wall a constant companion to his right. Never had he felt so unburdened; not even on hunts with his father or when he'd first been allowed to ride alone.

The stallion also wanted to run and Bataar released it, whooping for joy, everything a blur around him. Watchtowers passed like massive sentinels. Clouds drew closer. Out of the corner of his eye he saw the naked Black Rider but for once didn't pity him. The man had also known this same freedom. If he died today he would have lived a life that no one on the wall could equal.

Bataar pulled his reins slightly to the left, angling his mount away from the wall. For a moment he faced north and imagined what it would be like to simply ride away. In a short time he could be with his people, his family. He would be truly and forever free.

But if headed north, Fan would die. And no matter how great the temptation was to escape, Bataar would never betray his friend. He continued to tug his reins to the left, swinging the stallion back toward the wall, toward the distant ramp.

The Chinese rider was shouting at him, but Bataar didn't listen. He raced toward Fan, glad that his friend could see his true colors, his true self. On the wall he was often a frightened, helpless boy. Here he felt so much larger. Here he was a man.

His father would have been proud.

Meng and Ping had walked all day through the forest, the trail undulating with the land, though rising more often than not. The Great Wall became larger and soon dominated the horizon, its watchtowers plainly visible. Meng could understand why people said that it resembled a dragon. The fortification wasn't always graceful but was sometimes rather hunched and crooked, depending on the contours of the mountain ridges it followed. Never had Meng seen anything as impressive. The wall seemed to go on forever, endless and serene.

As they had headed north, climbing higher, the land had become more arid and desolate. The forest thinned, tall trees gradually replaced by short and scraggly evergreens. The soil was rocky and somewhat red. For no apparent reason, the trail abruptly ended, forcing them to navigate around crags, shattered boulders, and clumps of thorny underbrush. The going was difficult but manageable.

The companions had walked until sunset and, finally exhausted, had made camp within a cave that Ping discovered. Part of a mountain's rocky face had collapsed at some point, creating a fissure that was partially covered by jagged stone slabs. The cave had been used before by other travelers. In the most protected and flat area, ashes from previous campfires were deep and plentiful.

While Meng had gathered wood, Ping built a fire. They only had a few leftover chestnuts to eat, which they roasted and tried to savor. Ping had thrown rocks at a rabbit but failed to strike it. Hunger would once again be their companion.

It fortunately hadn't rained. The fire had grown, warming them, casting shadows through the cave. Travelers had left their names scrawled on overhangs, and Meng had wondered what kind of lives these people had lived. Not a single woman's name was present, so she had written hers in a prominent place, happy to leave a bold and honest sign of her passage.

Now, as the companions sat in front of the fire, Meng used a damp cloth to try to clean stains from Fan's coat. She hummed as she worked, hungry and tired, but elated by the possibility of a reunion the following day. She wondered how he would react to her arrival. Since she'd be dressed as a man, he would have to temper his enthusiasm, but his emotions would be clear to her. And she was certain that he'd barely be able to restrain himself.

Thoughts of their reunion made her increasingly restless, and she rubbed stain after stain, dulling them slightly but making no great progress. Still she worked, regretting that she hadn't been able to better protect the coat on her journey.

"I wish we could eat that coat," Ping said, probing the campfire with a long stick. He sat on a smooth boulder with his sword by his side. He'd also made a spear in case the rabbit returned. "From time to time, I'm tempted to try."

"You'll be fine," Meng replied. "We'll get food tomorrow. Fan has been working on the wall for a year and surely he'll have money saved."

"And we're just going to walk up there and introduce ourselves?"

"No. We're going to do exactly what we agreed on. We'll pretend to be messengers sent by his mother, letting him know that his father has died. He owes taxes. Fan will have to help."

"And he'll leave with us?"

"Only to sign some papers. Of course, we won't come back. But no one will know that at the time."

Ping shook his head. "Except for you and me."

"But I won't speak. You'll do all the talking."

"We're going to get ourselves killed. You think the men up on that wall are fools? They haven't been beaten in a hundred years. We could be Mongol spies for all they know."

Meng set down the coat and stood up. "But earlier … you said the plan would work. You were confident."

"Of course I was confident. It was my plan. But now it doesn't sound so glorious. I don't believe in it anymore. I've never been good at plans, to tell you the truth. Anyone would agree with that. Still not convinced? Well, listen to this sad tale. I once saw the wind blow a rich man's hat from his head. It fell from a bridge, onto a frozen stream. I told the man that I'd get his hat if he gave me a few coppers. He agreed. And soon thereafter I was neck deep in icy water. I almost died."

"So? You were just a boy."

"See how much you know? That was last winter."

Meng smiled at the image of Ping standing in a frozen stream.

"It's not funny," he said.

"Yes it is."

"Water that cold hurts a man's … privates. I was afraid I'd never please a woman again."

"You needn't have worried."

He tossed his stick into the fire. "Sit down, will you please? I'm getting a kink in my neck from looking up at you."

She did as he asked, settling once again on a flat stone. "I'll go alone."

"You can't go alone because you can't speak. How would you ever find him?"

"I'll use paper. I'll write down my questions."

"Why would his mother send such a useless emissary? A small, feeble man who can't speak? No, I don't think so."

Meng bit her lower lip. Ping was right. It would be difficult for her to fool anyone by herself. "Then I'll think of something else," she finally replied, not wanting to force him into helping her. "There must be another way."

He grunted. "Did I ever tell you how my mother thought that I'd be a good monk?" he asked. "She whispered that to me, just once. Of course, my illustrious father had other plans."

"I think you'd make a wonderful monk."

"Why?"

"Because I've seen how you've helped me. I would have never made it so far without you."

The fire popped, causing Ping to flinch. He looked up, appearing to study how the smoke pooled against a sheltering rock before ebbing away. "My mother was wise," he said quietly. "I never realized that simple fact until years later."

"You could still become a monk. It's not too late. Then you won't have any need to steal. You could just help people. And talk. You could talk a lot."

He smiled, rubbing a sore on his ankle. "I'd like that. I do talk a lot."

"I've noticed."

"But it's only because I have a lot to say. I could never pretend to be mute, like you do. I'd explode like one of the emperor's cannons. As far as helping people, well, maybe I learned that skill from you. Maybe you've inspired me."

"I could do more."

"And I could walk on water. You do enough, Meng. Don't be so hard on yourself. It's exhausting to witness. You already make the rest of us look greedy."

She reached for her bedding, adjusting it among the rocks and gravel. She noticed that Ping had placed his blankets an arm's length from hers. A more comfortable-looking place existed on the opposite side of the fire, but he'd neglected the spot.

Weariness seeping into her, she lay down. Her thoughts drifted to Fan, and she reached for her necklace, stroking it with her thumb. She wished that he could see how she'd scratched her name into the overhang. He would have been proud of her.

"You're doing it again," Ping said softly.

"Doing what?"

"Every night before you go to sleep, you touch your necklace. Sometimes you even kiss it."

She nodded, then positioned the necklace back against her chest. "It's a habit, I suppose."

"No, that's not a habit. Habits are disgusting. Picking at your nose is a habit. What you do with that necklace, it's not a habit. It's something else altogether."

"Maybe you're right. Maybe it's more."

"Of course it's more."

"I don't even know I'm doing it."

He rubbed the fingers of his right hand together, as if he held something small and memorable. "What's it like ... to love like that? To think about someone so often that you don't even realize you're doing it, that you might as well be breathing?"

Meng started to answer, but stopped. She thought about the question, unsure how to describe how she felt. "At first we were just companions," she finally answered. "I was lucky in that my father found me a good husband, one who didn't mind my feet."

"Then what happened?"

"Then Fan ... he looked after me. He accepted me. He loved me even though I was ... different. And at some point I started to feel that I was a part of him and that he was a part of me. Maybe that's why I touch my necklace. Maybe I'm wanting to feel whole again."

"But it's not whole. He has the other half."

"When I touch it, I'm missing him."

Ping tossed a pebble into the fire. "But you're so strong. How can you be so strong when you feel incomplete? That makes less sense than saving snails. An incomplete wall doesn't keep anything out or in. A bird with one wing can't fly."

She nodded to herself, then smiled. "The best part of me is us."

"It's that simple? Love?"

"What more is there, Ping? Though love is just a word. And what I feel for him can't be described in a word. I don't think I could describe it in a thousand words. Nothing else compares to how I feel about Fan. I wouldn't trade that feeling for anything, not even to save myself. Walking this far to reach him, it's nothing. I'd walk across all of China if I had to. I'd walk forever."

"What you have ... I don't understand."

"Yes you do."

He smiled, or at least tried to. "What you have is magic. Maybe you'll let me steal a tiny part of it from you, when you aren't looking. I promise that I'll give it back."

"You don't have to steal what you can discover on your own."

"I've discovered a great many things on my travels. A golden coin once. A massive bone from a long-dead dragon. And there was even a blind courtesan who made me laugh until my stomach hurt. But no, I don't think I'll find the same magic that you have. I don't think most people do."

Meng studied Ping. He looked tired. She realized that this would most likely be their last night alone together. For a reason she didn't understand, that thought made her melancholy, despite her longing to see Fan.

Standing up, Meng walked to where she had written on the overhang. She added Ping's name above hers, then scratched a line on either side of their names, so that it looked as if the names were on a road that led into the horizon.

"We can still be friends," she said quietly, returning to her bedding.

"That would be scandalous," he answered. "A married woman and an unmarried man cannot be friends."

Meng shook her head. "And a woman cannot walk alone to the Great Wall. And a man cannot go from being a thief to becoming a monk. How many things, Ping, have they told us we can't do, but later, we've found out that we can?"

"You dream of a different day. A different age."

"I don't dream. Wherever Fan and I settle, you'll be welcome in our house. You'll arrive as if to visit him, but before you come I'll send the servants away, so that you and I can talk and laugh."

"And Fan would allow us to do so?"

"Of course."

A smile spread across Ping's face. "I'd like that," he replied. "Even if it's only a dream, it's a nice one."

"Believe in it."

"We'll fool them all again."

Meng grinned, then settled down onto her blankets. She closed her eyes. "Good night, my dear friend."

"Good night."

She tried to sleep, but darkness would not come to her. The fire popped. The wind whistled.

Much later, she cracked open her eyes and saw that Ping was still staring at her.

∗

The night groaned, as if alive and in pain. Though no rain fell, the wind was strong enough to bend trees and send fallen leaves tumbling. Fan hadn't been off the wall in more than five months. It felt strange, almost disconcerting, to have soil beneath his feet instead of stones. His legs seemed unsteady and his gait was hesitant. Even under the cover of darkness, he moved with great care, following Yat-sen as he slowly rode his white stallion south, toward his home. Fan had been to the home once before, when he had trailed Yat-sen under a similar sky. At the time, Fan had wanted to know more about the man who had so much power over him.

Now Fan had grander plans. He suspected that Yat-sen was stealing funds intended for his men, and Fan wanted to sit outside his adversary's house and study its intricacies. Somewhere within it, Fan believed, was a pile of silver *taels*. The treasure was most likely in his personal chambers, a realm usually inaccessible to prying servants.

Fan had never deluded himself into thinking that he was cunning. He was a craftsman, after all, not a spy or a scout. So he followed Yat-sen with a wildly thumping heart, his face perspiring despite the coolness of the night. He kept a hundred paces between him and Yat-sen and walked with an exaggerated limp. He'd also changed clothes and wore much darker robes.

The road, narrow and usually well traveled, was quiet so late at night. Since it was cobbled, Fan walked alongside it on a pathway that held beggars during the daylight. He paid careful attention to the cadence of the big stallion as its hooves clattered rhythmically. Though Fan might have been able to locate Yat-sen's home, he wanted to refresh his memory. If his escape went as planned, he'd run to the house. There would be no time to waste.

The farther they got from the Great Wall, the less wild their environs became. Merchants' stalls soon bordered the road. All of them had been closed and locked. Wooden shutters swayed in the wind, thumping against battered frames. Signs proclaimed goods of every sort—meat, fruits, rice, spices, clothes, weapons, and services. Of course, none of the offerings were present. Several merchants still worked within glowing orbs made by oil lamps hanging from their stalls. The men swept the ground or bent over low tables as they made repairs. Yat-sen paid these figures no heed, and neither did Fan. He walked the way he talked—quietly and with no excessive movement.

The stalls soon gave way to bigger structures—homes, stores, temples, and tea houses. Yat-sen guided his mount off the main road, turning down an alley. It wasn't paved and the clatter of hooves immediately ceased. Fan let him pull farther ahead, barely keeping him in sight. His broken arm ached, and he wished that he could have taken something to dull the pain. But he needed a clear mind tonight. A distraction might lead to his death.

The way was as Fan remembered, though several new buildings faced him, and he was glad that he'd snuck off the Great Wall. He imagined what might happen the following night. Once Bataar was safe, Fan would run. Yat-sen would know that he'd gone south, and would send many men. But would it occur to him that Fan would head for his home? As far as Fan was concerned, stealing Yat-sen's wealth was the final play in their game of *Go*. It would be so much easier for Meng and him to hide with *taels* of silver in their pockets. They could travel far from Beijing, offer bribes when needed, and find new lives for themselves. Lacking the silver, they wouldn't have the means to escape. Yat-sen would track them down.

Without warning, Yat-sen twisted in his saddle, turning backward. Fan immediately paused, suddenly as still as the home beside him. The alley was dark enough that Fan might have been a shadow. Yat-sen, replete in his red armor, was much easier to see. Still, Fan didn't stir. He even held his breath as Yat-sen continued to stare in his direction. For a terrifying moment, he thought that

Yat-sen would turn his mount around, but then the horse went forward.

Fan leaned back, looking at the untroubled sky. He then rubbed his aching arm and started ahead, thinking of Meng, aware that being with her was worth any risk. He was nothing without her—a song deprived of instruments, perhaps, beautiful in concept but worthless without the strings and drums that gave it life.

Yat-sen seemed to increase his pace. He turned down a few more alleys before arriving at his home. Fan watched from behind the corner of another dwelling as Yat-sen dismounted from his stallion, gave his reins to a servant, and then headed inside. The home was well lit, and light seeped through shutters and seams in the walls. Unlike the nearby structures, Yat-sen's residence had a large courtyard in front and was surrounded on all other sides by ample space. The home was its own castle, fully defendable. Fan continued to study it, unaware of several drops of rain that struck his shoulders.

Fan had never believed that he would have an enemy; that a man would exist whose very presence endangered his own life. But Yat-sen had become that man. And Fan knew that to free Bataar, to see Meng again, he'd have to defeat his foe—not through a battle of swords or horsemanship, but in a contest of minds.

Yat-sen emerged quickly from his house, surprising Fan. Instinctively he lurched backward, the movement too swift and graceless. Yat-sen paused, standing still. Hiding behind the corner of the nearby home, Fan slowly backpedaled, afraid that Yat-sen might round the corner, a weapon in his hand, at any moment.

Silently cursing himself, Fan turned and began to run. His

footfalls seemed unnaturally loud in the darkness, and he hurried down a series of alleys, taking a different route back to the Great Wall. He half expected to hear hoofbeats behind him, to see Yat-sen charging out of the night. His fear giving him strength, Fan ran onward, moving with as much haste as possible, heedless of the noise he created.

Everything around him seemed dead.

Without thought, he reached into one of his pockets, producing the wooden horse he'd found near the wall. He wasn't sure why he gripped the carving, but it gave him something to grasp, to clutch at.

He wanted to run toward a light, toward something that beckoned to him. But there was only darkness.

So he imagined that Meng was in the distance. He ran toward her.

*

Later, after rain had come and gone, Yat-sen sat on a lacquer chair in Yehonala's quarters, with her kneeling before him. They had just left each other's arms. Their hair was disheveled, their naked bodies shining with perspiration. Several welts and darkening bruises were scattered on their necks and chests.

Their lovemaking had been passionate and, at times, violent. Curses had been muttered, cries of pain and pleasure exchanged. In the end, when no higher summit could be reached, they had collapsed against each other, their bodies and minds spent.

Wishing that he possessed the stamina of a young man and

could dominate and be dominated by her once again, Yat-sen reached for a silk blanket. He draped it over his privates, then pulled his nearby sword from its scabbard. Without a word to her, he picked up his favorite whetstone and started to sharpen his blade. Unlike his lovemaking, his movements with the sword and stone were careful and precise. He used long, steady strokes to sharpen the blade's edge, smoothing out nicks and abrasions.

Yehonala made no effort to cover herself. She remained kneeling before him, her breasts rising and falling as her breathing finally slowed. "When will the silver arrive?" she asked. "For the new watchtower?"

He shrugged. "The craftsman found a plot of land suitable for building. We're all ready."

"No more than I."

"I know."

"So bring more silver," she replied, leaning toward him, her voice rising. She reached for his blade, running her thumb along its edge. "Otherwise you risk more than your sword growing dull."

He raised the weapon, unconcerned whether she was cut or not. Again, he began to stroke the whetstone against it, the sound of stone against steel comforting to him. "I'll bring the silver," he said. "Soon."

Yehonala stood up, moving behind him. She began to rub his shoulders, leaning close enough to him that her breasts brushed against his back. "Tell me of the craftsman's wife. Has she come for him?"

"No. But she seems to have left Beijing. No one there has seen her for days."

"Then she heads this way."

Nodding, Yat-sen considered the three men he had positioned to the south of the Great Wall. If the woman arrived, they would stop her. "I still don't think she'll come," he replied. "But if she does, she'll be detained."

"And what will happen to her?"

Yat-sen had asked himself the same question a hundred times. "If she comes, that means he's asked her to, that he's defied me once again."

"Tell me what you'll do."

"She'll disappear. Forever. And then, months from now, when I no longer need him, I'll let him go. He'll spend the rest of his life looking for her, blaming himself for her loss. He'll never know that I had her killed. All he'll know is that she died searching for him."

"What if he didn't ask her to come? What if she just came?"

"If she arrives, it's because he asked her. He's weak like that. He's lonely."

"You don't … want her for yourself?"

Yat-sen shook his head, surprised by the question. "I want you. Otherwise I wouldn't be here."

"And you're not envious of their love?"

He started to speak, then stopped. "They're different than us," he finally replied.

"How?"

"You've read some of her letters. You know."

"I know that their love must bother you. It's powerful. And you seek power, you covet—"

"Enough," he interrupted, still sharpening his sword. "Her words can be tedious. And so can yours."

"Yet you read them. You read them every day."

Yat-sen repressed a cough. "He's weak in so many regards. As weak as a child. Yet you're right—somehow his love for her gives him strength. It makes him formidable, in his own way."

"How so?"

"His love gives him passion that he otherwise wouldn't have, which makes him harder to break, which makes him unpredictable."

"Does he remind you of what you don't yet have, but long for?"

"And what is that?"

"A woman to call your own. A woman who loves you."

"I'm a patient man. Someday I hope to have a version of what he does."

"A version?"

"I'm not him and you're not her. So, yes, a version."

She continued to rub his shoulders. "As long as they remain separated, you don't need to fear him."

"Don't be a fool," he replied, stiffening against her touch. "I don't fear him. Or any other man for that matter. A time will come when I'll laugh at his memory, at how I destroyed him."

"You'll destroy him, and will do so much more. Your name will be golden again. Only it won't be your father's name that will be remembered. It will be yours."

"It's a single name."

"No. Your father's destiny was to die in that wasteland. Yours is to lead men. Once you build your tower, once you defy the

Mongols, men will bow to you."

"Men already bow to me."

She smiled. "A handful, yes. But surely you want more than that. Surely you want immortality."

His whetstone paused against his blade. "If she comes, I want to be there when she dies."

"Why?"

"Because then I'll have beaten him."

"Is a single craftsman such a challenge?"

Yat-sen nodded, thinking about Fan, about what to do with him. "He may have followed me home tonight."

"How do you—"

"I glimpsed a man. It may have been him. Or another."

"Ask the guards if he left. Surely they'll know."

"Those fools know nothing," Yat-sen replied, his whetstone moving once again. "If he wanted to follow me home, he could. Yet I'll find out, one way or another."

"And if he did?"

"Then there will be a reckoning."

Yehonala leaned closer to him, her breasts pressing against his back. Reaching over his shoulders, she began to rub his chest. She kissed the back of his neck, gently at first, but then again with more passion. "He occupies your mind," she whispered. "As does his wife."

"So?"

"To claim me, you'll need a free mind. You'll need everything you have."

He twisted on the chair, the sword dropping to the floor.

Before he knew what he was doing, he reached for her, his fingers tightening around her neck. He brought her to him, moaning at the presence of her lips on his, at the pain of her nails sliding down his back. "I claim you now," he whispered, his voice rough.

"Now and forever are different things," she replied, kissing him.

"Yes."

"So enjoy the now, but strive for the forever."

They twisted, dropping to the floor, heedless of the sword beneath them. Drawing closer together, they clutched and kissed and moved with haste, as if the world were dying around them, and only moments remained for them to conquer and embrace.

CHAPTER THIRTEEN

The Forsaken

Between Jinshanling and Simatai—October 22, 1549

Chuluun's second dawn on the wall was more somber than the last. The sun's colors weren't as vivid, and in his weakened state, he found it hard to rejoice in his survival. A light rain in the early part of the night had almost killed him. Again, he had thought about Bataar while twisting and struggling to stay warm, recalling how his son had raced in front of the wall on the gray and black horse, seemingly a part of the wind. Though Chuluun hadn't been able to see the rider's face, he knew it was Bataar. No Chinese rider could ride so swiftly and fearlessly.

The sight of Bataar taking flight had sent pride surging through Chuluun. He had wanted to shout his son's name, over and over, celebrating his freedom. But just as his lips parted, Bataar had turned around, heading back toward his captors. Chuluun stared uncomprehendingly as Bataar returned to the men who had imprisoned him. He went willingly, even thrusting his fist into the air and whooping as he had years earlier, when he'd first learned to ride.

Bataar's return had crushed Chuluun's spirit. He struggled to understand why his son would turn away from freedom. That choice made no sense. Bataar had been raised to despise the Chinese, to seek their deaths. Yet he had willingly gone back to them, forsaking his own people. What had the Chinese done to him? Chuluun wondered. How had they turned and twisted him? Everyone knew that the Chinese were skilled in science and medicine. Perhaps they had used their dark magic to change Bataar into one of them.

For much of the night, Chuluun had pleaded with the spirits, repeating these same questions, over and over. He was tormented by the thought that his son had turned away from his people. Perhaps Bataar even knew about his imprisonment but cared nothing of it.

Chuluun didn't blame his son. Whatever had happened to Bataar wasn't his fault; it was Chuluun's. He was the one who let his boy be captured, who took the word of a spy that he was dead. Spending a year with the Chinese was enough to break and twist any man, not to mention a boy who hadn't seen thirteen summers come and go.

His despair at Bataar's return had kept Chuluun alive through the night. But now, as the wind tugged at him, he sensed the approach of his own death. His leg ached from the arrow's bite.

His body trembled without end, perhaps from the cold, perhaps from the knowledge that he had failed Bataar.

Chuluun still tried to escape, tugging at his bonds, wanting another moment with his son, even if it meant that Bataar might betray him. But more ropes had been wrapped around his wrists and ankles. They were like dozens of serpents coiled about him, impossible to cast off. He had also gone two days with nothing to eat. The rain had satiated his thirst, but his body craved sustenance.

Groaning, Chuluun sagged against the wooden frame, his body and mind spent. He studied the northern frontier, wondering what his wife and daughters were doing. They would be up by now, feeding horses perhaps, asking the spirits what had become of him. Surely they believed him to be dead, and soon enough they'd be right. He asked for their forgiveness, again and again, pleading with the spirits to always watch over them.

Voices drifted to him. Chuluun glanced to his left, surprised to see a large number of horses and riders atop the wall. They were too far away for him to make out their faces, so he searched for the black and gray mount that Bataar had ridden the previous day. He thought he glimpsed it, but the horses were packed tightly together. Several of the riders carried large, red banners depicting golden dragons. Using chains and winches, foot soldiers lowered a wide ramp that ran from the top of the parapet to the ground. A horn sounded, and one by one the riders moved onto the ramp, proceeding down.

Chuluun squinted, searching for Bataar, silently mouthing his name. He looked from rider to rider, horse to horse. In all there might have been sixty horsemen, a sizeable force to be certain, though one that could be easily overwhelmed if caught in the open. The men were well-armed. Yat-sen, replete in his red armor, was near the front of the group. Yet Chuluun's gaze didn't rest on him. He continued to search for a smaller figure, finally finding him toward the rear of the group.

"Bataar," he whispered.

Once again on the black and gray stallion, Bataar headed down the ramp with grace and poise. He carried no visible weapon, but his hands gripped the reins, and he didn't look to be a prisoner. For a moment Chuluun lost sight of him when he reached the bottom of the ramp. The wall obscured his view. Blind to what was transpiring below, Chuluun tugged at his bonds, strength flowing back into him. He cursed, using his teeth to tear at a rope that encircled his shoulders.

Someone shouted from below. Riders started to appear, heading north, spurring their mounts time and time again. The Chinese were rushing forward. Chuluun strained to see his son, managed to do so, and fought back the urge to shout at him to flee. Bataar was near the end of the column and could have broken away from the main group. It was possible that a Chinese archer might have downed him if he made such a move, but in Chuluun's experience, the Chinese shot much better from a wall than a horse.

"Why ... why don't you flee?" he whispered as Bataar stayed in his position. "What have they done to you, my son? What have they done?"

The Chinese charged north, their red banners held high and proud, their horses swift and sure. Chuluun watched his son grow smaller, still pleading with him to flee, promising that he'd be welcomed home by his mother and sisters.

Bataar merged into the column, now a part of it, impossible to discern from the enemy. Chuluun screamed, thrashing against his bonds, opening scabbed wounds on his wrists and shins. If the Chinese stayed out too long, they would be slaughtered. Thousands of Chuluun's countrymen would arrive that night, bringing death and destruction to the wall. If Bataar was with the Chinese, he would perish alongside them.

Fear had never fueled Chuluun. He had fought with conviction, empowered by the belief that his cause was just. But now, as the ropes cut into him, as he despaired at the notion of Bataar's looming death, fear gave him enormous strength. His skin split, his nails ripped, and still he struggled, praying for the arrival of rain, for wetness that would allow the ropes to stretch.

Whatever the cost to himself, Chuluun must escape by nightfall.

*

Bataar pulled back on his reins, slowing his charging horse. He felt the stallion's yearning to pass its brethren and shared the sentiment. Yet he had been told to stay perfectly in line with his captors. Otherwise Fan would be killed.

The column was headed toward the rise of land where Yat-sen's tower would be built. He wanted to personally inspect the grounds before there was further talk of construction. The proposed horserace would still occur, regardless of his decision on the tower.

Even though Bataar knew that they would flee later that night, departing beneath a moonless sky, a part of him wanted to stay and participate in the race. He longed to beat the Chinese, to show them that they would never best his people. They could build their walls and cities, but they would never be a part of the land. That belief was held by Bataar's father, and he had passed it to his son. The Chinese would chase immortality by shaping mountains in their image. The Mongols would ride beyond these mountains, living and dying, rising and falling. Yet their bones were a part of the soil, the water, the air. Immortality was already theirs.

Someone shouted from ahead in the column. Bataar further slowed his stallion, patting its warm neck. The trail rose, steeper than most, a scar cut into the side of a peak. The hooves of sixty mounts clattered on rocks, sending them tumbling downward. The top of the rise seemed to have been cut off, forming a nearly level plateau. Upon reaching the vantage point, Bataar thought about how he would have won the race.

Men around him dismounted. Bataar smiled as Fan awkwardly climbed down from his mare, dropping to the ground. Yat-sen, Li, and other officers stood near one another, admiring the views in all directions. The Great Wall, even Bataar had to admit, looked majestic in the distance, gleaming in the sunlight, impossibly long and powerful. Its watchtowers seemed to rise forever, vanishing to the east and west, square columns that appeared to support the sky.

Bataar leapt from his mount, then tied his reins to a stunted tree. He wondered why Yat-sen had invited him on the journey, deciding that the commander wanted the race to be seen as fair. If Bataar failed, no one could say that he hadn't ridden over the terrain before.

Fan had moved far away from the soldiers and was looking at the Great Wall. He held something in his hand, his thumb stroking an unseen object. Bataar walked over to him, nodding in appreciation. "You're getting better," he said. "Only twice did you almost fall."

"It felt like twenty times to me."

Bataar laughed, excited by the prospect of fleeing that night. Fan still hadn't shared his full plan, but Bataar knew that it would be wise.

"You're going to race," Fan whispered, his words barely audible.

"What?"

"No matter how many times I've run it through my head, there's just no good way to get you down from the wall, with a horse."

"But I don't understand. I thought we would leave tonight."

"And I thought I might bribe someone, might gallop away with you. But you'll be better off escaping after the race. Just win it and keep on riding. They'll never catch you."

"And you?"

Fan sighed, rubbing the object in his good hand. His thumb moved against it, he lifted it into the light.

Bataar's mouth opened but no words tumbled forth. Fan held a small, wooden carving of a horse. Without thinking, Bataar reached for it, plucking it out of Fan's hands. He examined it carefully, holding it close to his face, his gaze sweeping over every notch and curve. "Where did you get this?" he asked.

"I don't ... "

"Where?"

"This one … I found on the wall. But there have been others."

"Others?"

"Yat-sen thinks the Black Rider leaves them."

Bataar nodded, abruptly unable to speak. He found it hard to breathe and was unsteady on his legs. The horizon seemed to spin around him. He reached for something to grasp, clutching at Fan's shoulder. Everything suddenly made sense, though clarity seemed to bring the world tumbling down around him.

The Black Rider was his father.

Tears dropped to his cheeks as he thought of the naked man tied to the wall—his father. How much had he suffered? Was he even still alive?

Bataar moaned, collapsing into Fan. His friend reached for him, asking questions, but a buzzing arose in his ears, the sound of angry hornets. He tried to stand, to hurry back to his horse, but Fan held him tight and immobile. Weeping, unable to hold back his emotions, he remembered the rains, the cold winds.

"He's here," Bataar whispered, his chest heaving.

"Who? Who's here?"

"We have to free him."

"Bataar, you're not making sense. Free who?"

"The man who made that horse," Bataar replied, his voice barely audible. "He's my father."

The approach to the Great Wall was less grand than Ping expected. A simple road led from Jinshanling toward the fortification, which dwarfed everything else in sight. The structure was much larger than he'd remembered, tall and thick, dominated by the graceful and soaring watchtowers. He now understood why the dreaded Mongol armies couldn't breach it. The wall was stouter than a million armed men. Its towers and parapets and sweeping sides had been designed with only one thought in mind—to keep out the Mongol hordes.

In the past two days, Ping had only eaten a handful of nuts. He was weak and weary. Placing one foot before the other seemed a monumental task. The weight of his sword, which he'd never felt before, dragged him down. Even his mind was drained of strength, and he paid less attention to the details around him than normal. His attention shifted between the Great Wall and Meng, who was also exhausted. Yet her weariness was obscured by her zeal to reach Fan. She pressed forward, seemingly unaware of the rise of the road, of the emptiness of her stomach.

Ping felt a sense of pride as they neared the Great Wall. He knew that Meng would have never made it alone and was immeasurably pleased that he had been able to deliver her. It had been many years since he'd done something good, something in which he could rejoice. He wished that his father and mother could know of his accomplishment, of how he had disregarded his own needs for the sake of someone else. His mother, at least, would have been proud.

Yet Ping was also saddened by the end of their journey. He didn't want to see Meng go. Once she was reunited with her husband, Ping would have to leave. He'd be alone again. Perhaps he would seek a position on the wall, or maybe even become a monk, as his mother had wanted. Whatever he did, Meng would drift away from him. She would have a husband, perhaps children, and they would never again walk alone on a road together.

"My empty stomach is making me melancholy," he whispered. "Our grand adventure is about to end."

She turned to him, slowing. "That's not true."

"You can say what you want, Meng the Believer, but things won't be the same between us."

"Maybe. But they don't have to be so different either."

"I like how you dream," he answered. "Such ambitious aspirations. You should write poetry, and let people dwell on your thoughts. Maybe you'll inspire someone to save a snail or to tame a thief."

"You're not tamed."

"Only tired. Still … these days with you have been some of my best. And now they're over."

She shook her head, her pace faltering. "I won't let you disappear from my life."

Her comment pleased him. He smiled, looking ahead. A hundred paces to the north, a broad stairway led to the top of the wall. The stairway was guarded by six soldiers. Ping had expected that they would have to pass through guards to gain access to the wall. He'd prepared himself, going over his explanation time and time again. Meng and he had also discussed her role—how she was supposed to act mute, using gestures and standing with confidence.

Ping wasn't overly worried that they would have trouble with the guards. He was a Chinese citizen, after all, and from what he had been told, officials often traveled to the fortification, bringing letters, supplies, and services. The soldiers would likely suspect nothing unusual and wouldn't fear a pair of weary travelers.

He nodded to Meng, then increased his pace, eager to get past the guards. They stood grouped together, more intent on a conversation than anyone approaching. The men wore old leather armor and carried sheathed swords. One was a full head taller than the rest. His armor was newer and he wore a helmet. Ping suspected that he was the leader.

When the guards finally took notice of him, Ping bowed slightly, said hello, and introduced himself. He said that he carried a message for a craftsman on this part of the wall—a man named Fan.

The big guard picked something from his teeth, then spat. "Give your letter to me," he said. "I'll hand it over to the craftsman."

Ping's heart seemed to drop, but outwardly he gave no sign of his distress. "I could give it to you, but then my master would have me whipped."

"And why would that concern me?"

"Because my master might also come looking for you. He's an official in the Forbidden City—not a man to trifle with. A vile, despicable worm, of course, but a powerful one. He's seen the emperor twice and is happy to brag about it."

The big man spat again, apparently unimpressed. "My name

is Kang, and I haven't met the emperor, but I command ten men here."

"Well, Kang, my congratulations to you for your—"

"What does your worm of a master want with the craftsman?"

Ping shrugged, trying to appear nonchalant, though he was increasingly uneasy. "I wouldn't know. I haven't opened his letter, and even if I did, I can't read."

"And what of your quiet companion?"

"What of him? He's mute, but he keeps me company. I like to talk, and he likes to listen. If you're ever in need of a good traveling companion, you should find yourself someone like him. Just don't expect him to—"

"Be silent."

"I'm weary, my friend. I've walked all the way from Beijing. I just want to deliver this message and go find myself a lonely, lovely lady. Is there a pleasure house nearby that you might recommend? I've heard the pickings here are quite good."

"Then you've heard wrong."

"Really? That's not—"

The big guard reached for the hilt of his sword. "Give me your weapon."

"Why?"

"Because if you don't, I'll cut your head from your body."

Ping nodded, suddenly desperate, but unsure of what to do. "That seems like an excellent reason," he replied, handing over his weapon.

"And you, draw your blade," the guard said to Meng. "Draw it and hold it out before you."

Meng leaned forward, shaking her head. The big man repeated his command, then pulled his sword from its sheath. He held it, tip forward, near her neck.

"There's no reason for rudeness," Ping said, stepping forward. "I think—"

"Restrain him," the guard commanded, and his underlings encircled Ping, reaching for him.

He put up his hands, defenseless, but they grabbed him from all sides, holding him tight.

"Now draw your blade or lose your sword arm," the big man said to Meng.

Ping shook his head, starting to fight against the men who held him, writhing in their grasp. "When my master hears how you've treated us, he'll feed your ears to his pigs!"

Someone punched him in the stomach, and he doubled over, unable to breathe, but aware that Meng was sliding her blade free of its sheath. She held it steady before her, though her feet were too close together, her hands too far apart on the hilt. She didn't look like a fighter.

Without any warning, the guard swung his blade at Meng. Ping shouted, lunging forward. But the big man's sword didn't cut her down, but instead knocked her weapon from her hands. She hadn't even moved during the attack and remained mostly still, though her hands trembled.

"Three of you take them and follow me," the big man said, then sheathed his sword and started to walk away from the wall.

Ping protested, saying that they were making a mistake. But the men didn't listen to him. At least until he insulted the blood in their veins. At that point, one of them struck him from behind, knocking him down, bloodying his knees.

"Stop protecting the woman," the big man said, then smiled. "I was told she might come, but I didn't think that she ever would."

"You're mistaken," Ping muttered. "He's a mute, that's all."

"Say another word, and you'll be the mute. I'll carve out your tongue."

Still held by two men, Ping looked around, desperate for a means to escape. He thought about lunging for one of the guard's swords, but they gripped his wrists, and if he made any such move, surely their leader would cut him down. He wanted to say something to Meng, to promise her that he wouldn't fail her, that she would remain safe. But she was turned away from him and seemed to have gone limp in her captor's arms. He was practically carrying her.

The soldiers continued to proceed down the road, finally turning toward some type of military barracks. Many other armed men were about—practicing swordplay, sharpening weapons, or asleep in patches of sun. Ping and Meng were dragged inside the stone structure, down a hallway, and thrown into an empty room. Immediately Ping rushed to Meng's side, sheltering her. He saw that her eyes were rimmed with tears, yet she still said nothing. She seemed to be in shock.

"Please," Ping pleaded. "You're making a mistake. It's true he's worthless with a sword, but he's no woman."

The big man stepped forward. "Then why don't I strip him naked and see what's under those robes?"

"No!" Meng screamed, throwing herself against the guard.

He tossed her aside with ease and disdain, sending her careening into a wall. Ping picked up a bamboo chair and swung it at his adversary, crushing it against his side. The big man grunted and stumbled backward, and Ping might have brought him down if not for the other men present. They poured into the room, leaping at him, knocking him backward. He struggled against them, reaching for a sword hilt, managing to pull a weapon half free.

But then the big man was upon him, his fists raining down. Ping tasted blood. He smelled his enemy's odor. He saw fury and hatred in the eyes before him. Then he was on the ground. Someone stomped on his chest. Gasping for air, he rolled up into a ball. Meng screamed, beseeching them to leave him alone.

The big man shouted and the blows stopped. Ping shuddered, still unable to breathe, his right eye already swelling. So much pain consumed him that he was unable to think. Yet he fought against blacking out, resisting the darkness that came for him.

"Yat-sen wants to meet you," the big man said to Meng, straightening his armor. "But I don't think you'll like him much."

The guard started to leave, thought better of it, and kicked Ping hard in the ribs. The pain was overwhelming, and he rolled away from his assailant, trying to escape the agony.

Again darkness approached him and again he resisted it. Slowly some of the pain dissipated and the room came back into focus. Meng was kneeling beside him, stroking his face, tears in her eyes.

"I'm so sorry," he whispered. "Please, please forgive me."

CHAPTER FOURTEEN

War on the Wall

North of Simatai—October 23, 1549

The middle of the night neared as five thousand Mongol horsemen trotted south, along a previously scouted trail. None of the men spoke. The few times that communication was needed, whispers or whistles were exchanged. Though the warriors wore their usual, studded leather armor, they were also dressed in loose-fitting black robes that concealed anything that might reflect a Chinese torch or fire. All of the men had longbows slung across their backs, but most also were armed with swords. Others carried grappling hooks and ropes. A few of the bravest horsemen were linked together by long bamboo ladders that were slung from mount to mount. Additional sections of ladders had been previously hidden closer to the wall. These would be assembled

369

and utilized as the fighting started.

The horsemen had spent the summer and autumn battling against the Chinese defenders. They had been repulsed on several occasions. Many had lost friends during the war, or had been wounded. All knew that once the snows fell, they would have to retreat north, fleeing to the safety and warmth of their *yurts*. Winter would be long, tedious, and difficult. While the Chinese relaxed within their vast cities, the Mongols would endure the winds and blizzards, barely able to care for their families and horses.

Knowing that this assault would be their final of the year, the Mongols had gathered many of their best fighters. Though they could have brought more than five thousand men into the fray, others were not far behind. The arrival of reinforcements at the wall would be contingent on how the fight was evolving. If the Chinese were not duped by the original attack or had ample men to defend the assaults, the remaining Mongols would return to their strongholds. But if their countrymen were successful in securing the two towers, then the reserves would rush forward, pouring onto captured territory.

When the lights on the faraway wall twinkled like a row of stars, the commander of the attacking force whistled. His men began to separate. One column of two thousand riders headed to the southeast. The remaining three thousand riders pressed forward to the southwest. These men were the best fighters. Once their countrymen had attacked the wall to the east, and drawn the Chinese defenders to them, the main force would assault two towers that stood upon a mountain's crest. One of these towers was Yat-sen's command post.

The two columns separated completely. Though many men in both groups were impatient for the battle to begin, their leaders cautioned against recklessness. No horse was allowed to gallop. No sword was unsheathed.

The two armies resembled little more than twin, elongated shadows that slid over the land, drifting toward the great, gleaming wall.

*

On that same wall, on the opposite side of Yat-sen's tower as Chuluun's position, Fan and Bataar stood next to each other and stared into the darkness. Bataar's eyes had dried of tears but were still red and inflamed. He had stolen a dagger, and, at Fan's insistence, had tucked it into the folds of his robe.

Upon returning to the Great Wall from their expedition, Bataar had wanted to rush to his father, to risk his own life to free him as soon as possible. Fan was forced to plead with him, physically restraining him at times, begging that he await the cover of darkness. The moonless night, he argued, would provide a perfect opportunity for an escape.

The main problem with freeing Bataar's father was that a single guard was positioned close to him. Fan knew the man, who was good-natured and had treated both him and Bataar well. Neither of them wanted to kill him, but he would have to be somehow subdued.

Fan had stolen a long rope. Once Bataar's father had been freed, the two Mongols would go over the wall and escape, on foot, to the north. There was no time to worry about finding them a horse. They would have to take their chances running. Fan, meanwhile, would leave the wall and hurry south. With luck, their absence wouldn't be noticed until dawn.

"Hit him over the head with the hilt of the dagger," Bataar said, shifting his weight from foot to foot, as restless as the wind.

"But I might kill him."

"You're not strong enough to kill him," Bataar replied, his words louder than Fan would have liked. "Just give him a good thump, pull him away, and I'll cut my father loose. Then you can help us go over the wall."

Fan shook his head. For months he had been thinking about how Bataar and he might escape. His plan had been finalized. But now, with no time to spare, he was being forced to rush recklessly forward. "I wish you had a horse," he said, whispering. "How far will you get without a horse?"

"That doesn't matter! My father might die by morning. They say he's already feeble. We can't wait another day. Once I get him on the ground, once I'm beside him, I know he'll find the strength to run."

"But they'll chase you, Bataar. And they'll be mounted."

"I don't care! We'll run until dawn and then find somewhere to hide. They won't catch us."

Fan reached for Bataar's shoulder with his good hand. He held his friend tightly. "Are you sure it's him? What if it's not? What if the carving was just—"

"It's him! Stop saying that. I know it's him!"

"If you're caught, Yat-sen will skin you alive."

Bataar shook off his hand. "Why are you saying these things? He's my father! I have to save him. Stop being such a coward! What if it was your wife who was chained out there? Wouldn't you run to her?"

Nodding, Fan noticed that Bataar had started to cry once again. He leaned forward, hugging the boy with his good arm. "You're right," he whispered. "I would run to her. Just as I would run to you, Bataar. That's why I don't want you to be caught. Because I can't imagine you getting hurt."

"I'll get hurt if he dies. No pain could be worse than that."

The wind gusted, causing distant lanterns to flicker.

"How will I know if you lived or died?" Fan asked. "You'll be with your people, and I'll be with mine. I'll never come back to this place."

Bataar looked up, then used the tips of his fingers to wipe tears from his eyes. "Yat-sen won't catch me. I promise. So you'll never have to worry."

Fan thought about the vast distances that would soon separate them. In all likelihood, he'd neither see, nor hear from, Bataar again. For so many long months, he had believed that his last night on the Great Wall would be a joyous occasion. And while he rejoiced at the prospect of returning to Meng, he also lamented leaving Bataar.

"I may never have a son," he said quietly. "In some ways, you've become one to me. I'm afraid to let you go."

Bataar started to speak but stopped. He sniffed. "Learn to ride a horse," he finally replied. "Then you'll never have to let me go."

Fan nodded, then glanced to his right. On the other side of Yat-sen's watchtower, the Black Rider awaited his savior, his son. "I'll learn," Fan said, then reached for his necklace and carefully pulled it over his head. He placed it around Bataar's neck. "Something to remember me by."

"But your wife—she has the other half."

"And I'll be with her soon. We won't need it."

"Are you sure?"

Fan smiled and then reached into Bataar's robe, removing the dagger.

Bataar stroked the necklace. "I'll think of you as my Chinese father. I'll remember everything about you—especially your stories. I want to tell them to my sisters."

"I'd like that." Fan examined the dagger, feeling the weight of its hilt, imagining how he might bring it down on the guard's head. "Let's go free him. Right now, before I lose what little courage I possess."

Bataar left the side of the wall, walking slowly toward the watchtower.

After hiding the weapon within his robe, Fan followed him, trying to slow his breathing, to steady himself.

Soon they would be dead or free. No other fate existed.

*

Chuluun had spent the early part of the night struggling against his bonds, trying to escape. Though he scraped the skin from his wrists, he hadn't been able to loosen the thick ropes that confined him. He'd also tried to bite a shaft of bamboo near his head, thinking that perhaps he could rip a fragment off and use it as a saw. All he managed to do, unfortunately, was bloody his lips, gums, and tongue. Even with a jagged splinter held between his teeth, he hadn't been able to fray a single rope.

But the blood that oozed from his lips onto his chin and chest gave him an idea. As the wind picked up, he sagged against his ropes, pretending to be dead. Blood continued to drip from his mouth, coating his chest and belly. When his wounds finally ceased to bleed, he bit his lips and tongue, reopening his injuries. More blood fell. Still, he made no move, even as the new position of his body made his hands go numb. He rested in the blackness, thinking of his loved ones, then creating a plan for how he would find and free Bataar. If his son resisted him, he would knock him unconscious and carry him back to his people.

His guards had always checked him from time to time, and it was his hope that they would believe him to be dead and would cut him down. He waited, resisting the urge to move, so used to the taste of blood that he no longer noticed it. The pain of his injuries kept him awake. Though his body was battered and weary, his mind rushed ahead. He knew that his countrymen would attack soon. Assuming that his plan was still in place, they would be nearing the wall. Soon the diversionary assault would begin.

Afraid that he would slip into a dreamless sleep, Chuluun imagined what he would do with Bataar, once they were free. They would hunt together, of course. They would track game, make their own arrows, and rest under the stars. No longer would they fight the Chinese. That battle would have been already lost and won. Instead they would lead their loved ones away from the southern frontier. They'd head north, into a harsher land, but one untroubled by war. It would be there that Chuluun and his wife would grow old. In a simple but comfortable *yurt*, they'd smile at their blessings, and the cries of their grandchildren. He would die first, most likely, a belief which comforted him. With her beside him, having forgiven him, he would not fear death. She had always been the stronger of the two. He might have fought their enemies, brought them down beneath his feet, but she had endured his absence, raising their children, keeping them fed, warm, and safe. As the spirits finally came to greet him, he would squeeze her hand one last time. Then he would drift away from her, leaving signs of his passage for her to follow one day.

When some Chinese guards walked up to him, Chuluun thought they were a part of his imaginings. He almost called out to them but somehow remembered that he remained on the wall, that he was a prisoner. His eyes still closed, he readied himself for what was to come. Sure enough, his face was slapped. He made no effort to resist the blows. Instead his head rolled from side to side. The Chinese spoke, their voices harsh and foreign. Something slammed into his wounded thigh. Though the pain was instantaneous, he made no noise, even as his eyes swelled with tears.

The Chinese started to cut him down. He let himself fall forward, leaning against the ropes that remained, then falling again. When only his ankles remained bound, he toppled to the side, gritting his teeth as the ropes twisted his flesh. The Chinese began to talk again. He had no idea if there were two, three, or even more. Someone kicked his belly. The blow had little force behind it, and he realized that they believed him to be dead. A guard started to cut the ropes around his feet. Soon he was free, but he made no move to attack. His hands tingled and ached as blood flowed back into them. Keeping his breaths shallow, he thanked the spirits for the moonless night. The darkness was his ally.

Chuluun prepared himself, asking his ancestors for strength. He cracked his eyes open. His vision adjusted quickly to the night, and he saw that two guards stood above him, facing north. Each was armored and armed. Yet their backs were to him, and as they spoke, he rose silently. The spirits must have been bored that night, for vigor flowed back into him. He pulled one man's sword from its sheath and then smashed its hilt into him, sending him careening over the wall. The remaining soldier drew his own weapon but didn't shout. He must have been so surprised by the sight of the waking dead that his voice failed him. Chuluun lunged forward, his sword extended. The guard tried to deflect his blade but was far too slow. He died almost instantly as the steel pierced his ribs and heart.

After glancing around to make sure that no one had seen the commotion, Chuluun stripped the soldier. He tied the naked body to the bamboo latticework in the same manner that he had been positioned. Then he dressed himself in the man's clothes and armor, which were too tight on him, but made him look like one of the wall's defenders.

For once Chuluun was grateful for the height of the watchtowers on either side of him. The guards atop them were either asleep, distracted, or couldn't see his part of the wall. Whatever the reason, no alarm had been sounded.

Though he had thought about walking into one of the watchtowers and searching for Bataar, he understood that such an approach was foolish. He didn't know the layout of the towers and couldn't speak the language of his enemies. How far would he get within what would quickly become his tomb? No, it was better to wait for the arrival of his countrymen. Once they attacked, he could run, with relative freedom, from tower to tower, searching for his son. With luck, his countrymen wouldn't kill him.

Walking to the edge of the northern parapet, Chuluun stared into the darkness. He wiped the blood from his face, he tested the weight and feel of the sword, and then he waited, praying to the spirits that his countrymen hadn't abandoned him, that they would arrive before the light of dawn.

*

East of Chuluun's position, the two thousand Mongol riders readied themselves to attack. The wall was nearly within an arrow's flight away. Many of the men had never been so close to it, and found themselves in awe of its proportions. They understood how their fathers and grandfathers had thrown themselves against it, always with great bravery but little success. The wall had resisted them, broken them, and yet remained standing and unmarred. To a man they wanted to bring it down, to knock a hole in it so large that their army could ride through unmolested. Bets and boasts were exchanged about who would be the first to reach its summit.

Though any man to attain that plateau would likely die, most of the horsemen would be pleased with such a fate. They would be immortalized, champions of their people—the men who slew the great dragon and changed the course of history.

Orders were repeated. Horsemen readied their weapons. Ahead of them scores of their countrymen were on foot, running toward the wall, ladders held among them. An alarm sounded—a powerful reverberation of wood against steel. The sound carried, soon followed by others. Warning fires surged to life. Men ran atop the wall.

The Mongol commander notched an arrow on his longbow. He gave his men no speech of encouragement. They needed none.

Instead he shouted the war cry of his father's father, spurring his stallion toward the dragon.

Men around and behind him screamed amid a sudden thundering of hooves. The ground seemed to tremble. The dragon lit up as cannons fired, exploding with light and sound.

The commander rushed forward, knowing he would die, fearing failure more than death, determined to climb the great beast and slay the men who had brought it to life.

*

The cannon fire startled them. Meng leapt to her feet, rushing to a barred window. She became aware of alarms and saw that fires had been lit on a distant watchtower. At first she thought the tower was aflame but then remembered that Fan had written to her once, describing how signal fires were used to announce the arrival and numbers of attacking horsemen. She saw four fires, each unusually bright.

Outside their locked room, men were shouting. Meng peered through the window and saw that soldiers were quickly donning armor and reaching for weapons. Horses were saddled and spurred away. Where there had been idleness and lethargy, chaos now reigned supreme. In their haste to prepare for battle, men knocked over tables, extinguishing candles and breaking dishes. Curses were exchanged, orders shouted.

"Is it a large attack?" Meng asked, steadying Ping as he rose from the floor.

Ping's right eye was swollen halfway shut. His movements were as stiff as an old man's. He nodded. "It's got them scared, that's for sure. And it's not easy to scare the emperor's valiant, magnificent defenders."

"Look, they're leaving us."

Ping peered through the window. "All but the big one. I think he likes me."

"Maybe this is our chance. Can you pick that lock?"

Ping grunted in disdain, kneeling in front of the door's keyhole. He asked Meng to look for a thin piece of iron—something he could bend and use to manipulate the lock. Without hesitation she pulled out a metal pin that had been holding up her hair. Though some of her hair fell to her shoulder, she paid the sight no heed, instead handing over the pin. Suddenly she was frantic with worry. Fan had never written about being in the fighting, but maybe he'd lied to her. Maybe he was expected to defend the wall like any other soldier.

"Please hurry," she whispered. "We have to get to him."

"And what of the giant? Is there a sword near the door? A weapon of any kind?"

At first Meng spied nothing of consequence outside their room. The small courtyard that bordered it was dominated by an overturned table. Broken porcelain was strewn across the ground. A *Go* board and its pieces were also scattered. As alarm bells continued to ring, Meng glanced to the right, then the left, her gaze finally stopping on a spear that remained propped against a nearby wall.

"There's a spear," she answered, noting that the big guard was only ten paces away. He stood, facing north, his hand on his sword hilt. "It's to the left of the door, behind the guard."

"And you want me to kill him, Meng? Is that what you're asking?"

His question shook her. She thought about Fan, his imprisonment, and how the guard had beaten Ping. "Can you just wound him?" she finally answered, wringing her hands.

"It would be safer to kill him."

"No, I can't ask you to do that, to put blood on your hands because of me."

"My hands are already bloody."

"But to stab him in the back would be murder. Don't do that, Ping. I'd rather turn around and leave than have you kill him like that."

He paused from his work, turning to her. "Don't be so dramatic. You're not performing on a stage."

"But I mean it."

"When have you ever not meant anything?" he whispered, resuming his work. "You're not exactly known for your lies."

"I thought you could open that."

"And I thought you could fool those guards into thinking that you were a man. Why didn't you hold your sword with strength, anyway? Didn't you see him shift his feet, twist to swing his blade? You stood there like a helpless child, and I know you're anything but helpless."

"I know. I'm sorry."

"Don't be sorry. Be strong. If you want to escape with your man, you'll have to be strong."

Meng nodded, aware that her hair was still partially uncovered. It fell to her shoulder. She considered hiding it once again, but thought about Ping's words. He was right. If she was to find Fan and flee with him, she needed to stand with strength. And hiding behind a mask of someone she wasn't would only enfeeble her. Besides, if the men on the wall were under a large-scale assault, the last thing they would be worried about was the sight of a woman among them. Perhaps her hair would even prevent her from being attacked.

"Should I try?" she asked, edging forward.

"You asked me to stop my thieving ways, I did, and now look what's happened. I can't even pick a lock. Maybe I should really become a monk. I certainly can't go back to my former ways."

"Perhaps you should just—"

"There," he whispered, as the lock clicked open. He stood up awkwardly, dropping the pin on the floor.

Meng put her hand on his arm to steady him. "Are you sure

you're alright? Maybe I should just sneak out."

"What I'm going to do is crack that big, bumbling giant over the head with that spear shaft. Then we're going to run to the wall. Everyone will be on its northern side, exchanging pleasantries with their Mongol friends. We'll hurry up the back side of the wall and no one will even notice."

"Are you sure?"

He smiled. "My plans are flawless, remember?"

She closed her eyes, envisioning the path that he had described. "Be careful, Ping."

"Stay close to me."

He gently pulled on the door handle. Though the hinges groaned, amid the clamor of the distant bells little else could be heard. Creeping forward, his feet barely settling on the ground, Ping stepped out of the doorway and headed straight for the spear. He pulled it away from the wall, his right hand on top. Then he moved toward the guard, who was still facing away from them.

Meng was certain that the big man would turn around. But he never did, and without a sound Ping raised the spear shaft high in the air and brought it down hard on the guard's head. Even though he wore a helmet, the blow stunned him. He fell to his knees, his hands rising to his ears. Ping swung the spear again, this time horizontally. Again, the thick shaft struck home, smashing the guard's head to the side. He toppled over, no longer conscious.

Ping pulled the man's sword from his sheath. He tossed Meng the cracked but unbroken spear. "Follow me."

She did as he asked, running down an alley and then onto a broader street. The area teemed with soldiers who were rushing toward the wall. No one paid them any heed. They were just two more warriors racing ahead, trying to do their duty, to prevent the Mongol hordes from laying waste to their noble kingdom.

*

The Mongol commander of the main invading force studied the attack to the east. He saw bursts of flames from cannons, heard the alarm bells, and could easily imagine what was transpiring. His countrymen were rushing forward, some on horseback, some on foot. Ladders were being thrust against the wall and arrows shot over it. The Chinese would surely be desperate to reinforce the besieged position, and their soldiers must be pouring out of nearby watchtowers, running along the wall, rushing forward to repel the attackers. Two thousand Mongols assailing the wall in the dead of night was an assault that would have to be dealt with head-on, with all available resources.

Though the commander wanted to relieve the strain on his countrymen, he forced himself to be patient. His overall strategy would only work if the positions around Yat-sen's tower were weakened by the loss of men. The Mongol officer needed the Chinese to rush east toward the fighting. When convinced that they had, he would lead his three thousand horsemen in a charge against the two watchtowers ahead of him. If they could capture those towers, the night would belong to them.

Turning in his saddle, the commander studied the troops behind him. Most were silent, though their horses were skittish, aware of the distant pounding of cannons. The heavily armed men were illuminated as flashes of cannon fire pulsated through the darkness. Never had the commander heard so many cannons firing, so close in succession to one another. He knew that his countrymen must be taking a terrible beating. Yet he could do nothing, at least for the moment, to relieve them. He must let the Chinese believe that they were winning, drawing them away from the position he craved to capture.

Tightly gripping his reins, he raised his voice, asking his men for their patience. Someone coughed. A horse neighed. The commander flexed his fingers, their joints swollen and aching. He had seen more than fifty winters come and go, and he didn't mind the prospect of dying on the wall. He was ready. His wife had perished earlier that summer, drowned in flooding while washing their clothes. Their sons and daughters were grown, and he was eager to join her. At least in death they could be together once more.

Squinting, the commander strained to see if any of his countrymen had reached the top of the wall. The cannons continued to fire, which made him believe that they had failed. The goal of every Mongol upon straddling the wall was to knock out the Chinese gunners. Without their devastating cannons, the wall's defenders were vulnerable.

The rate of the firing cannons seemed to further intensify. Aware that his countrymen were surely getting butchered, the commander raised his fist. He repeated his previous orders, lifted his longbow into the air, and spurred his mount. Behind him, men screamed war cries. The vast column of riders and mounts surged ahead, then split, each group heading toward one of two adjacent watchtowers.

The commander's aches suddenly forgotten, he smiled as younger, fitter men charged past him, straight toward Yat-sen's tower. Many held their longbows aloft. Others carried ladders between them.

Though they were now only a few hundred paces away from the wall, not a single cannon had opened fire. The night, so dark, cloaked them.

Believing that victory might finally be theirs, the commander shouted at his men, beseeching them to make their ancestors proud.

They rushed at the wall like a giant, black wave, finally striking against it, flesh pounding against stone. Cannons burst into life, arrows flew, men screamed.

It all began with a sudden, desperate swiftness.

*

As he struggled to subdue the initial attack, Yat-sen heard the new pounding of cannons and released an arrow, not watching to see if it downed the Mongol horseman below. He spun on his heels, staring to the west, up the wall toward his command post. He saw bursts of flames as more cannons fired. The ground below the wall, his wall, was illuminated, and he cursed at the sight of hundreds, if not thousands, of horsemen.

Screaming at the officers around him to pay heed, he commanded several to stay and protect their current position, but demanded that most gather their troops and follow him to face the new, and likely larger, threat. As he ran toward his stallion, the reins to which were held by a servant, Yat-sen felt an arrow glance off his armor. He vaulted onto his mount, spurred it forward, and was soon charging atop the wall, glad that he had left Li in charge of his command post. The big, capable man was surely preparing his defenses and sending couriers to ask for further reinforcements. These fresh men would pour out of nearby barracks to the south and watchtowers to the west. If Yat-sen could hold the wall against the initial assault, the Mongols would surely be beaten back.

His stallion began to clatter up the short, wide steps that led to the next watchtower. Yat-sen shouted at men to let him pass, and they leapt aside as he and his mount squeezed through the tower's door. Inside, soldiers were donning armor and grabbing weapons. Yat-sen cursed them, screamed that they follow him, and exited the tower, the stone door frame scraping against his shoulders and his stallion's sides. His mount neighed, and he spurred it again.

Men were running ahead of him toward the fighting. One didn't hear his cry of warning and was trampled. Yat-sen paid the soldier no heed, continuing to rush forward, aware that he still had to pass through four more watchtowers before arriving at the conflict. Alarm bells continued to sound. Cannons thumped to the east and west. Scores of Chinese ran forward, their hands on their sword hilts, their feet agile and swift.

Though his men had been trained to fight on two fronts, and this Mongol tactic was nothing new, Yat-sen was close enough to the second attack to grasp its scale. He was certain that thousands of the horsemen were beneath his tower. He could see their ladders against a curve in the wall. Men climbed up, toppled, but were quickly replaced. The Mongols rose higher, nearing the summit, their screams reaching his ears.

Racing forward, he pulled his sword from its sheath, knowing that he would soon be fighting in hand-to-hand combat. He entered another tower, swore at the men who leapt out of his path, and continued on.

As he exited the tower and was once again on the wall, he thought of his father, wondering how he had felt as the Mongols overran his force. They had trapped him, beaten him to the ground, and tarnished his name for a generation. Yat-sen had sought to reclaim that name, the glory that had been a part of his heritage. But the Mongols once again threatened. If they captured his section of the wall, he would kill himself rather than endure the humiliation of another defeat.

The prospect of failure filling him with sudden, uncontrollable rage, Yat-sen beat his sword hilt against his stallion. The horse lurched ahead, clattering up another series of wide, short steps.

He was nearing the fighting. Soon his enemies would recognize him. They would seek to cut him down and become legends in the process.

But Yat-sen was certain that it would be they who fell. They would die with him standing above them, his sword bloody and blurring, his screams of victory the last sound they heard.

*

Still clad in his Chinese armor, Chuluun stood amid throngs of enemy soldiers, shooting arrows toward the approaching horde of horsemen, though always careful to miss them. He pleaded silently to the spirits to give the attackers strength and courage, to let them finally slay the dragon that had reigned over their land for so long. He watched, in awe, as his countrymen threw themselves at the wall, shattering against it, yet rising up, ladders sweeping toward the stonework as nearby cannons seemed to shake the very world.

When his countrymen reached the top of the wall, Chuluun ripped off his Chinese helmet and rushed forward to help them, calling out in their language, encouraging them. He wrenched a defender's sword from his grasp, threw the man over the parapet, and reached down to pull up a horseman. Two Chinese soldiers screamed at him, enraged by his betrayal. Their blades flashed in the darkness. Though still weak from his imprisonment, Chuluun stepped forward, managing to cast aside one sword with his own while twisting away from the other. He shouted his son's name, slew both of his attackers, and then dropped to one knee and picked up a fallen longbow. The weapon instantly became a part of him. He notched, drew, and shot an arrow in a single, fluid motion, cutting down a nearby gunner. The cannon fell silent, even as other Chinese scrambled about it. Chuluun brought another gunner down, again shouting for Bataar.

Chinese reinforcements were pouring out of the watchtowers on either side of Chuluun as well as from stairways on the southern side of the wall. Even though more of his countrymen reached the wall's summit, Chuluun wasn't sure they could hold their position. He screamed at the horsemen to rally around him. Some did, protecting the tops of the ladders, allowing more attackers to climb over the parapet. Chuluun continued to fire the longbow, almost all of his arrows striking home, shot with such force that they were able to pierce all but the thickest armor.

The thought that Bataar might somehow be trapped within the fighting terrified Chuluun. Again and again he shouted his son's name, far more concerned with Bataar's absence than the numbers of Chinese soldiers. An arrow smashed into his longbow, nearly knocking the weapon from his grasp. Chuluun spied his attacker, drew back on his bow, and brought the man down. More and more cannons seemed to be firing, creating a series of thunderous booms that echoed off stonework and nearby mountains. Swords flashed, men screamed, and ladders were thrust from the parapet. Several mounted Chinese rode along the wall, each heavily armored and wielding a sword. These riders cut down Mongols with relative ease. Chuluun stepped toward one, ignoring his charge, his own longbow twanging as an already bloodied arrow took the Chinese in the throat, sending him toppling backward.

Chuluun eyed the horse, tempted to leap upon it. But suddenly three Chinese soldiers rushed his position. He was forced to step backward toward a surge of his countrymen, who jumped over the parapet, pressing ahead, screaming war cries, their blades adding to the carnage. Chuluun's injured leg buckled. He fell and was immediately trapped beneath the combatants. They grunted and bled and died above him. Rolling to his right, he tried to escape the press of bodies.

"Bataar!" he shouted, still on the ground. "It's me! Your father!"

A nearby cannon exploded, sending men and stonework hurling in every direction. Chuluun reached for his ears, covering them, the blood of friends and foes on his face and chest. His head rang as if the inside of a vast, iron bell. He tried to stand, fell, and saw that his left forefinger was gone. Only a bloody stump remained.

The fighting was so fierce and overwhelming that his mind threatened to simply shut down. But he thought again about Bataar, believing that he was close, that if they were not brought together in this moment that a vast distance would always separate them. The fear of such an abyss gave him strength when he had none, focus when his mind was still reeling.

Chuluun saw a piece of smoking iron on the ground near him. Needing to stop the bleeding from his missing finger, he pressed his wound against the hot steel, screaming from the pain. He almost blacked out, but managed to clear his mind and reached for a fallen sword. As soon as he staggered to his feet a wounded Chinese soldier attacked him. He brought the man down without thinking, calling out to Bataar, stumbling toward a nearby watchtower. The stonework was slick with blood, and he slipped, fell, and rose again. Several horses were running wild, trampling both Chinese and Mongols. Alarms sounded, cannons fired, and the night seemed to have turned to day. The dragon was alive, thrusting this way and that, injured and furious.

Chuluun called for his son, stumbling ahead. He wept, afraid that Bataar was already dead, killed by his own people.

"Please, no," he pleaded with the spirits, his sword flashing, cutting down another defender. A Chinese officer then rushed him, their blades meeting, sparks flying. The man was skilled and determined, but Chuluun deflected his every sweep and thrust, finally sending the man's sword tumbling into the darkness. The officer fell to his knees, pleading for mercy. Chuluun killed him without pause, again calling Bataar's name, shouting it with such force that his throat burned.

Something unseen struck him from the side, crushing the air from his lungs, knocking him down. He tried to crawl forward, his bloody hands now weaponless, his body driven by instinct and love, not rational thought.

The dragon rumbled, shooting fire into the night.

Chuluun pleaded with his unseen son to run, to flee from this place of despair and death, and never look back.

Much to Chuluun's anguish, Bataar would have to go forward alone.

*

The attacks, especially the second, had taken Fan and Bataar by surprise. Aware that the very spot where Bataar's father was being held captive was under a full assault, Fan struggled to keep up with his companion as he rushed into Yat-sen's watchtower. Inside its smoke-stained walls, chaos reigned supreme. Men scampered up and down ladders, shouted instructions, and donned armor. One room contained a slew of injured Chinese and a physician who tried to staunch bleeding bodies and save mangled limbs. Screams echoed. Cannons rumbled. The stench of burning wolf dung and expended gunpowder dominated the air.

The press of men in the narrow passageways made it hard for Bataar and Fan to run. Several times they were pushed aside as sword-wielding defenders battered their way forward. Bataar shrieked at these men, striking them with his fists, desperate to move beyond them. An immensely powerful explosion boomed to the west. Officers shouted at men to hurry, saying that the Mongols were atop the wall.

As he struggled forward, Fan tried to keep pace with Bataar, rushing to his aid when he smashed into a soldier and was about to be beaten down by the side of a sword. Grabbing Bataar with his good hand, he demanded that the boy follow him, not waiting for a response, but pressing forward once again, his heart threatening to burst from his chest.

Outside Yat-sen's watchtower, a battle raged. In the darkness it was difficult to distinguish the combatants, but men fought, maimed, and killed each other. Most of the nearby cannons had been silenced, though a few continued to thunder and burst into light. Fan tried to discern the wooden scaffolding that had held the Black Rider but couldn't see that far, even with the flash of explosions that allowed him to glimpse ahead.

The noise of the battle stunned Fan. Thousands of men struggled, screamed, and wailed. It seemed that Mongols were still pouring over the wall, despite vast numbers of Chinese reinforcements who rushed forward to face them. Swords flashed. Arrows flew. Groups of men surged toward one another like waves trapped within a confined harbor.

Bataar tried to hurry ahead, but Fan grabbed him, pulling him back. To enter the fray as a boy, on foot, was to die. As Bataar cursed and kicked, Fan spun around, looking for a horse. At first he saw nothing, but then, twenty paces ahead, he noticed that a mounted Chinese messenger had been trapped in the fighting. The man, dressed in red robes and holding a sword, swiped ineffectively at an attacker.

Before Bataar could utter a word, Fan dragged him toward the white horse, which only now did he recognize to be Yat-sen's. With each step Fan took, the fighting seemed to thicken. Men swung bloodied blades, fought on the ground, and screamed like fiends. Arrows flew with wicked precision or complete uncertainty, downing foe and friend alike.

Fan had never swung a blade in his life and didn't pause to pick up fallen weapons. Instead he continued to stumble onward, his mouth agape as the Chinese messenger was cut down and yanked from his saddle. A Mongol warrior tried to mount the stallion, but Fan pulled on his sword arm, dragging him down. The man swung at him and fell, his head striking the stonework.

"Go!" Fan shouted at Bataar, motioning for him to mount Yat-sen's horse. "Find him!"

Bataar nodded and leapt up onto the stallion. He started to speak, but his voice seemed to have left him.

Fan had always thought that he'd have time to say a proper good-bye to Bataar, that they would embrace, and speak fondly of their many months spent together. He'd wanted such a parting. But there wasn't time for embraces or declarations. At any moment, either of them could be cut down by a sword or an arrow.

Debating if he should climb up and ride with Bataar, Fan looked ahead, trying to comprehend the mayhem. He longed to protect his young friend but knew that he would only slow him down. If he was a soldier, Fan would have gone with him. He'd have shielded Bataar from men and steel. But he could offer no protection, and, by further encumbering the horse, he'd only add to Bataar's vulnerability.

"Farewell, my Mongol son!" Fan shouted, his voice barely audible above the clamor.

"I'll miss you, my Chinese father."

"Go find him!"

"Go find her!"

Fan squeezed Bataar's knee, then slapped the stallion's rump. It didn't move, but then Bataar kicked it with his heels and suddenly the horse lurched ahead, scattering men who had been fighting near it.

Standing still, unaware of the flashing blades around him, Fan watched Bataar ride. Amid the vast ugliness of war, the boy and the white stallion created beauty, moving as one, rising and falling with each progression of strides. Somehow, seemingly with the aid of magic, Bataar and Yat-sen's horse avoided masses of men and weaponry, racing forward, hooves appearing to strike air, not stone. Fan had never seen anything move so swiftly. He shouted to Bataar, urging him onward.

The sight of the boy and the stallion unchained something deep within Fan. He saw freedom, he felt its wondrous madness rush through him, and he shouted again, exalting in the spectacle of beauty amid blood, hope amid hell. Cannons boomed, illuminating Bataar, who was perched above the stallion, bent forward, seemingly carrying the great beast instead of being a burden to it.

Fan thrust his fist into the air, yelling triumphantly as Bataar burst ahead. No arrow could touch him; no sword could bring him down. He had been a prisoner for too long to be recaptured, not even on this night. Whatever goodness remained in the world, Fan was certain that it would protect Bataar. Otherwise, why was he able to move like the wind? No boy, no man, could move with such speed. Surely greater powers aided his escape.

The cannons roared, dominating the battle. Bataar disappeared.

Convinced that his friend was safe, Fan thought of himself once again, then thought of Meng. Filled with newfound strength by the sight of Bataar's departure, Fan stepped back, away from the death and despair. He also wanted to flee, to rush toward the woman he loved. This moment belonged to him, to them, to everyone who yearned for freedom.

A stairway on the southern side of the wall beckoned to him. Escape was so near. Heedless of the fighting, of the many miseries and dangers around him, he ran ahead, the stairs nearing. He imagined himself on a horse, charging forward, diminishing the distance between himself and the woman he loved. Even amid so many horrors, he smiled.

The explosion knocked him from his feet, sent him flying sideways as if he were no more than a grain of sand in a gale.

He tried to call out to her, to let her know that he would always look for her, cherish her. But his mind could form no words, no thoughts.

While the battle continued to rage, a terrible, irresistible weight pressed down on him. Whatever freedom he'd imagined had been no more than a dream.

Ping had always mocked soldiers, ridiculing them for what he saw as laziness and corruption. But as he raced up one of the southern stairways leading to the Great Wall, he realized that he'd been wrong. Hundreds of his countrymen also ran toward the raging, vast battle between the two watchtowers. The soldiers shouted cries of war and showed no fear as they pulled swords from sheaths and notched arrows. Ping had never been proud of his country, but he felt a sudden strength surge through him, despite his wounds and aches. These men were rushing forward to defend their land, their people, their way of life. Each ran as if chased by the fires of the underworld. They ran toward their deaths but didn't alter their courses, holding swords and banners aloft, slamming like a spearhead into the underbelly of the Mongol force, penetrating deeply.

Having never been in love, Ping didn't understand what drove Meng. After all, she could have waited for the fighting to end before searching for her husband. Waiting would have been infinitely safer than rushing to join the madness ahead. But like the soldiers around her, she also seemed immune or perhaps oblivious to her own fears and vulnerability. Her hair completely unpinned, she ran forward as a woman, shouting her husband's name, asking wounded Chinese where he might be. Some men looked at her uncomprehendingly. Others spoke of the craftsman, pointing ahead.

Ten days earlier, Ping would have fled from the fighting. But now he was drawn toward it, like a butterfly to nectar. He wanted to be a part of something bigger than himself, more important than himself. Perhaps in this very moment, he would finally make his father proud. More important, he could help the woman who had shown him that he was more than a thief, more than a failure. The blood in his veins was as pure as any, and whatever shame had befallen him for the first part of his life, his latter years could be different. His legacy could be grand.

Picking up a fallen sword, Ping hurried to catch up to Meng. She continued to shout for Fan, avoiding groups of fighting men, but moving among the wounded, surprising them with her presence and her questions. In the darkness, amid the flashing cannons, she must have appeared to the soldiers as some sort of magical incarnation. Their wounds were suddenly forgotten, their screams stifled. A woman could never be present in such a battle, yet there she was, promising that they would survive, asking about a man named Fan. She shared her name with them, and they told her what they could; reaching for her hands, reveling in their warmth. "Thank you," she whispered, again and again. On the street, beyond the fighting, these men might have shackled her, imprisoned her. But on the wall, so near death and despair, they saw her as a reincarnation of their own mothers, wives, and daughters. Though her face wasn't beautiful or her fingers covered in jewels, she sheltered them with her presence and her words. She was a gift amid horror, a treasure worth more than gold.

Meng's affect on Ping was even more pronounced. He sensed the urgency in her voice, saw how her gaze darted between groups of fighting men. Now that she was so close to her husband, her love for him seemed so much more palpable. Ping wanted them to be together. Whatever jealousy he had felt at their union was gone, replaced by understanding and awe. She had gone where no woman could go, risked so much, only to be with him.

A large, badly wounded officer named Li nodded as she spoke, replying that he'd seen Fan fall, not far from where he lay. Li said that he had heard of her, that rumors existed on the wall about their tested, yet enduring love. Meng wept at these words, holding the officer's hands, squeezing them tight. He told her to hurry, to run to Fan, to leave this place with him and never look back. Meng nodded, stood up, and rushed forward. The stonework was slick with blood, and both she and Ping slipped as they waded deeper into the fighting.

Cannons thundered. More Mongols poured over the wall, screaming, blades flashing in their hands. A line of Chinese soldiers broke and suddenly three horsemen ran toward Meng, howling in delight. Ping knocked her aside, thrusting his sword ahead, impaling the largest of his foes. He ducked beneath a blow meant to take his head, but the maneuver left him vulnerable to a downward strike, and the third adversary's sword blurred, slicing deeply into his left shoulder. Pain was instantaneous, horrific, and all-encompassing. As Meng screamed and threw herself against his attacker, Ping struggled to his feet and stabbed his blade into the man's groin. The horseman went down with her on top of him. Then steel flashed again, and Ping pitched backward, his chest gashed and bleeding. A Mongol stood before him, his teeth bared, his sword coated with Ping's blood. As the blade began to descend once again, an arrow struck the Mongol in the arm, spinning him around. A second arrow brought him down.

Ping collapsed, his sword clattering on the stonework. He tried to stand, but his body wouldn't respond. Though his legs appeared uninjured, they didn't seem to work. Groaning, he rolled to his right, looking for Meng. She was trapped under the dying Mongol but managed to push him aside, then crawled toward Ping, reaching for him.

"No," she muttered, shaking her head.

"I look ... worse than I feel," he lied, grimacing. "It's mostly their blood."

She reached under his shoulders and started to drag him away from the fighting. As cannons thundered, he looked up at her face, glad that her hair fell toward him, that her true nature was finally revealed.

"Don't ever ... be a man again," he whispered.

"What?"

"You're better as a woman. So much better."

Continuing to drag him, she wept, her tears dropping to his face. He had never tasted tears before, but he tasted hers, remembering how he'd shared his salt with her. How very long ago that night seemed. Had it truly even existed?

Meng pulled him to an area near the southern parapet that was free of fighting. To Ping everything suddenly was peaceful. Though his wounds burned, the pain seemed less than before. He was wet, and he looked up, searching for rain. Only then did he realize that it was his blood that covered him.

He weakly shook his head. "I'd rather ... it be rain."

Meng was pressing something against his chest. Her coat? The one she had made for Fan? He hadn't realized that she'd carried

400

it here after their capture and escape. But she had. "Don't," he whispered. "You'll ruin it."

"I don't care."

"All your work … for nothing."

"You're not nothing, Ping," she replied, holding the coat against his shoulder and chest, trying to stop the bleeding. "You're everything."

He smiled, glad that she was leaning over him. He liked the feel of her tears against his face. "Don't be melodramatic. I'm much closer to nothing … than everything."

"I need to leave you. I must find a physician!"

His hand tightened around her wrist. "Please don't leave."

"But I have to!"

"Stay. Please stay."

"But Ping … "

Something rumbled in the distance. Thunder? A cannon? Ping closed his eyes, then opened them, hoping that she was still there. "How we fooled them," he whispered. "A thief … and a woman. We came so far together."

She lowered herself to him, pressing against his chest, sobbing. He remembered how he had touched her as they hid under the boat. Then he saw himself as a child, running though a rice paddy, blue skies overhead. How he felt as if he could run forever, charging forward, his spirit light and free.

"You should run to Fan," he said, his voice weak and unsteady. "Run with … those big feet of yours."

Meng rose above him, even as her hand fell to his face. Her fingers swept across his jaw, caressing him. "Your father would be proud of you," she said quietly. "I'm proud of you."

"You know me better … than he ever did."

"How lucky for me."

His eyes swelled with tears. "I think it's time … for me to go."

"Please, please don't."

"Someone calls for me. A lonely courtesan … I hope."

She cradled his face with both hands. "No. You're wrong. It's only me."

"I won't become a ghost, will I? I've heard … such dreadful stories of wandering ghosts."

"You've already wandered enough, Ping. You don't have to worry about that."

He nodded. "Thank you. That's reassuring. Even though you're … hardly an expert on ghosts."

She bit her bottom lip, her tears falling, her hands about his face. Shuddering, she continued to hold him. "I want to walk farther with you, to go to new places with you."

A response formed in Ping's mind but fled just as quickly as it had arrived. He tried to speak but felt as if he was drawing closer to sleep. Everything, even his pain, seemed to grow dull. His eyes fluttered open and shut. He saw Meng, then a flower, then Meng. Were they one and the same?

"I think … I'll rest," he whispered. "I've walked … long enough."

She leaned down, kissing his forehead. "I would have never made it so far without you. You brought me here. You did what no one else would do."

"And … I'd do it again."

"Please don't go. I want to hear your voice. There's still so much for you to say."

"Such a beautiful flower … you are."

The ground beneath them trembled. The dragon seemed to move, as if trying to escape a relentless pain.

Meng's mouth opened, and surely she said something, but Ping didn't hear her. He tried to speak, though his voice failed him. He faltered.

Now, as darkness closed in on him, he wanted her to kiss him again. To his delight, to his amazement, she did just that, leaning down, pressing her lips against his cheek. Her touch brought a flood of warmth into him, lifting him up, infusing him with her goodness and grace. He smiled, glimpsing something bright and beautiful—a flash of tranquility in the distance, a vision he had never seen before.

He died with her lips still pressed against him.

*

Bataar had never ridden a horse like this one. Though he'd known many strong, durable, and swift mounts, the white stallion beneath him was something more. Yat-sen's beautiful mount seemed incapable of fear, or perhaps was even spurred forward by the chaos around it and not the thumping of Bataar's heels. Whatever the case, the stallion leapt over bodies and navigated groups of struggling men without pause or protest. Bataar felt as if he were riding the very wind, rising over the dead and dying, immune to the woes of mortal men.

He called for his father, charging toward the broken latticework of bamboo that had once held him. To his relief, his father's body didn't sag against the splintered bamboo. He was gone. But where was he?

A ladder was thrust from below to fall against the nearby parapet. Immediately Chinese soldiers rushed forward, into a storm of Mongol arrows, to try to push the ladder away. Four defenders fell from the airborne onslaught. But two others made it to the ladder, throwing themselves against it. Without thought, Bataar kicked Yat-sen's horse ahead, sending it charging into the Chinese. They fell, screaming, beneath its hooves. Bataar yanked his reins to the right, forcing the stallion away from the parapet.

Once again Bataar shouted for his father, as Mongols poured over the wall behind him. Chinese reinforcements rushed forward, and suddenly he was trapped between two large groups of combatants. Arrows flew, men fell, and banners swayed. Bataar kicked the stallion again, clucking his tongue, trying to lead it out of the mayhem. For the first time since the fighting began, he feared for his life. He couldn't die with his father so close, with freedom only a few feet away.

"No!" he screamed, twisting in his saddle, avoiding the thrust of a Chinese spear that was meant to skewer him. He pulled back hard on his reins, causing the stallion to rear up on its hind legs, its front hooves battering his attacker. The man grunted and fell.

"Father! Where are you?"

Soldiers closed about him. An arrow darted through the night to bury itself in the stallion's neck. It shrieked in agony, throwing back its head, nearly knocking Bataar from the saddle. The horse began to leap and buck, as if trying to rid itself of a sharp-clawed predator. Bataar hung on desperately, unaware of how the stallion cleared an area around it, of how its hooves dented armor and sent both Mongols and Chinese to their deaths.

Wrapping his arms around the stallion's neck, Bataar held onto it tightly. Still, even he wouldn't have remained on the horse if someone hadn't leapt onto it behind him. The additional weight served to settle the horse. It stopped bucking but continued to twist in small, tight circles.

"Let him run," a familiar voice said.

Bataar spun in the saddle, his eyes tearing. His father reached around him, holding him tight.

"Father!"

"Save us, my son."

Bataar looked ahead. They were encircled by scores, if not hundreds of combatants. To stay here was to die. Without another word, Bataar spurred the stallion ahead, sending it careening into a line of Chinese soldiers. Several men swung their swords at it, and while their cuts were not fatal, their blades sliced deeply, causing the mount to surge ahead. Bataar and his father were nearly thrown from the saddle but somehow remained upright, moving as one, staying low and forward.

The top of the wall was brighter now, illuminated by fires from within the nearby watchtowers. Cannons continued to boom. Chinese reinforcements ran up stairs on the southern side of the fortification. Mongols leapt over ladders. The two armies pressed together, howling and hacking atop the fifteen-foot wide span of stonework. Bataar didn't know where to go. Everywhere he looked, men were fighting and dying. Another arrow struck the stallion, this time in the flank. It stumbled but somehow, miraculously, remained upright, charging ahead, even as it shuddered and shrieked. The stallion would fall, Bataar was certain. Not even its breathtaking speed or bravery would save it.

A thick wave of Chinese surged toward them. More arrows flew, one clipping Bataar's ankle, gouging his flesh. He cried out in pain, yet the agony of the steel was a gift, for suddenly he knew what must be done. As countless swords and spears darted toward him, he yanked hard on the reins, swinging the dying stallion to the left, toward the northern parapet. He kicked it once, screamed at it for a final burst of strength, and then leaned backward as the mount leapt over the parapet. Abruptly they were flying into the darkness, twisting ahead, toward an unseen mass of men below. Bataar let go of the reins, threw his arms around his head, and closed his eyes.

The impact was violent and cruel, hammering the air from his lungs, ripping his flesh, bruising his bones. Writhing in agony, Bataar rolled on the ground, trying to breathe, unaware of the fiery dragon above him, or of his father. All he knew was pain. He tried to flee from it but failed, shrinking before the blackness, gasping like a fish torn from water, clutching at himself, as if he could suffocate his own misery.

Finally, when death seemed about to claim him, Bataar's lungs drew in fresh air. He straightened, still wheezing, still afire with pain. Yet he lived.

Rolling over, he looked for his father, and saw that he also moved. Men ran around them, many carrying ladders, others firing longbows at the defenders above. Bataar didn't care about these sights. He was done with the wall, with the fighting. Grimacing, he crawled toward his father, reaching for his hands, feeling the strength of his grip and weeping in relief. Somehow his father had remained on top of the stallion. The mount had broken his fall, dying in the process, crushed from the descent before the sting of the arrows could kill it.

His father pulled him up, over the horse, so that their faces were close. "Are you ... broken?" his father whispered, holding him tight.

"No," Bataar answered.

"I saw you ... roll. You rolled like a rock."

"My hip. I think I landed on my hip. And my backside."

Large hands cradled Bataar's face, thumbs stroking his cheeks. "I thought you were dead. That's why I never came. Please forgive me, my son. How I failed you."

Bataar shook his head. "You came. And I knew you would."

His father began to weep, shudders dominating his large frame. Bataar had never watched his father cry. He didn't know what to think of it. Wanting to see his father smile, not weep, Bataar squeezed his forearm. "Can you ride, Father?"

"Yes ... I think so."

"Will you take me from here? Will you take me home?"

Nodding, his father moved slowly from the dead horse. Bataar stroked the stallion's neck, whispering his thanks. He then tried to stand, but the pain in his hip was too great. He let his father pick him up, and carry him away from the besieged and burning wall. His father limped forward, kissing the top of his head, promising that he'd never be left alone again.

They found an idle horse. Bataar felt himself rise upward, over the saddle. He remained in his father's arms. Though his hip and backside ached, it felt good to be moving again, to have a horse beneath him. Above, a sea of stars shimmered.

The clamor of battle gradually faded. Bataar thought of Fan, hoping he had also made it to safety, that they would both forever remain free.

The stars continued to twinkle. Bataar wondered how Mongols and Chinese could live beneath the same beauty and remain at war, generation after generation.

"I don't want you to go back to fighting," he whispered. "Please tell me that you'll never go back."

"I left my weapons at the wall. I'll never retrieve them."

"Good, Father. That's so good."

"We'll hunt and live on the land together, my son. With your mother and sisters. I'll carve you horses and everything will be as it should."

Bataar grimaced, his hip now throbbing. "How far away are they? Can I see them tonight?"

"Tomorrow, my son. You'll see them tomorrow. Tonight, it will be just the two of us."

"That's fine. Don't hurry."

"Should we stop and rest?"

"Yes. Let's do."

Bataar felt himself being lifted once again. He grunted, suddenly very tired. He wanted to sleep.

The stars seemed brighter than ever. Men whom Bataar had

known as a child had claimed to see horses among them. Bataar could see no such images but was pleased that he and his father looked upon the same sight.

"When I was told that you were dead, a part of me died too," his father whispered, wrapping something around his bloody hand. "The best part."

"I'm not dead."

"And I feel alive. More than I have in a long, long time."

"Good."

"I love you, my son, my lord of the stallion."

Bataar smiled. He then closed his eyes, at peace in his father's arms, grateful for the bond and warmth between them.

★

Though the watchtowers on either side of him were filled with flames, and hundreds of Mongols were still on the Great Wall, Yat-sen felt as if the tide of battle was turning. His soldiers appeared to be more numerous. Cannons still fired. And the enemy had failed to secure a defensible position. Dawn would soon unfold, and when it did, the Mongol's great ally—darkness—would vanish. Thousands of Chinese reinforcements would also arrive, having been summoned from nearby cities and other parts of the wall.

While these tidings should have pleased Yat-sen, he fought with rage, not elation. He'd earlier been knocked from his stallion, and the horse had been stolen from him. From time to time he had seen it running atop the wall, sometimes bearing a rider, sometimes not. Every single one of his men knew that the stallion was his, and all would realize that he'd been bested.

To make matters worse, later Yat-sen had seen the slave boy spur the wounded and bloody stallion over the parapet, perhaps to die in the plunge, but nonetheless escaping into the darkness. Accompanying him was the Black Rider. At first Yat-sen hadn't understood why they fought and rode together, but with a sickening realization he'd deduced that the Black Rider was the boy's father. That's why he had attacked the wall, day after day, month after month. That's why he'd targeted Yat-sen, blaming him for the boy's internment. Yat-sen berated himself for his stupidity, for having not realized what was so obvious. If he had known about their relationship, he could have used the boy to extract information from the Black Rider. The man must have known about the looming Mongol attack.

Aware that he could have planned for and annihilated the barbarians who now stood on his wall, Yat-sen rushed toward the fiercest fighting. He glimpsed Li's body, cursed a Mongol who tugged at his armor, and ran toward the horseman, engaging him with a flurry of sword strokes. The Mongol was strong, determined, and skilled. Their blades locked, disengaged, and clanged once again. As they struggled, both men slipped and slid on the bloody stonework. Yat-sen ignored an arrow that ricocheted off his helmet. Grunting, he slammed his knee into his adversary's groin. As the man instinctively bent over, Yat-sen struck him on the head with his sword hilt. The Mongol crumpled.

Yat-sen hacked at his immobile adversary, then waded through bodies and discarded weapons toward the northern parapet. He shouted to his men, extolling them to throw the barbarians back into their wasteland. Two Mongols heard his cry and confronted him. He killed the larger man, then turned to face his wounded companion. Somehow the Mongol's blade slid past his guard and opened up a gash along his forearm. Yat-sen bellowed in pain, killed the horseman, and was about to help a cannon's crew when he heard a woman's voice.

The woman, whoever she was, shouted for Fan. Suddenly Yat-sen remembered Yehonala's prediction—that Fan's wife, who had disappeared without a trace, would come looking for him.

"No," Yat-sen whispered, spinning around, searching for her.

Cannons boomed. A group of Chinese soldiers near him were decimated by a blast. Though Yat-sen knew that at least one of his cannons had been captured by the Mongols and aimed at his own men, he could only think of the woman. He needed to find her, to tell her that he, not her husband, had read her words. Then she would fall beneath his blade.

The woman could never live. Not when she bestowed such love to the one man who had defied him, not when their union was something he would never experience.

Her voice came again, drifting through the tumult of battle. He looked to the west, then east, seeing only men—endless waves of men that came together and fell. A cannon exploded, sending stonework and steel hurtling in every direction. Soldiers screamed and writhed. Something struck Yat-sen in the shoulder, spinning him around, knocking him off his feet. He toppled, looked for his sword, and winced from the ringing within his head.

He heard her voice again. She was screaming Fan's name, over and over. Each cry might as well have been a sword that hacked down upon Yat-sen. Yehonala, he knew, would never wade into battle for him. He would be abandoned, no matter that he cared for her, that he wanted her to be his.

His family's name, tarnished for so long, would never again gleam in the sunlight. Too many Mongols were on the wall, too much killing. Even after he won this battle, he would be replaced. Officials in Beijing would cringe at how close their precious wall had come to being overrun. He would be blamed.

All that was left for him to do was kill the craftsman and his wife. Grunting, his body bleeding in a dozen places, he struggled to his feet and wandered toward her voice, his sword in hand.

When the lovers had died, he would kill the Mongols until none remained on his wall. Then he would go to Yehonala. He would see if she could save him.

*

In the darkness of his mind, where he had tried to flee from the fighting, Fan heard her voice too. It came to him as if on wings, as if carried by something warm and bathed in light. He heard her say his name, again and again. She sounded as if she was calling to him from a vast distance, searching for his presence across infinite reaches of time and space.

Fan was afraid that the dream would end and didn't open his eyes, even as cannons thundered and the aches of his wounds returned. He fought against consciousness, lingering in the void between realities, listening to the voice of the woman he loved. He might not ever hear that voice again, might not be lifted to such a great height.

Someone touched his face. He turned away, moaning.

"Fan. It's me. Please, please wake up."

"No."

"I'm here, Fan. I came for you. Just open your eyes."

Still he resisted, falling back toward the blackness, fading away.

An unexpected warmth pressed against his lips. Her voice found him again, pleading with him to open his eyes, to look at her.

He did.

She knelt above him, her long hair falling toward his face. He'd always thought that she was beautiful, but now her presence overwhelmed him. He blinked, certain that his eyes betrayed him, that he was drifting toward death. Whatever powers ruled the spiritual world had been kind enough to grant him one final vision of her.

"It's me, Fan," she said, nodding, tears in her eyes. "It's really me."

"Are … are we dead?"

"No. You're hurt, that's all. But I've come for you. I've come so very far for you."

"You're a ghost."

"I'm real."

He started to cry, shaking his head. "It can't … it can't be true."

"It is true." She took his hand and pressed it against her chest, between her breasts. "Feel me, Fan. Feel my heart beating. I'm here."

He sensed movement beneath her skin, a rhythmic, wondrous

thumping. Darkness still lingered within his mind, and he shook his head. "I don't understand. How? How are you here?"

"I walked. All the way from Beijing. I brought you a coat."

"A coat?"

She looked away for a moment. "It's gone. But I'm not."

He began to believe that she was here, that a miracle had befallen him. Rising awkwardly, heedless of the booming of cannons and the screaming of men, he sat up, reaching for her. He brought her hand to his lips, kissing each finger, tears dropping to his cheeks. "You're here? You're really here?"

"Fan, we have to leave. People are dying."

"I know."

"Can you stand?"

"I think so."

She helped him get to his feet. The world swayed back and forth. For a terrifying instant he feared that the Great Wall was collapsing. But then he realized that only his legs were unsteady. Meng put her head between his arm and chest, helping to keep him aloft. She started to shuffle toward a stairway near the southern parapet. Around her, men were fighting and dying.

Fan saw Yat-sen, twenty paces away, replete in his red armor, struggling against two smaller men. Yat-sen staggered, but the men fell. Suddenly there was no one between Fan and Yat-sen. They looked at each other. Yat-sen screamed, limping forward. Fan turned from him, finally finding strength, hurrying ahead, stumbling over bodies and weaponry.

Yat-sen shouted again. Then a pack of Mongols descended on him and a few other Chinese soldiers. Swords flashed.

Fan gripped Meng's hand. They staggering down the stairs, bumping against Chinese reinforcements who rushed toward the fighting.

Reaching out, Fan touched the Great Wall, knowing that it would last forever, but that he would never feel it again.

Yet before the stonework became a part of his past, before he and Meng could escape forever, there remained one thing left to do.

Yat-sen must be vanquished.

CHAPTER FIFTEEN

Dawn

Jinshanling—October 24, 1549

The fighting had stopped just before the sun broke. Despite his wounds, Yat-sen had rallied his men and thousands of reinforcements, ensuring that every last Mongol who remained on the wall was cut down and cast into the wasteland below. Chinese soldiers shouted in victory, firing cannons in celebration, holding banners high and vowing to one another that their position would never be captured. The wall, they said, was immortal and would protect their land until their bones were but dust.

Though Yat-sen should have remained behind to compile reports and await the inevitable arrival of his superiors, he was too weary to linger on the blood-splattered stonework. Besides, the men above him would never understand what had happened.

Most were born into privilege. They had never fought against the Mongols, witnessed their prowess on horseback, or felt the ground tremble to the beat of ten thousand hooves. They would stand on the wall, see the carnage around them, and realize how close Yat-sen had come to being overrun. He would be questioned, blamed, and dismissed. Whatever honor he had restored to his family's name would vanish.

Yat-sen rode a brown mare toward his home. Much to his dismay, his white stallion had been killed by its plunge off the wall. Worse, the boy and the Black Rider were gone. Yat-sen had seen his dead mount not long after the craftsman and his wife had also escaped, rushing away from the maelstrom, fleeing together, hand in hand.

The memory of their departure further embittered Yat-sen. He gritted his teeth, trying to forget the craftsman, instead watching those on the road around him. Soldiers hurried north, eager to add their numbers to what remained of the defenders. He ignored them, even when they spied his bloody armor and asked what had happened. Though dawn had arrived, the sky was still dark, smeared by fires on the wall. The stench of burnt wood, leather, and flesh was carried by the wind.

Yat-sen knew that his life as an officer was finished. Yet, tainted as his name was, perhaps he could escape the way Fan had. He would offer most of his silver to buy Yehonala's freedom. They could leave the northern frontier and travel to a place warm and free of memories. She would never love him as the plain-faced woman loved Fan. But she might care for him enough.

His home appeared. To his surprise, no servant boy rushed

forward to take the reins of the mare. Yat-sen dismounted slowly, his joints stiff, his wounds aching. He dropped to the ground, took a deep breath, tied the mare to a post, and limped ahead.

Never had his home given him any solace and that morning was no different. Yet he expected a warm fire, an offering of tea, and no servant came forward to meet his needs. He called out, heard his voice echo, and drew his sword, heading toward his private quarters. His room looked undisturbed. He was about to turn around when he saw something unusual on his desk. He stepped toward it, his brow furrowing when he recognized the circular black stone as a game piece from *Go*.

"No," he muttered, picking up the piece, realizing that Fan had once touched it and had brought it here.

"No, no, no!"

Yat-sen hurried to the corner of his desk. He lifted it up, unscrewed the hollow leg, and pounded his free fist against his chest when he saw that his silver was gone.

Shouting a curse, he threw the desk away from him, stood up, and limped out of his home, into his courtyard. After untying his mount, he climbed upon it, asking himself which path Fan would most likely take, trying and failing to keep his panic in check. There were many roads that led from Jinshanling. Some ran toward distant mountains. Others headed in different directions, like the tendrils of a spider's web. Fan had at least a half day's head start and could have gone twenty ways. To his horror, Yat-sen realized that it would be nearly impossible to quickly locate the craftsman. Only through a slow and methodical search, one in which he questioned merchants and beggars in Jinshanling about two travelers, would he ever get an understanding about where they had gone. But Fan was no fool. He would have dressed his wife once again as a man and himself in ordinary robes. They would have made a rather unremarkable sight.

Fear surging deep within him, causing his hands to tremble and the horizon to sway as if he were drunk, Yat-sen spurred his mount toward Yehonala's tea house. He had to tell her that he was leaving and would likely be gone for weeks, perhaps months. She'd have to be patient. When he found Fan, he would return with the silver. He would buy her freedom.

His heartbeat thudding as hard as his mount's hooves, Yat-sen cursed, thinking of the *Go* piece. Surely Fan had planned his escape for many months. He'd waited, as he had in that one game of *Go*, for the perfect time to act, surprising his foe. Whatever moves he had made had been done so with extreme care and cunning. His tracks would be covered.

As Yat-sen neared the tea house it occurred to him that in all likelihood he would never find Fan. If he hadn't abandoned his post, perhaps he could have gathered his men and sent them after the craftsman. But now, having deserted his position, any return to the wall would involve a lengthy examination from his superiors. They would want to know why he had left, why his wall had almost fallen. In the end, even if they let him go free, days would pass.

Believing that his only choice was to hunt down Fan alone, Yat-sen limped into the tea house. His breathing ragged, he ignored the madam's greeting and hurried into Yehonala's quarters. Dressed in turquoise robes, with her hair pinned atop her head, she sat at her desk, fresh ink on the paper before her.

"What happened?" she asked, rising to her feet.

He took her hands in his. "We were attacked."

"I know. But still, why do you come to my quarters covered in blood and stinking of death?"

"My … my silver. It's gone."

"What?"

"The craftsman. His wife came for him … the way you said. And they stole my silver."

Yehonala shook her head. "No, that can't be. That—"

"They stole it last night, when I was still fighting. I have to go now, to follow them."

"But where … where did they go?"

"I don't know."

"You don't know?" she asked, pushing him away. "How can that be?"

"I'll be gone for weeks. You'll have to wait for—"

"Weeks?"

"He'll be difficult to find. I need time."

"No! He can't have beaten you!"

"He's no fool."

"But you are! To let him steal your silver! Our silver! You'll never see that treasure again! He could go in a hundred different directions, and he's twice the man you are!"

Yat-sen struck her without warning, an openhanded blow that split her upper lip. "Be silent!"

"You … you weak, simple man! How I hate you! How I endured your tedious embraces for nothing!"

"Stop it," Yat-sen muttered, her words stealing his strength, wounding him as much as any blade. "Please ... you don't mean that."

"You think I would ever care for you, without the silver? Never! I'd rather drown."

"But ... but we were to be together."

"In wealth! Not in poverty!"

"I'll find him. I'll—"

"You're just like every other man!" she screamed, blood flowing down her chin from her ripped lip. "Strong on the outside, but weak, so weak deep within. You let him beat you and you'll never touch me again! No man will ever touch me again!"

He lowered his head, finding it hard to breathe, as the room swayed about him. He knelt before her. "Please."

"No!"

When her hair suddenly fell upon his shoulders, he reached for it, lifting it to his face. He didn't realize that she had pulled the long, silver pins from her locks, that they were descending toward his neck, driven by her rage.

The pain of her strikes sent him reeling backward. He reached up, trying to defend himself, but the bloody pins darted at him again, one piercing his right hand, the other plunging into his chest. She stabbed and stabbed, the pins as sharp and deadly as daggers.

He fell away from her, no longer protecting himself. She tumbled against him, then pulled back, her robes awash in blood. She was weeping.

Yat-sen lay on the ground. The deep wounds burned as if

someone had poured hot oil into him. He grimaced, weakening quickly, watching her face. He tried to convince himself that her tears were on his behalf, that she would miss him more than she expected.

When she reached into the desk drawer and pulled out an ivory container, he tried to ask what she was doing, but his voice emerged as nothing more than a garbled whisper. She ignored him, opening the box and removing what he recognized as raw opium. The drug was meant to be smoked, but she began to stuff dangerous quantities of the black, tar-like substance into her bloody mouth. Yat-sen whispered at her to stop, but she only consumed the opium faster, her fingers and lips darkening from its residue.

Even as he faded, Yat-sen watched her. The rage on her face dissipated, and he was pleased for her. He saw the loveliness of her features, but also a beauty much deeper within her. She looked younger, as if she'd never entered the tea house but was still at home, dreaming of a pleasant future.

Yat-sen thought of Fan. He would have liked to have killed the craftsman, to have stuffed the *Go* piece, then a sword, down his throat. Instead, as Yehonala had said, Fan had won. He'd pretended to be nothing when he was so much more.

Imagining his silver in the craftsman's hands, Yat-sen began to gag, choking on his blood. He realized that Yehonala had fallen beside him. The light seemed to be fading from her eyes.

He reached for her and found her fingers, squeezing them tight. No response was given.

Yat-sen wanted to die in her arms, so that at least poets might write about them—famous lovers who had fought and perished after the Great Wall was saved.

But to his misery, he could no longer move. And as much as he tried to keep his mind on Yehonala, his swirling, waning thoughts drifted back to the craftsman. He wished that he could play him another game of *Go*. He wished that he had won.

*

The land was even more beautiful than Bataar remembered. Though the mountains were no longer lush with foliage, subtle colors still abounded within them—the gray of stone, the brown of dried grasses, and the white of frost. The air was unburdened with the stink of men or cooking fires. Gusts rolled forth, buffeting his face, hinting of approaching snows and storms. Even the sounds of nature seemed acute—the cry of a hawk, the gurgle of a stream.

Bataar had never felt so liberated, not even while on the swiftest of horses. Though his hip and backside still ached from his fall, his mind was clear. He'd broken nothing, his father had assured him, and his future would be unmarred by his past. Whatever he wanted to do, he would do. The wall, he suspected, would never been seen by his eyes again. It was no longer a part of his life, and he felt no pull toward it.

Fan did make appearances within his thoughts. He wondered about his friend, holding the necklace, believing that Fan had escaped the battle but unsure what would become of him. Most likely he would find his wife and they would escape together. Yat-sen would never locate them. Fan was too smart to be ensnared once again. But where would his friend settle? Near a tower or a temple where he could find work? Or had he discovered Yat-sen's stash of silver, and would never have to worry again about money? Perhaps most important, would Fan have a son or daughter? Would he name his son Bataar, as he had once promised?

Bataar knew that his questions would be forever unanswered. The world was too vast for them to meet again. But he imagined a warm, happy future for Fan, a future free of war, angst, and doubt. His Chinese father would live a contented life, as he deserved.

Thoughts of Fan compelled Bataar to consider his own father—the man who rode behind him, who pointed out a scampering hare and a nest of forgotten eggs. Once their wounds healed they would hunt together again, laughing, racing each other over uneven ground.

Though other Mongols they had seen earlier that morning had bowed in respect to his father, Bataar knew that he would never fight again. The war would be waged without him. Perhaps someday the Mongols would win, but Bataar didn't care much for the fate of his nation. He only wanted to be with his family.

"Father, have you ever played *Go*?" he asked.

"What's *Go*?"

"A Chinese game. It's played on a board, with black and white pieces. There are battles, but no blood; victories, but no killing."

Their horse snorted as it stumbled on a loose rock.

"You played it?" his father asked.

"No, but I watched them play, almost every night. And I'd like to play it with you."

"You could teach me?"

"Of course. And I'll teach Mother too. She'd be good at it."

"Then we'll play. You'll both enjoy beating me."

Bataar smiled. "Maybe I'll let you win a few games. My Chinese friend, he taught me how to do that."

"So you'll pity me, now that you've rescued me?"

"Maybe. At least in *Go*."

"The Chinese like their games. Perhaps, if the war ends someday, you can travel to their cities and play against their champions."

Bataar considered his father's words. He couldn't imagine ever returning to China, but then again, he'd never imagined jumping off the wall on Yat-sen's beautiful, extraordinary stallion. He wouldn't have had the courage without his father behind him. In his father's arms, he knew that he would be safe.

"Can we go faster?" he asked, tightening his grip on the reins, wishing that the stallion hadn't died.

"I've been waiting for you to ask."

Bataar thumped his heels into the mare's sides. He felt her muscles contract, her speed increase. "I love you, Father."

Chuluun smiled, kissing the back of his son's head. Bataar's words were a gift. The biggest failing of his life had been put to rest by those four words.

Though his enemies had called him the Black Rider, Chuluun didn't want the name. What he wanted was to be a good father and husband, to be charging across the plains with his son.

The landscape blurred around him. Chuluun wrapped his arms about Bataar and held him tight. He knew then that he wouldn't die beneath the blades of the Chinese, as he'd believed for so very long. Death would claim him beneath an open sky, while he was surrounded by his loved ones, content in all things, great and small.

The spirits had been generous to him. His misdeeds had been forgiven.

＊

Fan had forgotten what it was like to travel freely, on an open road. He sat on one of the two stallions that they'd bought with some of Yat-sen's silver. Though he still wasn't comfortable on a horse, he was pleased that his skills were progressing. Bataar would have been proud.

As he had several times already that day, Fan wondered what had happened to his young friend. He was certain that he had escaped. The Mongol attack had been a gift. Surely the arrival of thousands of his people would have provided opportunities for Bataar. With luck, he had found and freed his father and climbed down the wall.

A part of Fan wished that he had gone with Bataar, fighting toward his father, witnessing their reunion. But another part of him, the more practical side, understood that he would have merely encumbered his friend. Bataar had ridden like the wind. With Fan alongside him, either on the saddle or on foot, Bataar would have been slowed down. And if there was ever a time for speed, it was that night, with everything hanging in the balance. Fan had needed to let Bataar go. The choice had been agonizing, and not without remorse, but Fan believed that his decision was the right one. Bataar, like a caged hawk, required releasing.

It wasn't difficult for Fan to imagine Bataar riding on the plains, alongside his father. That was the image he held in his mind whenever doubts about his choices circled his consciousness. He saw them, racing over uneven land, toward a collection of distant *yurts*. They were laughing, their shadows taking flight, their joy infectious.

Fan believed in the promise of all of their futures. He looked from time to time at Meng, smiled at the radiance of her hidden, disguised face, and bowed to whatever powers dwelled above. Despite Yat-sen's strength and ruthlessness, Fan no longer feared him. Bribing his servants had been easy. Finding his silver had proved more difficult, but Fan had been certain that it was somewhere in his room. The hollow desk leg had been a clever ruse.

Though Fan was not a prideful man, it had been with some delight that he'd left the *Go* piece on Yat-sen's desk. He'd lost their contests of wit, so many times, when victory could have been his. He'd waited, month after month, planning his escape, as concerned about Bataar's fate as his own.

Yat-sen's only recourse, without his silver, would be to strike out toward Beijing, hoping to extract information from Fan and Meng's relatives. But three weeks earlier, Fan had sent coded letters to Meng, as well as to her mother and his parents, beseeching them to immediately sell their belongings and travel to Shanghai, a booming port city to the south. He would meet them there, near an old sea wall that had once been described to him. With Yat-sen's silver, Fan could buy a home and would never need to work on a wall again. He would change his name, and learn to properly ride a horse. Yat-sen wouldn't find him, no matter how steadfast his efforts. China was simply too vast and populous.

The road upon which they traveled was narrow and didn't head toward Beijing, but to the east, toward the coast. At times, the passageway was crowded but was now empty and serene.

Fan studied Meng's disguise, wondering how she could possibly pass for a man. "People must see what they want to see," he said, leading his horse closer to hers.

"What do you mean?"

"You don't look like a man."

"And I don't feel like one either. But until we get to Shanghai, I'll be one."

He smiled. "How you tease me. When will I ever get to kiss you?"

"Soon, I hope."

A blackbird settled into a nearby pine tree, calling loudly.

Fan sighed, at peace with his surroundings for the first time in more than a year. "You're braver than any man, Meng. You traveled so far to see me, to save me."

"I wasn't alone. I had help."

"I know."

"He wanted me to be with you, Fan. He understood how much I love you. I told him once how you made me feel complete. How the best part of me was us."

"What a gift you are. In so many ways." Fan reached for the reins of her horse, pulling them back, stopping her mount and his. "Someday, when I'm old and no harm can come to us, I'm going to find a girl who seems downcast. I'm going to tell her your story."

"Why?"

"Because I want her to know what you did, what she can do. I want her to spread the word."

"And she'll spread it. Girls want to hear such stories."

Fan took her hands in his. "I love you, Meng. How lucky I am that in the wall of life my stone was placed next to yours. I'll be beside you forever."

She brought his hand to her lips, kissing it. His smile warmed her. "Will you do one more thing for me?" she asked.

"What?"

"Ping. The man who helped me, who gave his life for me … for us. I want to honor him."

"Of course. What can we do?"

"He and I stopped at a temple. The monks there ran a hospital. Ping wanted to go back to it, to help them." Meng took a deep breath, steadying herself, wishing that Ping could have made the journey. "I want to find another temple like that one. I want to give half of our silver to its monks, so they can care for the sick."

Fan nodded, stroking the back of her hand with his thumb. "We'll tell the monks that the gift is from Ping. That it was his wish to do this."

"It was."

"Good. Then let's start looking."

Meng bowed to him. "Thank you, Fan."

"You don't need to thank me. He helped you, the woman I love. Of course I want to honor him."

She considered what Fan had said about their stones being placed together. They had both seen the vastness and beauty of the Great Wall—which was really nothing more than a collection of countless millions of neatly stacked bricks. She could have been placed so very far from him, never sensing his presence, never feeling the overpowering need to hurry toward him. The Great Wall was infinite in its wonders, but also in the span of its reach, the distance between its peaks.

"Why were we so lucky?" she asked.

"I don't know, Meng. I really don't."

Nodding, she looked at how her fingers intertwined with his, imagining how that embrace would appear many years from now, when both sets of hands were old and worn.

The stones would linger.

So would their touch, the feeling of him against her.

Whatever journeys lay ahead, they would make them together.

AUTHOR'S NOTE

There are many legends about the Great Wall of China, which is hardly surprising considering the tumultuous times during which it was built, defended, and revered. The story of Meng and Fan intrigued me when I first stumbled upon a few lines pertaining to it (which is about all that exists). Meng's bravery and travels contradicted everything I had ever heard about women in ancient China. I remain unsure if she existed, but I like to think that she did. In any case, I enjoyed bringing her to life on the page.

The history of the Great Wall, of course, did not end during the final days of the Ming Dynasty. During the 16th and 17th centuries, the fortification was besieged by the Mongols, as well as another powerful foe, the Manchus. Yet perhaps the deadliest threat to China came from within. In the 1640s a civil war raged, and in 1644, one of the factions within China allied itself with the Manchus. Its leaders opened crucial gates of the Great Wall to welcome in hundreds of thousands of their comrades. The Manchus soon marched on Beijing, occupied the city, and ended the Ming Dynasty.

It is interesting that the Great Wall achieved one of its most notable successes during the early chapters of what would become World War Two. In 1933, the Japanese attacked China from a variety of staging points, many of which required passage through the Great Wall. In some cases, the Chinese defenders held their positions on the wall, repelling larger and better-equipped numbers of Japanese—though the invaders ultimately broke through the fortification. Yet for years thereafter, the Chinese used the Great Wall to move soldiers and weapons, ambushing the Japanese at strategic mountain passes and other fronts.

Today the Great Wall is a shadow of its former self. Millions of its bricks have been carted away to build homes and streets. Cities stand in its previous path. In other areas, desert sands have buried ramparts that once stood tall and proud. But in some places, like Jinshanling and Simatai, which are settings in this novel, the Great Wall stands as it has for centuries, enduring the elements and the passing of countless feet. Its watchtowers are still grand and mighty. Its bricks remain hard and steadfast.

Perhaps ghosts or memories linger on the Great Wall. So many people died building and defending it. Walking upon the graceful structure, mile after mile, one has the sense of moving through history, of the fleetingness, but also permanence, of dreams and actions.

If such a wall could be built, so can anything else.

ACKNOWLEDGEMENTS

In many ways, writing is a solitary process. When I'm about to start creating a novel, I feel like I'm looking up at an immense mountain—one that I'm going to climb alone. If I look hard enough, peering over endless terrain and through thin clouds, I can discern the peak's summit. I know that it will take me many months of climbing to rise up, pass the timberline, plow through fields of snow, and finally reach the top. The view will be rewarding, I believe, making all the hard work worthwhile.

Of course, while at times I feel alone on this journey, I'm not. I'm blessed to have a wonderful network of loved ones, friends, and strangers who support me. Heading that list is my adventurous and lovely wife, Allison, who has been with me for countless climbs. We've experienced many peaks and valleys together, and she's a noble companion. Our children, Sophie and Jack, are also eager explorers, and I take immense joy in their discoveries. Seeing the world through their eyes inspires me.

I would also like to thank my parents, John and Patsy Shors; as well as my brothers, Tom, Matt, and Luke. Their collective support has been steadfast and significant. I wouldn't be who I am today without each of them.

Booksellers, librarians, and readers are deserving of my profound gratitude. There isn't a day that passes without someone contacting me about my work, and describing their reading experience. These wonderful people tell their friends about my novels, post online reviews, help me support my charities, and are always there for me. They are as important to my writing career as anyone.

Cheers also to Doug and Mary Barakat, Bruce McPherson, Pennie Ianniciello, Paula McLain, M.J. Rose, Jamie Ford, Elizabeth Donoghue-Armstrong, and Shawna Sharp.

Finally, to whoever is reading this note—my very best wishes to you. Thank you for your support. I'm truly grateful for it.

ABOUT THE AUTHOR

John Shors is the bestselling author of *Beneath a Marble Sky*, *Beside a Burning Sea*, *Dragon House*, *The Wishing Trees*, *Cross Currents*, *Temple of a Thousand Faces*, and *Unbound*. He has won numerous awards for his writing, and his novels have been translated into twenty-six languages. He also leads groups of readers on overseas trips to the places that he writes about.

John lives in Boulder, Colorado, with his wife and two children, and he encourages reader feedback.

CONNECT ONLINE

www.johnshors.com
www.facebook.com/johnshors
shors@aol.com

READER'S GUIDE

A Conversation with John Shors

Q. Unbound is your seventh novel, and like your other books, it takes place in Asia. Why did you decide to write about the Great Wall of China?

A. I've been fascinated by the Great Wall of China for many years. Part of the fascination stemmed from so many conflicting stories that I'd heard about it. Was the fortification built to keep people in or out of China? Was it really a single wall or a series of connected walls? Was it ever breeched? Questions like these had intrigued me for a long time, and I was eager to uncover as many answers as possible.

Q. Why did you set Unbound toward the end of the Ming Dynasty?

A. That's an interesting question in that I could have set *Unbound* at any point over a period of many centuries. I settled on the Ming Dynasty for several reasons. One, it was during this period that wall building was at its peak. The sheer magnitude and architectural splendor of the portions of the Great Wall that were built during these years impressed me greatly. Moreover, China during the late Ming Dynasty was at a crossroads of sorts, especially when it came to women's rights.

Q. Let's talk about women's rights. Meng is in many ways a strong, somewhat modern character. Can you discuss why you wrote her in this fashion?

A. My research led me to conclude that during the late Ming Dynasty many women were eager to become more active participants in society. For generations, women had been somewhat out-of-sight, out-of-mind—destined to remain indoors, forever supporting their husbands. And while even toward the end of the Ming Dynasty cultural expectations remained restrictive and repressive towards women, many wives, mothers, and daughters— especially those from wealthy families—stepped over boundaries established by past generations. Limited, but influential numbers of women, wrote poetry, supported charities, and perhaps most important, traveled. Meng embodied these women and the challenges they faced. I tried to create a certain level of conflict within her in terms of her role within the world. She isn't sure how the world sees her, or how she should see herself. Surely some Chinese women at this time must have had similar thoughts.

Q. Yehonala also struggles with her role in a male-dominated society. Can you talk about her?

A. Well, courtesans and concubines obviously played a large role in ancient Chinese society. From what I have read about foot-binding, most of the affected women remained in perpetual discomfort. As I thought about Yehonala's character, I wondered how that discomfort, coupled with her pre-determined station, may have affected her personality. I decided to make her bitter and resentful. In her case, she is aware that a few women are gaining personal freedoms, but she isn't one of them. As a strong, ambitious young woman, she finds her inability to escape her situation maddening.

Q. *We've discussed some of the pressures facing women at this time. What pressures did men face?*

A. Men obviously had much more freedom than women, yet they also dealt with enormous anxieties. Chief among those was perhaps the ability to excel, or to advance one's station, by passing extremely difficult imperial examinations. The few young men who passed the exams became state officials—high-ranking members of society. The many who failed dealt with that shame for the rest of their lives. In some cases, entire villages would financially support a young man's efforts to pass the exams. If he failed, he not only failed himself, but everyone else.

Q. *Yat-sen and Fan have a sort of understated personal battle that runs throughout the novel. Can you talk about these characters and what they represent? Also, how do you use the game of Go to move the story forward?*

A. I wanted to create a complex villain who certain readers might see a few admirable traits within (and who other readers would completely despise). Yat-sen is cruel, selfish, and untrustworthy. Yet he also is willing to sacrifice his life to protect his country. He believes in China and what it represents. Fan is a much more pure and noble character, but he also has his faults.

These two men represent different factions within ancient China. The military machine, obviously, was powerful and would stop at nothing to keep the Mongols at bay. Other parts of that society, however, were open to the possibility of trade with the Mongols. Yat-sen and Fan are symbolic of these two factions. As far as how *Go* plays a role in their relationship, *Go* is the one arena where they are equals. They are both vulnerable and powerful while playing, and *Go* provides Fan with opportunities to prove himself. Whether or not he capitalizes on those opportunities is up to him.

Q. You make an interesting comparison between Chinese and Mongol cultures. Were they really that different?

A. Yes, I think so. The Mongols were powerful nomads whose culture centered around life on a horse. They led difficult lives— forever moving and enduring the elements. The Mongols craved trade with China, but were denied access to Chinese goods, which would have made their lives easier. Consequently, their leaders pursued a long and often fruitless war against the Chinese. Yet this war made Mongols strong and feared. Rather than battle against some of the best horsemen the world had ever seen, the Chinese opted to fortify their cities, and in the case of the Great Wall, much of their kingdom. And while the Mongols perfected the arts of war, hunting, and gathering, the Chinese made breakthroughs in science, medicine, manufactured goods, and agriculture. Their cities became some of the greatest that the world had ever seen. While I would never say that one of these cultures was superior to the other, they were definitely different.

Q. What impressed you most about the Great Wall?

A. I was lucky enough to spend a few days walking the wall,

and I probably covered about twenty miles. What amazed me the most was how the wall followed the contours of the land as if they were not two separate entities, but one. The tallest mountains and ridges seemed to be targeted, not avoided, by the wall's builders. In places the wall's steepness surprised me. I couldn't imagine how anyone could build a seemingly endless structure that summited peaks and spanned waterways. I also admired the watchtowers, which were so plentiful. Each of these small castles provided amazing views in every direction.

Q. *What was the most difficult part of writing Unbound?*

A. Probably conducting the research necessary to even contemplate my story. By no means would I profess to be an expert on ancient China, but I tried to learn as much as I could about why and how the Great Wall was built, how it was defended, and the important and, at times mythological, role that it played in Chinese history. I also read about women's rights, or lack thereof, during this period. Many other details of the book, such as the frequent soup lines, were taken from first-hand accounts of famous Chinese writers.

Q. *The title, Unbound, is unusual. What does it mean?*

A. I encourage readers to also answer that question. But as for me, *Unbound* worked as a title on several fronts. First of all, Meng's feet are unbound. If they hadn't been, she would never have been able to even begin her journey. Secondly, as her trip unfolds, she becomes unbound in various ways. She feels freedoms that few of her peers experience. Within this liberated state, she is able to examine herself, her future, and her society. In many ways, she is reborn.

Q. As a novelist, you're well known for writing about exotic lands, and for going to great lengths to connect with readers. Can you describe some of those efforts, and why have you pursued them?

A. It's always been important to me to connect with readers as much, and as strongly, as possible. I've always felt that if readers are going to support me, I need to be supportive in return. To accomplish this goal, I've set up a variety of programs that provide bridges between readers and me. For instance, I've chatted (via speakerphone) with more than 3,000 book clubs. These book clubs have been from all over the world, and I've really enjoyed these interactions. Recently I've launched a program that gives readers the opportunity to travel with me to some of the places that I've written about. I've taken groups of readers to China, Japan, India, Thailand, Vietnam, and Cambodia. And of course, I always answer every single email that I receive, usually within the same day. If people are going to reach out to me, I need to be available.

Q. You've written about some of the wonders of the world, namely the Taj Mahal, Angkor Wat, and the Great Wall of China. What attracts you to such places?

A. I'm fascinated by the accomplishments of men and women who lived a long time ago. Untold millions of people devoted their lives to carving stone, copying religious scriptures, or preserving their culture in some other form. Today we create bright, wonderful buildings and monuments, but I wonder if any of them will endure the passage of time with as much grace as some of these ancient designs. Why did so many powerful and old civilizations feel the need to leave monuments to honor their cultures, their gods, their people? Do we attempt to accomplish the same feat today? Questions like these intrigue me.

Q. *What endeavors are you pursuing these days?*

A. I'm currently writing a young adult, science fiction trilogy that is set in some of the most beautiful places on Earth. The series has been a fun change-of-pace for me, and I'm excited to see its release.

QUESTIONS fOR DISCUSSION

1. Which of John Shors' novels have you liked the best, and why?
2. Which character did you most strongly connect with? Describe that connection.
3. Discuss the issue of women's rights. How far have we come? How far do we have to go?
4. Which story line did you find the most compelling? Why?
5. If you were Meng, would you have traveled so far alone to find Fan?
6. What mistakes does Meng make on her journey? Do those mistakes serve a purpose in the story?
7. Discuss Chuluun's character. Did you like him? How did his presence impact the story?
8. *Unbound* explores a clash of cultures. We see similar clashes today. Do you think history has a tendency to repeat itself? If so, why?
9. Many people believe that China will be the world's next superpower. How will that ascension affect you, if at all? How will it affect humanity?
10. John Shors makes himself easily accessible to readers. Does this matter to you? Do you think more authors should do the same?

CPSIA information can be obtained
at www.ICGtesting.com
Printed in the USA
FSOW02n2007250917
39187FS